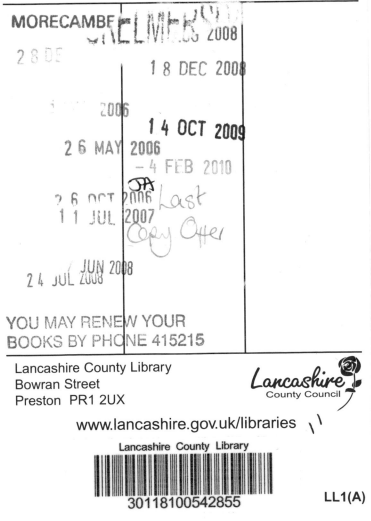

Time and Fate

Lance Price

© Lance Price 2005

ISBN 09549137-4-4

Published by
Polperro Heritage Press
Clifton-upon-Teme
Worcestershire WR6 6EN
United Kingdom
polperro.press@virgin.net

Cover design by Simon Reynolds

Printed by Orphans Press
Leominster HR6 8JT
United Kingdom

To Colin and Jean

We are not now that strength which in old days
Moved earth and heaven; that which we are, we are;
One equal temper of heroic hearts,
Made weak by time and fate, but strong in will
To strive, to seek, to find, and not to yield.
Tennyson, *Ulysses* 1.44

In politics, there is no use looking beyond the next fortnight.
Joseph Chamberlain, 1886

A week is a long time in politics.
Harold Wilson, 1964

Time and Fate is a work of fiction, nothing more, nothing less. Any similarity to real events in the past, the present or indeed the future, or to actual people involved in politics and journalism is, as they say, entirely coincidental. The truth, in the experience of the author, is often a lot harder to believe than fiction.

1

The Deputy Prime Minister put the remains of the toast in her mouth and used both hands to roll the stocking slowly up her right leg. Satisfied the seam was straight she readjusted her glasses and squinted at the security briefing propped up on the mantelpiece, before turning and examining herself once more from behind in the long gilt mirror. Joanna Morgan was a very particular woman. Details rarely escaped her but this morning she was concentrating on the overall effect.

"You know, for a woman of fifty-four, I have remarkably good legs."

"That, my love, is quite beyond doubt." Ray Morgan's curiously old fashioned turn of phrase and unfailing courtesy were always greatly appreciated by his wife. He had come into her life late but ever since that day he had never seen any good reason to disagree with her. That was something she appreciated even more. The Foreign Secretary knew her strengths and, occasionally, her weaknesses. Among the latter, although she was unwilling to admit to many faults, was her frustration that she couldn't always have what she saw as her just deserts. A man less admiring than Ray might have seen that as evidence of her immaturity or vanity, but as he thought she deserved whatever she wanted, he simply found it endearing. Ray was more than her rock, he was her plinth. In a world where loyalty was spread as thinly as the butter on her toast he was there for her day and night, in good times and in bad, right or wrong. That is if Joanna Morgan was ever wrong.

Her remarkably good legs were the first thing to catch the eye of her Private Secretary when he put his head around the door to remind her that she had a meeting at Number 10. She nodded and he disappeared back into the corridor.

"Can you find me the blue suit Ray? I may have to be interviewed and it always looks so smart on TV."

On that particular day in August Joanna Morgan was the most powerful woman in Britain. No, she was the most powerful *person* in Britain. And Joanna Morgan liked being powerful. She liked it a lot. She liked it perhaps a little too much. And the blue suit made her feel completely in control, which was just how she liked to feel. Ray handed her the suit and stood back as she carefully put one remarkably good leg and then the other into the skirt and pulled it up. She disappeared into the bedroom and came back with a simple gold chain around her neck, adjusting her neat shoulder length hair and checking her teeth in the mirror for traces of lipstick.

"Foreign Secretary?" The head had reappeared without knocking.

"Yes, Charles?"

"Fifteen minutes, Foreign Secretary."

"Charles?"

"Yes, Foreign Secretary?"

"Have I ever, since you've known me, been late for a single meeting?"

"No, Foreign Secretary, I don't believe you have."

"Thank you, Charles."

She picked up the security briefing and let her eye travel along the row of photographs on the mantelpiece. Joanna Morgan with the Secretary General of the United Nations. Joanna Morgan with Presidents and Prime Ministers from every continent. Joanna Morgan with King Charles and Camilla. Joanna Morgan with Paul Sinclair, their hands clasped together, held high in victory. "Sorry, darling, could you just fetch me the press summary? It's on the bedside table."

In the three years since this last photograph was taken, Paul Sinclair had only ever left the country on official business. Almost as if the job that came to him so unexpectedly could be taken away just as suddenly if he ever took a holiday. The Prime Minister had a remarkable ability to let every challenge and crisis wash over him and had shown no signs of even needing a break. But Joanna Morgan, who had a sense of history and a capacity for patience that her husband found extraordinary, knew it couldn't last. She had a sense that things were already beginning to change, if only by degrees imperceptible to those less, well less perceptive than the Foreign Secretary.

This summer Sinclair had decided to holiday abroad. His poll ratings had slumped badly but he seemed to think that was only to be expected. It was more the fear of being a bad father than any political pressures that had convinced the Prime Minister to take his son to Spain. And so it was that today Joanna Morgan was not just Foreign Secretary. Not just Deputy Prime Minister. But, in the absence of the man himself, in charge.

Her Private Secretary was waiting for her outside the door. She checked herself one more time in the large mirror at the top of the stairs and began the long, almost regal, descent to the hall below. The Foreign Secretary's residence in Carlton Gardens is one of the best addresses in London and none of its occupants, whatever their political persuasions, had ever seen fit to change it. True, there were portraits of Nelson Mandela and President Suu Kyi alongside Gordon and Grey on the walls these days but the dead weight of Victorian grandeur was still clinging to the drapes, pressing down on the deep pile carpets and being reflected in the perfectly polished silver. Ray Morgan rubbed his nose as he followed two steps behind his wife. It had taken him a very long time to work what it was that made his nostrils itch. It wasn't the aroma of polish and servility, it was what the place didn't smell of that got to him. No homely odours rising from the kitchen, no wet clothes drying in the hall, no dog hairs or half-finished cups of coffee. They were living in a museum. Ray was the kind of man who felt uncomfortable letting somebody else carry his bags to a hotel room. Opulence embarrassed him, but he knew his wife thought differently and had no doubt that she deserved the best.

The media often described Joanna Morgan, and she did nothing to discourage them, as the keeper of the government's conscience, a woman of principle compared to Paul Sinclair the man of action. But there was no principle she knew of that said Labour ministers had to live in any less style than their opponents.

"Are we walking, my love?"

"Of course, Ray. It's only ten minutes away, and the park looks so lovely first thing. Before all the tourists arrive."

"Right you are," he said. The doorman gave the merest hint of a bow as they passed out into the sunshine.

The pedestrian crossing that leads across the Mall to St James' Park is no respecter of office or of power. Everybody must wait. The Private Secretary glanced anxiously at his watch. He looked up and saw a taxi driver swing in towards the kerb and brake suddenly. Instinctively he took one step back but the Foreign Secretary held her poise. The driver slid down his window. "Miss Morgan, isn't it? Jump in, go on. The ride's on me. Where you off to?"

"That's very kind of you," she said, "but it's only just across the road."

"Downing Street eh? Well I ain't allowed up near there anyway. Tell you what though Miss Morgan, and I hope I'm not speaking out of turn, but it's you should be in there not you know who. I mean, he's lost the plot if you ask me. Started out all right, but he's lost the plot. As for you, you might be a bit la-di-da, but I reckon you know what the working man thinks, you do. Shows a mile off. Sorry if I'm speaking out of turn. Just my opinion like. Get 'im out, get you in and we'd all be better off."

She took a short, sharp breath but the lights changed at last and she had no time to reply. She didn't know what answer she would have given, something suitably diplomatic probably, but she did have to admit as the taxi pulled away that the man had summed up the facts with remarkable clarity.

2

Detective Sergeant Terry Woods leant back against the stone wall of the tower and wiped his brow with his handkerchief. Even in the shade of the building it was over 35 degrees. The stone felt cool but its rough edges pressed into his skin and he shifted his position to try to make himself more comfortable.

Staring at the gentle movement of the sea was starting to make him feel a little giddy. The heat didn't help. He rubbed the back of his neck and stretched his head forward a little to restore his concentration. The boy was kicking a football against the far wall and seemed to be quoting some kind of poem to himself in a loud voice, which struck Terry as an odd thing to do at any time of the day. Something about Lucifer and the fires of hell by the sound of it. Maybe it was the heat. Thank God for the tower, though. There was no doubt they'd chosen the best spot.

What was it? A lookout of some kind. A bit like one of those Martello Towers on the south coast. It was certainly in the right place for one, with nothing but miles of open sea on three sides. Two hundred years old? Three? Terry had no idea, history not being one of his strong suits. Maybe he should ask Joshua, he'd be off to university soon, but he didn't want to interrupt him.

The Sergeant could see the Inspector out of the corner of his eye and he was looking very uneasy. He'd been looking that way for the best part of two days now. Detective Inspector Derek Smyth wouldn't have been Terry's first choice for company on a job like this. Constantly on edge, always expecting something to go wrong. But then, thought Terry, he's an ambitious man, on his way up to much higher things. While Terry took his job seriously, nobody could argue with that, he knew by now he wasn't destined for the top. Even so he couldn't help feeling that for a protection officer Derek Smyth was a little too concerned about his own protection. Maybe that's what came from making Detective Inspector before the age of thirty.

Terry reached down for the binoculars propped against the wall. With his other hand he lifted up the two litre bottle of water they'd carried with them onto the cliff top. The sound of the football bouncing off the stone had stopped. "Want a drink Joshua?"

No answer. A second later the boy appeared around the edge of the tower with headphones in his ears. Terry waved the bottle and he took it, swallowed a long drink and then poured more onto his head. He was dressed in shorts and a vest. His curly hair was matted to his forehead where the water and his sweat had combined. "Are you sure you don't want a kick about, Terry?" His voice was a little too loud.

Terry shook his head as Joshua removed his headphones. "Too hot for me. Maybe later when it's cooled down a bit. Anyway, I don't know why you didn't go out with your dad. It would have been more fun than hanging around with a couple of old guys like us." He saw the Inspector's frown but ignored it.

"Nah. You know him. There's no peace when he's around. It's not easy having Action Man for a father, you know. Tennis before breakfast was bad enough, and of course I had to let him beat me." He grinned. He wasn't yet quite good enough to win and he knew it. "But I'm all right. Don't worry about me."

"Where is he?" The Inspector, who was sitting on a rock a few metres away, had a large scale map of the coastline spread out on the ground.

"Eleven o'clock. He's a bit beyond the bay." Terry pointed a finger down towards the sea and squinted into the sun. The canoe was just visible with the naked eye.

"I hope he knows what he's doing."

"He's been coming here for years, Derek, I think he'll be all right." Terry caught Joshua's eye and winked.

"Yeah, but the sea's cutting up pretty rough beyond the headland." The Detective Inspector marked a cross on the map and noted the time. 10.30. With luck, thought Terry, they'd be back in the air-conditioning before the midday sun deprived them of what little shade they now had. "Keep an eye on him anyway," said his boss.

This was the Derek Smyth's first visit to Moraira, which went some way to help explain his edginess. Although Terry Woods was the junior officer he'd already been to Spain on duty twice before, a few years ago when Sinclair used to come every summer. He picked up the binoculars again, convinced the Inspector was worrying needlessly. From here they had an uninterrupted view of almost the entire coast from Moraira old town to the cape. And while the canoe was just at that moment disappearing from view behind the rocks of the headland below them, he knew Paul Sinclair was familiar with every contour of the cliffs. The newspapers might have their fun with his Action Man image, but he wasn't the kind of guy to do anything stupid. He'd been given the detailed weather and shipping forecasts over breakfast. Detective Inspector Smyth had insisted on reading them to him twice.

A scurrying noise from behind the tower heralded the appearance of a large brown dog. It ran towards them, nose to the ground as it came. They watched as it raised its leg against the wall of the tower and then, as grateful as they were to have found some shade, gave them a cursory sniff and sat down looking back in the direction it had come. Thirty seconds later its owner made her own entrance around the curved side of the building, a tall woman in her thirties wearing flannel shorts and a grey blouse, both of which look a little too expensive and well cut for walking a dog in the heat. The dark rings under her arms were the only acknowledgement of the steepness of the climb.

She greeted them in Spanish and Joshua sprang to his feet and held out his hand, then felt awkward at having done so. But she took it readily and he offered a quick "hola" before looking down at his feet and admitting defeat with a more reticent "no parlo espagnol."

"That's okay," she said with grin. Her teeth were perfect, he thought. "Although my English is not so good either." Joshua thought her English was delightful. She looked at the two older men with their formal shoes and matching khaki shorts. She took in the binoculars and the map and what looked like a two-way radio laying between them on the rocks. Terry Woods brushed the dust from the back of his shorts. "It must be very hot to be out in a fur coat," he said nodding down at the dog.

The woman smiled again. "Yes. Yes, it must. He led me up here, more or less. He belongs to a friend but he certainly seemed to know the way. Do you happen to know if there is a shorter route down?"

Joshua was just wondering if he dared offer to walk her back down to the village, or if the detectives would even let him when the Inspector cut in. "Sorry Madam, but I believe there is only the one path." He knew it for a fact. They had checked for any alternative on their advance visit and had found none. "I'm sure the going will be a lot easier on the way down. Good morning."

The woman's English was good enough to recognise a polite dismissal and she smiled rather less engagingly than before. "Well, I must be going." She pulled at the dog's collar and it followed her with considerable reluctance round the side of tower and out once more into the heat.

"You didn't have to be rude." Joshua was watching her disappearing back. "She was fit."

"Your type is she then?" asked Terry.

"I'm sorry Joshua," said the Inspector, "but we're not here to help damsels in distress. We've got your father to worry about. Now where is he?"

Terry picked up the binoculars again and looked down towards the spot where Paul Sinclair had disappeared behind the rocks a few minutes earlier. He moved the lenses to the right and then back further to the left in case the Prime Minister had, despite promising not to, continued on the other side of the headland.

"Well?"

"No visual contact, Inspector."

"Give them here." The younger officer brought the binoculars up to his face and fiddled with the focusing ring. "Shit. Can't see him anywhere. You sure he didn't go the other side of the point? The waves are pretty big out there."

"He said he was going as far as the headland and then back to the village."

"Well, where the fuck is he then?"

Terry shrugged, scanning the sea while using his spare hand to keep the sun out of his eyes. Derek Smyth had picked up the radio. "PS One, do you read?" There was a crackled acknowledgement. "PS One. Lost visual contact with Red Admiral. Last known position 38.45.00.05. Please alert coastguard. Repeat alert coastguard." He lowered the radio as a voice confirmed the order. "How long will it take us to get down there?"

"Twenty minutes maybe."

The woman waved awkwardly as they approached but they swept past her without a word. Only Joshua looked back over his shoulder. The dog made a half-hearted attempt to follow but quickly decided against trying to match their pace in the heat.

The path curved around the side of the hill and then off to the right along the cliffs. The final stretch down to the sea was rough and unstable. The Inspector who, despite being younger, was noticeably less agile than his Sergeant, fell twice, scraping his hand on the loose stones. He sucked on his palm as he ran.

The wind had splashed the path with spray, slowing the two detectives down further. Joshua was the nimblest on his feet and was the first to pass the headland. For the first time he shared some of the Inspector's concern. The yellow canoe was upside down on the sand in a little inlet. The paddle lay alongside. There was no sign of his father.

The helicopter pilot already had the headland in sight. The flying time from the base was only ten minutes and they had been on a high state of alert ever since Paul Sinclair and his son had arrived at their holiday home. The co-pilot could see the canoe clearly and the two men in shorts approaching it from the west but there was no sign of anybody else.

3

Danny Oliver put his head around the door to the Private Office. He was having a good day. He'd spent a long time persuading the Prime Minister that the government wouldn't collapse altogether if he took a couple of weeks away, and so far he'd been proved right. Sinclair had been on the phone just yesterday to say that if August stayed as quiet as this Danny could have a pay rise. But he'd been in and around politics long enough to know that the summer months could mean disaster for any government, not just one as unpopular as Sinclair's was right now. Most ministers were out of the country and all the senior reporters on the newspapers were also sunning their pallid bodies leaving their up and coming juniors to cause as much trouble as they could manage.

With the government going through a rough patch, Danny was doing his best to keep politics out of the news altogether during the long summer recess and, to his relief, even the publicity hungry Foreign Secretary appeared to be behaving herself, although you could never be too sure.

Danny had already flicked through that morning's papers. Most of them were doing what they always did when news was thin on the ground, raking over the latest twists and turns in the love lives of the House of Windsor. It was the one thing that stopped Danny becoming an out-and-out republican. The story of the Prime Minister's meeting with his Spanish opposite number had produced some good pictures of a bronzed and fit looking Sinclair eating tapas but with no real story to go with it. Only the *Daily Mirror*, which never missed a chance to make life difficult for the government, had added a sour note: 'Paul Sinclair looked like a man without a care in the world as his sunshine holiday entered its second week. But back home the storm clouds are gathering.' They might very well be right, thought Danny, but they hadn't yet burst and there was a good chance he'd be able to take Luke for dinner tonight undisturbed.

"Don't start worrying yet, Sir, but they've lost him." Rebecca, the diary secretary, didn't believe in crises. They made for an untidy day.

"Who's lost who?" It was an unnecessary question. Around here 'he' was always the Prime Minister.

"There *might* have been some kind of accident, we don't know. He's been out in his kayak again."

Danny slumped into an empty chair. Rebecca had a phone pressed against her ear and, for a woman just back from her own holiday in the Dordogne, a very pale face. The son of Ghanaian immigrants, Danny was as black as the Queen of Spades. He felt like that was the card he'd just been dealt and wondered if this was what white guys meant when they talked about feeling the colour drain from their cheeks.

Three sets of binoculars were now scanning the waves either side of the spot where the canoe had been abandoned. Abandoned or washed ashore? Terry was fairly sure that because it was at ninety degrees to the sea it had been left there deliberately. When he said as much the Inspector just moved his range of vision a little further out to sea.

From the hovering helicopter the co-pilot was examining each indentation in the cliff in turn with a steady eye. He had no reason yet to share the growing feeling of panic of the detectives on the ground. The local fishermen knew the British Prime Minister as a competent oarsman who understood the sea and shared their respect for it. He was a good swimmer too. Word had got around.

Rebecca put in a call to the Deputy Prime Minister. Joanna Morgan was in her own room across the road in the Foreign Office when the alert came through. She listened carefully and promised to be in Downing Street again in fifteen minutes unless she heard otherwise.

"Ray?" Her husband appeared from the side room where he'd been working on correspondence. "Paul Sinclair has disappeared."

"Disappeared?"

"Lost at sea in a canoe by all accounts."

"That's terrible, my love."

"Yes, it is. Quite terrible. I think we were wise to go for the blue suit."

The Deputy Prime Minister, the most powerful woman, the most powerful person, in the country, opened the drawer to her desk and took out her make up bag.

~

"Where is Kneejerk when we actually need him?" asked Danny, his voice a little too shrill for his own comfort.

"Colonel Neilson is in the United States, Mr Oliver. On the West Coast at the Webber Research Laboratories we think. Switch are trying to find him."

"Oh great." Danny was feeling a lot less self-confident all of a sudden.

~

It was Joshua, perched on top of a rock, who spotted his father first. He was just a few yards out to sea. The detectives needn't have bothered with their binoculars.

The Prime Minister waved. "Josh, are you coming in? The water's beautiful."

"Great, Dad, yeah. Why not? Shall I bring International Rescue in with me or do you think it might be bad for their equipment?"

Sinclair waded ashore. The water ran off his shorts and down his legs pulling the dark hair into little pony tails. He rubbed his hand over his face and shook his head to clear the seawater from his ears. Inspector Derek Smyth, who'd never seen the Prime Minister in nothing but his shorts before, was startled by how totally at ease, fit and tanned he looked. Surprisingly muscular, too, for a man who took as little regular exercise as he did these days. Even so the Detective would have liked to give him a piece of his mind if only he could.

"Magnificent crabs. Just round the corner there. It's a tiny little crevasse, barely big enough to squeeze into but it's wonderful. They always seem to be there when I come out here. It's sheltered from the waves in both directions you see. They just get on with their lives completely unnoticed by the rest of the world. It's rather beautiful in a way."

Sinclair looked up startled as the helicopter appeared around the headland.

The Inspector had to shout above the noise. "We were a little concerned, Prime Minister."

"Oh you didn't call them out, Derek, did you? You shouldn't have done that. I told you where I was going."

"We can't be too careful, Prime Minister."

"Well sometimes I think maybe you can." Sinclair waved at the pilots, clearly visible at fifty feet. They gave him a thumbs up and swung the craft around to return to the airstrip.

"Red Admiral, se ha encontrado y salvo." The co-pilot's message that Paul Sinclair was safe and sound was passed onto Downing Street in just under three minutes. The Deputy Prime Minister was still in her office.

4

Colonel Henry Neilson took off his glasses and scratched his head. "And tell me again. You can do it with this kind of accuracy anywhere in the world?"

"Well no, Sir." In the experience of the Downing Street Security Supremo the Americans were always unfailingly polite. "The US may be the only global megapower for now, but even we can't stop that globe going round on its axis. And we can't stop nightfall either, Sir, much as we might like to. But if it's daylight and the bird is in the right hemisphere we can read the cards in a man's hand. The Chinese claim to be able to do it even if the cards are face down, but we think they're probably bluffing on that one, Sir."

"So if I gave you some coordinates you could bring up an image of this quality in, what, five minutes?" The terminal was currently showing a colour picture of the Reagan Memorial. A young man with a red baseball cap was putting his arm round a girl with ponytails.

"More like thirty seconds, Sir."

"Can I see?"

"We can give it a go."

The Colonel handed the man a slip of paper. "Try this."

The picture came into focus after less that twenty seconds. The operator lifted his eyes from the screen for a brief moment. "We prefer to under claim and over deliver, Sir. If we can."

The Colonel watched as Paul Sinclair's Daimler pulled up outside Casa Cosecha, the holiday home he'd owned for almost twenty years. Neilson had been told immediately by the Downing Street switchboard that Sinclair was safe but it reassured him to see for himself. He watched Detective Sergeant Terry Woods jump from the passenger door before the car had come to a complete stop. Joshua Sinclair beat him to it, it was a game they had, and was out of the back seat before the policeman could heave open the armour plated door. That boy, thought the Colonel, has never appreciated the importance of good security.

"Will you join us for a drink, Derek? Terry?" Terry Woods looked undecided but the Inspector was quick to say no. "Are you sure? I'm safely out of harm's way now."

"It's kind of you to offer, but you know what they say, rules are rules."

"The Colonel can't see you now, you know Derek. But I appreciate your professionalism. Josh and I will be having dinner out on the terrace this evening." Paul Sinclair went inside to pour himself a glass of rioja while his son clicked on the remote control to bring the TV to life. He groaned as the opening titles for *David and Victoria* rolled and the camera zoomed in on the special guest. Joshua flicked through the channels in search of something better but to no avail. The Beckhams reappeared with a promise that their viewers were about to be the first to hear the next number one. "Turn it off, Josh. You get enough of that when we're at home."

"You got it. Can you believe that guy? The *Reverend* Michael Jackson, I mean Jesus. I thought you could ban undesirable aliens, Dad."

"I can. But it's not a crime being today's answer to the Singing Nun, you know."

"The singing what? Well, whatever, it should be. A very popular new crime measure that would be, Dad, you should think about it. What's the point in being Prime Minister if you can't protect us from freaks like that? Mine's a beer, by the way."

Paul Sinclair put an arm round his son's shoulder and led him out onto the terrace. Joshua picked up an olive from the table and landed a perfectly aimed shot into the lap of Terry Woods at 20 metres. The Sergeant's hand twitched a fraction towards his holster before he mouthed an obscenity in the direction of his assailant.

"Screw you too."

"I'm sorry?"

"Not you, Dad."

"How are you, Josh?"

It was Joshua's turn to be perplexed by the turn of the conversation.

"I'm fine. What do you mean?"

"Not too bored?"

"Well, it's not exactly Club 18-30."

"You're seventeen."

"I'm mature for my age."

"You could have brought a friend out, you know. I did suggest it. Or we could go into the village. Have a couple of drinks."

"No, you're all right Dad." He thought of how his friends would have reacted to the idea of two weeks in a Spanish fishing village with two policemen and the Prime Minister for company. It was enough of a struggle to get them to treat him like a normal human being at the best of times. "I've got loads of work to do for school and my lines to learn and stuff. I'm cool."

"Your first leading role."

"Title role. It's different. Mephistopheles is the lead, I reckon. The devil always gets the best parts."

"So they tell me." Sinclair looked back into the empty sitting room. "Maybe we should have gone somewhere else. I was thinking of selling this place anyway."

"You're kidding me? I thought you loved it."

"I do. I did. But things are different now. I thought maybe your mother would use it more." Sinclair was rotating his wine glass slowly in his hand. It was the first time he'd mentioned his wife since the holiday had begun.

"Come on, what did you expect? It's where we came for happy family holidays. We don't play happy families any more, do we?"

Sinclair said nothing. He wanted to discuss all these things with his son, knew that he should, but he couldn't bring himself to do it just yet. Sometimes he felt just so, well, English. It's true, Joshua was mature for his age. Who knows, he probably already understood more than he was letting on. But here was the Prime Minister, never lost for words when he had to address the House of Commons or a packed conference hall but unable to find the words he needed to speak to his own son. "How is your mother?"

"Guess what? I haven't seen her for a couple of weeks so I don't know. Shall we find out?"

"What do you mean?"

"Telephones. Web-cams. Remember those? I know you have other people to make calls for you these days, but hey, let's just ring her up. I'm sure you can remember how to do it if you really try."

"Very funny, Josh. But it may not be a good time. She may be busy."

"Dad. Give her a call."

The laptop was set up on the kitchen table but Ruth hadn't typed a word for half an hour. The counter was littered with half drunk cups of tea and the remains of a chicken salad that she'd toyed with at lunchtime. There was a pile of unopened post propped up beside the kettle. She would have to give up soon anyway. If she wrote after she'd had more than one glass of wine she always had to redo it in the morning.

She cursed her agent quietly under her breath. *No extension to the deadline, darling, sorry, the publishers won't have it.* She knew why. Ruth Sinclair, author of rather dry but accurate historical fiction, was selling well at last. Better than she had in twenty years. *No, of course they're not marketing you as the Prime Minister's wife, but they can hardly stop people knowing it for themselves, can they? It isn't exactly a state secret, darling. And it's winning you thousands of new and loyal readers, you should be pleased. The back list is doing well, too.* These people weren't stupid. They saw the polls, read the pundits who said Paul Sinclair's hold on the top job could be the shortest since Jim Callaghan's almost forty years ago. *Sorry, darling, but they're holding us to the contract.*

Ruth poured herself a second glass. Mrs Fitzherbert could wait.

The kitchen at the back of the Sinclair's constituency home looked out on a wide expanse of green with the Birmingham skyline just visible in the distance. Through the window Ruth would occasionally catch sight of a solitary brazen fox or even a more timid badger. The badger's bark, so distinctive in the middle of the night, would take her thoughts into more comfortable territory, as often as not the Sussex countryside of her childhood. Ruth slept badly these days and didn't like to nap during the day, although if she had a drink at lunchtime she could find to her annoyance that she'd nodded off for an hour or more.

Eventually after several nights of wakefulness her body would drag her deep into unconsciousness and she would begin to catch up, but this hadn't happened for over a week now.

Ruth looked at the pile of post. Paul's local party office was closed for August and the correspondence was being redirected. It was Danny Oliver who had announced, not long after the General Election, that Mrs Sinclair would be spending more time in Aston where she could better attend to the Prime Minister's work as a constituency MP. There was nothing unusual in that, he'd told the media. End of story. In fact, no story at all. But if Mrs Fitzherbert was going to have to wait, so too could the post. She took a mouthful of her wine and tried to picture what might be inside the fridge when the phone rang. Against her better judgement she picked it up.

"Mum?"

"Josh, what a lovely surprise. Where are you?"

"You know where I am, Mum. Moraira. We were just talking about you so we thought we'd give you a call to see how you were."

"I see."

"So how are you?"

"I'm fine. Just a bit tired, I suppose. I've been working very hard. You know how it is."

"Do you want to put the web-cam on? We can talk properly."

Ruth hadn't looked in the mirror all day but she didn't need to. "Sorry, Josh, it's not working very well. And anyway, I was just, I was just going out. Are you having a good time?"

"Yeah it's cool. Dad was a very naughty Prime Minister today and went off without his minders for all of thirty seconds. But apart from having half the Spanish rescue services scrambled to find him in his swimming trunks, it's been pretty quiet."

"Josh, I can never tell when you're joking. Is he all right?"

"Yeah, Superhero lives to fight another day. Do you want to talk to him?"

"I would sweetheart, but there's a taxi waiting outside. Tell him I'll call him in a day or two. Enjoy the rest of your holiday. I really must dash, I'm sorry."

"Mum?"

"Yes Josh?"

"Nothing."

5

Ruth took a deep breath and held it. She had always impressed on her son the importance of honesty and tried to make it as easy as possible for him to be open about his feelings. She knew he didn't tell her everything, what teenager would? But he had none of that instinctive secrecy that she'd seen in other boys his age. She looked at the phone with an emptiness in her stomach that had little to do with having had almost nothing to eat since breakfast. She realised that lying to her son came almost naturally to her now. Until recently she'd have blamed her husband for making that even possible, but now she was starting to wonder. She looked around the kitchen, at the dirty crockery and the half-empty bottle of wine and slowly let her breath escape. She tried to picture Paul and Joshua alone at *Casa Cosecha* but it wasn't easy. Her memories of the house in Spain were full of people and noise and an optimism that now seemed naïve.

They'd all felt at ease there, able to speak their minds and say things that back at Westminster would have had to be uttered in code. And Ruth had been a part of it, although she'd made it her business to keep the food and wine coming so the political debate would never be held back by hunger or thirst. Joshua would run between the kitchen and the huge oak dining table caught up by the excitement of an adult enthusiasm he didn't begin or need to understand.

The cast list was always the same though their roles changed over time. Taking the lead from the start was Paul, a young Secretary of State for Culture, Media and Sport. He would joke that it was a job-share as Ruth was far better qualified for the post than he was. Joanna Morgan, tipped for promotion to the Cabinet herself any time now. Helen Griffin, perhaps Paul's oldest friend who was now in charge of his Westminster office. And Danny Oliver, then Political Editor of the *Independent on Sunday*. Ruth's mother, Olive, and Ray Morgan, never far from his wife's side, would help with the catering and keep the young Joshua out of too much mischief while the others talked.

Ruth remembered Joanna Morgan as the one who always had one eye on policy and the other very firmly trained on tactics. Her politics were a good few degrees to the left of Paul's but her thirst for power verged on the Stalinist. She had a simple philosophy: work out what you want and then work out how to get it. There had been a cold determination to her even then as she talked of the need to build alliances and establish a political network that could be activated as soon as the opportunity arose. And yet, with the benefit of hindsight, it was obvious that Joanna was already looking to find others to do the dirty work. Joanna Morgan didn't believe in leaving her own fingerprints where they might be discovered.

Paul on the other hand loved nothing more than discussing values, principles, policy. "It's the ideas that count," he would always say.

Danny Oliver brought a little journalistic detachment to the table. He knew governments could come and go and great white hopes be transformed into vague memories with a sudden change in the wind direction. His advice was to keep a low profile. He had no doubt Paul and Joanna were the ones to take the party forward but if they were too obvious about it they'd be torn to pieces, if not by their political rivals then by the media.

Paul would always ask for Ruth's opinion and she never hesitated to give it. She loved her husband for his intellectual energy, but she would often side with Joanna on the need to be practical. You can have the best ideas in the world but who are they going to help if you can't put them into effect? He always listened to his wife with great care and she knew what she was doing. She was giving him permission to get his hands dirty.

The other woman at the dining table, Helen Griffin, was never very comfortable with policy. She wasn't an intellectual and didn't pretend to be. Helen had a catchphrase, much over-used although nobody had the heart to tell her. "Let's cut the crap and get on with it", was her way of bringing the conversation back to where she was in her element. As the backroom person she volunteered to start laying some of the foundations for a leadership campaign that they all knew couldn't be long in coming. At Joanna's insistence she reluctantly agreed to work with Ray Morgan, though she wasn't sure what use he'd be.

Ruth had always rather liked Helen, although they'd never become friends in any real sense. She wasn't the sophisticated political operator that Joanna was, but she got results and wasn't squeamish about fingerprints so long as Paul was never incriminated. Helen Griffin's absolute loyalty had never been in question. Like Joanna, Helen had known her husband longer than Ruth had, if only by a year or two. He would say Joanna and Helen were as alike as marmalade and marmite. He could appreciate both but rarely in the same mouthful.

After only a few sessions of essentially speculative musings around the *Casa Cosecha* table it was Ruth who took the call that moved things up another gear.

The others were deep in a discussion on how to make subtle but important changes to Britain's foreign and security policy. Joanna was taking the lead, arguing forcefully that the terrorists were winning as long as civil liberties were being undermined. She was proposing a shift back to civilised values like democracy and freedom, whether the United States liked it or not, when Ruth answered the phone. None of them had even heard it ring.

"Paul, it's Switch." The Downing Street switchboard could find anybody at any time of the day or night. The room had fallen quiet.

Two minutes later Paul Sinclair had come back into the room and sat down, his deep green eyes scanning each of his friends in turn. The Foreign Secretary had just resigned, he said. Helen had muttered a barely audible 'fuck' while everyone waited for him to continue. Two other Cabinet ministers and four from the junior ranks had gone too.

Danny Oliver, who knew he'd have to get on the phone to his news desk, had been the first to ask why. Ruth had listened with half an ear to the explanation. Apparently he'd said he wanted to argue for a different approach to Europe from the backbenches and Danny confirmed that he'd been telling anyone who would listen that he'd felt bounced into taking Britain into the euro. Helen had had a few expletives to describe what she'd thought of that, but it was Joanna who'd asked the important question. What about the reshuffle? Paul had seen where she was coming from and told her to expect a call herself very soon. She'd made the Cabinet at last.

And him? "Oh. Me? Well, apparently I'm the new Foreign Secretary." Ruth had put her arms around his neck while Joshua tugged at her skirt and asked what all the fuss was about. He'd been the only one in no mood to celebrate that evening. He was twelve years old and if his dad's new job meant no more free tickets for the football he couldn't understand why the news was supposed to be good.

Now, at seventeen, Joshua was alone in the same house with his father. Time and fate had reshaped them all and given them so much of what they'd asked for.

In Birmingham Ruth squeezed washing up liquid into the sink and reminded herself once more of the futility of self-pity. They had all known there would be a price to pay and so it had proved. She had willed Paul on with as much determination as anybody else around that table so how could she complain now? With one arm she swept the dirty plates into the sink and then picked up the half empty bottle of wine.

6

Danny Oliver's editor had been delighted with his scoop. The first interview with the new Foreign Secretary. Although Danny had thought it better not to advertise too widely that he had been Paul Sinclair's house guest in Spain at the time of the appointment. Not that his pro-Labour sympathies were any big secret. The world of the Westminster lobby journalists was so small and claustrophobic that there wasn't much the hacks didn't know about each other. And so, just a year later, after Sinclair's victory in the leadership election took the political world by surprise, there were few raised eyebrows when Danny became the first black, and quite possibly the first gay, Communications Director at Number 10.

He hadn't been sure he was cut out for the rough and tumble of active politics, but when the job offer came it was simply too exciting to turn down. Since then he'd surprised even himself by proving extremely good at it. He worked closely with Helen Griffin, who was made the new Prime Minister's Chief of Staff, and Danny figured they had all the bases covered. Nothing much moved in the political undergrowth without one or other of them picking up the scent. He had his own personal Media Rule Book stored away in his head. Rule number one was never get taken by surprise. Rule number two said that if you were you should never show it.

Danny's quiet unflappability was just what Sinclair wanted. If his Communications Director ever did raise his voice or resort to expletives then the Prime Minister knew something out of the ordinary was going on in the parallel universe inhabited by the media.

"Alastair, I've never heard such bullshit in my life. You're not going to publish that story and I'll tell you why. Because you know as well as I do that it's 100% unadulterated rubbish."

Sinclair and Joshua had been back from their holiday in Spain little more than thirty-six hours. It was another of Danny's rules that journalists, like nature, abhorred a vacuum. If you don't make news, others will do it for you. So the Prime Minister had barely unpacked his swimming trunks and tennis shorts before Danny had him up on his well-tanned legs speaking to Royal Institute of British Architects. Nothing too controversial. Danny could have written it in his sleep. But the message, that you needed a properly drawn-up plan and the wherewithal to turn it into reality, had gone down well enough. Just the thing for the start of a new political season when the polls are grim and you need to give the impression that you're confidently getting on with the job all the same.

They were in the Daimler heading through the West End when Danny's mobile rang. Sinclair was looking out of the window wondering which of the many theatres he'd go to if he ever got the chance. "Trouble?"

"I don't think so. The *Daily Mirror*."

"I guessed that much. What's the story?"

"Are you ready for this? Alastair is threatening to lead tomorrow's paper with the news that you're having an affair. He won't tell me any more, not even who the lucky woman is supposed to be. He's bullshitting." Danny's dark face was silhouetted against the lights of St Martin's Lane but Sinclair could tell he was more worried than he was letting on. "Unless, of course, you want to tell me otherwise."

"Well, actually…" Sinclair was enough of a performer to know when to pause for effect, but Danny knew him too well to rise to the bait. "…actually, no. Perhaps Alastair would like to tell me where I might find the time or for that matter the opportunity. Even assuming I wanted to, of course."

Danny's phone rang again. This time he offered nothing beyond the occasional 'Go on, I'm listening.' He put the mobile away and looked at his watch. "He says he's got e-mails sent by you to the mystery woman. Her husband found them and for some reason thought the best thing to do was to ring the *Daily Mirror*."

"Well it can't be too hard to prove I didn't write them, surely?" Sinclair picked up his own phone, which was built into the seat beside him. "Switch? Get me Helen can you?" The Chief of Staff was on the line in seconds and Sinclair switched the phone onto the speaker. "Danny's got a little story you might want to know about."

As usual Helen Griffin's reaction to what she heard was immediate and direct. "People are going to believe it," she said. "You're a man in the prime of his life, still in reasonably good shape."

"Don't overdo the compliments."

"I wasn't going to. It's no big secret that Ruth is miles away living her own life and that you hardly ever see her. So people are going to think you probably are shagging someone else. It's what politicians do. So the question is, what do we do?"

"How about ignore it and let it go away?" Sinclair didn't sound particularly convinced by his own suggestion.

"Not an option," said Helen. You know what the Westminster Village is like. Left up in the air, something like this will keep the rumour mill going for weeks. We can't afford that kind of crap. So either you let them run it and allow people to think it's true. It might do wonders for your poll ratings especially among working class men, a group I don't need to remind you that we need to win back badly..."

"If it's all right with you, I think we'll dispense with that option."

"If you say so. In that case you have to kill it. Stone dead. Stake through the heart, the works. Can you do that, Danny?"

"I've told them it's not true, but Alastair says he's got evidence."

"Well I know what I would do." Danny and Paul looked at each other, both trying to guess what was coming next. "Go round there, tell Alastair his paper is a pile of shit and his story is just another lump of turd. How long are we going to the let the Daily Fucking Mirror give us the run around day after day? Sorry, Danny, I know this is your territory, but what does he think he's doing dumping this on us on a Sunday evening?"

"I think if he was here," said Danny, "he'd say he was doing his job."

"What about the Press Complaints Commission?" asked Sinclair.

"About as much use as Tetley's condom."

"Helen's right about that," said Danny. "It might be an option in the long run, if all else fails, but it's not going to help us tonight."

"Well then maybe Helen's right and I should go round there. How far is the *Mirror* from here, Derek?"

Detective Inspector Derek Smyth looked back over his shoulder. "About ten minutes. The traffic's pretty light."

"The only way to deal with bullies is to stand up to them." Helen had a way of dominating a situation even at the end of a phone. "Give him my love if you see him."

News of a possible scoop had been buzzing around the newsroom since early afternoon, but nobody outside the Editor's closest circle knew what it might be. There was nothing unusual in that. After all, tabloid newspapers lived or died by scoops, whether real or at least partly imagined. The dozen or so journalists still at their desks in the large open-plan office weren't exactly holding their breaths. This particular Sunday evening most of the rest of the paper was done and dusted and there were two other perfectly creditable stories that could make a front page splash if the Editor's baby turned out to be still born, as it so often did.

At first nobody raised their heads when the two men came in through the swing door by the lifts. It was only when Derek Smyth, so obviously a policeman, followed them a few paces behind and started scanning the newsroom that anybody looked up. By the time Paul Sinclair had been recognised he was through the Editor's door with just a cursory knock.

"Paul. What a unexpected surprise." Not entirely true. The *Mirror's* own security people had rung ahead to say the Prime Minister was on his way up. "I'd offer you a drink, but…"

"Don't worry," said Danny, "it's not a social call."

"No, I didn't think it was. Look, Paul, a story's a story. I couldn't sit on this if I wanted to. If we don't print this then your friend's husband is going to take it somewhere else. That's how it works, as I'm sure Danny will tell you."

"There is no friend, Alastair. No woman. No affair. If you or anybody else says there is then you're going to look very, very stupid, believe me."

"I'd like to believe you, Paul. No, really I would. But I have e-mails sent from your own computer at Number 10 and they don't leave a lot to the imagination."

"Can I see them?"

"I can't do that. I have sources to protect."

"Oh come on, Alastair. It's me you're talking to. How can we have a serious discussion about this if you're going to start that holier-than-though routine? What you're threatening to print isn't just any other story."

"What the Prime Minister is trying to say," cut in Danny, "is put up or shut up. If you'll excuse the cliché."

"We have the proof we need. Our lawyers have been all over it. Okay, so you're denying it, but if we're in the cliché game, you would say that wouldn't you?"

The two men were visibly sizing each other up like two dogs with their hackles up. One would have to back down and while Sinclair was the shorter he was younger by a decade. He also had the most to lose, but if he was going to prevail it was going to be by the force of his argument. "No, Alastair, that's where you're wrong. If the story had a shred of truth in it, I might leave it to Danny here to deny it and apply the thumbscrews in his usual, very polite way. But I am standing here in your office, looking you in the eye and telling you personally that your story is untrue. Think about it. All three of us in this room know the history of political scandals. It's always the cover up that gets you in the end. I could survive the revelation of an affair. Some of my people even think it would do me some good. Could I survive having stood in the office of a national newspaper Editor and lied through my teeth?"

There was a tap on the door and it opened a few inches only to be greeted by a sharp "Not now." The three men stood in silence for ten long seconds before the Editor spoke. "You've got bigger balls than I'd ever have given you credit for, I'll tell you that for free. Okay, you win. But it's not going on the spike. I'm going to keep investigating this one."

"You can investigate it all you like. You won't turn a fiction into the truth."

~

Helen Griffin hugged him tighter than he'd been hugged in a very long time. "I'm glad to see you've still got it in you. And there was me thinking you were starting to go soft. It sounds like it was quite a performance."

Sinclair was stretched out on the sofa sipping a beer. He looked genuinely perplexed. "It wasn't a performance, Helen. It was the truth."

"Well, whatever it was, it was impressive. So now the real questions need to be answered."

"I don't understand."

"What Helen means," said Danny, "is where did they get the story from? Who's behind it and why?"

Helen had an answer to that one. "Jo Morgan. As sure as night follows day."

"You can be very predictable sometimes," said Sinclair. "You guys seem to think that Joanna is spending her every waking hour looking for ways to destroy me. And sure, once you start thinking like that, then every bit of trouble can be traced back to her."

"That's about the size of it," said Helen.

"Danny?"

"Well, she does have very close links with the *Mirror*. I've lost count of the number of stories they've run recently that damage you and just so happen to reflect well on her by comparison. We all know what a clever operator she can be. When she was part of the team it was something we all appreciated. She hasn't lost her talents you know, she's just not using them to help us anymore."

"To help me, you mean. Look I know life would be a lot easier if Jo had stayed on board, but she didn't. She had her reasons. And, yes, she'd like to be Prime Minister. Well so would a lot of people. It doesn't follow that she'd go around fabricating something like this. Don't forget, I've known Joanna Morgan a hell of a long time. This isn't her style."

Helen took a swig of her drink. "I wish I had your confidence, Paul. Somebody had access to your computer, presumably while you were away sunning yourself. The acting Prime Minister perhaps? Or one of her cronies doing her dirty work for her as usual. It amounts to much the same thing."

The Prime Minister ran his fingers through his hair and yawned. "Look, I'm tired. There have been enough unsubstantiated allegations for one night. I'll see you guys in the morning. Get some sleep and let me worry about Jo Morgan. Okay?"

The Editor of the *Daily Mirror* was not a man who liked to be faced down. Nor did he want the story he was chasing to become widely known in case his rivals picked it up. So as Helen and Danny left the Prime Minister's flat, he was on the phone to his best asset, the source of most of his paper's political scoops. And for the second time that evening he didn't like the way the conversation was going. "Look, PJ," he said, "I know you don't do this kind of story. I'm not asking you to. But you've got the best contacts of anybody on this paper and we do pay your wages, remember? All I'm saying is, keep your ear to the ground and if you hear anything come straight through to me. I don't think that's too much to ask."

At Number 2 Castle Terrace, London SE1 the Mirror's star columnist put down the phone and rolled over in bed.

7

Castle Terrace was on the corner of Wilson Crescent, one of a thousand similar rows of houses built with municipal zeal in 1960s. But even by the standards of this largely undeveloped part of South London, the last house on the corner was nothing short of a disgrace. Number 2 hadn't been built as an end of terrace but had become one the day the house next door fell down under the combined assault of dry rot and a roof so badly maintained that every shower washed away more of its will to live. The whole structure had given an almighty sigh and collapsed in on itself allowing its inhabitants just enough warning to escape out into the street. It had tired of propping up the rest of Castle Terrace, a task that was now assumed with great reluctance by PJ Walton's own house, known improbably as the Castle.

Never had a building been less deserving of its name. Shortly after the demise of the neighbouring property a lanky figure had emerged to inspect the damage and see if the whole terrace was about to share the same fate. Digging through the rubble next door before the Council excavator arrived to clear the site, all he'd found of any conceivable value was half of the metal sign that had carried the name Castle Terrace for almost half a century. He wiped it on his shirt and reached up to hang it on a nail above the front door of the new end of terrace. Nobody had bothered to take it down again and the house had been known ever since as the Castle.

It was without doubt the only castle in England to have the remains of a gas fire clinging to its side wall, ten feet above the ground, surrounded by a particularly nasty shade of lime green wallpaper. Vinyl wall covering had been one of the more enduring products of the 1970s and the paper had survived all the rainfall that had done for the rest of the building. Below the fire, within reach of Bermondsey's thriving community of fly posters with their buckets of glue and soggy brushes, was a variety of hastily pasted advertisements for rave nights, political demonstrations and car boot sales. None lasted more than a week or two while the lime green held its own with as much dignified superiority as it could muster, which was very little.

Mrs Alma Gundry saw no dignity at all. Castle Terrace was immediately opposite her own house, which was situated on the south side of Wilson Crescent. All she could see as she stood on her step with the morning paper in her hand and looked across the road was a monstrous affront to her ambitions for the neighbourhood. She was convinced the area was at last on the way up. It had only been a matter of time. Mrs Gundry had been bemused as the rest of SE1 was gradually gentrified and Wilson Crescent had remained stuck in a mid twentieth century time-warp. But now people, most people, were making an effort to smarten the place up.

It had started when the run down warehouses by the river had suddenly been transformed into highly desirable apartments and workers in the City of London and Canary Wharf had discovered to their surprise that Bermondsey was just a short taxi ride away. Unlike some of her neighbours, Mrs Gundry didn't resent the arrival of so much unaccustomed wealth on her doorstep. She had high hopes that some of the class that had come with it would ripple gradually down as far as her street.

She had come to the conclusion that it was the Castle that had single-handedly arrested the otherwise irresistible tide of progress. The door looked as if it was ready to fall off its hinges at any moment. It was so long since it had been washed that she couldn't even remember if it was supposed to be dark blue or black. Mrs Alma Gundry despised the place and all who lived in it.

It was going to be another bright late summer's day by the look of it. On the way back from the newsagents she'd noticed that the African violets in the window boxes at number 37 had lost none of their colour. She pulled her cardigan tight around her chest and turned to go indoors. As she did so the door to the Castle creaked open. The man in the hallway called back over his shoulder, bent down to pick up an old leather briefcase and stepped out into the street. It was the respectable one. Relatively speaking, of course.

Mrs Gundry hesitated for a second and then decided to engage him. "Mr Walton."

PJ Walton had told Mrs Gundry his name once in an effort to be neighbourly and had regretted it ever since. "Good morning Alma."

"You know how as how I don't like to interfere."

PJ did his best to keep his face straight. He tightened his stomach and lowered his chin in an effort to close his windpipe to the splutter that was threatening to escape. Mrs Gundry wondered if he was constipated. PJ brought up his free hand to cough and relieve some of the pent up pressure. He didn't want Mrs Gundry to think he was laughing at her. Since his fortunes as a columnist had taken a turn for the better PJ Walton had been making a good living standing up for the ordinary citizens of Britain against an interfering state. Mrs Alma Gundry was a great believer in interference. "Of course not, Alma. I don't want to be late, but how can I help you?"

"I'm not at all sure you know what goes on around here while you're at work Mr Walton."

PJ looked up and down Wilson Crescent then back at Mrs Gundry. "Around here?"

"In there." She nodded towards the Castle. "There's some very unsavoury sorts. Not what the area needs." She realised she was having difficulty expressing herself. Her neighbour was clever with words, she could tell that, and it made her feel tongue tied. She knew what she felt, though, and that building was dragging the area down. She watched the street all day from her chair by the window and had no doubt Wilson Crescent deserved better. She had no idea what they got up to in there behind the filthy net curtains, but was sure it wasn't the sort of thing that should be happening in an area that was on the way up. "They drop litter and everything," she added, realising as soon as she said it how feeble it sounded.

"Litter?"

"What we need is more police on the streets." Mrs Gundry had just posted a letter to Downing Street saying the very same thing.

"I don't think the police collect litter, Mrs Gundry."

"Your friends don't seem to have no respect for the environment. I thought you was supposed to be all ecologists or something?" She pointed at the faded Green Party sticker in the downstairs window, next to that of the South London Freedom Alliance and the Anti-Nazi League. They had been there so long PJ had no idea who had put them up or when. Mrs Gundry was starting to get into her stride. "The police has had to be called more than once, you know. Takes them half the morning to get here, mind you." She believed it was a good citizen's duty to keep the local constabulary on its toes.

"Come along Alma, be fair, that was a long time ago. And even then they didn't find anything to trouble them. Given that there's nothing the police like more than trampling on people's liberties, don't you think they'd have been back if they had any good excuse? The house may be a bit of a mess but it's not a den of iniquity I can assure you." His column in the *Daily Mirror*, The Naked Prophet, regularly took the authorities to task for working against the people they should be protecting.

Mrs Gundry wasn't sure she understood but she was pretty certain she didn't agree. "I don't know about that Mr Walton."

PJ made a move as if to leave. He liked to spend the morning talking to his contacts and thinking through his article for the following day. He was certain his neighbour had never read a single word he'd written. Had she known that he was the author of one of the most widely read tabloid newspaper columns in the country, she'd be even more determined to pass on her sadly unenlightened views. Mrs Alma Gundry, in his considered opinion, made Paul Sinclair look like a liberal. Not for the first time he was delighted that the identity of the Naked Prophet, *The Man Who Tells the Naked Truth*, was the best kept secret in journalism. But Mrs Gundry hadn't finished yet. "No, no, you're wrong there Mr Walton. If it weren't for the police this place would have gone to blazes long ago. What we need is more of them."

PJ looked at his watch. He needed to be by the phone in half an hour at the latest. He should be able to keep his editor off his back provided he came up with something good to make the Prime Minister feel as if he'd never had a holiday. "Well, I really must be getting to work." He smiled feebly and shrugged as if to suggest that despite all the evidence to the contrary they were both on the same side really. "There'll be no more trouble with the police Alma, I promise you. And I'll have a word about the litter."

8

"Come in, Inspector." Colonel Henry Neilson's voice grated like a badly maintained gearbox. He used to be a sixty a day man, although the total ban on smoking in public places had forced him reluctantly to cut his intake to five or six. He didn't ask Derek Smyth to sit down. "I've read your report and I've taken the time to give it some thought."

"Yes, Sir. Thank you. It really was really little more than a false alarm."

"I see that's the conclusion you have come to here. I'm not sure I entirely agree, Inspector."

"Colonel…"

Neilson had swivelled on his chair to type something into the console on his desk. He turned back in an instant. "Allow me to continue, Inspector, if you wouldn't mind." When he was angry the Downing Street Security Supremo's clipped Scottish consonants became even more pronounced. "We have a tradition in this country and it's one I prefer to maintain. We do not lose the Prime Minister. Not even for a minute. I believe you lost sight of him for the best part of twenty minutes, is that correct?"

"He came to no harm, Sir. And he wasn't lost, not strictly speaking."

"Then why did you call out the Coastguard?"

"As a precaution, Colonel."

"I'd like to share your, shall we say untroubled attitude to this whole affair." Derek Smyth tried to interrupt but Neilson signalled him to be quiet with the flick of a wrist. "But we no longer live in a world where such complacency can be afforded. Do I need to remind you that three years ago this country was subject to the most callous attempt at mass murder anywhere in the world?"

"No, of course not."

"Do you think the terrorists who thought nothing of bringing chemical warfare to London would hesitate for a second to exploit our weakness, your weakness, to kill the Prime Minister while your back was turned?"

This was no time to remind the Colonel that the Circle of Death Bombers hadn't actually managed to detonate their lethal cocktail. To Neilson the very fact that the device had been planted could be used to justify almost anything. "It won't happen again."

"I wish I could be sure of that. I have to fight the kind of complacency I see in your report here almost every day. Single-handed. Lessons have to be learned, Inspector. And besides, I don't like loose ends. You were the senior officer at the time, I believe? It was just you and Sergeant…" He looked down at the file on his desk.

"Woods."

"Ah yes, Sergeant Woods. Well, as I said, I don't like loose ends. It's important when lapses like this occur to demonstrate that action has been taken. Loopholes closed. Any risk to security has to be addressed, I'm sure you understand." The Inspector nodded, fearing the worst. "Your service record is exemplary, Inspector. You're a man with a great future ahead of you, I'm sure of that. Which leaves us in a bit of a quandary. Clearly somebody must take responsibility. It may be that parts of your report here could be, shall we say, revisited? "

Derek was finding it hard to concentrate on what he was being told. This office always made him feel slightly sick. Behind the Colonel's balding head a bank of monitors flashed up image after image of the Downing Street periphery. The highest of hi-tech scanning devices looked into and sniffed the bags of passers-by without them even knowing they were being probed. A terminal over his left shoulder was checking the registration plates of every vehicle on the roads within a radius of a mile or more. Photographs of their drivers and a summary of their police and intelligence records scrolled continuously along the bottom of the screen.

Ever since a person or persons unknown had planted a phial of deadly chemicals less than half a mile away at Westminster tube station, Downing Street had been closed off behind the most sophisticated defensive security system anywhere in the world. Colonel Neilson, known to just about everybody behind his back as Kneejerk, was very,

very proud of every sensor, every lens, every listening device. But even the best technology he'd been able to purchase from his American friends benefited from the addition of human eyes and ears at strategic points. It was, in Kneekjerk's view, a great privilege to be asked to serve as part of such a system.

"Revisited, Colonel?"

The following morning Sergeant Terry Woods found a note in his inbox when he checked in for work. He had been taken off Personal Protection for the Prime Minister and would, with immediate effect, have the privilege of standing and serving on the gates of Number 10.

~

"Shit."

Paul Sinclair looked up from his papers and out into the hallway. The bathroom door was half open. "Thank you, Josh, but I don't need a running commentary on what you're planning to do in there."

"Very funny." Joshua squinted in the mirror at the new spot that had broken through overnight. He pondered whether to burst it. He gave it an exploratory squeeze but it clearly wasn't going to give in without a bloody fight. One that he'd probably end up losing. He knew from all the experience of his teenage years that launching a full-scale assault now, while it would make him feel better, would only make matters worse. Better to wait and see how things developed. He could always deal with it later if he had to. But the discovery had got the day off to a bad start. He closed the bathroom door behind him with a bang and stomped across the hall and into the kitchen.

The Prime Minister's flat above Number 11 Downing Street was spacious and comfortable. The huge central hallway with stairs leading up and round to the bedrooms and main bathroom gave it the feel of a much larger property than it actually was. Light poured into the reception rooms from across Horseguards and St James' Park and the thick security glass made it almost unnaturally quiet. It was even possible, just occasionally, to forget that it was only a connecting door away from the labyrinth of offices and corridors of Number 10. Sinclair liked to work on his boxes here first thing before going down to meet his staff. Since Ruth had left he had an occasional twinge of guilt at holding on to so much space, but when the morning sun hit his face as he sat on the sofa surrounded by his papers the Prime Minister was very much at home.

And yet, roomy though it was, the flat could still feel crowded when it was being shared with a seventeen year old boy and a marauding army of uncontrolled hormones. It didn't always make for good concentration.

"Why are there no Cheerios?"

"Well, let me see. Possibly because you didn't put them on the list?" His father was standing in the doorway in his dressing gown. "You can't expect people to be mind readers, Josh. And, anyway, you're quite capable of stopping off and buying a packet of breakfast cereal yourself, you know."

"Too busy." Joshua didn't look up from the book he had open on the breakfast bar. Paul Sinclair bent over and tousled his son's thick blond hair but was pushed away by a bony shoulder. Evidently this was not the time for one of his Ordinary Dad bonding sessions.

"This couldn't be an attack of first night nerves, could it?"

"No."

"Have you learnt your lines?"

"Yes." He glared up at his father. "Of course. Unlike someone I know I've got no intention of standing up and making a fool of myself in front of hundreds of people." His face softened into the beginnings of an impish grin as he returned to the script. "But then I don't insist on writing my own speeches, do I?"

As he'd emerged from the constrictive cocoon of puberty Joshua Sinclair had started to grow into the rather angular face he'd inherited and had even learned how to remove its harder edges with the warmth of his smile. It was the distinctively long, narrow but perfectly symmetrical nose he'd also been handed down that was currently harbouring the teenage acne. His father was sometimes accused of exploiting his own 'boyish' charm but Joshua was the genuine article. He had yet to develop that slight tightness around the jaw and the eyes that came from knowing the world was looking at you for most of your waking hours.

As a schoolboy actor, Joshua could switch easily from anger to fear to passion with little of the self-consciousness of the average teenager.

43

His father, on the other hand, had long since grown weary of putting on the faces that people expected of him. Those closest to him, Helen Griffin and Danny Oliver in particular, could usually divine how he was feeling from the hint of a furrow on his forehead or the subtle shifts in the muscles around his mouth, but for most people the Prime Minister was infuriatingly difficult to read. He didn't do it on purpose, his face was naturally passive. When he was Joshua's age it had made him look self assured to some but self satisfied and smug to others. Later in life, once he'd embarked on a career in public life, people took it as a sign of a shrewd political operator, a man who knew how to keep his thoughts to himself until he was ready to reveal them.

When, during the leadership campaign, one columnist had described his features as "showing all the intelligence and character of a jelly mould" he had briefly tried to change, grinning and frowning at the slightest provocation. Helen and Danny soon told him to go back to being himself.

"You will be there, won't you?"

"Hey. I said I'd be there and I'll be there. I also said I'd make a modest attempt at running the country again today, so I'd better go."

"What is it today then? The Emergency Powers Must Give Your Name And ID Number When You Answer The Phone Act?"

"Very funny."

"Or the Anti-Terrorist Put Your Hand Up Before You Go To The Loo Bill?"

"Stick to the classics, Josh. Comedy isn't your style."

"You think I'm joking. I had an iris scan and my digital thumb-print taken on the way into school last week."

"You want me to be sorry about that? Well I can't be, Josh. I'm pleased to hear it, I really am. Do you think I would sleep at night if I thought we weren't taking every possible precaution? How do you think I would feel if something happened at your school? Or at any other school for that matter? You don't see all the intelligence stuff I get on a daily basis. It's terrifying."

"But you can't move out there without having your photo taken or being asked for your ID. No not asked, asked would be okay. Having it demanded of you. Everyone's looking at everyone else like they could be the next Circle of Death Bomber. It's okay for you. You get driven around in your nuke-proof Daimler or whatever it is. You've got no idea what everybody else has to put up with."

"I do, you know. I get a thousand letters a day about it."

"Yeah and you have somebody else to read them for you."

"Josh, this is serious. Do you want me to ignore all the warnings, forget what's already happened, just cross my fingers and hope for the best? Do you?"

"I just think you need to get it into proportion. But what do I know? I'm just seventeen right?"

"Now don't be stupid."

"See what I mean? Later, Dad. Go and run the country. I'm going to go and try to live in it. If I can fight my way out of Kneejerk's little fortress that is."

9

Helen Griffin spat out a mouthful of toothpaste, looked first at her watch and then in the mirror. Neither gave her any comfort. She applied a neat circle of bright red lipstick, puckered her lips and hobbled into the bedroom looking in the half light for where she'd kicked off her second shoe the night before. The duvet shifted slightly, grunted and stretched itself out. One foot appeared and then vanished just as quickly back into the warmth.

Helen bent down to look under the bed. She had just retrieved the missing shoe when a hand darted out and held her wrist, drawing it under the bedclothes. She stretched out her fingers and brushed against firm evidence that at least part of him was awake.

"I've got a cab waiting downstairs."

He grunted and kicked the duvet to one side. His eyes were still closed while Helen's were admiring his lean, almost hairless body. He tugged again on her wrist and arched his back. It could have been a stretch but it looked to her more like an invitation. She knew she'd left him alone, yet again, last night. He'd been asleep when she'd got back from seeing Sinclair. So she bent down and exhaled in a gentle silent whistle over his scrotum. As she lowered her head further he let go of her wrist and moved his hand to her leg. With his eyes still closed he edged his fingers upwards, pausing only for a second as he felt her tongue dart over him. He was deftly pulling aside the elastic when the taxi hooted just under the bedroom window and made him jump.

Helen lifted up her head and looked at the almost perfect circle of red lipstick that her mouth had left behind. "A little something to remember me by, darling."

"You know, just for once, I'd rather not have to rely on memories." It was, thought Helen, a surprisingly long sentence so early in the day.

"I'll call you when I can."

The taxi tooted again in the street below. She stuck her head out of the window and her words were lost in the morning traffic. Inside her bag a mobile phone was ringing. She found it, clasped it to her ear, pulled her jacket off the back of a chair and headed for the door.

"Sorry sweetheart," she called back over her shoulder, "Next time. Don't forget it's Washington tomorrow. But I'll see you tonight. I promise."

Ruth Sinclair was used to her mother's kitchen being freezing cold first thing in the morning. She pulled at the coffee machine, trying to extricate the plastic filter from its housing, but soon gave up the struggle and reached for the jar of instant. It smelt stale. She must have bought it the last time she was down here in Brighton. She put it back on the side. Her mother would want tea anyway.

Ruth had enough on her mind without worrying about what was going on sixty miles up the M23 in London. Had she been able to see the scene that was about to be played out in her husband's little office she would have felt more embarrassed than surprised. Colonel Henry Neilson, a man Ruth had loathed from the moment he first gave her his thin smile and shot out his hand like a weapon for her to shake, was at that moment clearing his throat and preparing to knock on the door.

As Helen Griffin slammed her own front door behind her, the taxi was already starting to pull away. She waved frantically with one hand, still holding the phone to her ear with the other.

"Switch? I'll be ten minutes," she said, throwing her bag onto the back seat of the cab. Buying a flat in Stockwell, just across the river from Westminster, had been one of her better decisions. She took out her lipstick and pouted over the driver's shoulder into his rear-view mirror.

Kneejerk's security update was always Sinclair's first meeting of the day. The Prime Minister had his back to the window overlooking

47

the Downing Street garden and appeared to be doodling on a pad of paper. He signalled to the Colonel to take a chair without looking up. He thought he knew what was coming having already been through the various intelligence reports while his son was monopolising the bathroom.

The Colonel sat down stiffly and coughed. For him Ruth was a security issue and nothing more. As he started to speak the woman herself was carrying the tea and her mother's newspaper up the creaky stairs of the house in Brighton.

"If you don't mind, Prime Minister, I think perhaps we should start with the question of your wife."

~

Helen Griffin looked at the digital clock on the taxi's dashboard and decided she had just enough time to grab a coffee.

"You can drop me here."

She pushed a five euro note through the window and took advantage of a gap in the traffic to cross Whitehall without having to dodge half a dozen homicidal motorcycle couriers. The staff in Churchill's were watching her through the large glass window and her cappuccino was ready for her when she came in.

"Pay me later, Miss Griffin. You'll be late." They were well used to this Monday morning ritual. She took the polystyrene cup in her right hand, shuffled her bag higher up on her shoulder and headed back across the road searching for her pass with her left.

~

Colonel Henry Neilson gathered up his papers and rose to his feet. At just five feet six, with his rigid, agonisingly thin body and almost bald head, he looked more like an undernourished pigeon than the man in charge of protecting the country's safety. He carefully cleaned both lenses of his reading glasses before sliding them into the breast pocket of his suit. Paul Sinclair watched his precise movements with a mixture of amusement and admiration. He'd never thought of the Colonel as a natural diplomat, he hadn't been hired for his charm, but nobody could have handled the matter with greater tact. The Prime Minister slid the beige file marked West Midlands Police Confidential Report under a pile of papers.

"Thank you, Colonel. Would you ask Rebecca to show the others in?"

"Prime Minister, I hope…"

"Don't worry. Thank you."

10

Sinclair liked the intimacy of his little office. The Den, as it was known, was hardly big enough for all his closest advisers to squeeze into at one time. Two sofas faced each other in front of the ornate fireplace and for those not lucky enough or early enough to get a seat on them, a dozen hard backed chairs lined the walls. Anybody else had to stand.

He loved the light that poured in across the Downing Street garden on a bright day. The view was much improved since the climbing frame, mountain bikes and paddling pool had been removed. Inside he'd replaced the rather unsettling modern art with some more figurative works. He'd struggled as best he could with the latest wave of new British art when he'd been the Culture Secretary. Now he was Prime Minister he could hang what he liked on the walls.

Ruth Sinclair was sitting at the foot of her mother's bed as her husband's staff filed in from the outer office. It would have surprised her to know he was thinking of her just then and, after what he'd just been told, with genuine concern. Danny Oliver noticed his eyes fixed somewhere in the middle distance. He hesitated before handing him the media brief.

This was the inner core, the small group of men and women who were the Prime Minister's eyes and ears to the outside world. He encouraged them to speak frankly, told them they were no use to him otherwise. Danny took the corner of the sofa opposite the window, the morning light adding unexpected shadow to his black skin. He flicked quickly through the papers in front of him and unable to find what he was looking for got up again, pushing past the rest of the team as they found themselves seats or stood against the wall.

"What's up with him?" someone asked. "It's not like Danny to let a few bad headlines get to him."

Sinclair shrugged and looked around the room.

"And where is my esteemed Chief of Staff?"

"It's Monday," said a voice from the back of the room, as if that were explanation enough.

"Thank you for that," said Helen opening the heavy door with her shoulder. "I'm all too well aware what day it is. I'm also aware, because unlike some people I can listen, think, walk and talk all at the same time, even on a Monday morning, that we have work to do. So let's cut the crap and get on with it." There was a groan at Helen's familiar injunction but if she heard it she didn't react.

A uniformed messenger was handing out cups of coffee. The Prime Minister shook his head. "I've had too many already this morning thanks, Jean." Danny Oliver pushed his way back into the room and placed a single sheet of paper on the desk in front of Sinclair. The Prime Minister read it quickly and put it to one side. Helen Griffin was already in full stride.

"Welcome back to the real world. I hope you all had good holidays and are refreshed and ready for the battles ahead." They all knew who she meant and a few eyes flicked involuntarily towards Sinclair who despite his tan was looking unusually tense. "Danny can tell us about the latest dismal polls. In case anybody has failed to notice, the unions could have half the hospitals in England on A&E only by the end of the week. Wasn't somebody supposed to be coming up with some ideas for making the health reforms popular, or have we given up on trying to do anything that people will actually support?"

Suddenly Sinclair's staff were taking a keen interest in the cleanliness of their shoes. "Well, we're running out of time," she went on. "The health debate is next week and as it happens to be the central plank of our legislative programme it would stop us looking completely incompetent if we managed to win it. So far as I can see, we can't even be sure enough of our own MPs will back us, never mind anybody else. In the meantime you," she addressed the Prime Minister directly for the first time, "have got a speech to deliver in Washington that hasn't even been started yet."

"I've been working on that."

"Well that's something."

"Danny?" Sinclair was impatient to get the meeting moving.

"The papers are full of the health story. As Helen says, they're all predicting a close vote. The *Mirror*," there was a flash of triumph as his eyes darted from Paul to Helen and back again, "has talk of a Cabinet split as its lead story. They're quoting a senior Labour backbencher…"

"Senior backbencher my foot," chipped in Helen. "More like some has-been or never-will-be with an axe to grind."

Danny picked up where he'd left off. "A senior Labour backbencher who says the Conservative Party is now closer to the founding principles of the NHS than the government. The BBC, as ever, has been pumping up the same line with knobs on, hauling in the usual suspects. The Health Secretary put up a good show at ten past eight, though."

"Stephen Piggin? A good show? There's a first time for everything, I suppose." This time Helen's interruption earned her a stern look from the direction of the Prime Minister's chair.

"I was more concerned about the inside pages, though," Danny went on, digging out a folded newspaper from the pile on his lap. "Our favourite columnist has a detailed account of the row at the Cabinet Committee on Health. It's remarkably accurate too."

"Somebody has been talking to the Naked Prophet and it doesn't take a genius to work out who," said Helen.

Sinclair scratched his head and ran his hand down the back of his neck. Helen and Danny were becoming so obsessed by Joanna Morgan that they saw her hand in everything. "Maybe we can talk about all that later. Now what's all this about?" Sinclair picked up the report he'd been handed. "Danny?"

"Associated Press agency report out of Asmara. A group of aid workers feared taken hostage. They disappeared from their camp late last night. They're from Poverty Action, which I have to admit I've never heard of. A small charity with a base in Cambridge, so there's a good chance there are Britons among them but we don't know for sure yet."

"Poverty Action?" Like any politician, Sinclair had had dealings with most of the major charities at some time or another. "Doesn't ring any bells. Do we have any idea who might be holding them?"

Danny shook his head. "We're relying on the news wires for the minute, but our guys are trying to find out more."

"Asmara?" The Prime Minister was looking perplexed.

"Capital of Eritrea," said Danny.

"Funnily enough I do actually know where it is," replied Sinclair, "I've even been there a few years back, in my days on the International Development Committee. Very good food, I seem to remember. Lots of pasta. But I thought their rather nasty little border dispute was finally settled a year or so ago."

"It was – officially." Helen Griffin was reading from a Foreign Office briefing paper. "But they and the Ethiopians have been carrying out raids into each other's territory ever since the UN turned its attention elsewhere. It's become quite brutal again, by all accounts. The aid agencies have been pushing us to do more to help."

"Okay. Let me know as soon as we learn more. We'll leave it there."

Sinclair motioned to Danny Oliver to stay behind as the others left. The Prime Minister looked out on the late summer sunshine. The gardener was busy sweeping the leaves that were already starting to fall. "You were looking pretty grim in there. Is everything Okay?"

"Beyond all the usual stuff, you mean? I don't know. Alastair was on the phone again this morning. He's still smarting at having to pull his lead story. He insists the e-mails he has were sent from this building. He's had them compared with others that were undoubtedly sent by you and they match. Some computer code or something, don't ask me, I'm not very into all that."

"No, well nor am I. Is he going to run the story?"

"I don't think so. Your eyeballing routine worked better than we thought. He knows you're not having an affair with anyone, but he still thinks he's on to something. He's just not sure what."

"In the current climate I think we can file that under Small Mercies."

"Indeed. I didn't want to say this in the meeting," said Danny as he came up behind his boss, "but Joanna Morgan had lunch at the *Mirror* only last week."

Sinclair turned round and cut him off short. "I expect my ministers to keep on good terms with the newspapers, it's part of their job. Don't you think you and Helen might be making the same mistake as Alastair? Things aren't always what they seem." Danny looked shocked. It was part of his job to keep Sinclair abreast of these things.

Sinclair noticed his reaction. "I didn't mean to snap. But I think I can handle Jo. I wanted to ask you about something else. When did you last see Ruth?"

So that was it. Danny had had a feeling there was something going on that he didn't know about. "I spoke to her on Saturday. She sounded fine. But it's a few weeks since I've actually seen her. Why, what's up?"

"I'm not completely sure. That's why I'd like you to go and see her if you can manage it. I know you've got a lot on your plate."

"We've all got a lot on our plates, Paul, but some things are more important than others. It'll have to wait until after Washington but of course I'll go. It'll be a pleasure." It always was.

11

"That's him."

Ruth turned her neck slowly to see where Sandra Burch was indicating. The tall, muscular black man gave them both a little nod and broad, toothy grin.

"Isn't he wonderful?"

"Undercul". Ruth was afraid if she opened her mouth more than a fraction to speak the mask would crack.

"You made a big mistake, Ruth, you really did. Half an hour under those huge hands and you'd have gone away feeling twenty years younger."

And he'd have felt something at least thirty years older, thought Ruth as Toby disappeared through the swing doors. "Gagee you're wight".

"He's not cheap but, honestly, I'd pay it just to be in the same room with him for thirty minutes." Sandra was warming to her theme.

"An wat's Grian gonna think agout that?" Sandra's husband was famously jealous of any other man who so much as stole a glance at her in a crowded restaurant. Never mind a strapping young masseur alone in a locked cubicle for an hour.

"Brian? Oh I told him all the masseurs down here were gay. I mean Toby might well be for all I know. He's awfully good looking, even you must see that darling, and he takes care of himself. Did you see how smooth his skin was? Frankly I couldn't care less one way or the other but the idea helps put my beloved's mind at ease, bless him."

"Don't ache ee lark."

"Oh this is ridiculous. You've had that thing on for at least forty-five minutes. I'm sure that's enough. I see you rarely enough to have you talking like a Dalek with toothache all afternoon. Come on, you can wash it off and we'll have one more go in the steam room before tea. I'll be gasping by then."

55

The health spa in the basement of the Grand had been Sandra's idea. Most of her contact with Ruth was by e-mail or telephone, but she liked to have a bit of personal time with her authors occasionally. Ruth Sinclair wasn't the easiest woman to represent at the best of times and today Sandra had something very delicate to discuss.

Along with half the publishing companies in London, Sandra's agency had moved to Brighton in the first decade of the new century. Taking a couple of hours out of the office to wrap herself in a towel in the interests of literature was a price she was always ready to pay. And Ruth, who had intended to spend the whole day in the library, had proved surprisingly easy to talk round.

Sandra hiked her towel up, tightened the knot under her left armpit and led Ruth off in the direction that Toby had taken towards the wet area. Ruth watched her agent's chubby thighs as she followed her out. They were about the same age and she couldn't help looking down at her own legs and wondering why time had been kinder to her. It certainly wasn't that she took particular care of herself. Upstairs, after their final go in the sauna cabin, Ruth felt a tremendous glow in her cheeks as she ordered a pot of Earl Grey and a slice of chestnut and chocolate cake. "Come on, Sandra, are you sure you won't?"

"No thanks, honestly, I'm not hungry." She smiled bravely at the waitress and shook her head before getting down to the business in hand. "So how is the writing going?"

Ruth pulled a long face. "Not too bad, I suppose. Well, I'm struggling a bit, if you want the truth. What with mother's illness and all the constituency work, it's been hard to find the time to make as much progress as we'd hoped. Are they really going to hold me to the letter of the contract?"

"They will if they can, darling. Although they know they can't strap you down and make you write. Much as they might like to. I might be able to hold them off for a bit though. Especially if I told them you were busy with something else that might be an even bigger seller."

"But I'm not."

"That's what I wanted to talk to you about, darling. You know Janine Clairmont…"

"Do I? The name sounds familiar."

"She's a journalist. Political Editor of AM-TV. Put the telly on any morning and you'll see her."

"I'm afraid I can't stomach television in the mornings."

"Well anyway, she's writing a book."

"So?"

"It's a biography of Paul." Ruth took a mouthful of her cake but said nothing. "An intimate biography. You know, the real man behind the politician, all that kind of stuff. The publishers love it. "

"And let me guess. You're her agent too?"

"Well as a matter of fact, yes I am. Look, don't worry, it'll be very positive. She's a big fan of our Prime Minister. And she's great friends with that woman who runs his office, what's her name, Helen something-or-another."

"Griffin."

"Griffin, that's it. So she'll be getting plenty of help there."

"And what exactly does this have to do with me?"

"Well you are married to him, darling."

"You cannot seriously be suggesting that I sit down and talk about my private life with Paul to some TV journalist I've barely heard of? You know me better than that, Sandra. I'm amazed that you can even suggest it."

"Ruth, hang on."

"No, you hang on. You know the rules. We don't talk about the family. Not Paul, not me. It's off limits. Now we've finally got the papers to understand that I can hardly turn round and start pouring my heart out for a book. Even if I wanted to, which I can assure you I do not."

"It would be off the record. Nobody need know."

"You're not listening to me. Why on earth would I want to talk to her?"

Sandra paused. "Look, Ruth, I know things haven't been easy between the two of you recently. And you're right, the press have left you alone pretty much so far. But how long is that going to last? I thought you might want to, well, get out your side of the story."

"That is very thoughtful of you. But you can tell Janine Clairmont and whoever her publishers are that I most certainly do not."

"You're happy for Helen Griffin to tell it her way?"

"Meaning?"

"Well, from what I've read in the cuttings, they go back a long way."

"That's true. Helen knew Paul before I did. They were in Oxford at the same time."

"Precisely."

Ruth bit her lip as the waitress placed the cake down in front of them and then, sensing the tension, moved quickly away. "Sandra, if you've got something to say why not just come out and say it? I'm getting a little irritated with all this."

"Okay. We've all read the gossip columns. Unless you know differently, it seems your husband was a bit of a lothario before you came along. Janine Clairmont has told the publishers that she's going to reveal the story of Paul Sinclair's dark lady. The woman who awakened his sexuality and who's had a hold over him ever since. That's Janine's take on it anyway. It's the kind of story that will make the book fly off the shelves. The passion behind the power, all that kind of stuff. Well if Helen Griffin is the dark lady it explains a lot. Even so, people would understand your point of view. You could come out of it all very well in the end, but only if you're willing to put it across."

"Forget it, Sandra. Just forget it."

"All I ask is that you think about it. If you're not careful, you'll get pictured as the frumpy academic wife who couldn't compete with the fiery dark lady and so ran away home and refused to come out. Is that what you want?"

Ruth stood up and put on her coat. "This conversation is at an end. Mother will be waiting for me."

"Ruth, wait. Just remember one thing. It's always the winners who write the history books."

"Goodbye Sandra."

Ruth Sinclair went out through the revolving doors, crossed the busy street in front of the Grand Hotel and took the steps down onto the beach. She tried to put the conversation with Sandra out of her mind. Over to her right the lights of the huge West Pier Casino were reflected off the dark September sea. Thirty years ago the pier had been little more than a cast iron shell, its majestic frame serving as huge perch for a thousand starlings. It was here that she'd stood with Paul not long after he'd appeared on the Sussex University campus as head of the visiting Oxford debating team. From the start it was his passion for ideas that had attracted her, far more so than his effortless charm and self-evident good looks. That this bright, passionate, thrilling man wanted to see more of her had startled her at first. But his enthusiasm was so infectious and his manner so reassuring that when he said he wanted them to get together she forgot her usual caution and made no attempt to hide how delighted she was. And yet she felt he should know what he was taking on. So while they had leant against the railings and allowed their bodies to lean into each other she told him where she stood. When she talked about integrity and trust and honesty he hadn't shied away or told her to lighten up, as she'd feared he might. Emboldened by his reaction she'd told him that if he wanted her, she was his, but that she would never share him. Two days later he'd called from a phone box in Oxford High Street to tell her she was the only woman in his life.

12

The Foreign Secretary had her remarkably good legs up on her desk. She leant back in her chair in a way that her husband found irresistibly attractive. There was nothing that pleased him more that being the bearer of news that brought a smile to her face. She fingered the pearls around her neck as she spoke. "What do you think, Ray? Do you think he's having an affair?"

"My dear," he answered in a quiet voice, "I really have no idea. You know PJ. He wouldn't give me any details and sounded quite cross that he had to mention it at all. That beastly editor of his had been on to him about it late last night and again this morning. Our PJ gets quite moralistic about these sorts of thing, we have to remember that. Apparently he told the editor that if he asked him to get involved in stories about people's private lives again he would take his column elsewhere."

"Oh dear, Ray, that would be most unfortunate. You're quite right of course. We must be mindful of PJ's sensibilities. He's a good boy. A very good boy indeed. We don't want to upset him."

"No, my dear, I quite understand. Whatever you say."

The Prime Minister stuck his head out of the Den. Rebecca, whose desk faced square onto the doorway so she could guard all access and listen out for any cries for help from within, raised an eyebrow.

"Can you find Helen for me? And send in some tea maybe?"

"How was your sandwich?"

"I'm not really all that hungry. I'll eat it later." Rebecca raised both eyebrows. "I promise." As he disappeared back inside she thought to herself that he was looking a bit off-colour. She had to resist the temptation to mother him sometimes because it only made him uncomfortable, but she knew she was the only person in the office who saw him as a man first and a politician a distant second. Helen would only get him more worked up, but if it was Helen he wanted then Helen he would get.

"I can't get this bloody computer to work," he said as soon as she appeared at the door.

"I know you can't."

"What? Are you psychic all of a sudden? You've only just walked in the room."

"I'm your Chief of Staff. It's my job to know what you're thinking even before you think it. And anyway, I've had the access codes changed."

There were furrows of incomprehension across the Prime Ministerial forehead. "I thought you wanted me to finish this speech?"

"I do want you to finish the speech. It's just that when you're delivering it four thousand miles away or whatever it is I don't want anybody else sending e-mails in your name. Is Joanna coming with us to Washington? No, she isn't. Do we want any more late night scare stories courtesy of the *Daily Mirror*? No, we do not."

He sighed deeply and sat down. "I've told you, I know Jo, and no matter how paranoid the rest of you get, she wouldn't do something like that. Besides we've killed that story."

"Wrong on both counts." Even now, she took inordinate pleasure in telling him he was wrong. "Do you want to know how I know?"

"Does it matter what I want? You're going to tell me anyway."

"I know because, unlike you I still have some friends in the media. You remember Janine Clairmont." The furrows in his brow deepened. He couldn't put a face to the name. "Well she's just had lunch with our Stephen Piggin and like a good girl, the first thing she did when she got back to her office was to call me. Now we all know that Piggin is pond life and he's only in the Cabinet because Jo insisted you keep him and you caved in. Actually, for once it was a good move because if we didn't have our beloved Health Secretary we might know rather less about what Ms Morgan was up to. Like all pond life, he's severely deficient in brain cells. He also likes a drink and has a pathetic weakness for even half-way attractive women. I mean no disrespect to Janine, who's actually more than half-way attractive, when I say that after a bottle of wine over lunch he was singing like a canary."

"Canaries don't live in ponds."

Helen was enjoying herself too much to be irritated by his sarcasm. "Stephen Piggin is zero without Joanna Morgan. He has no thoughts of his own and no role in life other than to do her bidding until such time as she gets to sit in that chair and repay him for his mindless loyalty. So when he leans across and confides in Janine that there are rumours you're having an affair then we know where he got it from."

Helen's eye went straight to his wedding ring as Sinclair held up the palm of his left hand to interrupt her. "Hang on a second. You guys keep telling me what good contacts Jo has with the *Mirror*. She's more likely to have got the story *from* them than to have given it *to* them."

It was a good guess but Sinclair had no way of proving it and Helen had no interest in even considering it. "The best is yet to come. We've all been getting a little twitchy in case Jo's supporters turn out in force to rebel against the health reforms. We'll lose the vote if they do. Well, according to Piggin, she hasn't said what she wants them to do yet."

"You're making my argument for me, Helen. Jo is cunning but she's not brave. She'll nurse her grievances and grumble like hell, but she hasn't got it in her to strike."

"That's not Piggin's take on it. He says she has something on you that's so explosive it could destroy you overnight. They call it the Big One. Ruth's not afraid to strike, Paul, she's just biding her time for the best moment knowing she can take you out any time she wants."

He shook his head and laughed. "And you believe that? Come off it. If there was something that big then you, or who knows maybe even I, would know about it. The Big One?" he scoffed. "It's more like the Big Bluff. Trust me, I can keep Joanna Morgan where I want her." He realised there was nothing more he could say to persuade her. Besides, he didn't want to make her paranoia disappear altogether. It was a useful insurance policy just in case he was wrong. "Now, if it's all the same to you, could you start worrying about things you can do something about? Like getting my bloody computer to work."

13

"The old trout."

At the second floor window Pete Morley's long thin body was bent almost double as he watched PJ Walton shrug his shoulders and turn to go through what passed for the Castle's front garden and up to the door. Mrs Alma Gundry crossed the road, went up to her own porch, gave the brass knocker a wipe with the sleeve of her cardigan and went inside to make a cup of tea.

"Trout," said Pete again to her disappearing back.

There was a small forest of wooden staves propped beside the wardrobe and Pete had to step over a pile of home-made posters to get to where Helmut was sitting. The 'Sweet F.A.' logo of the South London Freedom Alliance was in the top right hand corner of every one. On the top floor of the Castle was the workshop. PJ rarely ventured up here these days. There was a time when he was happy to believe his lodgers were shut away busily planning demonstrations in peace, although these days he wondered if the workshop was put to much productive use at all.

If he had gone up the stairs, however, rather than making himself a sandwich and going to his own study on the first floor, PJ would have had more than the nagging of Alma Gundry to worry about. Despite his solemn promise to his landlord, Helmut had started using the cover of the workshop occasionally for some subversive activity of a very different kind. He didn't like to have secrets from PJ, but there were some things the Naked Prophet could be very conservative about despite his professed liberalism. And none more so than drugs.

Helmut Feldhofer had done his time as a fully paid up anarchist and revolutionary. He was still remembered as the most hardworking leader the South London Freedom Alliance had ever had. But in his bitter experience the British masses were just about impossible to arouse. Even now the worst excesses of Sinclair's police state weren't enough of a provocation for them to get up off their knees. Helmut was happy to let PJ think he was still true to his beliefs, working for that great day of liberation while making ends meet in the meantime as a club DJ. But the truth was that he'd proved no more successful at getting the proletariat on the dance floor than he had in getting them to the barricades and had fallen back on what he knew best, his chemistry set. If he couldn't get them to fight for their freedom then he'd just have to sell it to them instead.

In his early twenties Helmut had trained as a chemical engineer in Munich but had soon fled to London, disillusioned by the demands of his capitalist employers. He hadn't budgeted for the city's astronomical rents, however. So when he saw how easy it was to replicate and even improve upon the cocktail of chemicals the capital's club scene was ingesting in industrial quantities every weekend he decided to make use of his talents as best he could. It had been intended as a temporary career change that helped subsidise his other interest in radical politics but he was a remarkable and almost instant success. By the time he'd met PJ through the Freedom Alliance and been invited to rent a room at the Castle at a very fair rent indeed, Helmut Feldhofer was hooked on his own reputation. He justified it by mixing some radicalism into his famous recipes. Market Anarchism. Pills with a Purpose. Every packet of tabs or powder came wrapped in a leaflet from the Freedom Alliance with a quotation from Chomsky, Gramsci, Trotsky or Marx. He had no illusions that they were ever read, but the 'Sweet F.A.' logo had raised a few smiles. Then it had all gone sour and, under strict instructions from PJ, he'd given up his profitable sideline. For a while. Until he realised that his total absence of rhythm made him the worst DJ South London had ever experienced and the clubs where he had once been so welcome started to close their doors to him. He then took the only decision a market anarchist could take. He went back to supplying what his customers demanded.

So, as his landlord turned on the laptop to put the finishing touches to the following day's Naked Prophet column, Helmut Feldhofer was laying out his chemicals on the makeshift table against the back wall of the room above his head, his chubby face rigid with the effort of intense concentration. Although he was now well into his thirties, Helmut had the look of an overweight, ill at ease schoolboy. His face was almost completely without lines due in no small part to the fact that Helmut never smiled. What he did do, for most of his waking hours, was frown. But the furrows in his forehead were hidden beneath his extraordinary hair. Not strictly speaking a haircut. No professional cutter had been anywhere near it in at least fifteen years. Helmut had little interest in outward appearances and preferred to just take a pair of scissors to his fringe when it threatened to obscure his vision, hacking away at the sides and back as an afterthought.

"The old trout."

"I heard you the first time, Peter. And the second. But I am not sure I understand you." Helmut was sorting the little sachets of powder into piles. His surprisingly delicate hands looked anaemic in the translucent plastic gloves he wore.

"The old trout from across the road. Mrs Gundry. She's been giving PJ a hard time again."

These days the Metropolitan Police had the Castle on their computer records as a Grade 4 risk, almost as low as it gets before it falls off the bottom of the scale. If it hadn't been for the periodic complaints from Mrs Gundry it might have been removed from the register altogether. It was several years since the building had been used as a regular meeting place for some of South London's more hardened would-be revolutionaries. When PJ had his big break into national journalism he'd made it clear that the Castle was no longer a safe haven for those dispossessed of anything better to do with their lives than hang around, drink second rate coffee and talk third rate revolution. Helmut was delighted. He'd already started to question his faith but hadn't the heart to admit it. His relief was so obvious that the Special Branch agents who made up more than fifty percent of the membership of London's far-left groupings soon reported that Helmut Feldhofer had declared the British working class beyond help and had broken off contact with his former comrades. So far as the forces of law and order were concerned, the Castle had pulled up its drawbridge and was no longer any threat to national security. PJ Walton wanted to keep it that way.

This afternoon, therefore, Helmut, with Pete's connivance, was taking a risk. Helmut knew he was on to a good thing every time he had to pay PJ the paltry rent, so he usually worked on his production line at his girlfriend's house half a mile away. But they'd had a dramatic row the night before after he'd been caught for a second time in the arms of the long-suffering girl's mother. As of today Helmut was single again. He didn't understand sexual jealousy but now at least he understood how much anger it could generate. So until he was allowed back, or until he managed to find another home for his chemistry set, he would have to make do by working out of a suitcase at the Castle.

Pete, who was rather in awe of his friend, had made no objection. In many ways Helmut set an example that Pete struggled to follow. He had no real interest in the drugs business but Pete longed to know how such a social misfit as Helmut was able to enjoy a successful and complicated sex life without appearing to try, while he, who tried very hard indeed, was left constantly frustrated. Clearly there was more to Helmut Feldhofer than met the eye but Pete had no idea what it could be.

Helmut liked to work in silence so Pete was able to hear the sirens when the police van was still half a mile away. Mrs Gundry, who was just settling down with a second cup of tea, heard them a few seconds later. They were both looking out of their respective windows when the van drew up and were equally startled when two policemen and a large Alsatian jumped out of the back doors.

"Jesus, Helmut, the old trout has called the Old Bill."

"Please, Peter. I don't have time for your riddles."

"The police. Here. Now. Put that stuff away."

"You won't be needing that," said Mrs Gundry aloud to herself as one of the officers approached the doorway with a large steel jemmy. She was right. The door gave way without a whimper of protest as soon as he put any weight against it.

By the time four pairs of heavy boots and four impatient paws were clattering up the stairs to the first floor, Helmut had the contents of the chemistry set back in the suitcase. He surprised himself by having the presence of mind to wipe his sleeve across the table in case any traces had been left behind. PJ Walton came out of his study at the noise but the Drugs Squad knew just where they were going and brushed straight past him. While Pete cursed Mrs Gundry again under his breath, Helmut's former girlfriend watched from the end of Wilson Crescent. An hour earlier her mother had asked when that nice boy with the funny accent was coming round again and she'd decided that Helmut had not yet suffered enough.

Well he was suffering now. Pete, six foot eight and agonisingly thin, had already pulled his long legs up into the loft opening like a metal tape measure retracting into its holder. Helmut had passed the case through the gap and was now trying to follow with his own much heavier frame. Pete grabbed him by the collar and yanked him up, kicking the hatch closed behind them.

Under the eaves a large sheet of blue plastic covered a hole a metre across. Miraculously this temporary repair had lasted over two years, deflecting all but a few drops of rain onto the vacant plot next door. Pete reached up and pulled the sheeting down into the loft space. He was dazzled by the bright light but quickly turned and pointed Helmut towards the hole.

"Up there."

"Is this some kind of humour, Peter? I don't think I am ever getting through there."

From the sound of it, the boots and paws had now reached the second floor. Pete looked down towards where the noise was coming and then back up at the gap in the tiles. "It's your choice mate."

Two large palms against the soles of his training shoes propelled Helmut out onto the roof where he stumbled and tried to get himself upright without letting go of the case. Pete was behind him in a second.

"Now where?"

"Follow me."

Pete ran along the ridge of the roof with an agility and sense of balance that took Helmut by surprise. He did his best to follow as he'd been told. At the far end of the roof Pete knelt and looked over the edge. Huge iron bolts stuck out from the eaves where the residents of the other end of terrace had taken measures to make sure their house didn't fall down too. Pete swung his Lowryesque legs over the edge and jumped down onto the flat roof of the newsagents next door. He reached up for the suitcase and saw the blank look of panic in Helmut's eyes.

"Come on mate, it's only a small gap. You can do it."

Helmut hit the roof with an almighty thud. The newsagent's wife, who was ironing in an upstairs bedroom, looked up half expecting the ceiling to give way. All she saw was the cobwebs vibrating as the two men ran to the rear of the building. She put the iron in its cradle and went through into the back bedroom. As she looked out the window into the garden Pete was struggling to untangle his limbs from her rotary washing line which had broken his fall. Thirty seconds later something large and heavy flew through the air from above. Pete, now free of the plastic wire and assorted undergarments, caught the suitcase in both arms and set it down on the grass. In a second he was upright again, gesticulating wildly. He looked like an enormous praying mantis, shaking his head from side to side and waving his extraordinarily long arms up and down. The woman heard a strangled scream from above her and something even larger and heavier crashed into what was left of her washing. She watched, unable to take her eyes of the performance, as the two men moved, one striding the other limping, towards her back gate and out of sight.

The doorman at The Prince of Wales was perched on a stool at the corner of the bar. The afternoon session, one of the most popular of the week, was already well under way and the place was starting to fill up nicely. Not that he cared much. The busier it was the more often he had to get up off his seat and go to the front door, behind the wide black curtain that rang the full length of the pub's front wall, and let the punters in. From where he sat he could see them approach on the CCTV cameras that pointed both ways down Callaghan Grove. Some people would stride up purposefully, press the bell beside the door and wait impatiently to be admitted, defying anybody to challenge what they were doing there. Others would approach more tentatively, pretend to be examining the times on the bus shelter and then dash quickly to the door casting nervous looks over their shoulders as they waited for him to open up. He liked to think he could tell The Prince of Wales's customers, both the confident and the uneasy, from ordinary passers by without fail at twenty metres, the point at which they came into the range of the cameras.

"Awight mate?" he greeted one of the regulars as he patted him on the back. Most of them were white, very white indeed, while most of the staff were black. He shook his head at the offer of a cigarette. "Jus' put one art mate".

When he looked back up at the TV screen he saw two guys hurrying down the street like something out of one of those black and white comedy shows they used to put on on Saturday mornings when he was a kid, one tall and gangly, the other much shorter and heavier clutching a suitcase to his chest. He fiddled with the gold stud in his ear lobe and settled back onto the stool. These two were definitely not up for The Prince of Wales.

Pete stopped and looked back at Helmut. Behind him in the distance blue lights were flashing at the end of the street where it turned left into Wilson Crescent. He looked up at the peeling black painted shutters on the windows of the pub. You'd have thought the place had long since gone out of business if you didn't know better, but Pete had heard on the streets about The Prince of Wales.

"Come on, in here." Pete pressed hard on the bell.

"What is it?"

"Gay bar. They'll never think of looking in here."

The doorman looked up at the screen in disbelief. He'd never been wrong before. But sure enough the lanky one was pressing the doorbell again. Well he thought, looking around him at the customers on either side of the bar, they sure come in all shapes and sizes. He got up and went behind the curtain. When the front door was opened nobody in the street could see what was going on inside.

"Yuh?"

"Er, we'd like to come in."

These guys just didn't look the part. "Yous know waddit is?"

"Sure." They were both sweating visibly but then some people got more than a little nervous on their first visit. "It's um, a gay bar right? We're er…we'd like to come in."

The doorman was all but invisible against the black material as Pete put on what he hoped was a knowing smile. It seemed to work as the man stepped back even further into the darkness to let them step inside.

"Boosonly wight?" The doorman's words were obscured by the music from the bar behind the curtain.

"Sure. Yeah. Right."

"What did this man say?" Helmut wasn't at all sure he liked the way this particular plan of Pete's was developing, but he'd come with him this far and he didn't have any better ideas. They were following the black guy the length of the curtain towards the smell of stale sweat and beer.

"Booze only I think."

"What is that supposed to mean?"

"I dunno. Either no diet cokes or none of what you've got in that case, I guess."

"Five euro."

Pete fumbled in his pockets for some cash. Helmut kept his eyes fixed on the carpet.

"K guys." The doorman handed Pete his change. "Lockers r'over there."

"Lockers?"

For the first time Pete looked around at the bar and the forty or so men that were in it. Some were propping up the bar, a pint glass in hand. Others were walking about looking at who else had chosen to leave the afternoon sunshine for the darkness of a bar with no windows. One or two seemed to have come with somebody they knew but most were on their own. And not one of them had any clothes on at all.

Pete realised he'd be staring for just a little too long and looked back at the doorman who gestured at a notice pinned to the wall behind the bar. Pete flicked his eyes over it. Fridays – Leather. Saturdays – Sports Kit. Sundays – Slaves and Masters. Mondays - Boots Only.

Boots. Only.

14

The Prime Minister held a large mug of tea between his palms. Helen never ceased to be amazed at how perfect his nails were. Not once had she ever seen him chew them. Danny Oliver put his head round the door. "You wanted me?"

"Yes, come on in. Rebecca," Sinclair called through the open door, "ask the Colonel to come through would you? What news on Eritrea, Danny?"

"Not much. We're a bit short of reliable information. The only journalist we're getting stuff from in Asmara is some guy from the Associated Press. His last report said there were thought to be five hostages. It's all happened in some really remote spot up in the mountains, close by the border apparently."

"Helen?"

"I've spoken with the charity, Poverty Action. There's a very helpful American woman who runs the show in Cambridge. She seems to understand the sensitivities and says she'll run everything by us before talking to the media. They've got a team of about twenty people in different parts of Eritrea. They travel about in Land Rovers a lot of the time and communications aren't easy. But there was one group up in the mountains and they've heard nothing from them for twenty-four hours. There are three Brits among them. I think we have to assume they've been taken captive."

There was a knock on the door. "Come in Colonel." The Security Supremo's expression was always some variant on grim so it was hard to tell how serious he thought the situation was. "Do you have any fresh intelligence?"

"We're rather thin on the ground in that part of the world. We're relying on satellite surveillance and even with the Americans' latest kit the mountainous terrain makes it almost impossible to track what's going on."

"Who controls the territory?"

"The Eritrean Government in theory. But there's a local militia linked to remnants of the old guerrilla movement. They've been skirmishing with an equally shadowy bunch on the Ethiopian side for months now."

"So cut the crap." Helen, of course. "We're in the hands of the Yanks, is that what you're saying?"

The Colonel was momentarily taken aback. He'd always thought of Helen as the most practical of Sinclair's inner team. She wanted results and never usually troubled herself with too many qualms about how they were achieved. "Not entirely. There's a Royal Navy frigate within a day's sailing of the Horn of Africa. I would recommend diverting her and flying out an SAS unit to join her offshore. As for intelligence, if you can find me a few billion pounds for our own satellite network, we can go it alone Miss Griffin. But I'm not sure we'll be able to do it in time to help these hostages, do you? The CIA will share whatever they have. I think we should be thankful that our relations with the United States are back on a sensible footing. And, of course Prime Minister, you'll be seeing the President tomorrow."

Sinclair nodded. "Well, I agree with your suggestion about the naval deployments and the SAS, Colonel. If you wouldn't mind passing on the necessary orders. And I want a briefing every two hours. There's not much else we can do right now, by the sound of it. Helen, what else have we got on?"

"You're meeting the health unions in ten minutes. When they've bullshitted you for half an hour there's a run through the Washington schedule and then a Policy Unit presentation on the pensions stuff that I can never get my head around."

"Try coming along. You'll find it fascinating."

"I wish I could. If only you knew how much. And then tonight you have an evening at leisure. Master Joshua Sinclair in tights and a false beard. That one I'm definitely coming to."

~

The Foreign Secretary held her finger on the intercom. "Ask Ray to come through, would you?"

Joanna Morgan had the *Daily Mirror* spread open on the desk in front of her. PJ's article giving a blow by blow account of Cabinet divisions over the Health Bill had been given particular prominence by the Editor after he'd been forced to change his front page. Ray, who was never separated from his wife by more than a door's width was soon at her shoulder. "Are you still reading that? You must be pleased with it, my love," he said.

"It is unfortunate, Ray, that we have to use unorthodox methods to help give the party back its sense of direction. But it is our duty. The Prime Minister gets a lot of advice every day and it must be a terrible strain trying to decide what to do for the best. It would be nice if he chose to pay a little more attention to his Cabinet ministers and a little less to what the papers say. But we must accept the world as it is and exert a little influence where we can. In the interests of the party, of course."

"Of course. Nobody with this party's true interests at heart could ever fault you for that, my love."

"Thank you, Ray. Now, I've just taken a very interesting phone call and I think we may have a very good story coming up for the Naked Prophet. Could you suggest to him that he keeps his column for Wednesday free? Of course the Prime Minister will be in the United States by then, but that may be no bad thing."

"I'll speak to him right away." Ray rarely asked his wife for more information than she was ready to impart. He had complete faith in her judgement and was proud to do what he could to help her achieve what she wanted. If you couldn't rely on your family to give unquestioning support, who could you rely on?

The walk from the West Pier up to Kemptown had taken Ruth less than an hour. The city was still full of late summer holidaymakers, some huddled on the stony beach in jumpers and coats trying to get what they could from the thin sunshine, others crowded around the hot dog vendors. Much of Brighton had become very trendy and expensive but down by the sea it still had the feel of a seaside resort for those unable or unwilling to fly abroad. By the time she'd passed the second pier, where the roller coasters and dive-bombers seemed to call out to the tourists that the summer wasn't yet over, the crowds had thinned. She could walk under the cliffs of Marine Drive and let the cool sea breeze clear her head a little. She could still feel the after-effects of the sauna in a tingle on her skin. She was sorely tempted to linger, but walked up the steep steps to the road above as fast as she could. She'd promised she wouldn't be long.

Ruth closed the heavy oak front door behind her and called up the stairs. "Mother?" There was no reply. She could hear the television in the kitchen but the room was empty. A packet of biscuits lay on the table and Ruth could see where her mother had torn away at the cardboard packet but had been unable to prise open the cellophane wrapping inside. She threw her bag down on a chair and went back out into the hall.

The bedroom was on the first floor overlooking the narrow street below. The door was ajar and Ruth could hear what sounded almost like a struggle coming from inside. "Mother, are you okay?"

Mrs Olive Reynolds was sitting on the edge of the bed. There were tears of frustration in her eyes and she looked exhausted. One arm was in the sleeve of a dark blue cardigan and she was pulling at the garment with her free hand and her teeth. When she saw her daughter her body relaxed and she let the fabric fall from her mouth. "I was cold," she said, "I wanted another layer.".

"Come here, Mother, let me help you. You've got it all back to front." Ruth started to pull her left arm out of the right sleeve.

The old woman looked up at her daughter with unmistakable anger. "I do know how to put on a cardigan, young lady."

Ruth sat on the bed and put her arm around her. "I know you do, Mother. I know you do." The old lady resisted a little and then allowed her daughter to pull her in close. As a family they'd never been used to much physical intimacy and sooner than Ruth would have liked the embrace was over and the practical business of getting Olive properly dressed resumed.

"Where's Josh?"

"He's at school, you know that."

"I thought he was coming to see me." Normally when Ruth was in Brighton over a weekend Joshua would take the opportunity to see his mother and grandmother at the same time.

"Not this time, Mother. Joshua's very busy at the moment. He's got a big part in the school play. Remember, I told you last night?" It had got to the stage where she was never sure how much Olive was taking in. It was something else she would need to discuss with the specialist in the morning. "Now come along, let's get you some tea."

15

The residents of the Harvest Hill Estate had become used to the unmarked police car that sat, almost permanently, at the end of the road. Mrs Pinney at number 19 often took them coffee in the mornings and one of her home-made scones each at tea-time. But they'd said a polite no thank-you this evening, nodding at the uniformed officers now stationed outside Harvest Hill Comprehensive.

"Maybe tomorrow, Mrs Pinney, if you're baking."

The Prime Minister's Daimler was just turning off the dual carriageway and entering the estate. For a few seconds the windscreen wipers seemed to be keeping time with the music on the radio.

"Five minutes," said Detective Inspector Derek Smyth, as if into thin air. He kept both hands on the steering wheel.

"Five minutes," crackled the reply. In the back seat Helen Griffin was creased forward and laughing. Beside her Paul Sinclair was doing his best to look serious but his face, too, quickly loosened into a smile.

"I can't believe you chose such a fucking awful record," said Helen, wiping away a tear. A few bars of a long-forgotten hit from the seventies played out and were cut short by the voice of Dame Sue Lawley.

"Billy Don't be a Hero. Not the kind of thing most people expect Prime Ministers to spend their time listening to."

"Well Sue, I don't exactly spend a lot of time listening to it, I can assure you. But I think it's the first record I remember buying with my pocket money as a kid."

"And does it have any significance beyond that?"

"It's only a pop record after all. But...and I know people get a bit tired of me talking about this all the time, but it does represent what I mean when I say that life is all about some really tough choices. And often there's no right answer, but you still can't run away from the decision. Billy has to choose between the woman he loves and going off to war. If we make the

right choice then we can maybe make our lives and the lives of those around us a bit better. If we get it wrong…well, it's a big responsibility."

"Does that mean that you… I mean, you must have to make a dozen tough choices a day, do you find that hard?"

"It never gets any easier, but it's just what you have to do."

"Choices between family and duty?"

"Well like I said Sue, it's only a pop song."

"So what's record number six?"

"Turn it off, Derek."

"She saw straight through you," said Helen still wiping away the tears. Paul Sinclair looked wounded.

"But I meant it. One of these days the rest of you will realise that I do occasionally mean what I say."

"Maybe. It was still a crap record, though. And you seem to be forgetting that, if I'm not mistaken, poor little Billy gets blown to bits by the end of the song. Doing battle with his conscience didn't do him a lot of good, did it?"

"Okay, okay, let's just drop it shall we?

As the car pulled into Harvoot Hill Sinclair looked at his watch. "How late are we, Derek?"

"About forty minutes, Sir."

Outside the school entrance a small group of people stood huddled under a large umbrella. Helen Griffin dabbed at her eyes with a handkerchief and straightened her jacket. Sinclair was already shaking hands with the Headmaster by the time she'd gathered her things together and clambered out of the deep leather seats. She brought up the rear as they made their way towards the shelter of the entrance hall.

"I hope you didn't wait for me, George."

"We couldn't really, Prime Minister. The other parents. You understand."

"Yes, of course. I'm just sorry I missed the start. I wouldn't have disrupted the opening night normally, but I'm off to the States in the morning. Has he been on yet?"

"He's been on from Scene One. It's a big part. He's good you know. I mean seriously, very good. You've met Mr Clements, I think, our Head of Drama?"

"Yes. Jim, good to see you." Sinclair reached out a hand to the young man in jeans and a cotton open-necked shirt decorated with what looked like enormous red azaleas. "I hope he's word perfect. He had me up till midnight going through his lines with him."

"He's a very conscientious young man, Prime Minister." Jim Clements, thought Sinclair, didn't look more than a few years older than his son himself.

"Paul. Please, call me Paul. I seem to remember that's what you called me before. Before all this." He waved his hand back at the Daimler and the ever-vigilant detectives. "Do you know what I'm called in all the official documents back at the office? PS. It makes me feel like an after thought. It's just one of the crosses I have to bear, I suppose. Another is always being late for the things I want to be on time for, but we had to cram in yet another meeting."

"Nothing too serious, I hope."

It was the kind of question the Prime Minister never knew how to answer. Three British people with their lives in danger on some remote Eritrean mountainside. Was that serious? Of course it was. Serious enough to keep him in his office an extra half an hour, and yet not serious enough to make him miss the play altogether. Power did curious things to your sense of priorities and it was better not to dwell on the consequences. "Hadn't we better go in?"

Jim Clements led the party in through two large sets of glass swing doors, doing his best to hide his eagerness to get back inside. They entered the hall from the back while Joshua was in full flow. He was barely recognisable under a heavy coat that trailed behind him on the floor and a beard that seemed to move independently of his jaw as he spoke. His teenage acne had been well and truly upstaged.

Joshua had inherited a powerful speaking voice that carried easily to the back of the hall. "The god thou serv'st is thine own appetite, Wherein is fix'd the love of Beelzebub, To him I'll build an altar and a church, And offer luke-warm blood of new born babes."

"And people accuse us of being authoritarian," hissed Helen.

The headmaster indicated a row of empty padded seats at the front of the hall but Sinclair shook his head and took one of the wooden chairs that were still vacant at the back. A few faces turned to look at the latecomers but most people were too engrossed by the Prime

78

Minister's son doing battle with temptation. Two angels, one evidently good dressed in white and the other made up like a demon, were hovering around him, pulling him this way and that.

"Contrition, prayer, repentance what of these?" asked Joshua.

"O, they are the means to bring thee into heaven."

"Rather illusions, fruits of lunacy, That make men foolish that do use them most."

"I'm with the bad guy," whispered Helen just as her pager, which was clipped to the shoulder strap of her bag, started to vibrate. She got up and headed for the door, leaving the battle of good and evil to sort itself out.

"Sweet Faustus, think of heaven and heavenly things."

"No, Faustus, think of honour and of wealth."

The heavy door swung shut behind her. She already had the phone pressed to her ear and was speed dialling the familiar number. At the other side of the anteroom two women who were laying out the cups for coffee watched open mouthed as if she were on the stage herself performing a manic, disjointed monologue complete with exaggerated expressions and sweeping arm movements.

"Switch? Hi, it's me. You paged me. Yeah, put him through. Danny? No, of course you can't bloody well talk to him. He's only just sat down. I don't know, Shakespeare or something, hang on."

She looked at the poster sellotaped to the wall. It showed a drawing of Joshua's character looking forlornly up to the skies with a copy of the Bible discarded at his side and flames gently toasting his shoes.

"Doctor Faustus. Is that Shakespeare?" Helen moved towards the counter. "Danny, you worry about your own soul and I'll look after mine. I'm still not disturbing him. What's going on anyway?" She listened intently. "They're threatening to shoot them? How long have we got?" One of the women dropped a cup onto its saucer and slapped her hand over it to deaden the noise. Helen gave her the briefest of glances. "Yeah, I'll tell him. Yeah, okay. Look, Danny, I'd better go. Much as I love talking to you, there are souls at stake here. I'll call you later."

The Prime Minister's Chief of Staff went over to the counter and asked the women for a coffee. The machine had only just started spitting into the jug but they could sense her urgency and poured her half a cup straight away. She drank it back in one gulp and grimaced as if it had been a neat spirit.

"Thanks."

"That's okay. So, if it's all right to ask, do you work for him then?"

Helen shrugged. "Yeah, you could say that."

"He seems a nice man."

"Sometime, I suppose. But I'll tell you a little State secret, he's not always as nice as he looks. But then have you ever met a man who is?" The two women shook their heads sadly. "I thought not. But yes, I'd say he was a nice man more often than most. Maybe too nice for his own good sometimes."

"I suppose you must see all sides of him," chipped in the second woman.

"Darling, I've known Paul Sinclair for thirty-five years. I've seen him every which way and, believe me, it's not always a pretty sight. But then can any of us put on a good face all day every day?"

The two women nodded this time in simultaneous agreement. By now the coffee machine had produced enough for a full cup and Helen accepted it eagerly, drinking it down as fast as she had the first one.

"You must have an asbestos throat."

"It comes from years of not having enough time to taste anything on the way down, I'm afraid."

"You should slow down, it's not good for you."

Helen gave the women a resigned smile. "I wish. Anyway, I'd better go and see whether Sinclair Minor has been swallowed up by the gates of hell."

She switched her phone off and watched its illuminated screen slowly fade then clipped the pager back onto the strap and threw her bag over her shoulder. Four eyes watched her back as she pushed open the heavy door and disappeared. The Prime Minister's own deep green eyes picked her up on the other side and followed her to her seat, the creases on his forehead asking her if anything was wrong. She whispered in his ear and saw the muscles in his face tighten. He looked as if he was about to get up and leave, but she put a hand on his arm and signalled for him to stay. There was nothing they could do in the next hour that was going to make any difference. She settled into the wooden chair as best she could and tried to fathom out who was on top in the battle of good and evil.

The television set looked out of place in the opulent sitting room of the Foreign Secretary's official residence. During Paul Sinclair's brief tenure in this particular job he'd been happy with a much smaller set that could be hidden away inside an antique armoire. He'd rarely watched it anyway. When Joanna Morgan took his place after his elevation to Number 10 she had insisted on a much larger and more sophisticated affair, complete with a state of the art recording device. Ray, who's eyesight wasn't what it used to be, appreciated the big screen and Joanna liked to be sure every news bulletin was recorded. Just in case.

This evening, however, they were watching the Channel Four News live and the Foreign Secretary was pleased with what she saw. The story of the Cabinet split had been picked up and there was a gaggle of Labour MPs queuing up to say how they were grappling with their consciences over the Health Bill.

"Oh dear," she said as she sipped her tea, "The Prime Minister will be disappointed. He does so hate to see party divisions played out in public." The item ended and she muted the sound. "Did you speak to PJ again?"

Ray Morgan was drinking a small lager from a cut glass tumbler. "Yes. He's a little anxious at the moment, but I don't think it's anything for you to worry about."

"Anxious? In what way?"

"Apparently the editor has now decided he wants him to start writing the Naked Prophet column under his own name. Go public, so to speak. He says that now he's established himself he doesn't have to be anonymous any longer. I think he wants him to go on the television and the wireless sometimes to get a bit of extra publicity for the newspaper. PJ's not awfully happy about the idea."

"And he's absolutely right, Ray. I want you to speak to him right now and tell him that it's out of the question."

"Yes of course. I did tell him that I didn't think you'd approve."

"That is an understatement. This is a complete, one hundred percent, bottom line issue so far as I'm concerned. Tell him to inform his editor that if the Naked Prophet's real name becomes public the inside information dries up the very same day. What use will he be to their precious circulation figures then?"

"Yes, my dear."

"Now, Ray."

"Yes, my dear."

"Oh, and Ray?"

"Yes, my dear?"

"Get hold of Stephen Piggin and some of our friends on the backbenches. I want to have a little discussion about the Health Bill. I'm very concerned about these divisions. I think while the Prime Minister is out of the country, it's only right for his deputy to have discussions about this crucial piece of government business, don't you?" The Foreign Secretary stretched out her shapely legs and put down her tea cup. "We really must be sure that the vote goes the right way. For the good of the party."

16

"Where's Terry then, Derek?" Joshua was fond of Derek's usual partner. At least Terry Woods was able to do all the security stuff without losing his sense of humour.

Inspector Derek Smyth ran a finger under the collar of his shirt. "He's switched to door and gate duty. He likes the open air, you know." He tried to make a joke of it but Joshua didn't look convinced. "We all get moved around in this job, there's not much we can do about it."

"Kneejerk's been throwing his weight around again has he then?"

"I wouldn't say that, Sir."

The mention of the Security Supremo's name roused Helen from her slumbers. She was in the back seat. Joshua, still in his make up minus the beard, sat between her and the Prime Minister. "Morning, Helen," said Sinclair.

"I was not asleep, thank you very much. I was thinking."

"With your eyes shut."

"Yes, with my eyes shut. Jesus."

"Sorry, Josh, but she was asleep. I'm sure it was no reflection on your performance."

The Daimler turned off the Hammersmith roundabout and headed for Hyde Park. They never took the same route between the Harvest Hill Estate and Downing Street, but tonight Derek had been asked to get his passengers back to Number 10 as fast as he could, so the Inspector avoided any unnecessary detours. "Actually," Sinclair went on, "and I'm not just saying this, I thought you were really very good. Sorry we were a bit late."

"You've already apologised twice, Dad. If I was going to get upset every time you were late for something I'd have had a breakdown by now. But you did miss my wicked opening speech." Joshua turned to face the windscreen and threw his arms out wide, catching Helen on the ear. "Sorry."

"Don't worry about it. I'll get you back." But the performance was already underway.

"All things that move between the quiet poles shall be at my command: Emperors and Kings are but obey'd in their several provinces."

"I'm not even sure your dad is obeyed in all his several provinces, are you?" asked Helen turning to Sinclair. "Did I tell you what the Scots are doing with the health reforms? Sweet F.A."

"You'll have to forgive my Chief of Staff, Josh. She has a thing about our colleagues north of the border at the moment."

"Is this the face that launched a thousand ships and burnt the topless towers of Illium?" Derek Smyth looked at Helen Griffin in his rear view mirror. It seemed unlikely. Joshua turned and threw his arms out in her direction. "Sweet Helen, make me immortal with a kiss."

"Well done, Josh, that woke her up. I don't think Helen is used to having young men quote poetry at her."

"How do you know?" she asked. "Anyway, I told you, I was not asleep."

"Come Helen, come, give me my soul again."

"Don't overdo it, Josh. I might get to like it."

"That's all right. I'm quite into older women." His father gave him a sidelong glance but put the thought out of his mind.

"Fifteen minutes," said the Inspector into thin air. Then to Helen, "We'll have you in bed soon Ms Griffin."

"I'm afraid not. Kneejerk wants to see us as soon as we get in."

"You know, Josh," said Sinclair, "Helen may have a point. If you really want to feel powerful I'd stick to the stage. At least actors get a lay-in most mornings."

Colonel Henry 'Kneejerk' Neilson was already standing outside the door to Number 10 awaiting their return. He liked to linger here and admire his handiwork. It had taken someone like himself to insist on the ring of steel, correction, an alloy much stronger than steel, that now surrounded the street.

Any visitor, whether on foot or in a vehicle, had to enter an immense airlock known as the Vortex. The Colonel had found a manufacturer in California and had the whole thing flown over and reassembled in Whitehall. There had been predictable howls of anguish from the

84

likes of English Heritage but Kneejerk had had little trouble getting them overruled. Joanna Morgan had mounted a ferocious campaign for a European supplier but he'd seen her off too. In his experience the Foreign Secretary never wasted an opportunity to try to undermine relations with the USA, the one country capable of keeping Britain safe.

A wall almost fifteen feet high had replaced the once familiar black gates. It was slightly concave when viewed from the street but was otherwise featureless. The front door to Number 10 was now hidden totally from the main road. Even when the Vortex slid silently open like an enormous lift, nothing was revealed of its inner workings except darkness. Once inside and out of sight, visitors were subjected to dazzling light that was suddenly illuminated as soon as the doors closed behind them. What they couldn't see as their eyes adjusted to the glare was the most sophisticated electronic screening anywhere on the planet. Tiny cameras took their pictures from three different angles. The Colonel could view them all from his office inside the building. By the time the inner door opened to let them pass these images had been compared with the suspect lists on not just the UK national database but those of the CIA in Washington, Interpol in Paris and Mossad in Jerusalem.

At the Colonel's insistence all unnecessary callers to Number 10 had been banished. No more delegations with their worthy little petitions opposing a by-pass here or a hospital closure there. No more groups of school children wanting their picture taken against the famous black door. And no more journalists getting off on feeling they were close to the centre of power by standing in the street in all weathers.

The sight of the two uniformed Metropolitan Police officers on either side of the door to the house itself always made Neilson smile to himself. They were, of course, just window dressing. No possible threat could penetrate this far. He gave them both a cursory nod. Sergeant Terry Woods couldn't bring himself to meet the Colonel's eye.

The Prime Minister's Daimler was the only car permitted to pass through both ends of the Vortex without stopping. Helen was on her mobile phone. "Sorry, honey. Yeah, I know I said I'd try to be home early. Okay, I said I *would* be home early. I don't know how long. Before midnight I'm sure. Try to stay up "

"How is he?"

"Not the happiest of bunnies."

"You go on home, Helen, I can do this one by myself."

"No, it's okay. He's just going to have to get used to it." Just like the last one had never got used to it, nor the one before that. For longer than she cared to remember Helen had been going from lover to lover, searching for that certain someone who'd be happy to trade intense periods of fiery and rather creative passion for the somewhat longer periods of absence. The whole situation mystified her. What she was offering should have been a pretty good deal, especially to the kind of man she was attracted to. They got an older, more experienced woman, great sex, plenty of freedom, a nice flat they could use as their own. But time and again they seemed to crave what she couldn't offer, an uninterrupted morning going round Sainsbury's or an evening at home in front of the telly. "From what Danny said, I think it could be important. You don't need a Chief of Staff who isn't fully on the case."

"Nor do I need a Chief of Staff who isn't happy. Or one who's distracted by problems at home."

Helen thought about that for a second. "I can handle it."

17

Colonel Neilson stepped inside the Entrance Hall as the car pulled up and the Prime Minister's party came in. Sinclair gave Joshua a hug and watched him walk off to the left towards the stairs to the flat. He thought of telling him not to make a mess of the bathroom when taking off his make-up but decided it wouldn't sound very Prime Ministerial. There was something about Neilson that always made him want to appear as Prime Ministerial as he could.

"Henry," Sinclair shook his hand while Helen kept hers wrapped around her bag. "It was good of you to wait for us."

"Not at all Prime Minister. It shouldn't take long." The Colonel's clipped Scottish consonants echoed around the hallway as he watched Joshua disappear from view. No son of his would have been allowed to parade around in public with powder on his face and makeup round his eyes.

Paul Sinclair followed his Security Supremo down the silent corridor towards the Den. The house was always rather eerie at night. All the paintings, busts and sculptures along the walls made him feel like an intruder in an exclusive private museum. Ruth had been astonished when she first saw the quality of all these art works hidden from public view. Now, he thought, not even she was here to appreciate them.

The Duty Clerk was waiting for them in the outer office. "Mr Oliver is on the line, Sir. Shall I put him on the screen?"

"Yes, please." Sinclair led them in and signalled for them to sit down. He took three glasses from the side cabinet and poured each of them a sizeable Scotch. "Good evening, Danny."

"Prime Minister." Danny Oliver's voice entered the room as if from nowhere. A few seconds later the image of him in his shirtsleeves at home in Battersea appeared on the plasma screen in the corner.

"I've got Colonel Neilson and Helen here with me. Has the ransom demand been made public?"

"Yes. Two million euros in development aid, but we know where the money would really end up. It came through too late for the first editions," the Communications Director had a pile of newspapers on his lap, "but Sky, Fox and the BBC are running it. They've been on the phone trying to get an off the record steer from us on whether there are Britons among the hostages so they can decide if they need to send crews out to cover it. If it was only foreigners they wouldn't bother."

"Henry?"

"Well I think Danny's friends will soon be checking the timetables for flights to Asmara, Prime Minister. We now know there are definitely three Brits among the hostages as well as an Australian and a Canadian. The ransom demand was passed to us while you were with your, er, your son." The note of reproach was unmistakable. "They say they will kill them all but they haven't said when."

Danny's voice cut in again. "Do we even know who they are for certain? Or where?"

"I'm afraid not. We think they're hidden in caves or deep ravines so the satellites can't pick anything up unless they move," said Kneejerk.

"What about the diplomatic side, Helen?"

"Both Asmara and Addis insist it's nothing to do with them. It's a weird neck of the woods. It seems they never really agreed a border when the two countries separated. Kind of like a couple who thought they got on so well that they didn't need to worry who owned which CDs. Well now they're arguing big time. Apparently the two Presidents are even distant relatives of some kind. Both former Marxist guerrilla leaders too. It's been going on for decades. Makes our relations with Scotland seem like a marriage made in heaven."

"Thank you for that characteristically illuminating assessment. Well Colonel? What next?"

"Very clear, Prime Minister. First, find out who we're dealing with. Second, scare the living daylights out of them."

"What's that going to achieve?" asked Helen.

"We have to make them realise that the cost of shooting the hostages will be a hell of a lot higher than the price of letting them go. If they release them they lose face, which they won't want to do. They need to understand that if they don't, they stand to lose a lot more than that."

"How do we get a message back to them if we don't know who they are?"

Danny had the only answer. "Through the media I'm afraid. These days the one thing we can be sure of is that wherever they are they'll be watching satellite TV."

"Okay. Get me something ready to release first thing in the morning. Thanks guys. Get some sleep. I can't see that we can do much more tonight."

As Danny's picture faded from the screen Kneejerk caught sight of a young man in a dressing gown putting his arm round the Communication Director's shoulders. He frowned but had no time to dwell on it. "A quick word if you don't mind, Prime Minister." He paused. "In private."

Helen looked up at the ceiling with ill-disguised contempt. Was the man really so stupid that he didn't realise Sinclair would tell her everything anyway? She picked up her glass and went outside. By the clock over the fireplace in the outer office it was 11.32. She might just be back at the flat in Stockwell in time to keep her promise.

When the door closed behind the retreating Chief of Staff, Neilson adopted a stage whisper. "Have you had an opportunity to consider the situation regarding your wife, Prime Minister? The West Midlands Chief Constable is going to need some guidance soon."

"Of course I've considered it, Colonel. I'll give you an answer in a couple of days."

"Forty-eight hours?"

"You'll get your answer. Now is that everything?"

"Thank you, Prime Minister." Paul Sinclair left the Colonel standing where he was and made his way as fast as he could up to the flat. The bathroom sink was a gooey mess of stage make up and the remnants of a beard. The sound of gentle snoring was coming from Joshua's bedroom.

Helen was still standing in Whitehall trying to find a vacant taxi when the Colonel was spewed out from the Vortex onto the pavement outside. Only Kneejerk could emerge from that monstrous, disorientating cavern looking as if he'd just had the best experience of his life. For a former marine and MI6 officer he was not much to look at. Not for the first time, Helen took in his short frame, pinched features and that quite revolting tuft of hair that sprouted above his collar and wondered if he'd sprung from a different gene pool to the rest of humanity. But in politics you couldn't expect to enjoy the company of everyone you had to work with. No doubt plenty of people had strong feelings about her too. Best just to cut the crap and get on with it. It didn't even hurt to try to be nice occasionally and Stockwell wasn't far. She could afford to be civil with this man for ten minutes in the back of a taxi. "Would you like to share a cab, Henry? There don't seem to be many to go round tonight."

"Oh no thank you, Miss Griffin." From the look on his face anyone would have thought she'd just suggested that he accompany her to a lap-dancing club. "No, no. I always take the tube. If I possibly can."

At that he looked both ways along Whitehall and strode with great purpose in the direction of the underground. Helen watched his retreating back as he pushed past the customers who were finally being evicted from the Black Lion. That, she thought, is a man who carries his responsibilities like a sack of coal.

She was momentarily lost in thought as the taxi came towards her, but her hand went out instinctively and she clambered in. After a swift U-turn in the middle of the road they were heading back towards Westminster Bridge. Colonel Neilson was just disappearing down into the mouth of the tube station, his biometric tube pass complete with photograph and fingerprint and DNA code held tightly in his fist when they passed. It was then that it occurred to her that maybe he was still on duty, still looking for clues. It made sense, after all. The London Underground must have looked to him like a massive affront to everything he believed in. It had thrown up the Circle of Death bombers and swallowed them again as if they had never existed. Despite all his high-tech equipment and his emergency powers the tube represented the challenge he'd utterly failed to conquer.

Ten minutes later Helen paid the driver and opened her front door. It was ten to midnight but the flat was in total darkness.

18

Helmut Feldhofer brushed his teeth with meticulous care and looked in the mirror at his friend who was standing out on the landing. Pete Morley had never shown much of a grasp of revolutionary theory but tonight it seemed he was turning the concept of freedom inside out.

"No, but come on, Helmut, you've got to admit it was kind of liberating."

Helmut wondered if he was confusing liberation with humiliation. They had been forced to wait for over an hour in The Prince of Wales until the doorman's security cameras had shown that the coast was clear. Helmut had spent the whole time even more taciturn than usual, perched on a stool with his legs crossed. Pete couldn't understand what his friend was so upset about. Helmut's flabby body hadn't raised a lot of interest amongst the bar's clientele in any case. Indeed now that he'd seen his friend naked, Pete was more mystified than ever by what women saw in him. No, it was Pete who'd been forced to reveal that being six foot eight and lanky had other physical compensations. He'd turned down six offers of a drink and three invitations to go 'back there', whatever that had meant.

"Liberating?" Helmut spat a mouthful of toothpaste into the sink in disgust.

"Yeah. Not my cup of tea, of course. But at least those guys had found their own way of throwing off the shackles of the police state." Maybe, thought Helmut, this was another of Pete's attempts to teach him about humour. He said nothing. "I mean with their ID cards locked away with the rest of their gear and out of sight of prying eyes, they were sort of free."

"Promise me one thing, Peter."

"What's that?"

"That however liberating, as you put it, you found the experience you will never talk about what we have just been through with anybody else."

"Sure thing, Helmut, whatever you want. It was something else though."

Pete went into his own room and closed the door behind him, his efforts at lightening the mood having been so firmly rebuffed. He didn't like it when there was an atmosphere in the Castle and tonight was the worst he could remember for a very long time. If Helmut was his usual humourless self he was positively light-headed compared to PJ Walton. Their landlord had been monosyllabic with fury when they'd finally arrived back home. Pete fumbled for words that might pass for an explanation or at least an apology while Helmut stood in silence.

"I don't want to know," said PJ.

The police, fortunately, had found nothing except a few leaflets and some posters from the South London Freedom Alliance depicting Paul Sinclair stamping a boot on the head of a defenceless nurse. PJ had told them he had no idea why his lodgers had fled. Maybe they had panicked thinking it was another raid on political activists. The officers had looked dubious, muttered something about a tip-off and said they'd be keeping an eye on the place.

Helmut was more taciturn even than usual tonight because he realised he was going to have to unpack his politics and rediscover the joys of futile protest. He and Pete were lucky not to have been evicted. Instead PJ had said in no uncertain terms that as he'd told the police they were harmless idealists, then harmless idealists they would have to be.

At seven o'clock the following morning as they emerged from the tube and set off up Whitehall Helmut's mood had not improved. It was raining. Not hard, but he didn't like the rain. He didn't like the sun much either for that matter. Helmut wasn't an outdoors sort of person, but he was earning his penance.

Pete followed Helmut a few paces behind, his long arms clutching three large rolled up banners to his chest. They had barely exchanged a word since their painfully early tea and toast. But if they could get themselves on breakfast telly staging a demo in Whitehall then maybe PJ would be mollified.

Helmut was the first to reach The Compound. This was Kneejerk's sole concession to the rights of the faceless masses who wished to challenge the power of the state. The Security Supremo had astonished the Prime Minister by agreeing to relax the ban on demonstrations at the end of Downing Street. Despite appearances, however, it had little to do with the right to protest. While they were penned inside the narrow confines of the Compound, a twenty foot square enclosed bit of pavement at the end of the road, the Colonel's cameras could scan them, his sensors could sniff them and he could get a detailed profile on every single individual so they weren't faceless any more. They could wave their banners and shout their slogans for as long as they liked. In return Kneejerk had opponents he could see and put a name to. He preferred it that way and liked to watch the demonstrations on the screens above his desk. In his own private lexicon these were ODMs. Ordinary Decent Malcontents. They were in a wholly different category to the SCEs, serious criminal elements, and PTSs, potential terrorist suspects, that really did pose a threat to the nation's safety. The Colonel actually had a bit of a soft spot for the ODMs. He'd even been tempted to become one himself when the smoking ban had felt like a threat to his own freedom. But while he was no great fan of the Prime Minister's politics, he believed in discipline and the rule of law. So long as Paul Sinclair stayed tough on security then the Colonel was happy to get on with doing his job.

With the touch of a switch one of the cameras swivelled to show the back of the breakfast TV reporter who was just finishing her report for the seven o'clock news.

"Paul Sinclair leaves for Washington in a few hours' time. But these demonstrators mean to remind him that his troubles won't go away as soon as his back is turned. With the health vote just days away, the Prime Minister knows that his biggest challenge is yet to come. Janine Clairmont, AM-TV News, Westminster."

Danny Oliver could see the Compound's rag-bag protesters as he walked up Whitehall. There couldn't have been more than a dozen of them. One very tall character waving his arms around in a demented fashion, a couple of women looking suitably cross and the rest of them just huddling to keep warm and, from the look of them, wishing they were somewhere else. It was pathetic. Danny didn't always agree with the Colonel, but as they both surveyed the protest neither saw it as a real threat.

Danny looked up at the massive bulk of the Foreign Office as he passed. Joanna was always at her desk early, but she was unlikely to look out from her office and agree how pathetic it was. He'd heard her tell Sinclair in that prim little voice of hers that while of course she would support the changes and urge her supporters on the backbenches to do so too, there was a powerful groundswell of public opposition. Well it hadn't swelled very much so far as he could see.

Danny felt a gentle tug on his sleeve and looked around. "Mr Oliver?"

"Yes."

She had an envelope in her hand. "Could you possibly take this in for me?" Evidently she knew who he was and where he was going.

"I'm sorry, if you want to demonstrate you have to be in there." He gestured towards the Compound.

"No, it's not that."

"Well, all letters for the Prime Minister have to be handed in at the gate."

"It's not for the Prime Minister."

They'd reached the entrance to the Vortex and Danny was taking out his electronic pass. Sergeant Terry Woods, spotting his embarrassment, had come up to help extricate him. "Over this way, Madam, if you please." As she was led away, the woman reached back and tucked the letter into the crook of Danny's sleeve. He was too busy digging out the pass from his bag to notice at first. When he did spot it he saw that it had just one word written on the outside: Joshua. He really couldn't be bothered running after her and giving it back so he slipped it into his pocket.

Janine Clairmont turned her mobile back on as soon as she was off air and it rang immediately.

"Thanks for that, darling. As if we needed reminding what a hole we're in."

"Good morning Helen."

"Are you all packed?"

"Of course. Although why I'm bothering beats me."

"I'll meet you at the corner of Parliament Square at three."

"What?"

"I'm offering you a lift, darling. We can talk about this fucking book of yours."

Helen had been in the office since six thirty and she was in a state of nervous anxiety that was unusual even for her. Unlike Paul Sinclair, who was reluctant to believe anything until he'd seen the supporting evidence, Helen Griffin trusted her instincts. And her instincts told her that all was not well. Not well at all. Even the gorgeous Otto had been behaving oddly, waking her at five in the morning with an urgency that had taken her by surprise. He normally slept through solidly until long after she'd left for work, but this morning he'd attacked her body as if he thought he'd never have the chance again. Not that she was complaining, but she hadn't been able to get back to sleep and had been feeling a profound sense of foreboding ever since.

What had changed? The information Janine had gleaned from Stephen Piggin over lunch for a start. The Health Secretary was easy to dismiss as a buffoon but even he wouldn't have blabbed his mouth off with such indiscretion if the Morgan camp wasn't feeling very confident indeed. If there was a Big One, a story that could sweep them all out of Downing Street, she couldn't think what it could possibly be. Joanna's style was usually more low-level. Stories that chipped away at Paul's credibility and enhanced her own by comparison. Helen was still convinced she was somehow involved in the smear story of an affair. But it was something more than Joanna's backstabbing that was troubling Helen this morning. For the first time since he'd got the job, and whether he could see it himself or not, Paul Sinclair was looking shaky. She couldn't put her finger on what had caused such a swift change in his fortunes, but he was starting to appear vulnerable and she knew she wouldn't be the only one to have noticed. When political authority starts to ebb away you could suddenly find the tide too strong to counter and Helen had no wish to be Chief of Staff in the court of King Canute.

Paul was right about one thing. He knew Joanna Morgan better than any of the rest of them. And yet she'd confounded him once by turning against him so dramatically. What was to say she couldn't do it again by going in for the kill? Helen tried to view the political scene through Joanna's eyes. There was going to have to be a General Election within a year or so whatever happened. Would she be willing to wait and risk another contender for the leadership gathering unexpected strength just as Paul had done himself? Or would it be better to strike now while he was weakened by a party revolt, poor poll ratings and a hostile media. If she really did have the Big One in reserve, why not detonate it quickly and step forward to pick up the pieces?

Helen was no historian but she didn't need to be. Common sense said that political leaders were at their most exposed when they weren't around to defend their flanks. She looked at her watch. Paul would still be upstairs in the flat. There was time to catch him and tell him the Washington trip had to be called off. After all, he saw enough of the President at the endless summits and conferences they had to attend in all corners of the world. 'Bunny' Warren liked to have these cosy chats in his log cabin occasionally but that didn't mean it was in Paul's interests to go. Maybe they could use the hostage crisis as an excuse to cancel.

She was half way to the door of her office when she stopped, turned and caught herself reflected in the darkened window. She looked tired. No. Cut the crap woman. Cancelling the trip would be like taking out huge adverts to tell the world Paul was in trouble. As if he'd ever agree to stay at home anyway. It was time for steady nerves and, she looked at her watch again, another cup of strong black coffee.

19

Downing Street's response to the ransom demand hit the news wires just before 8am. Producers on all the TV and radio outlets had a moment of panic but the newsreaders were soon delivering the message that Britain would never negotiate with hostage takers and would respond with force if any of the captives were hurt. 'According to Number 10, there are thought to be three British citizens among those being held somewhere in the mountains of Eritrea.'

The morning meeting was just getting under way when Danny Oliver, satisfied that the statement had been reported fairly, came in. He nodded to Sinclair to indicate that all was well and stood at the back of the room. The seats had already been taken.

Helen was in mid flow, as usual the first to give her take on the events of the day. "From what I can see, the papers can't think of any good reason why we're all decamping to the States. I'm with them there, incidentally." She could let it be known she thought the trip was a bad idea, even if she couldn't stop it. "They've decided you're running away from the health row, which is apparently the toughest challenge of your political career. Why is it always the toughest challenge, Danny?"

"That's the way it goes. The media can only deal in superlatives. The toughest challenge, the most crucial speech, the worst week," said Danny. "The second or third toughest challenge doesn't sell papers."

"What about the hostages, Danny?" asked Sinclair.

"Our statement is running on all outlets. We've confirmed that the majority of the captives are Brits. Poverty Action are still trying to contact all the relatives. They won't name the hostages until they've told their next of kin, so the media don't know anything more. We'll have to give an update later today."

"Maybe it will distract a bit of attention from this pointless trip." Helen's acidic observations could sometimes come across as crass cynicism.

The visit, whether she liked it or not, had created an extra buzz of excitement around Number 10. Coming through the front door and seeing the baggage piled up for collection, all neatly labelled, meant a change to the usual routine for all concerned. Helen couldn't get into the almost holiday atmosphere of the place, but even she was relishing the prospect of five hours enforced inactivity with all the trimmings of First Class service. Nobody outside of here ever believed her when she told them how austere British politics could be. Even Sinclair was probably secretly looking forward to the in-flight catering. He never complained but more often than not his lunch was eaten at his desk and consisted of a *Prêt à Manger* sandwich that somebody had to be sent out to buy. Helen rarely had anything at all unless she took herself up to the Cabinet Office canteen to sit amongst the civil servants tucking into food that had welcome connotations of school dinners for most of them. So a large comfy seat with constant attendance and even, if all the work was done, a few drinks was the nearest thing she could think of to Downing Street Heaven. She would have to settle Sinclair down and make him feel his time was being profitably spent, but she knew him well enough to be able to keep him occupied.

And there was always something special about a trip to the United States. The hospitality people over there were the best in the world so, as usual, the welcome was bound to be both warm and a little overpowering. The Americans were never quite able to disguise their relief at having guests who understood them, spoke more or less the same language and weren't there simply to make extortionate demands on Washington's largesse. And the Americans did motorcades like nobody else on earth. Even Helen got a buzz from that.

Like Helen, Danny Oliver had looked at the piles of luggage on his way in with a distinct feeling of unease. He was less concerned about the problems they'd be leaving behind than by the pressures of the trip itself. He'd have thirty-two members of the travelling media to keep happy and very little by way of a story to pacify them. Hostage crisis or no hostage crisis, he was enough of a journalist to know that this was not going to make for an easy time.

The walk up from Bloomsbury Street to the Royal Sussex County

Hospital was no more than fifteen minutes, but Ruth Sinclair had ordered a taxi. Her mother was waiting inside the front door. She had insisted on putting on her thick winter coat although the forecast on the radio had promised the unseasonably warm late summer weather was set to continue.

"I don't like to keep the driver waiting. It's such a narrow street and they can't stop without blocking the road." She looked out of the big curved bay window but there was no traffic to be seen.

"We only called a minute ago so they can't possibly get here that quickly."

"Do you think it will be cold? Where did I put my scarf?"

Ruth adjusted the scarf that was already around her mother's neck as the old lady took another look out onto the street. Ruth could see that she was anxious and impatient. She'd heard her moving about at 5.30, opening cupboards and drawers in the bedroom below. When Ruth had come down to join her at six there were clothes scattered about on the bed and Olive was already sitting in a heavy skirt and thick woollen cardigan. Ruth had noticed she usually wore things she could pull on easily these days. Anything with buttons or fasteners caused her problems. Although some days were better than others, there was no mistaking the deterioration in her condition.

She had refused Ruth's offer of a cup of tea, worried that she might need to go to the lavatory as soon as they got to the hospital. "It takes me such a long time these days and what if I was in the cubicle when they called my name? I don't want to miss my appointment."

"I could come and find you, Mother."

"I'd still keep the doctor waiting and he's a terribly busy man. No, dear, I'll wait. It's for the best."

Sandra Burch had promised Ruth that after just an hour at the Albion Club she would sleep like a baby for a week. Well it just hadn't happened, unless by that her agent had meant waking up every few hours wondering where her mother was. Perhaps she should go back later and have one of Toby's massages after all. There would be time after the consultation and before the drive back up to the Midlands. Ruth stretched her back and looked out of the window herself. She was convinced her mother hadn't changed the guest room mattress in thirty years. Whenever she stayed Ruth woke up with a collection of aches and pains that never troubled her anywhere else. She had expected to be woken early by the mad squawking of seagulls. That was just one of the joys of living near the sea. As a child she had loved their cries. They had sounded so free and so impatient. But this morning she was already sitting up in bed with a book listening out for Olive when they started their dawn cacophony. There was a half finished bottle of port on the bedside table which she had told herself would help her get a decent night's sleep.

Ruth knew in her heart that her mother might not be able to look after herself for very much longer, not even with a daily help. But persuading her to move would be hard. She complained bitterly at the way Brighton had changed in recent years, taken over she said by young people down from London with no respect for the place, but this was home and always would be.

As they stood by the window the taxi driver turned off King's Cliff and pulled up to the house. Olive pulled her coat tighter. "Here it is."

The front door was already unlocked. It took her a lot of time and effort even to do something as simple as slip the large brass key in the lock and turn it these days. She waved at the taxi and called out to the driver that they would only be a minute.

"Come along dear, we mustn't keep him waiting."

Ruth joined her mother on the porch.

"Are all the lights off?"

"Yes, Mother. Come on, I'll help you down the steps."

Ruth locked the door behind them and took Olive's arm. She looked at the bright yellow car in the street, some sort of Japanese model, and wished she'd thought to ask the taxi company to send one of the big London cabs that were so common down here now. But Olive managed to get into the back seat without too much difficulty and Ruth slipped in beside her.

"The Royal Sussex please."

The driver looked at Ruth in his rear view mirror. The fare was hardly worth his while, the hospital was only three streets away. He couldn't help noticing, though, that the younger of the two women, although she must be fifty if she was a day, was really rather good looking.

20

Danny tried Ruth's number again, but it went straight through to the answering service. He wanted to catch her before they left for the States so as to fix a time to see her as soon as they got back. Maybe lunch at their favourite restaurant, The Light of Nepal, if Subash the head waiter could fit them in. He put his mobile back into his pocket and pulled out the letter.

"Rebecca, what should I do with this?"

The Diary Secretary looked up with a scowl. There was still some last minute scheduling to be done and she had no time for distractions. "What is it?"

"I don't know to be honest. Some rather persistent woman handed it to me on my way in."

Colonel Neilson, who was waiting for the Den to empty so he could start his own meeting with the Prime Minister, was looking over Danny's shoulder.

"May I?" He took the envelope without waiting for a reply and tore it open.

"I don't believe that was addressed to you." Danny's membership of the Kneejerk Fan Club had lapsed along with that of most of the Prime Minister's immediate entourage.

"You know the procedures, Mr Oliver. All communications for the Prime Minister and his family whether marked personal or anything else have to go through security first." He took out the handwritten note and read it to himself. "You say this woman was outside when you came in?"

"Yes, she came up to me outside the gates. I just figured her for one of the usual rabble. But she pretty well thrust this on me. Are you going to send me to the Tower for not handing it in at the Vortex? I'm afraid I forgot."

"Very funny, Sir. But think we should just see if she's still out there.

Come with me for a second if you wouldn't mind, Mr Oliver." Danny looked for sympathy from Rebecca but she was deep in concentration. He was dragged along in the wake as Colonel Neilson swept past him and out into the corridor. There was a trace of shoe polish in the air wherever Kneejerk went that Danny found very off-putting.

Neilson's personal command centre had been established down a short flight of stairs less than five yards from the entrance to Sinclair's outer office, much to the disgust of Helen who'd had to move to another room on the floor above. In many ways Number 10 resembled a palace in ancient Rome. Power and influence were all too often measured by sheer proximity to the man at the centre.

There was a bank of small television screens against the back wall. Colonel Neilson was able to sit at his desk and watch them all day long if he chose to, and sometimes he did exactly that. He pressed a couple of buttons on the number pad beside his telephone and five different angles on the Compound and the Ordinary Decent Malcontents inside were displayed in an instant. Danny squinted at the screens.

"Can't see her." Colonel Neilson looked so disappointed that Danny felt obliged to take another look. "Actually, that could be her. Outside the Compound, just there," he said pointing his finger at one of the images.

The Colonel said something softly into the microphone on his control panel and the camera started to pan a little to the left and zoom in. The woman, who was standing alone about fifteen feet from the gaggle of protesters, came into focus.

"Well?"

"Yeah, that's her. Looks harmless enough to me."

"Oh, appearances can be most deceptive," said the Colonel in his most irritating just-you-leave-all-that-sort-of-thing-to-me voice. "It won't take a minute to be find out."

It took 33 seconds.

A single sheet of paper slid silently out of the console into the waiting tray. Neilson picked it up and scanned it quickly. His disappointment was all too evident. "No matches. Not even a history as an ODM."

"A what?" Danny hadn't heard the phrase before.

"Colonel Neilson?" Rebecca was standing at the open door. "The Prime Minister is waiting."

Paul Sinclair signalled to the Colonel to sit down. The Prime Minister had not been disappointed when his Security Supremo had announced that he could spend the next few days more profitably in London than Washington. Maybe Neilson had seen enough of America over the summer as he toured all his favourite haunts seeking out new ideas for boxing the Prime Minister even more tightly into his own little pen.

Sinclair didn't think he made too many bad judgements, not in his working life anyway, but he now realised he should have been a great deal more specific when appointing Neilson to the job. He'd hoped that by having a Security Supremo reporting directly to him he could respond to the new threat of chemical terrorism without launching a wholesale assault on civil liberties at the same time. His promises on 'Civilised Values' and restoring some basic democratic rights had been sincere, even if he did have a less black and white view of the issues than Joanna Morgan. And who better than a tough ex-MI6 man to get the Circle of Death Bombers brought to justice quickly, tighten up essential security measures and overhaul Britain's intelligence gathering? But three years on and the Colonel appeared to have given up all hope of finding the perpetrators. His policy seemed to be to turn Downing Street into a fortress in the hope that he could protect the Prime Minister if nobody else. It was almost as if the Colonel saw Paul Sinclair as the embodiment of the democracy they were all fighting to preserve.

Sinclair had hoped the hostage crisis might give the Colonel a chance to show what he was worth. So far, though, he had little to offer the Prime Minister by way of new information.

"*HMS Achilles* is under full steam and should be off the coast within twenty hours. But in targeting terms there's still nothing from the satellites, I'm afraid, Prime Minister. These situations do call for patience sometimes."

Patience was the one thing Sinclair was running short on with regard to his Security Supremo. He had defended the Colonel's trans-Atlantic policies for three years in the face of strong opposition from the Deputy Prime Minister and much of the Labour Party, but he wasn't sure how much longer he could keep it up. He was sure of one thing, however. That the President would have been far less patient if any of the hostages had been American. "Well let's hope that by the time I see John Warren we have something to go on."

"There is another pressing matter, Prime Minister." Sinclair braced himself for another instalment on his wife's brush with the police, but instead the Colonel produced a letter from his pocket. "You should probably know about this." Sinclair took the envelope and opened it as Kneejerk continued. "It was handed to Mr Oliver on his way into the Vortex this morning. It appears that your son has been drawing some unwelcome attention."

Sinclair was no longer listening.

'Dear Joshua, Sorry to write you like this, but I couldn't think what else to do. When you stopped answering my e-mails I knew somebody in there had found out about us and stopped you. Maybe they've been blocking your replies without you even knowing. When you told me how they rule your life I didn't realise it could get this bad. But I wanted you to know that I'm still thinking of you, and that I hope we can find a way to start again where we left off. I could tell how much you were enjoying it, you naughty boy. I hope they aren't being horrid to you because of me. Writing like this makes me feel as if we've got some big guilty secret, which of course we haven't. But I couldn't think of any other way. Try to get in touch…I'll be waiting! Soon I hope. HH.'

There was one of those little smiley faces drawn beside the initials. Sinclair looked at the Colonel and waited for him to explain.

"The responsible party is a white woman, aged about thirty-five. We don't have a name as yet Prime Minister, but we're working on it."

"Responsible for what exactly?"

"Well it's clearly an inappropriate communication of some sort. We do have to look into it."

"Leave it with me, Henry. I'll speak to Joshua." He folded the letter and put it in his jacket pocket. "Do you have children of your own, Colonel?" When his Security Supremo failed to reply he added, "I thought not. Now if you'll excuse me I have three more meetings before we leave."

21

The Royal Sussex County Hospital was a sprawling complex of buildings on a site that commanded a fine view of the English Channel. Its various additions and extensions reflected almost every building style since the eighteen hundreds and, while it had been extensively modernised in recent years, parts of it still had the feel of some venerable old charitable institution. The Outpatients Department was across the road from the main building. Outside it a group of nurses was collecting signatures on a petition under the close supervision of two uniformed policemen.

"Sign here to save the NHS," called one of the nurses as they approached. Ruth looked apologetic but didn't stop on her way in. The waiting room was already very busy. The illuminated sign on the far wall told patients to expect a delay of approximately thirty-five minutes.

Olive sat with her hands crossed in her lap, ignoring the pile of magazines on the table in front of her. She looked around at the other people waiting but recognised nobody except the Indian lady whose husband ran the newsagent in St George's Road. She was trying to get her young son settled in the chair beside her by tempting him with a packet of sweets. Ruth, meanwhile, had collected a cup of coffee from the machine by the door and was making her way back to her seat.

The waiting room was hot and stuffy and as she sat down Ruth felt the drowsiness of a night with too little sleep nag at her eyelids. She took out her book to give herself something to occupy her. She still found it unsettling to look around and see her husband's name and often his picture too on the front of the newspapers that people held in their hands or laps. But she couldn't concentrate on the book and allowed her eyes to close for a minute.

"Mrs Reynolds? This way please." Ruth woke at the sound of the nurse's voice and was momentarily disorientated. She hurried to help Olive to her feet. The nurse was pointing to a door off the main corridor. "Dr Gill is ready to see you now."

Ruth straightened the jacket of her suit and put a hand up to her hair as she followed her mother towards the open door.

Dr Donald Gill stood up behind his desk as the two women entered. He was a tall, averagely built man with slightly sloping shoulders and a broad tanned face. The tan covered not just his face but every inch of his scalp as well. Dr Gill was completely bald, although he didn't look more than forty or forty-five at the most. Ruth wondered if he shaved his head. It looked as if there were some areas where hair might still be willing to put in an appearance if it was allowed to. It suited him, though, and it was obvious he took pride in how he looked. His eyes were a rich shade of blue. Was it a coincidence that he chose to wear a shirt of almost exactly the same colour? The doctor gestured towards the two chairs in front of his tidy desk and Ruth noticed that his wrists where they emerged from what looked like a very expensive shirt were surprisingly hairy.

"Mrs Reynolds, do take a seat. And Mrs, er…"

Before Ruth could think about introducing herself, her mother interjected. "I thought I was going to see Dr Salamon."

"I know you did, Mrs Reynolds, but unfortunately Dr Salamon has had to go to Boston for a conference. We didn't want to put your appointment off any longer." He smiled across at Ruth. "So I hoped you wouldn't mind seeing me this time." There was no hint of condescension in his voice, which, although it betrayed an educated accent, was still unmistakably from Sussex.

"But Dr Salamon knows me well."

Ruth thought her mother was probably reluctant to have to explain her medical history for this new man. "You know, I'm sure Dr Gill has got everything he needs in your file, Mother."

"I certainly have, Mrs Reynolds. And most importantly I have the results of the tests Dr Salamon ran on your last visit." Olive was looking intently at him now, her hands once more folded on her lap. "First of all, though, tell me how you've been getting on with the steroids."

"Oh they help a bit, I suppose, but Dr Sal…" she sighed.

"They've obviously been reducing the swelling and making you feel a little better, but they're not doing anything about the basic condition,

Mrs Reynolds. I'm sure Dr Salamon explained all this."

"Oh yes, he always explains things in a way I can understand."

"Well let's see if I can manage to do the same. We're learning more and more about your illness, Mrs Reynolds, and the more we learn the better we think the chances are of stopping it getting any worse and maybe even reversing some of the damage already done." Olive nodded. Her daughter hadn't taken her eyes off the doctor since he'd started speaking.

"Are you going to give me something new to take?"

"No. Pills aren't always the answer Mrs Reynolds. This new treatment is basically an injection."

"Oh no, I don't like injections." Olive had her head down and was staring into her lap.

"Well it's not like an ordinary injection. We'd attach a catheter to you that would take very small amounts of a new drug straight to the affected area. Does that make sense?" His patient looked uncertain. "It means that the overall dose would be very small but it would be targeted just where we need it. I can't promise you anything as it's all very new, but the signs are good. The treatment has been on trial in the United States for a while and seems to be doing remarkably well, especially with the over seventies. Dr Salamon is in America now reviewing the case studies. That's why he couldn't see you himself. We're hoping to get permission very soon to use it here and if that happens we can start you on it almost immediately."

"What is this new drug, Dr Gill?" Ruth asked.

The doctor held her eye for a split second longer than felt comfortable. There was something about this man that slightly unsettled her. He was evidently sincere. Ruth had been around politicians long enough to spot false sincerity at a hundred metres. She admired his confidence and was ready to buy into his optimism but she had a feeling there was something he wasn't telling them.

"Well it's essentially a derivative of uranium…"

"Uranium? Is that safe?"

"Perfectly." He was now sounding almost too confident. "It's not dangerous at all. As I said, just a stable isotope. The American trials have been running for over five years and there have been no significant side-effects."

Olive had picked up her daughter's unease. "I think I'd like to talk to Dr Salamon."

"Of course. He'll be back in a few days."

Olive stood up abruptly and ran her hands down the front of her coat. "Thank you, doctor. We really should be going now. There are lots of people waiting."

Dr Gill stood and came around the front of his desk. He shook them both by the hand and Ruth noticed how firm his grip was.

Out in the corridor she turned back and looked at Dr Gill's door as her mother went off in search of the lavatory. She was still looking at when it opened and the doctor came out. He looked taller away from his desk.

"I'm so sorry, she doesn't mean to be rude."

"No, of course not. I didn't think she was rude at all, believe me. She's never met me before so of course she's a bit wary. And, if I'm right, she wasn't the only one who might still need some convincing."

"Well, I've always thought that dementia or whatever it is was basically a one way street. I'd never thought of mother coming back."

"That's what we all thought Mrs Sinclair," So he did know who she was. "But it looks like we may all have been wrong." He looked down the corridor to where Olive had emerged from the ladies and was looking lost. "You'd better go and help your mother. But I'm glad I caught you. I have another appointment now, but if it's not a terrible imposition I wondered if you might be free for lunch."

Ruth still had half a mind to call the Albion Club to see if Toby had a spare appointment over lunchtime, but there was something about this man that made her say yes to his invitation. He gave her his card with his mobile number printed at the bottom and suggested a vegetarian restaurant a short distance away. Ruth put the card in her pocket and when she looked up again the doctor had gone. She found Olive standing by the exit looking impatiently at the taxi rank across the road.

22

Helen's car emerged from the vast silver doors of the Vortex and pulled out into Whitehall. The small group of demonstrators inside the Compound made a half-hearted attempt at a collective jeer but soon gave up when they didn't recognise the red-headed woman in the back seat. A uniformed policeman held back the traffic as they turned right towards the House of Commons.

Janine Clairmont was standing with two large suitcases just before the traffic lights. "There she is. Jesus, how much is she taking? Just pull in here a second can you?"

"I shouldn't really Miss Griffin."

"I know but it won't take a sec." Helen opened the door before the car had come to a complete halt. "Come on, get in." As usual Janine had a phone to her ear, so Helen got out and threw the bags into the boot before pushing her friend into the back seat. "We're only going to be away two days, you know."

"I'll call you as soon as we land. Yes, of course." She brought her hand up to cover the mouthpiece. "I love you too."

Helen raised her eyebrows and tilted her head to one side as the journalist put her phone away. "Someone new? Do tell."

"It was the office."

"Mixing business with pleasure again are we, darling? You know that only means tears in the long run. Well?"

"I'll tell you about it later." The two women took a keen interest in each other's untidy private lives. Neither was very surprised or for that matter particularly disappointed when things didn't work out. Being an unmarried woman over forty is an experience more palatable when shared.

"Suit yourself, Janine."

"I think it might be time I did suit myself for once. Much as I love you, I've got to tell you you're not very good at the give and take business. Especially the give bit." The car turned into Piccadilly and slowed to allow a group of tourists to cross in front of them. She waited for her friend to fire back, but Helen wasn't her usual combative self so Janine pressed home her advantage. "Look, I've been bloody good to you. If people knew just how good then whatever reputation I've got left as a journalist would be down the drain in a flash. What do I get in return? A lift to the airport? I'd rather get a cab."

Helen knew she was right. Pathetic though it might be, the woman sitting next to her was her best hope of knowing what another woman currently sitting pretty as Deputy Prime Minister was up to. She needed to find something to offer Janine in return. "What do you want, darling?"

"We're going to have to talk about the personal stuff sooner or later. This book of mine is supposed to be an intimate biography. So far you've given me nothing more intimate than the kind of milk he puts on his Bran Flakes."

"I told you he wears boxers."

"I don't think that's going to be quite enough to satisfy my publisher, Helen. You know what I'm talking about. Let's start with the early years. Pre-Ruth. Paul Sinclair's so-called dark lady. Or is that getting too close for comfort?"

"We are not having this conversation now."

"Why not?"

"Because we're in the back of a government car on the way to RAF Northolt, that's why. Kneejerk has probably got the fucking thing bugged."

"There's always some excuse."

"Yeah, but you've got to admit that was a good one."

"Okay. So why did you offer me a lift?"

"Because we never seem to have enough time to talk. Let's stick to the political stuff, shall we? How far did we get?"

"So far, Little Miss Loyalty, all you've given me is Paul Sinclair as the shrewd Foreign Secretary, Paul Sinclair and his brilliant leadership campaign, oh yes, and Paul Sinclair the first sure-fire year in office. I'm thinking of calling the book *Walking On Water*."

"Well sometimes, let me tell you, it feels more like *Wading Through Shit*."

"Tell me about it."

"I will. All in good time."

"For a woman who claims to want to cut the crap all the time, you're pretty good at doling it out."

Helen sighed. She was doing her best. "Do you want my help or don't you?"

"Yes, of course I do. You're still my best source, God help me." She sighed, took out her notebook and summarised their last conversation. "Sinclair has been a clever old Prime Minister for a year, comfortably ahead in the polls, and he calls a General Election. The Tories and the LibDems are still fighting it out for second place and Sinclair looks like a shoo-in. He's riding high."

"Can you believe that all that was just three years ago? Mind you, to listen to him, you'd think he was still riding high. I don't think he realises how much trouble he's in. Maybe I should get him to watch your programme more often."

"Maybe you should. But don't change the subject. Tell me about the night of the Circle of Death. Let me guess, it was his finest hour."

"You can be as cynical as you like, Janine, but actually I think maybe it was. He can be completely crap sometimes, and yes I'll tell you about some of that too in good time, but I'd never seen him so impressive as he was that night."

"You were in Edinburgh, right?"

"It was the big Foreign Policy speech of the General Election campaign. The Tories had been banging away at us for being too anti-American, criticising our 'Civilised Values' campaign and saying we were putting Britain's security at risk by ending detention without trial and all the rest of it. This was Paul's answer, although to be honest it was always Joanna who'd really pushed the policy hard. And, being Jo, she couldn't resist combining it with a bit of anti-Americanism. Paul was never too happy about that, he thought it was playing into the Tories' hands, but he said he had to give her a bit of licence. As we all know, she has to remind people what a great European she is from time to time."

"It's not just that. She would have us all believe that she's the only one in your government who really believes in human rights."

"Yeah well, we're used to that too by now. But the truth is that

Paul had thought about the speech a lot. He genuinely believed…no, he genuinely believes that Britain is stronger at the heart of several alliances, not just one. And, for that matter, that's there's a balance to be struck between retaining our democratic values and fighting the terrorists. So he was getting ready to say that while we would continue to support America in the war on terror, we wouldn't do it slavishly. We'd tell them when they were wrong like good friends should. And, of course, it was a very popular policy. Critical Friends. The Yanks had tried to talk us round with the usual mixture of bribes and threats but Paul and Jo were holding firm."

"And yet he never made the speech."

"No. Jo made it for him. She was on the platform too so it made sense for her to pick up from him when he had to leave."

"In the dim and distant days when she was still his closest supporter."

Helen did her best to laugh. "You know the line, Janine. The Prime Minister and the Deputy Prime Minister are working hard together in the interests of the hard-working families of Britain."

"Yeah, right. Spare me the smokescreen stuff. So, when did you first hear about the bomb?"

"I took the call from Downing Street on my mobile. The chairman had just finished the introductions and Paul was doing his warm up bit before he got into the important section. I was in the wings and had to whisper into the phone. It was the Cabinet Secretary insisting on speaking to the Prime Minister personally. I told him he couldn't but there was something in his voice that made me realise this was serious. Normally I'd have told the old fart to bog off, but I didn't. I sent a steward on to the stage to get Paul off. He wasn't best pleased, I can tell you."

"I know. I was in the audience. We got it all on camera. A rare flash of anger from Mr Nice Guy."

"Paul was quite heavily made up for the TV lights but you could see how shocked he was when he heard about the explosion and that a chemical weapon was involved. He'd read all the top secret briefings as soon as he became PM, although he knew most of it already from his year as Foreign Secretary. He made it his business to understand sarin and the other compounds that had been used by terrorists in the past. It was sobering stuff. A chemical attack could kill thousands, tens of thousands of people and many of the newer compounds are almost impossible to detect. Until they go off."

"But it hadn't gone off."

"No, it hadn't, thank God. Indeed at first nobody was quite sure what had happened. They thought it might just have been an electrical fault. Some kind of short circuit. Several passengers had reported hearing a loud bang at the top of one of the escalators at Westminster tube station. There was no obvious damage and the duty manager had thought about leaving it for the overnight engineers to take a look at but he decided to play it by the book. Just as well he did. The safety regulations demanded the closure of half the station while an electrician was sent up a step ladder to investigate. You know what that place is like. Very late twentieth century with all the pipes and wires exposed but quite high up. So it didn't take him long to find the fault."

"But the country's top civil servant didn't call to tell you about an electrical fault?"

"No, of course not. He didn't ring us until they realised it was a bomb that had failed to detonate. I couldn't hear the other end of the conversation, but it was clear that even after everything London had been through before, this was something quite different. The electrician was a lucky man. He found that something had caused the plastic coating of two wires in the ventilation system to melt. When they had come into contact they had shorted out with a bang. He worked that out quickly enough, but then he spotted a McDonald's bag squashed up between two of the fresh air pipes just above the wires. He thought it was odd because it was too high for anyone to have reached it from the ground unless they were a fucking giant. He pulled it out and got a whiff of chemicals."

"What did he expect from McDonalds?"

"Yeah, very funny Janine. I'd leave that one out of the book if I were you."

"Sorry. Go on."

"Well he was smart enough to put it back where he found it very carefully and call his boss. Just before the election the station manager had been on some special security course and they'd put the willies up everyone about gas and chemical attacks and what have you. There was an attack on the underground in Tokyo, if you remember, long before all the conventional bombs in Europe."

"Don't worry, I did a full report on it all that same day. I know the history."

"Sorry, of course you do. Well this guy was familiar with all the contingency plans at least. They were drawn up so there would be some procedure to follow, although nobody could really predict what would happen if a big chemical bomb did go off. And it was just as well he did because he got the police down there sharpish and they called in the bomb squad with all their protective gear and stuff.

"As soon as he got their preliminary report the Cabinet Secretary called us. All very British and calm on the surface but Paul said he was obviously bricking himself. Scotland Yard had advised him that we had to assume there had been an attempt at a massive chemical attack on the London Underground."

"And the media were told nothing."

"Not immediately. It was the old problem of how to deal with the risk of panic. The Cabinet Secretary was afraid that if people knew there was the chance that chemicals were being released into the air all over London then this time there really would be mass hysteria. The device had been placed right next to the ventilation channels for the whole of the Circle, District and Jubilee Lines."

"Hence the 'Circle of Death'".

"Exactly. It was the *Evening Standard* that dreamed that one up, I think, and the rest of the media just latched onto it. So some headline writer has got his footnote in history. Anyway, the device was obviously intended to spread toxic gas across half the underground system. And we had no idea how many other devices there might be."

"What did Paul do?"

"He told him to trust the good sense of the people of London. He didn't flinch. He simply ordered the complete evacuation of the entire underground network and authorised the doomsday alert. Everybody but everybody to return to their homes as quickly as possible and close all doors and windows. Drink only bottled water and keep the radio on. I don't scare easily, as you know, but my skin froze as I heard him give the order. And believe it or not he even remembered to phone the

King, who was as drippy as ever incidentally. "

Janine nodded. "Sitting there watching Jo go on with the speech I had a feeling that something was seriously wrong. Feminine intuition maybe. I actually felt sorry for her later. She was up there talking about not over-reacting by letting the terrorists destroy our basic freedoms when she had no idea what was going on back in London."

"Well nobody covered the speech so no harm was done. And of course Paul was dead right. There was no panic other than in some bits of Whitehall and the intelligence services."

"Really? I'd have thought they'd have been all very calm and professional."

"On one level, yes. But they'd been telling us how they had all the terrorist cells infiltrated. So to discover, yet again, that there were some totally unknown madmen out there came as a shock. And then to make matters worse when they did an analysis of the McDonalds bag they discovered that the chemicals were some nerve agent they'd never come across before. They really had been caught with their collective pants down. The deadliest attack ever attempted anywhere in the world had just been averted but it was no thanks to them. Don't get me wrong. They do their best and it's an all but impossible job, but they obviously saw it as a massive failure."

Janine looked over at her friend. "And they never really made up for it so far as I can see."

"I wouldn't argue with you there. It wasn't the chemicals that terrified them at the end of the day. It was the fact that they never had any lead on who was responsible. They checked out every face on the CCTV cameras at the station. Some guy who had his kid on his shoulders was detained for nearly a week in case he'd made the little boy plant the bomb. All their contacts in the Muslim community and the hard left, and in Ireland and Palestine and everywhere else produced absolutely sweet F.A. Paul kept asking for answers and all he got was excuses."

"And yet he never stopped giving them his support, did he?"

"How could he? There was nobody else for him to turn to."

"Not that it did him any harm politically."

"Well, call me a cynical old bitch, but no it didn't. We were in the middle of an election campaign, remember. There was nothing much

I could do on the security front so I got hold of the other party leaders and persuaded them to agree to a political truce while the country was under threat. They had no choice, of course."

"It didn't last though, did it?" said Janine. "I've been covering politics long enough but even I can't believe how stupid the Tories can be. I mean, at least on law and order you expect them to get it right. If they hadn't turned round three days later and accused Sinclair of having invited the attack by turning his back on America we wouldn't have a Liberal Democrat as Leader of the Opposition today. Pretty ironic as it turned out."

"I expect you're right."

"I'm not political editor of AM-TV for nothing you know. Which reminds me, are we going to get a story out of this trip or not?"

"Not my problem, darling. Talk to Danny." She leaned forward to speak to the driver. "How much further?"

"Six miles, Miss Griffin. We'll have you there in ten minutes or so."

"Well, Janine, was that any help?"

"Yes. As far as it went. But what about the Security U-turn? I mean I can see why Paul had to shelve the 'Civilised Values' stuff but you're not going to tell me he wrote the new State Security Act single handedly on the back of an envelope on the plane back to London?"

"No. We have the Home Office to thank for that. They had a draft over to us within hours. I wish some of the other departments could work half that fast. Paul looked at the evidence and said he wasn't afraid to admit he'd been wrong. Frankly our guys had shown the limits of what they could do and the harsh reality was that the Americans did have the best intelligence network in the world and the best equipment. There was a bit of a set-to with Jo about it, but he told her that Britain's security was his primary responsibility and until the European Union caught up we would re-align ourselves fair and square behind the Yanks. To be honest, it was a relief. Jo was very difficult for a while, but I never quite bought her line that Europe could deliver on the security front. If you're going to try to stay one step ahead of those bastards you can't waste time negotiating every damn thing with thirty different prima donnas in God knows how many different languages. I mean, cut the crap. You need a clear line of command. Unfortunately while Paul understood that, he also decided to go down the American road and put a Security Supremo in charge. So we have him to blame for Kneejerk."

"Is the Colonel coming with us today?"

"No. I was a bit surprised about that. He usually can't wait to see his buddies over there but he's staying safely tucked up behind his bloody Vortex and all the rest of it, thank God. He can keep Joanna Morgan company. We decided not to bring any excess baggage."

"Can I quote you on that?"

Helen grinned at her friend. "Perhaps you'd better not."

"And Ruth?"

The smile was gone. "What about her?"

"She not coming either?"

"You know she's not." Helen could see the gates of the air force base ahead of them. The Prime Minister's personal Airbus was parked on the otherwise empty runway.

"Maybe next time you'll tell me why out of the three women in Paul Sinclair's life you seem to be the only one who's still standing by him."

The young Air Force officer on the gate saluted as the car passed through and was the subject off two pairs of appreciative forty-something eyes. "Now that," said Helen seeing her chance to change the subject, "is something I would be more than happy to stand by."

23

Ruth had no idea what to expect from her lunch with Dr Gill, but her curiosity had been aroused and she was ready to hear what he had to say. Besides, it was a long time since a man had invited her to lunch on any pretext.

The café was usually quiet at lunch times, which is why Donald Gill had suggested it. He rarely had time for more than a sandwich but today he'd made sure he'd be able to get away. He was already at the table when Ruth arrived and he stood up to make sure she spotted him. She came across and shook his hand rather awkwardly. The doctor took her jacket and placed it over the back of her chair.

"I'm so glad you could make it."

"Well, I don't have to get back until later."

"I hope you don't find this too unorthodox."

"Unusual, certainly. When I said I'd take Mother for her appointment I didn't expect to be sitting over a meal with her doctor a hour and a half later."

Dr Gill smiled. "Yes, well I suppose the whole situation is a little unusual, Mrs Sinclair."

Ruth stiffened. "I hope this has nothing to do with my being Mrs Sinclair?"

Before Donald Gill could answer, the waiter brought their menus and asked if they wanted something to drink. Donald ordered a mineral water, Ruth a glass of chardonnay.

The interruption gave him time to avoid having to answer her question directly. "Tell me, are you writing at the moment? I thought your last one was marvellous. You had Lloyd George off to a tee, and all that wonderful Edwardian hypocrisy and repressed emotion." Either this man had done some serious homework or he meant what he said. Ruth's finely tuned insincerity radar was currently giving him permission to land.

"Thank you. I'm currently up to my eyes in scandal of a different kind. A bit more historical. I had a rather snotty letter from one of the Lloyd George's great-great-and maybe great-again grandchildren so I thought I'd be on safer ground in the eighteenth century. A lot of it is based down here, as it happens."

"Brighton is pretty immune to scandal, you know. It must be something to do with the air."

She smiled. "Don't tell my mother that."

"I wasn't planning to. So go on, what's the story?"

"It's a fictionalised life of Mrs Fitzherbert…"

"The woman who secretly married the Prince of Wales? Or were they never really married, I can't remember."

Ruth was quietly impressed. "He denied it later, but they were yes. At least that was the Pope's take on it so who are we to argue? He was rather beastly to her at times, but he clearly loved her. When he died, they found a miniature picture of her in a locket round his neck."

"It sounds rather romantic."

"I suppose it was. I mean George III, his father, was going quietly bonkers and parliament and the press were giving him a hard time. I'm trying to be fair to him as well."

"I look forward to reading it."

"Not as much as I look forward to finishing it. But I'm sure we're not here to talk about my writing. How ill is she, Dr Gill?"

"Do you know exactly what is wrong with your mother?"

"I'm hoping you may be about to tell me."

He took a mouthful of mineral water and wiped his serviette across his lips. "Until not that long ago she would have been diagnosed with some catch-all thing like pre-senile dementia. Nothing that showed up on the scans except a little cranial atrophy. Stop me if I get too technical."

"Go on."

"Now the scans are a lot more accurate and our understanding of what goes on in the brain has progressed enormously. What we see with your mother is a kind of brain cancer."

"A tumour?"

"No. That would show up like a big black lump. Easy to spot but harder to deal with. No she has a sort of grey cloud over parts of her brain and it's getting bigger. Think of it as kind of liver spots but inside her head. Most old people get them. Fortunately the brain doesn't have nerve endings like the rest of the body, so cancers of this kind can get very serious indeed, fatal even, and the patient feels no pain. You're mother hasn't got there yet, not by a long chalk. This new treatment could mean she never does."

"I've been thinking about what you said earlier. Uranium does sound rather alarming."

"I didn't say so back there for fear of terrifying the pair of you, but we're actually talking about enriched uranium. Micro-bursts in a solution that's injected straight into the tissue of the brain via the catheter. Think of it as a combination of chemotherapy and radiotherapy. It's an ingenious technique and really not dangerous at all. We've been using radiation in medical science for a very long time. People thought Marie Curie was playing with fire too, remember."

I suppose that's true, but even so. I'm just surprised that I haven't heard anything about it on the radio or anything."

"Well it has been a bit hush hush, although God knows why. It all gets a bit mixed up with politics, I'm afraid." She tensed perceptibly as he went on. "You might remember that a few years ago the Americans were getting hot and bothered about the nuclear research programme in Turkmenistan. They couldn't prove it but they were pretty sure they were getting secret help from the Iranians. They had this fancy new facility they were building that they could never have afforded by themselves. Anyway, the government in Ashkhabad, is it Ashkhabad, I can never remember?"

"I really have no idea."

"I think it's Ashkhabad. Anyway, they kept insisting they were processing this uranium for purely medical purposes and, of course, the Yanks didn't believe a word of it. So the United Nations and the World Health Organisation stepped in and told these guys to prove to the experts that it really was medical research they were doing. In the meantime, of course, the Americans were preparing to deal with what they saw as a military threat in their own sweet little way. The plant was reduced to rubble but not before we found out that the scientists in this tin pot little dictatorship actually had made a scientific breakthrough or at least they were on the point of one. It's since been perfected with a bit of Western help, mainly American but the British were graciously allowed to take part too so long as we didn't say anything about where the discovery had really been made. It all stinks, of course, but it does mean we're now ready to start offering it to patients like your mother. She's ideally qualified."

"And is that the only reason you're talking to Mrs Sinclair and not the daughter of any other elderly patient on your books, Doctor?"

"Donald. Please."

"Donald. Well, is it?"

"I'm telling you this because I want to. Because it's right for my patient. But I'm not going to pretend it has nothing to do with politics. It does."

"Well I appreciate your honesty." There was something about this man that made her want to give him the benefit of the doubt. His deep blue eyes held hers just long enough to make her feel comfortable in his company. She took another sip of her wine and told herself she mustn't get tipsy.

"The government's being very cagey about whether it will fund the treatment if it passes the trials. The new Health Bill…"

Ruth put her glass down firmly and it clattered against her fork. "Dr Gill, let me make one thing perfectly clear. I may be married to the Prime Minister but I don't get involved in politics. We've all seen what can happen when that mistake is made and I'm not about to repeat it. If you have anything to say about the government's health policy I suggest you talk to the Health Department. It's their job and I'm sure Stephen Piggin is a very reasonable man. I'm very pleased that you've invited me here but if it's because you want me to talk to my husband about this then I'm afraid I really must be going. I'm sorry, I don't mean to be rude."

"No, please. It was me who was being rude. That isn't why I invited you at all. It's just that I get rather passionate about it all sometimes. I'm sorry. Really I am." The intensity of his stare was both a little unnerving and strangely exciting. He looked away and dabbed at his mouth with his napkin. It was the first time she had properly noticed his teeth, almost perfect but not too perfect and very, very white. He raised his eyes again and furrowed his forehead like a puppy. The waiter offered them both more bread and she took two slices.

Helmut was in a foul mood when they got back to the Castle. Try as he might, he couldn't remember why he'd ever believed standing around waving banners was going to dent the power of the ruling classes. They just laughed from inside their comfortable cars and passed by. When Paul Sinclair left, with his outriders and flashing lights, he hadn't even taken the trouble to laugh. He appeared not to have noticed them. Helmut was more convinced than ever that far from helping to free the masses from their servitude, demonstrations like that just reminded them of their captivity. But his humiliation wasn't over yet.

"I saw you on the TV boys. Well, I saw Pete," said PJ. He'd been hard to miss, standing a good six to eight inches above everybody else. "Let's hope the nice men and women of the Metropolitan Police saw you too. Now, I want you to go across the road and apologise to Mrs Gundry for the disturbance last night. She thinks you're bringing the area into disrepute and we don't want that."

Helmut couldn't believe what he was hearing. It was positively feudal. The Lord of the Manor graciously allowed them to remain as his serfs, and admittedly the rent PJ charged was negligible, but in return they had to do his bidding. And to think that he'd once looked up to PJ Walton as a vanguard of the revolution.

Even Pete, who was usually happy to go along with whatever PJ wanted, balked at this. "Aw come on, mate. Wave the white flag for the old trout? You're kidding aren't you?"

"No, Pete. I actually like living here but I'd rather do it without having to make excuses for my lodgers either to the forces of law and order or to their stout defender, Mrs Alma Gundry. You don't have to mean what you say, you just have to sound as if you do. Now, go on. She's expecting you."

The telephone started to ring in PJ's first floor study and he went to answer it. There was nothing further to discuss.

Mrs Gundry opened the door cautiously. She'd watched the two men come out of the Castle and cross the road to her side of Wilson Crescent, but she was no more convinced that this was a good idea than they were. Pete introduced themselves. "I'm Pete. This is Helmut." Helmut stood on the doorstep hunched and silent.

"You'd better come in." Alma looked down at their shoes to make sure they weren't bringing anything in with them. There was tea and a packet of bourbons on the table in the lounge. If making peace with these men meant the street had a chance of moving up, she was willing to make a few sacrifices.

"Do you take sugar?" The fatter one had taken a seat by the window. The tall, gangly one was still hovering uncomfortably. "Please sit down, only you're making the place look untidy."

Pete looked around the room and decided she hadn't meant it as a joke. He couldn't see a single thing that might have been said to be out of place. It was an averagely sized lounge, just like every other one in the street except that it was populated by a regimented army of tiny china and glass figures. They covered almost every surface and each had been placed in exactly the right position to give an impression of total order. Pete felt a chill in his cheeks and quickly chose a chair and sat down.

"Well?"

"Sorry, Mrs Gundry?"

"Do you take sugar or don't you?"

"Oh yeah, I mean yes. Thanks. One for me. Helmut takes three. He's German."

"Oh, I see." This wasn't going to be easy. "Mr Walton tells me you have something to say."

Helmut appeared to have nothing at all to say, so Pete did what he could. "We don't like the fuzz coming round any more than you do. It was a total misunderstanding. A friend of Helmut's trying to cause trouble."

"That's as may be…"

Pete wasn't going to let her get into her stride. "Well, she certainly caused enough trouble. But she's made her point now. We don't think there'll be any more bother, do we Helmut?" He looked over at Helmut for support but to no avail. His friend was looking around as if he'd found himself in an unfamiliar dentist's waiting room. He had more of an eye for detail than Pete. Apart from the figurines Mrs Gundry's lounge was neatly if conventionally furnished with a heavy emphasis on antimacassars and frilly tablecloths. A two bar electric fire sat in the grate guarded over by a couple of porcelain cats that looked vaguely Chinese. Helmut had seen the same cheaply painted creatures on Lewisham market and wondered who bought them. What looked like a complete set of Dickens, it was almost always Dickens with the English, was prominently displayed in the glass fronted cabinet by the door to the hall. A recent commemorative plate from the Coronation was set at an angle on the mantelpiece so it could be seen from the sofa.

"Well I do hope not." Mrs Gundry didn't look convinced and she was getting a little worried that the quiet one was looking for valuables. She congratulated herself on thinking to put the silver engraved tankard that her husband had won on bowls under the stairs for safe keeping. "It's not good for the area. No, not at all. It puts the better sort of people off of moving in. Biscuit?"

"It is a very nice room." Pete looked across at Helmut as if he'd just farted loudly, but his friend had clearly decided he did have something to say after all. "Very comfortable. It is clear to me that you admire tradition."

"Well of course. It's what we do best. I mean I know you're not from these parts, but you must have seen that by now."

Pete was tempted to cut in with some observations about the great British traditions of liberalism and live-and-let live, but Helmut was moving onto new territory. "You appreciate Mozart I think?" His sudden change of tack left both Pete and Mrs Gundry equally lost for words. "That is his portrait by the door. Am I right?"

Alma Gundry looked over her shoulder at the small gravure print. "I think so. I mean, it is, yes. Mozart, that's right." Mrs Gundry kept the picture because she thought it gave the room a touch of class. Nobody had ever commented on it before. "My late husband was keen. Do you like him then?"

"I do not think it is possible to like Mozart."

"Oh well, no. I suppose not."

"You can only admire, be in awe. Mozart changed the world. How many can say that?"

"Did he?"

"Do you know the Linz? You must."

"Well…"

"It is exquisite. Almost perfect. Mozart wrote it in just a few days, but I'm sure you know that too. You are obviously a woman of culture."

Pete was studying Mrs Gundry's face. He'd seen that look before many times when out with his friend. It was the look that came over women's faces when they started to really notice Helmut for the first time. When he stopped being an overweight man with a dreadful haircut and became, well whatever it was he became when he had them hooked.

"If you like Mozart then perhaps we can listen together. I don't believe it is the cup of tea of Peter here." Pete couldn't argue with that and he didn't try. He'd known Helmut for years and this was the first time he'd heard him mention Mozart.

Mrs Gundry busied herself with the tea and took a plate of biscuits over to Helmut. "Do tuck in, otherwise I'll have to eat them all myself. I still have my figure to think about." Pete tried not to think about it at all.

~

Across the road, PJ Walton replaced the receiver. Unusually Ray Morgan had been most insistent on meeting him face to face. He normally telephoned PJ once or twice a day with his, or his wife's, take on the political events of the moment. He was a political journalist's dream, always ready with the minutes of a Cabinet meeting or a secret memo that revealed the disagreements at the heart of the Sinclair government. PJ knew he was being used to help further the Deputy Prime Minister's ends, but nothing Ray had ever told him had turned out to be inaccurate. He was being given a line but he wasn't being fooled. The truth was that The Naked Prophet would be nothing without Ray and Joanna Morgan.

Before the Morgans had assumed such an important role in his life PJ had been a poorly paid sub-editor on *Tribune* with a vague ambition to write a column of his own. The first document he'd been leaked had shown just how much the suppliers of the Vortex at the end of Downing Street stood to make if they won the contract. "Naked profit," Ray had said. "It's not right. Joanna, incidentally, is supporting a cheaper European alternative." PJ had gone to his editor with the story and the first column by The Naked Prophet had appeared the same week. After a few months the exposés in PJ's column had come to the notice of the *Daily Mirror* and he was lured away on five times the salary.

Today, however, Ray had something for PJ that he said he couldn't give him over the phone. He suggested a walk in the park, which made PJ wonder if he'd been reading too much John Le Carré. But he didn't have a better idea so had agreed to meet near the pelicans in an hour.

"I didn't know you were into classical music, mate." Pete and Helmut were on their way back up to the workshop. They'd met PJ in the hall and had been able to report that Mrs Gundry had been very nice about it all and had invited them back for tea the following day. He was obviously in a hurry and had left without asking for more details of such an unlikely and speedy rapprochement.

"There are a lot of things you may not know, Peter, because you have never asked."

"Well maybe I should ask a few more questions then. I might find out what makes you such a wiz with the women."

"You might," said Helmut, "but also you might not." The truth was, he had no idea himself. "First I need you to do something for me. You remember how free you felt in that...that bar?"

"I never said I enjoyed it, mate. Don't get me wrong."

Helmut handed him a key. "My suitcase is still in the locker."

24

"The press are all aboard now, Ma'am. The Prime Minister's convoy is expected in about five minutes."

"Thank you." Helen went over to the table and poured herself another strong cup of RAF coffee. Janine had gone off to join the rest of the press pack in the back of the waiting Airbus leaving her to enjoy the benefits of the VIP lounge alone until Danny, who had travelled with the media on the official bus, came to join her. He didn't look as if he was about to cheer her up.

"You look as apprehensive as I feel," she said. "Maybe I just didn't get enough sleep, but all I see when I close my eyes are vultures circling. I can't believe I'm saying this but I actually wish we had Joanna with us. At least we could keep an eye on her."

Danny looked up from his papers. "Hard call, I know. I'll tell you one thing, though. If she wanted to make news, now would be the time to do it. We're going into this trip really badly prepared."

Helen, who was ultimately in charge of the preparations, bristled. "What do you mean? It's been in the diary for over a year. And I do know how to organise a successful visit. Everything is in place."

Helen could turn quite nasty if anybody questioned her professional ability, but that hadn't been Danny's intention. He knew better. "That's not what I meant. We inhabit different worlds sometimes, that's all. I don't think you understand, and I don't think Paul always understands either."

She was calmer already. "Help me understand then. I'm all ears."

"It's all in the Danny Oliver Media Rule Book. I sometimes think Joanna has read it and Paul hasn't. My world is full of these extraordinary creatures, charming and loveable one minute but liable to turn nasty a moment later. They're like over-active but intelligent children. If you give them something to occupy their minds you can keep them quiet for a while, but not for very long. They get bored easily and start looking for mischief and the only solution is to find them another toy to play with before they break something. But they're past the age when you can fob them off with just anything. If they don't like it, or they think it's not half as exciting as you said it would be, then they'll throw it back in your face without a second thought."

"For a gay guy you seem to know a lot about bringing up children. And I all I have to deal with is politicians. They can be pretty infantile too, you know."

"Oh I know that. That's why they get along so well. My lot, you see, they like politicians. They think they're fun to play with because they're provocative and unpredictable and full of surprises. And if one of them gets boring they can be sure that one of the others will be up to something to keep them entertained."

"Now we're speaking the same language, Danny. Politics as the playground. I know all about that. And our Ms Morgan, let me guess, is a politician who never gets boring."

"Well she knows how to keep the children happy, put it that way. Paul would do better if he took at least that one leaf out of her book. Today is a perfect example. The kids are already in a bad mood because they've been told to sit quietly for two hours on the bus and that's something they're not very good at. Right now we've even told them to turn off their computers and their other electronic games. That they really hate, believe me. So they're impatient to play with Paul Sinclair, although I don't think he's going to want to play with them."

"I don't suppose he is."

"So, you see, two days may not seem very long to you, but to me it's an eternity."

"You're a different man when you're dealing with the hacks, aren't you? Be yourself, darling, go and charm them. Butter them up and flatter them, make them feel important, that's what I always do."

"It's all right for you, you're the Prime Minister's Chief of Staff. They don't get to see you very often so it's a big treat when they do. Me they see all the time so I can't work the same magic no matter how hard I try. No, all they want from me is stories, preferably one for every deadline. Do you know how many deadlines there are in two days?"

"No."

"Nor do I. But it's a lot and all Paul has come up with is the latest draft, not the final draft but the latest draft, of a speech to the Washington Institute for Foreign Affairs on debt relief in Africa. My family are from Ghana and even I can't get to the end of it. I don't think it's going to be enough."

"I take your point, Danny. We'll have a word with him on the plane. I'm sure we can work something up."

"Well if we don't I can tell you what tomorrow's headlines will all be about right now. It'll be Action Man Sinclair flying off to strut the stage in America so he can avoid the mounting crisis at home. The nurses meeting didn't go well. They're planning a Day of Action to coincide with the Health vote."

"Yeah I know. Never take on the nurses. You can't win. The public love them whatever they do. And that's in the Helen Griffin Book of Winning Power and Keeping It. Page 2."

"You must let me have a copy."

"We'll do a swap. For Christmas, I promise. If we're not in opposition by then."

"Ms Griffin, the Prime Minister's car is just pulling up."

"Thank you." Helen handed her cup to the officer and gathered up her bag. "We'd better go and see what the main attraction has to say for himself. Maybe he's got some new toys in his bag, you never know."

The runway at RAF Northolt was being sprayed by a light rain as the armour plated Daimler stopped at the foot of the aircraft steps. Detective Inspector Derek Smyth jumped from the driver's seat and opened the rear door in a single movement. An officer with a large umbrella stepped forward to protect Paul Sinclair's head for the few seconds that he'd be in the open air. The station commander saluted and shook the Prime Minister's hand before he climbed up into the forward door opening. TV cameras were no longer allowed at Northolt so Sinclair was spared the need to wave into the middle distance as if he recognised someone.

Helen and Danny left the warmth of the departure lounge to cross the fifty metres or so of tarmac to the Airbus. They were offered umbrellas of their own but it didn't seem to be raining hard enough to bother.

In the First Class cabin Sinclair took off his jacket and was about to pass it to the waiting stewardess when he remembered Joshua's letter. He took it out of the inside pocket and quickly reread it while his jacket was taken away to be hung up for the duration of the flight. Something about it was nagging at him, but he couldn't think what. He settled into his seat and motioned to Helen and Danny to take the seats across the table from him. For the next five hours this would be his mobile Den, less intimate that the real one but scarcely less well equipped. Already the advance party had set up computer terminals and printers. The Private Secretaries were talking to their opposite numbers in Washington on secure lines. The Duty Clerk was amending the schedule setting out second by second what would happen when they landed, who would be assigned to which of the awaiting cars and how all the luggage would get to the right destination.

An RAF Captain appeared from the front of the cabin and passed the Prime Minister a sheet of paper. "The weather and flight report, Sir. It should be a comfortable crossing. There's just a ten minute delay before we'll get clearance for take off."

Danny looked out of the window. RAF Northolt wasn't exactly Heathrow on a busy afternoon. There was no queue of aircraft ahead of them. "What's the hold up?" The sooner they were airborne the sooner he could go back and try to pacify his charges.

"The Prince of Wales, Sir. On his way down from Balmoral." The Captain returned to the flight deck without further explanation.

"Sorry, Danny," said Helen, "but you didn't think we were living in a modern democracy did you? Of course the Prince of Smiles coming back from a busy few days shooting whatever it is they shoot up there takes priority over the Prime Minister on official business. The British people wouldn't have it any other way."

"And if the British people knew I was being advised by a secret republican cell I'd be out on my ear," said Sinclair. His features gave nothing away, but there was no reproach in his voice.

"It might give our friends in the rear cabin something to write about, though," said Helen. "Your Communication Director is worried that the gentlemen and ladies of the press aren't going to have enough to keep them out of mischief, aren't you darling?"

"Well…"

"Don't worry," said Sinclair, "they'll be okay."

130

Danny had never known a Minister, never mind a Prime Minister, less concerned about what the newspapers wrote about him. He put it down to the fact that Sinclair had never had to curry favour with them as an Opposition leader. They'd given him an easy ride in his first year, pleased to have the novelty of a new man at the top at long last. Most of the papers had backed him during the General Election, and the rest came into line after the Circle of Death. Only fairly recently had the government's problems started to affect the way the Prime Minister was portrayed, but Paul Sinclair seemed barely to have noticed.

"Perhaps you'll go back and talk to them during the flight?"

"If I really must."

Paul was quite happy to leave the journalists to get on with their job so long as he was left alone to get on with his. Danny found something admirable in that but it didn't help him with his own job very much.

"Are there any journalists you actually like?" asked Helen.

Paul Sinclair thought a moment and said, "Not particularly, but none I really dislike either. To be honest I don't know many of them terribly well. I used to give all my best stories to Danny here and since he crossed the great divide I've left all that up to him. It's good to have a team you can trust. I mean it. Both of you. I appreciate what you're doing."

There was a sound of engines being thrown into reverse and through the window Danny saw a light aircraft bumping along the runway towards them. It passed close enough for him to see the Prince at the controls, his bald head hidden beneath a flying cap. Immediately their own engines fired up and the plane started to move forward.

"About bloody time." In the rear cabin Janine Clairmont tucked her magazine into the seat pocket and did up her safety belt.

"How was he, Ray? No more nonsense about writing under his own name, I hope."

"He didn't mention it, my dear, and I'm afraid I forgot to ask."

"That was silly of you."

He knew she was right. "I know. You're right. But he was mightily intrigued by the cassette tape. Apparently you don't see them that often any more. I do hope he'll appreciate the contents too."

"He's a bright boy, he'll know what to do with it."

"I think he was hoping to meet you again in person soon, my love."

The Foreign Secretary was briefly lost in thought. Eventually she nodded and looked up at her husband. "Yes, of course, we must arrange something. I'd like that. Perhaps we could have him in for a drink or something. Let me think about it, Ray, would you? In the meantime, what about the others?"

"I spoke to Piggin's office. He'll be free after the vote at seven. I told the rest of them to meet us in your office at the House then. Is that satisfactory?"

"Perfectly, Ray. Perfectly satisfactory."

25

"I just assumed she'd be coming." The woman from the *News of the World* was sitting across the aisle from Janine. "She came on Sinclair's first Washington love-in."

"I know, it's a real bugger," replied Janine, "I did a nice little piece on the Fashion Battle of the First Ladies. We had a phone poll and everything. Ruth Sinclair 67%, Tracey Warren 23%, I can remember it now. My desk were hoping for a return match. I mean it's all right for these guys." She indicated the earnest young man from the *Independent* sitting beside her: "their lot will take a think piece on African debt relief or whatever it is, but it's not very AM-TV is it? Not without a pop star attached."

"So what will you do?"

"Oh, I'll think of something." Janine was relying as ever on Helen, whom she'd arranged to meet for a drink before the end of the day. "But if all else fails there's always the shops." She gave the man beside her a sideways glance. Without the glasses, he might be quite cute. He'd have to get rid of the geeky haircut. But there was something familiar about his face that unsettled her. Then she remembered. "It's you, isn't it?"

"Please…"

"The Bottle Man." The young man groaned. "So there is life after Uxbridge Magistrates Court."

He concentrated hard on his notes but Janine had turned to the man from the BBC in the row behind. "Hey, Jim, remember The Man with the Bottle? Well here he is, alive and, well I don't know about kicking. But alive at any rate."

The young man sank deeper into his seat. It was one thing to be respected by your peers for courageously going to jail to protect your sources. Defence of journalistic freedom you could wear as a badge of honour but he'd have been happy to forget all about his own brief moment of fame.

"You gave us quite a little story for a day or two." Janine was enjoying herself at last. "The intrepid tabloid hack who thought he'd make a name for himself by exposing the sham of airline security. You remember, Jim? He smashed a bottle of tax free plonk in mid-flight to show how crazy it was to take nail scissors off people but allow them to fly with glass bottles. Just so the airlines could make more money. If it hadn't been for the six months in prison for air rage, oh and losing your job of course, it might have worked."

The young man refused to rise to the bait. Jim Wells jumped to his defence. "Yeah, but he was right wasn't he? Remember all those protests in First Class when they had to drink their Chateau Whatever out of plastic bottles? Good on you, mate."

Janine hadn't finished with him yet. "But how did they ever let you on a flight with the Prime Minister?" She looked down at his pass slung round his neck and back up to the thick rimmed glasses. "Oh I get it. You changed your name."

"No."

"Well you weren't Jonathan Barrowman-Simon in those days. Johnny Simon, wasn't it? Well, I never. The Born Again Bottle Man. If we really get stuck we'll make another story out of you. Doesn't say much for all their security if they let you slip through the net, does it?"

"Please, no. I do serious features these days. We all have a right to put our pasts behind us, don't we?"

"Maybe he's having affair," the woman from the *News of the World* suddenly threw in as if from nowhere.

"Who, the Bottle Man?" Janine didn't think he looked the type, but then she knew better than to be fooled by appearances.

"No. Sinclair. Now that would be a story."

Janine leant forward to get a better look at the woman in the opposite row. "Have you been having lunch with the Health Secretary too?"

"What? Piggin? That old letch. I wouldn't sit across a lunch table with him for all the scoops in the world. No, I was just thinking. Maybe Sinclair's having an affair. He's quite fit. A lot of women would find him very attractive." She looked as if she would probably count herself among them. "Well if he is up to something you should know Janine, you're the one writing a book on him. Or are you saving it up for the serialisation rights?"

""I tell you what, why don't you ask his official spokesman, that might liven things up? Here he comes now and he doesn't look to me like he's bearing gifts."

Danny Oliver's face had appeared through the curtain that separated the journalists from the galley area and the First Class section beyond. His dead-pan approach with the journalists hadn't won him a lot of friends among the Westminster press corps.

"Is Sinclair coming to speak to us?" called out the man from the BBC.

"Am I not good enough for you, Jim?" Jim Wells was on the point of shouting something back about the organ grinder but he looked at the frown on Danny's dark forehead and stopped himself just in time.

"It's not that. You know we love you really," Janine came to his rescue, "but it is traditional for the Prime Minister to give us a few words. We haven't got much to go on, you know."

"I'll see what I can do, Janine. But Paul Sinclair is currently hard at work on his speech on debt relief, to which I'm sure you'll all be giving plenty of coverage."

"No he's not." Jim Wells again.

Danny was thinking of the best words with which to deal with this challenge to his authority when he heard a gentle cough in his ear. Sinclair had slipped silently through the curtain and was standing behind him. "Are they giving you a hard time?"

"No worse than usual, Prime Minister."

"Well that's good. Now ladies and gentlemen, how can I be of assistance?" Twenty hands shot up. "Jim?" The young man from the *Independent* groaned. The newspaper journalists hated the way politicians always asked the broadcasters first.

"What's the latest on the hostages, Prime Minister?"

"Well we're very concerned for their safety. We do know that three of them are British citizens. And I'm sorry, incidentally, that we haven't been able to release any names as yet. I believe some of the relatives have yet to be traced. But we've no reason to think they're being maltreated. However, hostage taking is not something we can treat lightly and whoever is holding them needs to bear that in mind."

"Who is holding them?"

"We've had no direct message from the captors as yet, Jim, so we can't be absolutely sure. As you know we have an excellent system of intelligence cooperation with the United States and this is something I'll be discussing with President Warren."

"You say you can't treat the matter lightly, Prime Minister. Does that mean you're planning a military response?"

"It means what it says. I can't go any further than that." He looked for who to call next. Two rows from the front, Janine was waving her hand wildly. "Er…"

Danny whispered Sinclair a prompt, "Janine Clairmont".

"Jean."

"Janine actually, Prime Minister."

"Sorry Janine, of course." Helen had told him about her book, but he had only the vaguest idea who she was.

"Isn't it normal protocol for your wife to accompany you on visits like this?"

Sinclair hadn't been expecting that one and was momentarily lost for a reply. "The Prime Minister never discusses his family arrangements," cut in Danny.

"It wasn't a question about the family. It was a question about protocol." Janine wasn't letting go.

"My wife has a very busy schedule of her own and much as I'm sure she'd love to spend a couple of days in your company I'm sorry to say that pleasure will have to wait." He scanned the expectant faces and started to understand what Danny was up against. "Now I'm sure lots of you have questions on my speech?"

Only the young man from the *Independent* still had his hand in the air.

26

In the back kitchen at the Castle, Pete Morley was leaning by the sink and watching the TV coverage from Washington when PJ got home. Unsure what mood his landlord was in, he went to turn off the set just in case but PJ told him to leave it on. Jim Wells was eagerly telling the viewers of the BBC news channel how the Prime Minister had given him a personal account of his concern for the British hostages.

"He told me he wasn't going to let the hostage takers get away with it. This was Paul Sinclair at his most resolute. I've rarely seen him more determined to get a crisis settled and settled quickly. Jim Wells, BBC, at the White House".

Pete turned back to the kettle and carried on making himself a cup of tea. The health demo hadn't even made it to the evening news bulletin.

"No Helmut tonight?"

"Nah. He's round at his girlfriend's having a kiss and make it up session." Pete muted the TV and did his best to curl his lanky body into one of the kitchen chairs. He gave up and settled for one leg in the chair and the other back on the floor. Helmut had run through the little speech he had in mind before he left. Jealousy was a form of self-imprisonment and she should free herself from it if she wanted to be happy. Pete thought she'd probably fall for it. If he had to, Helmut was ready to promise not to try out any new compounds on her mother and so far as Pete could see that was a small enough price to pay. The price he'd had to pay himself, five euro to get back into The Prince of Wales and retrieve the suitcase, had been a lot higher in his estimation. Slaves and Masters night hadn't had the same sense of freedom he'd felt the first time around.

"Well that's good," said PJ. "It's a lot quieter around here when Helmut has a love interest."

Pete didn't go in for a lot of introspection as a rule, but he was feeling sorry for himself tonight. He was always at a bit of a loss when Helmut was ploughing his own furrow and PJ wasn't much company at the moment. It wasn't that long ago that he'd happily spend an evening with a couple of bottles of wine talking about politics and society and how it could all be different if only people would get up off their arses and make it different. These days Pete only knew what PJ was thinking if he bought the *Mirror*, which he rarely did, and even then he couldn't tell whether the Naked Prophet column really reflected PJ's views. Maybe he'd invite him out for a pint tonight, see if he could get him to loosen up a bit.

PJ unplugged the old radio that had stood beside the bread bin ever since he'd moved in. It was the only thing he could think of that still played cassette tapes. He put it under his arm and went upstairs.

"Colonel, it's Kapolski. Are you clear to talk?" Since the Prime Minister and his party had left, a calm had descended on Downing Street. People were no longer on edge, wondering if they might be summoned in for a meeting at a moment's notice. Even Kneejerk, who never liked to let his guard down, was feeling more relaxed. He usually locked his door if he knew Kapolski was calling, but today he hadn't bothered.

"Yes, of course, Sir. All secure." He coughed. He'd just been outside for one of his few cigarettes of the day and it sounded more like a retch.

"Are you still a smoker, Colonel? That's not good. Reflects badly on a guy, let me give you that for free. Sign of weakness. But that's your problem. Look, we've got your Sinclair meeting the President in a few hours. Private face time, the way Warren likes it. But what he doesn't like is surprises. I hope your guy isn't planning to spring any?"

"Not so far as I am aware."

"Isn't it your job to be aware? He let us down once before. He'd better not let us down over this Africa thing."

"He won't. He learned his lesson, don't worry. We've got him in as good a place as we can hope for. He's clever enough to realise that he needs you." Kneejerk knew the Americans preferred to deal in absolutes, For Us Or Against Us. "Don't worry Sir. He's with us."

"I hope so, Colonel, I really hope so. Things are getting a little tense over here, I don't mind telling you. It's always the same at election time. I mean democracy is what sets us apart from the bad guys, I understand that, but it does take the politicians' eyes off the ball sometimes. Warren thinks he's behind in California. Pinko country, but he wants to win there. Anyway, that's not your problem. Not mine either, but the world is a safer place when the President is feeling strong. So your Mr Sinclair needs to be feeling, and acting, strong too, if you get my meaning."

Kneejerk got the message. "He will."

"Thank you, Colonel. Have a good day." The line went dead. Kneejerk picked up his cigarettes and left the room. Kapolski should have known better than that. Hadn't he, Colonel Henry Neilson, as reliable an ally as the CIA could hope for, brought the Sinclair government back into line after the Circle of Death? The Americans weren't very good at trusting foreigners, he thought to himself ruefully, and weren't up to much when it came to showing gratitude either. The Colonel had never been a supporter of Sinclair's politics, but he was sure the Prime Minister wasn't going to weaken on security again. He'd do the right thing. Besides, did the Yanks think they'd be better off without him? They would really be in trouble if Joanna Morgan took over. And as for the Liberals…

The Foreign Secretary's room in one of the narrow wood-panelled corridors behind the Speaker's Chair was a modest affair for the holder of one of the Great Offices of State. Only the Prime Minister had a suite of rooms within the House of Commons that could be described as even remotely adequate for the job. But it wouldn't have been appropriate to use the Foreign Office or her residence at Carlton Gardens for anything too overtly party political and Joanna Morgan liked to behave appropriately. She'd seen too many political careers shipwrecked on the jagged rocks of hubris.

She signalled for the Health Secretary to sit beside her on the old leather sofa. At least from there Stephen Piggin couldn't stare too openly at her legs. She never ceased to be amazed at how the older, fatter and less attractive a male MP was, the more of a predator he was likely to be. Yet anybody who thought that lechery wasn't a convertible currency in the market place of modern politics was a fool. And Joanna Morgan was no fool.

Piggin on the other hand was, in the view of most of those who knew him at all well, every inch a fool. Every government had a sprinkling of them, but Joanna was a little embarrassed that she had invested so much political capital in keeping his career afloat. Fortunately he had few illusions that he was better than he really was. Without Joanna Morgan there would be no Stephen Piggin and he knew it.

Among the other dozen or so MPs in the room there was a sprinkling of former ministers who believed their careers had been cut short prematurely, one or two congenital plotters who thought this was the best show in town but would have no hesitation in switching to any other pretender who stood a better chance, and mercifully one or two young backbenchers of real talent who actually believed in her.

Joanna Morgan trusted nobody except Ray, who sat at the back of the room and whom she trusted completely. As a result she never said anything that could be quoted back at her as evidence of disloyalty. It was a game played in the language of Humpty Dumpty for whom words famously meant whatever he wanted them to mean. The one thing that the men and women in the room all had in common was that they understood what the Foreign Secretary meant.

She asked Piggin to explain the parliamentary arithmetic in the run up to the vote on the Health Bill. After he'd rambled for several minutes nobody was much the wiser. The former Chief Whip, who knew exactly where all the bodies in the Westminster Village were buried and was more than ready to inter a few more, was far more succinct. "It's two or three votes either way."

"Thank you, Dick. Well this is obviously a very serious situation for the government and for the party." Joanna Morgan looked suitably serious. "The Liberals will vote against for perfectly good political reasons that many on our own side might be tempted to agree with. The Conservatives will vote against because that's what Conservatives do. So the question is what will our people do and what effect will it have?"

Politicians are the only breed of humanity who will allow one another to speak for more than thirty seconds without wanting to interrupt. Politicians like speeches in the way that vicars like parishioners. They can't get enough of them. "The Prime Minister has staked a great deal of his authority on winning this vote. That was his judgement. Some people say he couldn't survive if he was defeated, and I hear what they say. Certainly he would be gravely weakened and that would be very serious indeed for this particular administration. Stephen here will use all his skill to win over the waverers in the debate, but we must accept that many will remain unconvinced. And we shouldn't forget that it's sometimes good for a party to examine its fundamental beliefs in this way. We'd be foolish to deny the opponents of the Bill the right to have strong, principled objections to what it contains. It's perhaps unfortunate that the Prime Minister is in Washington at this crucial period rather than staying to help influence the outcome but that was his judgement. He has his convictions and I'm sure we will hear more about them before long." She caught the smile on her husband's face. "In the meantime we should all talk to our colleagues and do what we can to ensure that the result on Monday is in the best interests of the party and of our chances of re-election. Dick says two or three votes either way. Let's make sure it's the right way."

She didn't wait to answer questions. Only Stephen Piggin looked a little confused. Everybody else knew what they had to do.

27

The traffic on the M23 had been mercifully light. Ruth did her best to concentrate on her driving. She'd already had one uncomfortable brush with the police in recent days and didn't want to risk another. She thanked herself for not allowing the pleasure of Dr Gill's company to lull her into more than two small glasses of wine.

Her mobile phone lay switched off on the seat beside her so she wouldn't be tempted to answer it. Before leaving Brighton she'd listened to the messages Danny had left but it had been too late to call him back. There'd been a hint of urgency in his voice that convinced her that the meeting he was suggesting wouldn't just be a social visit. He had been at the airport when he called for the last time so at least she could be sure that Paul and his team were now out of the country. Again she felt dragged down by the weight of the situation she'd allowed herself to get into. It was almost a month since she'd seen Joshua. If it hadn't been for the play she was sure he'd have come down to Brighton but it was another fortnight before he was due for one of his regular trips to the constituency. She was lucky to have a son who was willing to make all the effort without ever really asking why.

She got herself into the inside lane and prayed that the M25 would be as kind to her. The school was an easy enough run up from the motorway and if she didn't get held up she should have plenty of time. She should probably have rung ahead to warn him she was coming and felt guilty at wanting to keep her options open. Who was to say who's fault it was but Ruth Sinclair had been forced to accept that she wasn't the kind of mother she'd always thought she would be.

Her luck held and Ruth arrived ten minutes before curtain up and took a seat by the tall windows of the school hall. Nobody had noticed her come in. Joshua looked so grown-up there on the stage as he held the world in his hands and savoured his power. He had his father's gift of playing to the gods, although Marlowe had always been a bit melodramatic for her tastes. Maybe it was the writer in her, but she couldn't just sit back and wallow in maternal pride. By the time of Joshua's fall from grace and come-uppance at the hands of bloodthirsty demons she was itching for the final curtain.

"See here are Faustus' limbs, all torn asunder by the hand of death."

"Well, about time too," thought Ruth. Nevertheless she felt herself beaming as he took his bows hand in hand with Mephistopheles. As the other parents left, she stood quietly by the door that led backstage.

"Mum, you came," Joshua spotted her in the corridor as soon as he came out of the changing rooms. "Why didn't you tell me?"

"Oh, you know. Busy, busy, busy. I didn't know what time I'd be able to get away from your grandmother and I didn't want to build your hopes up."

He was unconvinced. "How was I? Wicked, eh?"

"You were certainly that."

"So, what, are you coming home?" He'd been so bound up with the performance that it was only just dawning on him that his father wouldn't be there.

"I don't know, Josh."

"Come on, Mum. You must. I'm not even asking, I'm telling you. You can drive and I'll tell Kneejerk's men they can just follow behind." The adrenalin was still flowing and Josh was feeling assertive. "We'll be home in half an hour." Ruth rather liked having the decision made for her and followed her son out into the car park.

It was indeed thirty minutes later that they were through the Vortex and standing outside Number 10. Sergeant Terry Woods tapped once on the huge iron knocker and the door opened.

"Terry, how lovely to see you." Ruth was good at remembering the names of all the policeman and other staff, but she was especially fond of Terry Woods. "I didn't expect to see you out here. I thought you were on my husband's detail."

"Well things change, Mrs Sinclair, you know how it is. Life's swings and roundabouts. Sometimes you lose on them all." She couldn't tell if he was joking. "But it's not so bad. Sometimes I get to stand here and sometimes I get to stand down the road by the Vortex. I've always liked variety in life."

Ruth looked back down the street at the huge metal box that they'd just passed through. "It's not very attractive is it?" The failed chemical attack had been a very recent memory and the Vortex still under construction when Ruth had last been in residence.

"Needs must, I suppose. But it's nice to see you again, Mrs Sinclair. You've been missed." Terry had nodded towards Joshua who had gone inside ahead of her. "And not just by young Joshua either." She was touched by the obvious sincerity of his words.

Joshua looked around the hall warily but all was quiet. It was almost eleven and the only lights escaping under doorways were from the policy unit where one or two stakhanovites were still hunched over their papers and computer screens. "Welcome home, Mum," said Joshua but the words echoed around the empty hall and refused to settle.

She could sense his awkwardness and tried to take some of the tension out of the moment. "It's a funny sort of place to call home at the best of times, isn't it? You must get a bit stir crazy sometimes."

"Well I've formed an escape committee but so far I'm the only member. Dad's agreed to be honorary President but I think that was just to keep me quiet." He followed his mother as she walked slowly down the corridor that led to the Cabinet Room.

She stopped to admire a portrait of Ellen Terry and wondered who'd chosen to hang it there. "Now there's a woman who knew a thing or two about tragedy." She realised she was deliberately avoiding going upstairs to the flat.

Joshua had passed the portrait of the actress with her long hair billowing out behind her as if she were in flight many times but had never really looked it. He had no idea who she was. "Come on, I'm dying for a pee." He took her arm and she turned to face him. The bright lights in the corridor cast a dark shadow beneath her eyes and Joshua couldn't remember his mother ever looking so vulnerable. "I'll put the kettle on."

"To be honest, I think I could do with a drink."

When Joshua came out of the loo he'd washed away most of the remaining traces of his make up, but his mother took out a tissue and wetted it in her mouth. She was sitting at the breakfast bar with a tumbler in front of her. She reached out for him and dabbed around his eyes which he closed instinctively. He could smell whisky on her breath.

"I'm really glad you're here, Mum." Without opening his eyes, he put his arms around her waist and pulled her to him. For the second time in as many days she was happy to enjoy the physical warmth of someone she loved very much, but while her mother had felt so weak Joshua's teenage body felt wonderfully strong. She brought the tissue up to her own eyes before he released his grip.

"Does it have to be like this, Mum?"

"I don't know." She hesitated before going on. "It's just something between me and your father that we have to work out between ourselves. Or not, I suppose."

"You're not going to...you know, get divorced or anything are you?"

Ruth was taken aback. She'd never given the option, if it was an option, a moment's thought. "Oh no, I don't think so. Who ever heard of a Prime Minister getting divorced? That's more the Royal family really, isn't it?"

He could tell she was trying to make light of it and felt embarrassed about pushing her. "Can I get you anything, Mum?"

"No, I'm fine." She picked up her tumbler of scotch from the counter.

"Well, I think I'll go to bed then. Are you sure you're okay?"

"Of course I am, but it's sweet of you to ask. Good night, Josh. Sweet dreams."

She followed him out of the kitchen and watched him go upstairs. Taking her drink and topping it up, Ruth opened the door to the sitting room and turned on the light. There were papers strewn across the coffee table and an old jumper of Paul's was thrown across the back of the sofa. She saw her own photograph in a simple silver frame on the table by the window.

When Joshua came downstairs at three in the morning ostensibly to get a glass of water but in reality to check that his mother hadn't left, he saw the light still on and looked inside. She was curled up on the sofa with the jumper over her shoulders for warmth. He turned off the light and went back up to his room.

28

There was a loud bang from the grate which caused the two black labradors who had been dozing in front of the fire to jump to their feet. A piece of wood glowing orange on one side came shooting out and landed where one of the dogs had been laying half a second before.

"I told them that wood was too wet," said the President picking up a pair of cast iron tongs and putting the log back on the fire. "Come on Frankie, it's okay." There was a brown scorch mark on the rug which Warren rubbed with the toe of his boot.

John 'Bunny' Warren resumed his seat as the larger of the two dogs walked awkwardly over to the couch. He picked up his glass of bourbon and ran his hand around the dog's neck. "Did that scare you?"

"They're beautiful dogs."

"Yep, Paul, they sure are. This here is Frankie and that one over there is Teddy." Sinclair had been introduced to the dogs before, on his first visit as Prime Minister, but the President seemed to have forgotten. "Come on Ted. Frankie doesn't walk too well so we named him after Franklin D. Roosevelt. The thirty-second President. Elected four times and he was in a wheel chair. Can't see that happening today, Paul, can you? Not in this country anyway. Wouldn't look good on TV."

"That's a depressing thought."

"I guess it is. I hadn't really thought about it like that. So anyway this one here just had to be Teddy. After Theodore. One Democrat, one Republican and here's me, as I always say, I govern from the centre. Don't I boys?" Both dogs, who were now sitting in front of their master, looked up, their tails swinging in unison like windscreen wipers across the wooden floor.

"You don't have dogs do you, Paul?"

"No, it's not really practical in Central London."

"I thought you had that old mansion in the country, Chess House or something. You haven't invited me yet but I hear it's pretty special. A bit grander than Camp David, I'll bet."

"Chequers. I don't go there much. My wife was never fond of it and it's too big to rattle around in by myself."

"Well that's why you want to get dogs. You're never alone if there's a dog in the house."

Sinclair imagined Kneejerk's face when he told him he was buying a dog and that he'd be taking him for walks in St James' Park. It might be worth it just to see what he'd do. Bring the whole of the park inside his security cordon probably. The thought of the Colonel brought Sinclair back to the business in hand. It was getting late and they were already on their third glass of whisky each. But John Warren was showing little readiness for serious conversation.

"I love this place, Paul. Come out here just as often as I can. Makes me feel almost human again after life in DC. Roosevelt, Franklin that is not Teddy, named it Shangri-La, did you know that?"

"No, I didn't."

"Yep. And it is a kind of Shangri-La." The President's Mississippi accent made it sound like a voice exercise. Shang Ree Laa. "Well, it is to me anyhow. Then along comes Eisenhower and good ole Ike, number thirty four, goes and renames it after his grandson. I heard talk that Reagan was thinking of doing something sim'lar. Hell, we could of been sitting here in Camp Nancy if he'd had his way." The President chuckled and took another sip from his glass.

"Maybe we should be getting down to a little business, John."

"Oh there's plenty of time for all that. Just tell your guys to put out a press release with the usual bullshit about what a positive meeting we had. My guys have probably already put out mine already saying how America is proud to stand side-by-side with our old ally once again. It was good of you to come, Paul. Looks good. For me I mean. My opponents try to say nobody respects America anymore but you sitting here tells a different story. It doesn't matter much if all we do is play poker, so long as the great American public don't find out." The President laughed and then realised he might have gone too far. The British could be a bit funny sometimes. "I'm sorry, it's this damn election. Seeing me in campaign mode isn't always a pretty sight, but we have to do what we have to do. That's my point. Gotta get the image right. The reality can wait until I'm safely back in here again. It's just part of the game. If you wanna be in government where you can do stuff rather than out of government where you can do sweet nothing then you play it by the rules. But I didn't mean to get on my high horse."

Sinclair had long since learned what a tough operator John Warren could be, but this evening he was finding the President a bit hard to take. He tried, with only limited success, to manage a sympathetic smile. "That's okay. They tell me your race is proving tighter than expected. I know what that feels like."

"Is it? I hope not. I mean I always tell people it's close just to keep them on their toes, but I think we're on track. The good Senator has a shock coming to him, let me tell you."

"Didn't I read that California is on a knife-edge?"

"If you did it's because my spinners said it was. Working like a dream. The Senator is now spending half his time on the west coast and that's where he's gonna be buried."

"I admire your confidence, John."

The President looked at him as if unsure whether he was being teased. The British had a funny line in humour. "Confidence doesn't really come in to it. In this game it's all about control. Control of yourself, control of those around you, control of the agenda and right now control of the election. Lose that and you might as well go home and grow potatoes." He took another sip of bourbon. "It's all on the grid. All primed and ready to go. You want to know the killer blow? I shouldn't be telling you this, but it's so good. This is how to deal with political opponents." Paul picked up his glass. He had a feeling that he was going to need it. "In two weeks' time one of the Senator's old college buddies will suddenly recall a Frat House dinner at which the never-to-be President of the United States made a number of unflattering remarks about a local football player who'd been photographed baring his ass at some fag party. The guy just happened to be Hispanic so that's the gay vote, the ethnic vote and the whole goddamn liberal vote all bound up in one poor motherfucker."

It was Sinclair's turn to wonder if he was being teased. "Are you serious?"

"Sure I am. Listen and learn. I can't wait for the story to come out.

I mean politics can be dirty, we both know that, but it never stops being fun."

"But the other side must be on their guard for a smear like that."

"Of course they are. And I will immediately be accused of the most outrageous dirty tricks. Do you know who by? Because I do. A previously unknown organisation called Californians for Fair Play will attack me almost immediately and make so much noise about it that I'll be on the ropes for a day and a half while every liberal thinking person comes in behind them."

"And that helps you?"

"A small price to pay. All the stories about what my opponent said or didn't say will have been given plenty of coverage at the same time. The Shock Jocks love all that kind of stuff. My ratings in the State will fall, we reckon, by three points max. But then when Californians for Fair Play turns out to be run by another old college friend of his with a conviction for underage sex that the Senator, good liberal lawyer that he is, helped get overturned, it'll be too close to the election for them to recover. We've bought him up, everyone has their price. It's all in the grid."

The famous grid. It was something Sinclair was familiar with, a technique imported into British politics after being so successful in the States. Every step of an election campaign was plotted and marked on the grid, so nothing was left to chance. But no grid he had ever worked on had featured a deliberate smear like this one. He was starting to feel physically sickened by the President's cynicism. "All in a day's work, I suppose?" He tried to keep the contempt out of his voice.

"There's no room for faint hearts, Paul. Choose your own enemies and you can always defeat them. Not since Jimmy Carter has anyone won an election in this country by being nice. You have to make a choice. Who's going to be around to make the decisions and get things done, you or the other guy? But it's the only choice you have to make. Once you've made it, the rest comes pretty easy."

Paul Sinclair felt winded, as if Warren's onslaught had been directed at him. It seemed there was nothing he wouldn't do to hold on to power. "I'm just glad we still do things differently."

"Do you?" The President looked incredulous. "Well, maybe you can afford to. I'm just glad you're not an American, Paul, 'cause they'd love you over here. Good looking tough guy and all that. Why, even I might have difficulty whipping your ass."

Sinclair shifted his position in the chair and reached forward to stroke the dogs. He felt himself taking deep breaths and holding them. The clock over the fireplace struck one in the morning. He was tired and Warren seemed so fired up by his own potency that he might want to talk half the night. This was no time for an argument over the price of power. But then suddenly the President changed gear. He got up and collected a file from his desk. He had business to do too and needed Paul Sinclair more than he was letting on. "You should take a look at these."

"What are they?"

"Aerial photographs. I think you'll find them useful. Our boys reckon they've pinpointed the base used by the terrorists who've taken your people hostage. What are they, Eritreans?" Ay Ree Tray Ahhns. "Is that how you say it?"

"I don't think it's quite how they would pronounce it, John, but then they're not listening, are they?"

"I sure as hell hope not. This is the most secure log cabin anywhere in the world. Now look, here's the satellite surveillance stuff. Precise coordinates and the picture quality is great. I wish I could do as well with the family camera at Christmas, and that's a fact." He passed the dossier to Sinclair.

The Prime Minister's hands felt clammy as he took the folder. The pictures showed some empty buildings in a field. Sinclair was unsure what he was supposed to make of them. "They don't tell us much, do they? Is there nothing showing the hostages or even the people who are holding them?"

"You have to be patient, Paul." Sinclair had heard the very same line from Kneejerk. "They're still holed up in some cave somewhere. But we have radio intercepts from a guy inside this camp that say the hostages will be brought down from the mountains as soon as they feel it's safe to do so. Overnight would be my guess. All the transcripts are in the file. You just need to be ready to strike and strike hard as soon as they appear."

"Thank you, John. I'll have these looked over tonight."

"You do that, but don't forget. There's no room for faint hearts.

If I were you, I'd want to teach those Eritreans a lesson they'll never forget."

"Well, let's see what happens. I don't want to overreact."

"Jeez, Paul. You'll be giving me another of your lectures about civilised values next, whatever all that was supposed to mean. I thought we'd kinda moved on from there."

It was late and Sinclair had hoped to avoid an argument but he couldn't let that go unchallenged. Warren needed to know that while he was grateful for America's help on security he hadn't abandoned his principles when it came to democracy and human rights. But as he was searching for the right words there was a knock at the door and Tracey Warren appeared, a bright yellow dressing gown wrapped around her more than ample body. She came into the room and sat beside her husband.

"Come along sweetheart. We should let Paul get to his room. He's had a long day."

Sinclair's smile reflected his exhaustion. He was certainly ready for bed and thankful for the interruption. Warren probably wouldn't have understood what he wanted to say in any case.

"It's such a shame Ruth couldn't make it," the First Lady continued, "I was so looking forward to seeing her again. She's such a clever woman."

Sinclair's recollection was that his wife hadn't had quite such a high estimation of Tracey Warren's intellectual achievements. "I'm afraid she just…"

"Couldn't face it?" The President finished his sentence for him.

"That's not far off, John, to be brutally honest."

"I know how she must feel," Tracey Warren said, "I hate all the travelling and stuff too. I don't know what State I'm in half the time."

"That's why they give you cue cards, darling."

She ignored her husband's remark. "But this would have been like visiting old friends. Maybe I should call her and see how she is?"

"I wouldn't do that, really. I mean it's very kind of you, but there's no need."

"If there's anything we can do, Paul, you only have to ask, you know that," said the President getting up and putting an arm around his wife's waist.

Sinclair had no desire to prolong the conversation, but his question came almost of its own accord. "Has there ever been an American President who wasn't married?"

"Now you're asking, Paul, I can't rightly think of one. I guess there must have been but I couldn't tell you who. Sure as hell wouldn't happen now, though. I mean I know there's men getting married to men these days, if that's what they want to call it, and the courts let them get away with it. Plenty of regular people not bothering with the sacred vows any more either, but I don't think America's ready for any of that in the White House. Nor in Camp Nancy either come to think of it." Warren chuckled at his little joke and pecked Tracey on the neck. "If you're gonna win, Paul, you have to have a good woman at your side. It's not negotiable. There's three things the American people expect their President to believe in. God, marriage and the death penalty and fortunately I'm wedded to all three."

29

Inside Blue Monday, one of Georgetown's more fashionable new bars, Helen Griffin too was thinking it was high time she got some sleep. Janine Clairmont hadn't arrived until well after ten. AM-TV had insisted on her recording an interview with the editor of a men's health magazine about staying fit at the top. They were planning to run some footage of Paul Sinclair looking at his most virile and athletic and then have a discussion in the studio about how he managed it.

"Can you believe it? They asked me if I could get the Prime Minister to come on and talk about his fitness regime. These people are on another planet sometimes."

Helen was starting to understand what Danny Oliver was up against. She looked at her old friend and tried to see in the darkness of the bar how much make-up she was wearing.

"Mind you, you look pretty amazing yourself from where I'm sitting," she said. "What are you on?"

Janine took a deep swig of her margarita and leant forward conspiratorially. "Plenty of Clinique," she said in a stage whisper, "and plenty of sex."

"Oh yes, the tried and tested formula."

Janine raised her tweaked and dyed eyebrows. "And how is the gorgeous Otto?"

"Still gorgeous." She smiled at the memory, although five o'clock that morning seemed a very long time ago.

"Good for you. If I had a twenty-nine year old bricklayer with the body of a Greek god waiting for me at home I'd be smiling too." Janine was itching to tell her friend about her own recent liaison with Scott Bolton, the new reporter on AM-TV who just happened to be a mere twenty-five, but she wasn't ready to let Helen off the hook just yet.

"He's thirty-one, Janine. And he's an architect."

"I think my point still stands."

"I've got a feeling in my water that he isn't going to be around that much longer, though. I cancelled him three times last week. There's only so much you can expect a boy to take."

"Get a life, Helen. If you want my advice get out and get a life."

"That's easier than it sounds."

"No it isn't. It sounds easy and it is easy. People would be falling over themselves to offer a job to the Prime Minister's former Chief of Staff. You could name your own price and I'd make it a very high one if I were you. Condition number one, written into the contract, home by seven every night to shag the gorgeous Otto."

"I know it sounds strange to you, Janine, but I actually like my job. I just have to cut the crap and get on with it."

"That's becoming a bit of a cliché, Helen."

"Even clichés can be true. I mean, the hours I can cope with. And Otto will just have to work his cute little arse round it. Or not. It's up to him."

"Oh, stop playing Lady Diamond just for once, will you? You're not that tough, honey. Are you seriously telling me you're going to sit there and let him slip through your fingers just like all the others? Remember, one of these days there won't be a queue of virile young men ready to take his place. Quit while you're ahead, I say."

They were both a little drunk by now, Helen especially. She hadn't eaten since getting off the plane and had downed two margaritas before her friend had arrived.

"Or you could always try a little cocktail of work and entertainment. I can recommend it, believe me, and isn't power supposed to be an aphrodisiac?" Beating about the bush doesn't come naturally to many journalists. "So come on," Janine leaned forward again, "while we're on the subject, how is Paul Sinclair doing in that department? I asked him on the plane about Ruth and he looked very uncomfortable."

"Who's asking, Janine Clairmont, political correspondent of AM-TV or Janine Clairmont, old mate and life-style counsellor?"

"Come on, you know the answer to that. Have I ever let you down? Jesus, I've lost count of the number of stories I could have run but didn't because you're a friend. Even if you are a friend who never takes any notice of anything I say."

"Yeah but now you're a mate who's writing an intimate biography of my boss, who I happen to like. And respect. Even if he can be a total tosser sometimes. So how are you going to sit down at your little computer and wipe your brain cells clear of anything I might tell you in confidence before you start writing? Can't be done. Not even by somebody as talented as you."

"Look, I've already promised you that I'll go through it with you before I send it off."

"That's not exactly editorial veto now is it, darling?" Helen clasped Janine's hand and held on to it. The young barman, who had been toying with offering Helen a drink on the house before her friend turned up, wiped his hands on his jeans and decided he'd better try his luck elsewhere. Janine downed the last of her margarita and signalled to the boy for two more. He shrugged and reached for the frosted tequila bottle. These dykes sure knew how to put it away.

"You know I can't give you an editorial veto, not even if I wanted to. But you've got my word as a friend that I'm not going to stitch you up. That must count for something. And it's more than you'd get from anyone else in my position." Helen still didn't look convinced. "Look, you're the one who's always going on about cutting the crap. Well let's cut it, shall we? Paul Sinclair is in Downing Street. So is Helen Griffin, his oldest friend and now his Chief of Staff. Mrs Ruth Sinclair is strangely absent writing her own turgid novels and doing whatever else she does. Now why is that?"

"It sounds to me like you might have your own theory on that one."

The barman leaned across the steel counter to place a drink in front of each of them. "Go easy ladies. I should tell you there's a DC ordinance that obliges me to counsel you on the dangers of too many of these on a Tuesday night."

Janine looked from his well defined chest in the tight Blue Monday t-shirt and up past his prominent Adam's apple to his too perfect all-American-boy smile. "I'm sure you'll be able to handle us if we get out of control." The grin widened a little as his mind ran through the possibilities. "But in the meantime if you wouldn't mind giving us a bit of space." He moved down the bar to where other customers were trying to catch his eye. Janine's eyes followed him. "Very nice."

For once Helen was in no mood to be distracted. "Come on, If you've got something to say then say it."

"Okay. Let me just tell you what some of my colleagues in the press are itching to write but can't because they can't prove it. Ruth Sinclair is sitting at home hitting the bottle and nursing a bruised ego. Why? Because her husband wouldn't give up his dark lady. The woman who awakened his sexual appetite all those years ago and who he's never been able to forget or give up. The woman who, for all we know, is even now helping to make life inside that fortress of his a bit more bearable. You."

Helen Griffin pushed her drink to one side and stood up. She was a little unsteady on her feet. "If you only knew."

"Then tell me."

"It's late. I'm going to bed. And I suggest you do the same." As Helen turned and made for the door, Janine looked up and caught the barman's eye.

30

The Foreign and Commonwealth Office had a lot in common with the first woman to be at its head. It liked to think of itself as a cut above the rest of the government machine. Diplomacy, after all, is a finer art than administration. And as befits its status, the FCO was the only department of state with an entrance on Downing Street itself. This suited Joanna Morgan extremely well. She was, after all, Deputy Prime Minister into the bargain and so it was only right that she should be the sole member of the Cabinet who didn't have to pass through Kneejerk's wretched Vortex on her way to Number 10. Having failed to dissuade Sinclair from buying the monstrosity from the Americans she had made a point of arguing that all Cabinet Ministers should be able to come and go without being subjected to surveillance. She'd failed again but it was a defeat she could live with. She rather enjoyed her role as the Cabinet's unofficial shop steward and it was enough that the rest of them knew she'd tried. The story, leaked just a few days after the event, had been one of those that had helped the Naked Prophet make a name for himself as the best informed political columnist in town.

Sergeant Terry Woods watched her stride out of the Foreign Office courtyard and come towards him. Ray Morgan and her Private Secretary were a pace or two behind. Her arrival was expected but behind the black front door an unexpected departure was taking place. Ruth hadn't told the House Manager she was staying the night. It hadn't even occurred to her that she should. So her appearance in the Entrance Hall that morning had caused something of a stir. The Number 10 Messengers, whose job included not just delivering messages but a hundred and one other domestic duties in every part of the building, didn't like to be taken unawares. They had been bustling around her offering coffee and asking after her health. Joshua had gone back upstairs to collect something he'd forgotten for school when there was a single knock on the bullet proof door and it swung open.

Ruth look round at the noise. There was something in the way her body stiffened that made the Messengers take an involuntary step back and fall silent. Joanna Morgan came to an abrupt halt just inside the door, leaving her husband outside on the step. The loud ticking of the clock on the mantelpiece skipped a beat as the two women met each other's stare.

"Ruth, what a lovely surprise."

"Good morning, Jo." Insincerity was a concession that Ruth made only with tremendous reluctance and she was relieved when Joshua hurtled through the archway that led to the flat. He was in too much of a hurry to pick up on the glacial atmosphere.

"Come on Mum, are you giving me a lift or what? I'm going to be late." He took Ruth by the sleeve and dragged her towards the door. "Hi, Mrs Morgan." And then, over his shoulder, "if you're here to see Kneejerk, tell him he's a waste of space from me, will you?"

Colonel Neilson was indeed waiting for her in the Den. As usual, whenever Paul Sinclair was out of the country, he had his daily security briefing with the Deputy Prime Minister. In his view she was a naïve, stubborn and quite possibly dangerous woman. He held her personally responsible for the government's childish attitude towards the United States when Sinclair first took over. It had taken a lot of hard work, and the Circle of Death of course, to undo the damage she had done. Sinclair, thought Kneejerk, may not be able to choose his family but he could choose his Foreign Secretary and why he kept this woman was a mystery to him. "Good Morning, Deputy Prime Minister, shall I order some coffee?"

"Thank you, that would be very nice."

The television in the corner of the room was showing pictures from the White House. The 24-hour news channels were re-running shots of Sinclair's arrival from Camp David with the President and Mrs Warren half an hour earlier. The helicopter had barely landed when the door opened and two black labradors jumped out and ran into shot, one of them looking as if it was limping. John Warren appeared next, waving and calling after them. It was the first the cameras had seen of the Prime Minister and President together so there was much handshaking and some playful pats for the dogs as they ran back across the lawn. Helen and Danny were just visible on the edge of the picture. Joanna Morgan turned it off with the remote control.

"The real business has barely started, DPM, so there's nothing to report from there yet."

"That's quite all right, Colonel, my staff will keep me fully informed." My staff. The Foreign Office staff. The staff of the Foreign Secretary who should have been invited to accompany the Prime Minister to Washington but wasn't.

"I don't think we're expecting much in any event. There's not a great deal on the agenda. Although I'm sure the Americans will be very helpful on the hostage situation."

She bristled. "Perhaps." Whether they were helpful or not, and she doubted it, was scarcely the point. Her own absence would be noticed by the people who mattered. She was being kept in her box. And to make it worse, Sinclair was delivering a speech to the Brookings Institute later that day about Third World Debt. That was one of her issues and one that always played very nicely with the backbenches and the unions. No, Paul Sinclair knew what he was doing. There was no mistaking it, she was being snubbed and Joanna Morgan was not a woman who took kindly to snubs. "Well," she went on, "what's on our agenda for today?"

~

PJ Walton listened to the voice on the cassette one more time. Sinclair sounded relaxed and conversational. He was obviously addressing a fairly small group of people as he hadn't needed to raise his voice. There was some polite applause when he finished speaking and then some questions that the microphone hadn't managed to pick up. It was Sinclair's third answer that PJ had replayed now half a dozen times and transcribed word for word. The voice was so familiar there could be no doubt the recording was genuine, but PJ felt uneasy. He'd rung Ray Morgan early to ask him to check the exact date of the meeting and had been reassured that as Sinclair had only been Foreign Secretary for a year in total, it wouldn't take long to find.

PJ had the *Daily Mirror* laid out on his desk in front of him. He reread his latest article, a creditable enough piece about how it shouldn't take a hostage crisis to remind ministers of the ongoing suffering in Eritrea, but not one of his best. He played the tape one more time. This was a story the Editor was going to be very pleased to read.

~

Mrs Alma Gundry had a knack for knowing just when to open her front door. If she'd left it thirty seconds longer, PJ might have noticed her on the doorstep and chosen to delay popping out for a breath of fresh air. As fresh as it got in London SE1. As it was, she was fifty yards ahead of him walking down Wilson Crescent and, with a feline sense of another creature's presence she turned and waited for him to catch up.

"Good Morning, Mr Walton."

"You can call me PJ if you like, Mrs Gundry. Everybody else does."

She had obviously already given this some thought. "It's always a J isn't it?"

PJ's mind was racing to catch up. He was desperately searching for a way of bringing the conversation to a reasonably early conclusion, but then his curiosity got the better of him. "What is always a J?"

"When people use their initials, like instead of their names. There's always a J. OJ Simpson, that black footballer person. PJ Proby. Maybe you were named after him. Was your mother a fan?"

PJ had no idea who she was talking about. "I really don't know. I doubt it." He thought of calling GK Chesterton or TS Eliot as defence witnesses, but she didn't give him the chance.

"I feel so romantic…" Mrs Gundry appeared to be swaying slightly inside her heavy overcoat. He realised with relief that she was singing to herself. She could see his bewilderment and was enjoying having something to teach him. Since yesterday she had found herself in an unusually good mood. "Believe it or not I was quite a little rock and roller in my younger days. PJ Proby. One of the last of the greats. Before all the drugs and everything. I know you think I'm an old busybody, but we knew how to enjoy ourselves too, you know."

"I'm sure you did." Although it was very hard to picture and PJ wasn't sure he wanted to try. He was starting to think that dealing with his neighbour had been a lot easier when she was angry.

"It was just that we did it without spoiling it for everybody else."

PJ decided this was his cue to try to move her back on to more familiar territory "I do hope my lodgers apologised properly for all the inconvenience."

"Oh yes. Helmut and…and the other one. What nice young men. I can see I might have been a bit hasty, Mr Walton. That's why I wanted to speak to you, to say, you know, maybe we can put it all behind us."

PJ couldn't hold back his smile. He would have to congratulate the boys, although he hadn't ruled out the possibility that one of them had slipped something in her tea. He was now torn between curiosity about what had brought about this dramatic change and his usual urge to get away as fast as he could. The tingle of his mobile phone vibrating in his pocket made the decision for him. He took it out and answered it. Ray Morgan had found the date he'd been asking for.

PJ dug into his pocket for something to write on. He gave Mrs Gundry a shrug as if to say he would have been delighted to hear more about the many qualities of Pete Morley, Helmut Feldhofer and PJ Proby if only he could. She put an understanding hand on his arm and turned to go on her way. There still seemed to be a sway to her hips as she went round the corner towards Sainsbury's. "Go ahead." He scribbled down the date. "So that's what, three months before he became Prime Minister? Thanks, Ray, that's very helpful."

"You will be able to get it in today, won't you? Only…"

"Don't worry, Ray." He'd already written most of the article. "And could you just tell her that it would be good to arrange that drink soon? I've been missing her." He clicked the phone shut and looked down at the date. She needn't worry, he'd do her dirty work for her, but he was starting to wonder how much longer this could go on. He desperately wanted to see to her in person and surely she must want to see him too. How could she not? And yet he'd never known a woman who could keep such a tight control on her emotions. He understood that she was busy and had Ray to consider but he was still feeling neglected.

31

The coffee table was strewn with newspapers, empty CD cases and half empty cups of coffee. Joshua cleared a space with his heel and put his feet up. The cleaners had long since stopped doing any more than run a mop around the floor of the sixth form common room each morning. But Joshua loved the mess. He needed a bit of chaos to make life bearable.

Charlie Gauthier, Mephistopheles to Joshua's Faustus, was at the coffee machine lapping up the attention of the two girls generally regarded as the best looking in the year. Charlie had inherited all of his father's Gallic charm and ease with women. He had tortured Joshua with tales of sexual conquests since they had both been fifteen, accusing Joshua of using his professed taste for older women as nothing but an excuse for not getting laid with anyone his own age. Charlie's accent made getting laid sound both like the stuff that was nicked from church roofs and something impossibly romantic too.

The newspapers spread around Joshua's feet were just as Danny Oliver had predicted they would be. They were full of stories about strikes in the hospitals, the likely defeat of the Health Bill and a hostage crisis that seemed to be outside the government's control. Joshua had developed an ability to scan the headlines and not make any connection at all with his own life. Occasionally somebody would pin one of them up on the notice board as a joke. *Sinclair Popularity at All Time Low* had only recently been covered up by the results of the squash league. Most of his fellow pupils, however, had long since become bored with the fact that he had a famous father.

Charlie sauntered over with a mug of hot coffee in his hand. Even in baggy jeans his groin projected potency and promise. "So, just one more night on the boards, eh? Then we can relax."

"I can't wait. I've sold my soul so many times now that it wouldn't even raise a bid on eBay."

"And tomorrow night Mr Clements is taking us out to celebrate. Maybe even Josh Sinclair will get what's coming to him! I mean we have earned a bit of adulation for all our hard work, surely?"

Although he did his best to ignore it, sexual frustration was never far from Joshua's mind. "About bloody time, Charlie. Are you going to fix me up then? You keep promising."

Charlie Gauthier looked thoughtful. He pulled up a chair next to his friend. "You are a hard man to please, that is your problem."

Joshua leaned over and lowered his voice. "I am not. Just find me someone who's got something to say for herself, doesn't giggle all the time, and can teach a young man all he needs to know."

"I thought I'd already taught you all you need to know."

"You've done your best. I'm very grateful, Charlie. It's just time to move on from the theory, okay? Otherwise, if I ever get to uni, I'm going to be the only virgin on campus."

"I'll see what I can do." He stood up and threw out an arm. "This or what else my Faustus shall desire shall be performed in the twinkling of an eye."

A wet tea-towel flew through the air from the direction of the kitchen. "Are you two in love with each other or what? Fucking thespians."

Joanna Morgan had kicked off her shoes and her legs were crossed delicately at the ankles under the desk. She was studying the file on her lap and thinking. She sat without moving a muscle for all of five minutes until the civil servant from the East Africa desk started to wonder if the Foreign Secretary had something wrong with her. Then all of a sudden she snapped the file shut and swung her legs out to search for her shoes.

"Thank you, Michael, that's extremely helpful. There's no need to send it over to Number 10. I'll be going there myself later, I can brief them." The civil servant looked uneasy. Downing Street got very upset if they weren't made aware of things like this immediately. Joanna Morgan knew what he was thinking but stood her ground. "Thank you, Michael, that will be all. Would you send Ray in?"

Her husband's hearing wasn't all that it used be now he'd turned

60 but he could tune into her voice with ease from a considerable distance. He was already standing at the open door. "Did you want me, my love?"

She waited until the two of them were alone. She stood up and brushed down her suit. "Close the door, Ray. I've got a meeting at Party Headquarters in half an hour. I think it might be useful if, by chance, there was a camera crew or two outside the entrance. Can you see what you can do?"

Ray nodded. "Of course. Do you want to tell me what it's about?"

"I'm very concerned that the Prime Minister may be about to make a terrible mistake. I'd warn him personally if I could, of course. But he's so busy with all those meetings with the President. My mind is churning with the possible dangers, however, and when you're caught unawares by the cameras it can be so easy to say something you didn't really mean to."

"I think anybody would understand that. I'd better get on with it right away. It shouldn't take the BBC more than fifteen minutes to get a crew round there."

The Foreign Secretary picked up the file and held it to her chest.

A copy of the same report from the European Foreign Ministry was among the papers awaiting Paul Sinclair's attention. He'd been too busy finalising his speech on debt relief in Africa to see it yet. There was enthusiastic applause from the audience as he sat down. The American political establishment knew a class act when they saw one. But his Communications Director had been watching the British press pack while the Prime Minister spoke. They'd barely wasted the energy to make any notes at all, always a bad sign. Danny hadn't yet seen any reason to cheer up and felt a sense of deep foreboding about the news conference that was scheduled to follow. They'd got through the past twenty-four hours more or less unscathed, but it couldn't last.

The policeman at the end of the drive bent down to look through the driver's window and then waved Ruth's car through. Even if the Prime Minister didn't use his constituency home much it still had to be kept under twenty-four hour surveillance. She looked tired but, so far as the young constable could see, sober. The security detail had been warned to keep an eye on her. It wasn't their job to intervene but they needed to know.

She parked on the gravel drive and went in through the kitchen door. The house felt cold so she turned on a couple of gas rings to bring some heat to the room and went across the hall to turn on the pump that would kick start the old but efficient central heating system. It roared into life but she kept her coat on as she picked up the post in the hall and flicked through it. Not much for her, except an invitation to a book launch and a card from the dentists asking her to come in for a check up.

Ruth had never had many friends in the Midlands and at her age it was too late to start making them now. In any case, she rather enjoyed her solitary lifestyle. After being married for so long to a man in the public eye, it had come as a blessed relief to have nobody watching over her the whole time. She knew there were armed police at the end of the drive but it was very easy to forget about them. She could be in this house for a week sometimes and never speak to another soul. It was certainly good for her writing and on the motorway she had been thinking through some new plot lines that she wanted to get down while they were fresh in her mind.

She picked up the phone and dialled the number to activate the answering service. Three new messages. Danny Oliver, Joshua with the noise of the common room behind him asking if she'd got home all right, and Dr Donald Gill. He was thanking her again for meeting him for lunch although she felt certain she hadn't given him this number. By the time he was explaining that he had a Conference to attend in Coventry she realised he must have found it in her mother's notes. She was trying to decide if that was a breach of medical ethics when she heard him clear his throat before asking if she might be free one evening while he was in the area.

It was one of the things that Paul Sinclair had never got used to. That at any given moment of any day a preposterously huge number of people were actively thinking about him, quite possibly even discussing him or writing about him. It didn't make a lot of difference if they were for him or against him, it was a strangely humbling thought and one that he tried not to dwell on. It gave him no pleasure at all. It had flashed into his mind as he took the applause at the end of his speech which had been carried live across the States and back in Britain too. He left the podium and started shaking hands with the line of Senators, Congressmen and other dignitaries. Janine Clairmont, who was sitting in the front row leaned across and whispered to Helen Griffin that he still knew how to work an audience. Joanna Morgan switched off the car radio as her car took a turn round the block on its way to the party HQ. Ruth hadn't heard it but she was sitting down now in her badly worn armchair thinking of him all the same. The Prime Minister brought his hand up to his temple as if he sensed that every significant woman in his life now had him in her thoughts.

The synchronicity was over in a flash. Janine nudged her friend and pointed out the tall, frighteningly blond Marine who had just snapped his hand into a salute. Ray Morgan called the Foreign Secretary to say the camera crew would be another five minutes and she asked the driver to delay their arrival a little longer. Ruth was now thinking about Doctor Gill and trying to understand why the prospect of seeing him again was making her feel so shaky.

Only Danny Oliver was still focusing intently on his boss. The news conference should have started by now and, whether deliberately or not, the Prime Minister appeared to be ignoring him.

32

Janine Clairmont left her seat while the applause was still dying down and pushed her way to the back of the auditorium. The rest of the journalists were already waiting impatiently in the press room across the hall. Sinclair was twenty minutes late and many of them were on a deadline. As she looked for a seat Janine was joined by Jim Wells from the BBC who had just finished a live report back to London about the speech. They found two seats together near the front and Jim rang his news desk warning them to expect a further delay before the press conference started. The earnest young man from the *Independent* was typing furiously on his laptop.

Danny managed to get alongside the Prime Minister and whisper in his ear. Reluctantly Sinclair tore himself away from his appreciative audience and followed his Communications Director to where they both knew the reception would be rather more critical. As he and Danny spent five minutes in a side room going through what the journalists were likely to ask, Joanna Morgan was answering questions of her own, looking for all the world like a woman taken unawares by the presence of the cameras.

"Yes!" said Jim Wells, turning off his phone and lifting a clenched fist into the air in celebration. Janine looked at him for an explanation. "A fucking story at last," he said.

Just at that moment Danny Oliver walked up to the microphone. "Ladies and Gentlemen, sorry to keep you waiting. And, I'm afraid we'll have to keep it fairly brief. The Prime Minister."

Sinclair walked up to the lectern and Danny took his reserved seat next to Helen Griffin in the front row. After he'd given his few opening remarks off the cuff the Prime Minister asked for questions. For once the others weren't put out when he called Jim Wells first.

"Prime Minister, do you agree that military action in Eritrea would be, and I quote, *a grave error of judgement*."

"I'm sorry, Jim? I don't follow you."

"Well as I'm sure you know, Prime Minister, the Foreign Secretary has just said that, and I quote again, *history is littered with examples of military action taken in haste and then regretted afterwards.* She said your government knew better than to make a similar mistake. Can we assume that you agree with Joanna Morgan?" Jim Wells smirked and sat down.

Paul Sinclair looked down to Danny for some gesture of guidance but he just raised his eyebrows and shook his head with a look of blank incomprehension. "Well, of course Jim…" Of course, what? Of course she's out to undermine me? What would the President have said? Disowned her? Gone on the attack? Lied through his teeth? Exposure to such raw cynicism the night before had done Paul Sinclair no favours. He couldn't go there. "I, er, haven't had the chance to examine the Foreign Secretary's remarks yet, Jim."

"Well they've already been broadcast live by the BBC, Prime Minister." A small current of laughter eddied around the room.

"Well…er, you have the advantage over me there."

"It's a straightforward question, Prime Minister. Would military action be a grave error of judgement or wouldn't it?" A dozen more hands went up around the room. Danny slid a little lower into his chair and closed his eyes.

Travelling on the London Underground had exactly the opposite effect on Joshua than it did on his least favourite member of the Downing Street staff. Where Colonel Neilson saw threats and uncertainty, Joshua wallowed in the crowds like a hippo in a mud bath. He loved the idea that all these people had their own lives, their own loves, their own troubles that to each and every one of them was the centre of a different universe. All the biometric ID cards and security scans in the world couldn't take that away from them. He grinned at the spiky orange hair of the punk a few seats down. According to Charlie, who kept abreast of fashion better than he did, there was a fully fledged Punk Rock revival on the way and they'd soon have to learn to pogo, whatever that was. Somebody had been playing an old Sex Pistols album in the common room and while Joshua had very little idea what anarchy really was, he was starting to like the sound of it.

The tube was also a rare victory for him in his war of attrition with the Colonel. Kneejerk had tried to persuade the Prime Minister to ban his son from using the underground, but Joshua had persuaded his father that the chance of him being caught up in a random attack was minimal. All Joshua had had to do was promise not to take the same lines on a regular basis or establish a routine.

Whichever route he took, though, he had to pass through the Vortex eventually. Standing in the clear Perspex chamber that was hidden just inside the huge steel doors felt like being strip searched, which it very nearly was. Cameras and sensors photographed and probed and only when they were satisfied did the doors open again to let their captive out. It always made Joshua want to fart. He'd tried it once and had been sorely disappointed that no lights had flashed or alarms sounded. Maybe if he went in for a some serious body piercings the thing might blow a gasket. He could always say he'd decided to become a punk.

The walk from the Vortex to the Number 10 front door was only a hundred metres or so, but Joshua had put on his i-pod and turned it up full. Sergeant Terry Woods saw him coming and opened his eyes wide in warning but to no avail. The door swung open and Joshua stepped inside to where Colonel Henry Neilson was waiting for him.

The Prime Minister's son had been thrilled when he'd first heard Helen and Danny referring to the Colonel as Kneejerk. These days he found the nickname unnecessarily long. To him the Colonel was just a jerk.

For his part the Number 10 Security Supremo regarded all children and most women as unpredictable and so by definition potential security loopholes. One of the greatest challenges he faced was to try to work out what they were likely to do next so he could head off any problems before they got out of hand. Since yesterday he'd learned rather more about what young Joshua had been up to and it confirmed all his suspicions. When he'd watched the boy on the TV monitors inside the Vortex he'd been tempted to have it out with him while his father was still abroad. Just a gentle reminder that he was no ordinary teenager, and that he too had to take questions of security seriously. But he thought better of it.

"Good afternoon, young man." Joshua had taken his headphones off but was now wishing he hadn't. Patronising tosser. He too was keeping his thoughts to himself and simply looked at the Colonel to see if he had anything more to say. Unfortunately, he did. "How are you keeping?" The mock concern was painful to listen to. "Not too bored? It must be difficult sometimes, cooped up in here all by yourself."

What was he getting at? "Actually I don't mind being by myself sometimes. I've got a lot of work to do with my exams coming up and all that." He wasn't going to be able to humour the old git much longer, but he had a feeling there was an agenda going on here and wanted to know what it was.

"Even so, sonny, it must get a bit lonely sometimes."

Sonny! That was enough. If Kneejerk was the last man on earth Joshua could survive a lifetime of loneliness. He fitted his headphones back into his ears and walked towards the flat. He didn't trust himself to look back without giving away his anger and he didn't want the Colonel to have the satisfaction of seeing it.

Neilson walked back to his office quietly pleased that he had the boy on the defensive. For now there was more pressing business to attend to. A couple of clicks on his console and the main screen confirmed that a secure link was being established. Kapolski was seated at his own desk and turned to face the camera.

"Colonel Neilson, good morning. Although I guess over there it must be afternoon. How time flies. The last time we spoke, yesterday I believe, you told me I had nothing to worry about. Well, I've just been listening to your Foreign Secretary. Would you like to revise your opinion, Colonel?"

"Don't worry, Sir. I think we can handle Joanna Morgan. She's just a politician with her own game to play."

"It sounds like a dangerous game to me, Colonel. Where I'm standing members of the administration stick to government policy or they get out. Simple as that. Warren would have had her ass by now. Anyway your man Sinclair was given all the, er, intelligence stuff by the President personally. It's up to you now to make sure he uses it when the time comes. Do I make myself clear?"

Kneejerk didn't need reminding of his own responsibilities. "I think Mrs Morgan's intervention may actually help us there. "

"How so, Colonel?"

"She's a clever woman but blinkered. Like all these Euro-fanatics she'll swallow anything they say in Brussels. And if it contradicts the US, then so much the better so far as she's concerned."

"You're confusing me, Colonel. How is that good for us?"

Maybe the argument was too subtle for a CIA station commander, but Kneejerk pressed on. "It isn't, but this is our chance to show yet again that you people are the only ones we can rely on in a crisis. We just have to make sure we get the right outcome."

"I like your confidence, Colonel. I just wish I could share it."

He tried another tack, a language he knew Kapolski would understand. "Paul Sinclair is a politician with his back to the wall. They're all the same. When things are going wrong at home they like nothing more than a foreign crisis to show how tough and decisive they are."

"Gotcha, Colonel. Gotcha." Kapolski's guttural laughter could still be heard as the screen went blank.

33

The TV cameras panned around to catch the convoy as it crossed the tarmac towards the Prime Minister's plane. The President had decided to take the unusual step of accompanying Sinclair all the way to the aircraft steps so he could bid him farewell in person. This close to the election it could do him no harm at all to be seen standing shoulder to shoulder with an old ally.

"Jesus, Paul, I don't understand why you don't just get rid of the woman." Out of hearing inside the limo they were less shoulder to shoulder than face to face across the cavernous interior.

"It's not that easy. It's called Parliamentary Democracy. She has a lot of support in the Labour Party and I can't afford to ignore that. Wasn't it one of you guys who said it was better to have them inside the tent pissing out than outside pissing in?"

"Lyndon B. Thirty-sixth President of the United States and a good southerner too. Not that it did him much good in the end. But it looks to me like your woman is pissing all over her sleeping bag. Or yours."

"Well we'll have to see about that."

"Nobody's indispensable, Paul. You wanna be careful or people will start to think she's got some kind of a hold over you."

Sinclair looked away. They'd be pulling up beside the waiting plane in just a few seconds. "Thanks for your help on the hostages, John. I appreciate it."

"Yeah well, just you stand firm there at least. Get them out and get them out fast. Any sign of weakness and you'll never recover."

"My priority is to get them all home in one piece."

Warren sounded unsure. "And God willing, I'm sure you'll do that. Just don't forget, it's how strong you look at the end of it that counts." Warren's face was now in silhouette against the TV lights around the aircraft steps. Sinclair had no way of telling how serious he was being. Maybe the President didn't even know himself as he adjusted his tie

172

in the mirror above the door and then reached over and did the same for Sinclair. "Always gotta look your best, Paul. Hey, it's been good to see you, it really has. And you look after that good lady wife of yours, you hear?"

"Next time it's at our place, John."

"Chequers House right?"

The car drew to a halt and the locks disengaged with a loud clunk. A Marine opened each passenger door in unison and the President and Prime Minister emerged into the glare of the camera lights. Danny Oliver watched the handshake and then the warm embrace from his seat in the First Class cabin. Thirty seconds later Sinclair appeared through the curtain and handed his jacket to the stewardess. He looked at his Director of Communications and sat down opposite him.

"What's the matter, Danny? If it wasn't racist I'd say you'd been in a black mood ever since we left England."

"It pretty much reflects how I've felt. But never mind me, I'm paid to worry. What about you?"

"What's that supposed to mean?"

"I've never seen you so unsure of yourself as you were back there at the news conference. You were all over the place."

"I know. I've got a lot on my mind."

"You're the Prime Minister. You're supposed to have a lot on your mind. It's never affected your performance like that before."

"I appreciate your concern, Danny. I'm sorry, okay? What more can I say? I got through it, didn't I?"

"Just." The stewardess placed a glass of champagne in front of each of them and asked them to fasten their belts. Danny pushed his glass to one side. "It's not as if we've got much to celebrate."

"Oh come on. It's not that bad. One bad performance at a news conference isn't the end of the world."

"There's more."

"Tell me."

"A split with Joanna over the hostages we can cope with. After all, it's your responsibility at the end of the day and she'll have to go along with whatever you decide. It's embarrassing, though not as embarrassing as quotes from a very senior member of the government that could sink the Health Bill."

Sinclair mentally scanned the faces around the Cabinet table. Half of them would vote against the health reforms if they could, most out of cowardice, some out of a desire to show off their left-wing credentials and one or two even out of genuine conviction. Danny no doubt had a list of suspects ready to accuse of planting anonymous stories. "Tell me the worst. Joanna again? Piggin?"

"Not this time."

"No?"

"No. It was you."

"Me? What are you saying, that I've been leaking against my own government in my sleep?" Danny passed him a grainy fax that had just come through from Downing Street and watched the Prime Minister run his eyes over it.

The Naked Prophet
The Man Who Dares To Tell The Naked Truth.

Prime Minister Paul Sinclair has finally let the cat out of the bag. For months he's been insisting he has no plans to hand the NHS over to the private sector. His henchmen have been bullying Labour backbenchers into voting for the so-called "reforms" by telling them that they had nothing to fear. It was all about better hospitals. Now we know what it's really about – Naked Profit!

You don't have to take my word for it. Listen to the Prime Minister's own words. A tape revealing what he really thinks was recently passed to this column. You can hear it for yourself by going to my web-site www.naked-prophet.com. But I can give you the best bits right here.

Before I do, let me just be clear about one thing. After all, this is the column that gives it to you straight so you can make up your own mind. He wasn't Prime Minister when he said these words, but it was less than four years ago. Paul Sinclair likes to tell us he's a man of strong convictions. Could those convictions have changed so much or do his words reveal the real thinking behind this week's crunch vote?

This is what he told a group of students at Aston University when he thought nobody would notice:

"The Health Service today is a massive industry with a turnover

that runs into the billions and a workforce far bigger than any other company in the UK. Governments shouldn't be in the business of running an industry like that. We should leave it to the people who know what they're doing."

Get the idea? But there's more. Forgive me, but I thought the Labour Party was proud of having created the NHS. They go on about it often enough. But not, it seems, Paul Sinclair.

"After the war..." That's the Second World War, not any of the little ones Labour has delighted in taking us into in recent years. *"After the war we were given millions of pounds in aid by the Americans, and what did we do with it? While the Germans were rebuilding and modernising their industrial base, we were cosseting ourselves with hugely expensive programmes to pay ourselves something for nothing."*

Like the National Health Service you mean, Mr Sinclair. Something for nothing? Tell that to the millions of your own citizens who have been paying into the NHS all their lives.

People say the Tories aren't dead, they're alive and kicking and still running the country. After reading those words who can doubt that it's true? We can only hope there are still enough brave souls on the Labour benches with the courage to stop Paul Sinclair in his tracks by voting NO.

The Prime Minister put the shiny sheet of fax paper down and looked Danny in the eye. "Not good is it?"

"Do you remember saying it?"

"Oh yes, certainly. I remember it very well. It was supposed to be Chatham House rules, off the record."

"How many times do I have to tell you? Everything is on the record in the end. If you don't want it to appear in print don't say it. Secrets are a luxury you can no longer afford, Paul."

The plane started to rumble forwards. Helen Griffin had taken her seat at the opposite side of the First Class cabin. She'd kicked her shoes off and was on her second glass of champagne. She'd seen Sinclair's vacillating performance in front of the journalists with her own eyes and assumed that was what they were so deep in conversation about. There wasn't much point in her adding her own commentary on how crap he'd been.

Danny wasn't letting up. "What do you suggest I say?"

"I thought it was your job to come up with what to say? What do we pay you for?"

"Well let's start thinking." Danny signalled with his head towards the back of the plane. "Our friends in economy will need a statement before we get to London."

The plane's wheels left the ground with barely a shudder. Out of the window Sinclair could see the lights of the Presidential motorcade heading back into the city.

34

On the top floor of the Castle Pete Morley was just coming to. He stretched out his legs and let them hang over the end of the mattress, his size 13 feet poking out of the bottom of the duvet. Pete was so tall that he always had to sleep with his knees curled up. Rolling over in the night was no easy matter and he invariably woke up feeling stiff.

Helmut was still sound asleep in the room next door. His personal living space was uncluttered to the point of being austere. Pete sometimes wondered if he wouldn't have made a good monk, apart from his obvious sexual appetite of course. Almost all he had to his name was a futon on the floor and a bookcase containing a surprisingly catholic collection of books. Helmut regarded clothes as purely functional accessories and what few he had were stuffed into a sort of kitbag at the foot of his mattress. If any common thread ran through Helmut's adult life it was a search for freedom. He may not have got very far towards his goal but he remained convinced that possessions weighed a man down. He had no interest in buying or acquiring things he didn't need and he needed very little. The one thing he would find it hard to do without was once again in plentiful supply.

Helmut's girlfriend had taken him back with very little persuasion. She clearly hoped his narrow escape from the forces of law and order would be a warning to him to leave her mother alone. They had agreed that her act of revenge was best forgotten and he promised himself not to blame her for forcing him into contact with the Prince of Wales and its specialised clientele. Pete may have found the place liberating but Helmut was still having nightmares about it.

Pete could hear his friend's muffled snores through the thin wall that separated their rooms. His own sleep had been interrupted by terrifyingly lifelike dreams in which they were now so friendly with Mrs Gundry that Alma, as she insisted they call her, was knitting them winter scarves and taking them for days out by the river.

The rapprochement across the previously unbridgeable chasm of Wilson Crescent had certainly eased the atmosphere inside the Castle. The night before PJ seemed to be back to his friendly self, although he'd spent most of the evening shut away in his study. Helmut had been out keeping his girlfriend entertained and, as it turned out, playing with his chemistry set, so Pete had stayed in with a take-away vindaloo trying not to dwell of the fact that these two men were the only real friends he had.

He stretched and thought about going downstairs to make a cup of coffee. He dragged himself down to the foot of the bed, threw off the duvet and pulled on a pair of track suit bottoms and a sweat shirt. He heard the front door slam and PJ's voice in the street outside saying a hurried good morning to Mrs Gundry. He looked out of the window and saw an uncharacteristically friendly smile on their neighbour's face. Pete marvelled yet again at Helmut's way with women. He put on some socks and his enormous feet padded down the worn stair carpet to the kitchen.

The caffeine trail from Pete's stomach to his brain was so well marked that the first shot of the day reached its destination before he had taken a second gulp. Like a hyperactive child, Pete responded a little too readily to stimulants. As his brain became more alert he remembered Helmut coming home the night before. He'd been excited, or as excited as he ever got. It showed only in the way he rubbed his strangely delicate hands together with enthusiasm and in the faintest trace of a smile around his eyes.

It had been a very successful evening by all accounts. Helmut didn't say much about the sex, he never did. But in a whisper, in case PJ was still awake on the floor below, he told Pete that he'd mixed what he was sure would be a winning new blend for those young people who liked to spend their weekends unsure which planet they were inhabiting never mind which part of South London. He had wanted to try out the latest pills as soon as he got home. Helmut always liked them to try a small quantity themselves to check for adverse side effects before putting them on the market. But last night Pete had had the good sense to refuse. Experience had taught him that he might well find himself being kept awake all night.

Refreshed by a good night's sleep, Pete switched on the TV and decided to take Helmut up a cup of coffee too.

Janine Clairmont adjusted her earpiece and tried to fluff a bit of life into her hair. They hadn't had much sleep on the flight back to London and she'd had to spend a good fifteen minutes in the plane's toilet before landing making herself look presentable.

"Coming to you in thirty seconds," said the voice in her ear.

On the small monitor that sat on the ground beside her cameraman she could see pictures of Paul Sinclair's Daimler leaving the airport gates. Helen Griffin was clearly recognisable staring straight ahead in the people carrier behind. The picture cut to a presenter on a sofa, her blonde hair perfectly coiffured and her angular face contorted as she tried to look concerned.

"Our Political Correspondent, Janine Clairmont is at RAF Northolt where the Prime Minister's plane landed in the past half hour. Just how big a crisis is this for Mr Sinclair, Janine?"

"It's the last thing he wanted with the health vote hanging in the balance, Amanda," said Janine trying to block her contempt for the anchor woman from her mind. "But having said that he's refused to apologise for his reported remarks. It looks like he's hoping to tough this one out. According to his spokesman," Janine looked down at her notes, "the Prime Minister believes that sometimes difficult things have to be said. However his advisers tell me he remains fully committed to the NHS and the principle of free treatment at the point of use."

"But surely, Janine," the woman was reading from a list of questions she'd been given by the producer, "this could mean defeat in the House of Commons."

"Well, we'll have to wait and see. But it is clearly a gift to the Leader of the Opposition who can be expected to exploit it for all it's worth. Just as important, though, will be the reaction of those in the Labour Party and even in the Cabinet itself who are known to have serious doubts about the reforms."

"So what about the reaction in the Labour Party?"

The woman was an airhead. She hadn't been listening to a word Janine had been saying. "Well, as I said, Amanda," *you talentless bitch,* "as I said, the Labour Party's reaction will be critical. It could mean the difference between victory and defeat."

"We'll have to leave it there," the sound of relief in the presenter's voice was clear as she moved onto surer ground, "because it's time for our daily Neighbours from Hell feature. Scott is in Lincoln this morning, aren't you Scott?"

The picture on the screen cut to a young man in a leather jacket standing in front of a pair of semi-detached houses. Two very large motorbikes were parked in one of the drives. Although Janine and Scott had got to know each other intimately of late she didn't wait to hear what he had to say. She pulled the earpiece out and threw it on the ground before her lover had a chance to explain this scene of suburban discord.

Helmut's coffee was going cold on the floor in Pete's bedroom. He'd never developed the British taste for instant. As soon as Pete had woken him he'd sent him back to his own room so he could dress, a sign of modesty that his friend found both quaint and frankly unnecessary given recent events. A few minutes later he'd appeared wearing dirty jeans, an old and badly stretched t-shirt that looked too big even on him and socks in different shades of green.

"Are you ready now, Peter?" Between his fingers he held two little yellow pills.

Although Pete had his doubts about this so early in the day, he could see that his friend wasn't going to be deflected a second time. They each placed a pill on the backs of their tongues and swallowed hard, Pete washing his down with a large gulp of Nescafé. The effect was almost immediate. Pete felt a violent churning in his stomach. He looked at Helmut whose normally pale face had lost what little colour it ever had.

"I don't think this one is going to sell, mate. I feel like shit."

"I have to confess, Peter, that so do I." Helmut was trying to work out where he might have gone wrong but the pain in his gut made it hard to concentrate.

Pete contemplated a dash to the toilet on the first floor but wasn't sure he'd make it. By now Helmut was gripping his ample stomach.

Some colour was returning to his cheeks but it was an odd shade of puce. Pete swallowed hard and went over to the window. He pushed up the bottom of the old sash mechanism and leaned out. Helmut was already at his side. In one movement the two men emptied the contents of their indignant stomachs onto the front garden below. An appalling stench of curry, coffee and something sulphurous wafted back in as they sat down on the bed.

"That was awful. Fuck me, Helmut, what did you put in there?" Pete lay back on the mattress and then sat up again with a start. "Oh God, PJ will be back with the papers." Pete wiped his mouth, dragged himself unsteadily to his feet and headed for the landing. The cool air rising up the stairs made him feel a little better. He held onto the banister and propelled himself down the stairs two at a time. When he got to the bottom he stopped abruptly. Through the cracked panes of frosted glass on the front door he could see a figure on the step outside. He went quickly into the front room and pulled just a fraction of the old net curtain to one side. Mrs Gundry was looking straight at him. She had a homemade fruitcake in one hand. With her other hand she was holding a handkerchief to her nose.

35

Danny Oliver's little silver MG left RAF Northolt in the slipstream of the Prime Ministerial convoy, but as soon as Paul Sinclair's outriders turned left towards central London, Danny indicated right. He could be in Birmingham in little over an hour. A bit early for Ruth perhaps, but he could always kill time on the way. It would take Downing Street a few hours to reabsorb the PM and his travelling entourage in any case. But Danny had some absorbing of his own to do and he didn't get more than half a mile down the road before he had to pull over into a side street and turn off the engine.

Communications Directors should never to be at a loss for what to say or do, but that was how he felt. He had himself to blame in a way. Paul Sinclair had obviously taken to heart his admonishment that secrets were a luxury he could no longer afford. Danny had awoken a few hours after making the observation to find a Prime Minister ready to get something of his chest. Something very big indeed. If a journalist had told him the story he could have laughed it off as the stuff of bad fiction. Instead he'd heard it from the Prime Minister himself. And if he couldn't dismiss it he was going to have to work out how to deal with it.

They had sat together over breakfast with Helen sound asleep across the aisle. Danny had asked him if there was anything more he needed to know before seeing Ruth and then listened as Sinclair talked in a voice that was barely audible above the engines. Without touching his food, he had related events that put the immediate political crisis into perspective. When the Prime Minister had finished they had both sat in silence for a while, not yet ready or able to think through all the possible ramifications.

It had been obvious that Sinclair wasn't thinking about himself at all, a rare enough event for a politician. He's concerns were entirely about Ruth. Danny had expected, in the wake of what was going at

Westminster and in Eritrea, to be told to forget the trip to Birmingham, but on the contrary Paul was even more insistent that he should go. When the steward had cleared away his cold scrambled egg, the Prime Minister had gone on to explain how it was Colonel Neilson of all people who had brought home to him just how much pressure his wife was under. Danny knew about her drinking, although he hadn't realised how serious it had become. Sinclair had told him that since Kneejerk had walked into his office with the West Midlands Police report under his arm, he'd decided to face up to his responsibilities to his family. Only now had he accepted that to do that he would have to stop running away from his own past.

Danny sat staring out of the windscreen, unsure how he felt about what he'd been told, beyond dismay and disappointment that it had taken Sinclair this long to confide in him. Why did so many politicians, despite all the evidence of history, think that they alone could break the rules of journalistic gravity? Every story will hit the ground with a bump sooner or later. And this one stood to hurt more than a few people when it did, although none of Danny's experience could help him work out how much damage it would do his boss. Ruth held part of the answer and Danny was no longer in any doubt that by taking the time to see Ruth he'd be acting in everyone's best interests.

On the seat beside him was the stack of newspapers the ground staff had handed him as soon as they landed. They hadn't made for happy reading. He was going to have to help Paul to stay focused on the immediate crisis. Danny was more uncertain than he'd ever been about the long-term but decided to concentrate for a moment on those problems he could do something about. He rang the press office and told them what to say to in answer to questions about the NHS. The easy bit out of the way, he turned the key in the ignition and pointed the little MG back towards the motorway.

The road cut through miles of West London suburbia before breaking out into the Buckinghamshire countryside and climbing up into the Chilterns. This was one of Danny's favourite parts of the country but an area that had never fallen for the charms of New Labour either before or since Sinclair. Danny imagined himself pulling off and choosing a village at random. The car's fancy satellite navigation device offered up some enticing possibilities. Knotty Green or Beacon's

Bottom perhaps. They were just names to Danny but he was sure he could get a little focus group together in the local pub, introduce himself as the black, homosexual Downing Street Communications Director and see how they felt about the story the Prime Minister had told him over breakfast at 35,000 feet. No, he didn't need a focus group to tell him it wouldn't play well in Beacon's Bottom.

~

In the back of the armour-plated Daimler, Helen had given up trying to get any serious conversation out of the Prime Minister. From the moment they set off back to central London he seemed reluctant to talk at all and when she'd asked him what the matter was he'd told her about the President's plan for destroying his opponent. She assumed she must have disappointed him by being neither surprised nor particularly shocked because he'd quickly fallen back into a sullen silence. There was always a chance, she thought, that he was pondering how to pull his government out of its current difficulties, but it seemed unlikely. He used to so love discussions of strategy and what to do with power if he ever got it, but those long evenings around the dinner table in Spain felt like a lifetime ago now. Helen turned and stared out of the window. Had she known what was really on his mind, and that he'd seen fit to open his heart to Danny rather than her, she would have been devastated.

The Western approaches to London were a relentless succession of tedious housing estates interspersed with increasing frequency by industrial parks and shopping centres. Although Helen had slept fairly well on the plane, the car's heater, the deep leather seats and the absence of stimulation was making her drowsy. She couldn't even get on the phone for fear of irritating Sinclair. She figured he was going to be high maintenance for a while. As Greenford gave way imperceptibly to Ealing, Helen had her eyes closed and was allowing herself the luxury of imagining Otto beneath the duvet just as she'd left him.

"Pull over here, Derek."

Inspector Derek Smyth looked in his rear view mirror for confirmation of the order and saw Helen waking up with a start.

"Now, Derek, if you wouldn't mind."

Derek whispered a message into his sleeve, the indicators on the Daimler signalled left, and the entire Prime Ministerial convoy of police outriders, Special Branch Range Rover, back up cars and people carriers lurched into the car park outside a DIY superstore and a hamburger chain. Only the press bus that was following behind carried on its way with thirty weary journalists craning their necks to see what was going on.

"Paul, what are you doing?" Helen was looking at him as if he'd gone mad.

"Just hang on here a second." He tried to open the passenger door and realised that in four years as Prime Minister he'd never once opened it for himself. It didn't budge. Derek looked again in his mirror where Helen caught his eye and shrugged her assent. But once the door was open she slid across the seat and followed Sinclair into the car park where he appeared to be walking towards the recycling bins.

"What the fuck are you doing, Paul?" He said nothing and kept walking. When she came up beside him he brought his hand up to his temple but refused to meet her eye. "Paul?"

He pushed both his fists back down by his side, like a frustrated child. When finally he looked at Helen it was with eyes that were focused only on his own dismay.

"It's Ruth isn't it?" Helen knew where Danny was going even if she didn't know what he'd been told.

"How could I send him? What was I doing? I should have borrowed his car and gone myself. God knows what she'll think."

"She'll have the sense to know that the Prime Minister can't just run off to Birmingham on the spur of the moment, no matter how he's feeling. For Christ's sake Paul, we're starting to attract attention. Come on, get back in the car."

Instead he walked further away. A young woman with two small children looked as if she might come and introduce herself but clearly thought better of it. When Helen caught up with him again there was a trace of spittle on the side of his mouth. He rubbed it away with the back of his hand. "I don't know what to do."

"Paul, look around you. All these people on their way to work or about to do the shopping, all of them have more choice about what to do right now than you do. They can go home and call in sick, or have their hair done instead. You have one choice. To get back in the

185

car and hope that not too many people noticed you wandering about like a delinquent. Sometimes you're a very powerful man, Paul. When you're back in the office we need you to start using some of that power. But right now you might as well be on your way to starting a ten year stretch for all the choice you have." She took his elbow. "Paul, please."

His head was bowed as she led him back towards the waiting cars. As he got closer he straightened his back, aware of the dozens of pairs of eyes that were following his progress. He sat back inside without a word and Derek Smyth slammed the heavy door shut behind him.

~

Colonel Henry Neilson had noticed the unscheduled stop on the vehicle tracking system on his desk. A radio call failed to produce any explanation from the security team. Kneejerk became very uneasy whenever anything unexpected happened. Only when the black dots on his electronic map started moving again did he relax. The cameras at the end of Downing Street showed only four people inside the Compound. It was still too early and too cold for the Ordinary Decent Malcontents.

Even allowing for the morning rush hour, the Vortex was able to open its massive gates to admit the Prime Minister's car little more than thirty minutes later. From the front step Kneejerk watched the vehicles pop out into the street one by one. Sergeant Terry Woods who was on door duty yet again looked straight ahead. He hadn't exchanged a word with the Security Supremo for two weeks now and he wasn't about to start if he could help it. Kneejerk slipped inside. It wouldn't do to be seen to be too impatient.

The doors on the people carriers that brought up the rear opened as soon as the convoy pulled up outside the front door. Their occupants paused just long enough to allow Sinclair to go in first. Few people spoke, as if they'd been common witnesses to something that couldn't be discussed. Secretaries clutching laptops and fax machines, suitcases and overnight bags converged on the entrance eager to re-establish themselves after the disruption of the trip. The lucky ones had managed a little sleep on the flight home, but none enjoyed the Prime Minister's luxury of living over the shop. Nor would they have wanted to.

Paul Sinclair had walked straight past the Colonel without exchanging a word. As soon as he got up to the flat he slipped off his shoes in the hall and went into the bathroom. Under normal circumstances he would have folded his clothes neatly on top of the marble vanity unit and wiped away the ring of stage make-up that Joshua had left, once again, round the sink. Instead he shut the bathroom door behind him, threw his clothes in a pile on the floor, turned on the shower and stepped inside. He let the supercharged jets of water pummel his broad shoulders and back. The steam circled upwards towards the extractor fan in the ceiling, sucking up with it just a little of the accumulated stress. He reached out and turned on the radio above the sink. It was tuned to Sinclair's favourite oldies station and with his eyes tight shut he found himself singing along to the Monkees.

Alone at last, he was suddenly feeling strangely light-headed and wondered if he was actually starting to lose it. He knew that when the pressure got too much some people were tipped over the edge, but had never thought it could happen to him. He felt the urge to sing at the very top of his voice but took a deep breath instead and held it in. Maybe it wasn't stress but the opposite, a funny kind of relief. Danny now knew the truth. Things were going to change, one way or another. So, the Colonel wanted to see him as soon as it was convenient, did he? Well it wasn't convenient.

He turned around and let the jets fire their pellets of water at his face and chest. He watched the water bouncing off his upper body and then collecting in powerful rivulets that ran down his abdomen, split into two streams around his groin and coursed down his legs towards the shower tray. He wasn't particularly body conscious but he knew he was in good shape.

The music had given way to an advert for cut-price car windscreens.

Reluctantly he turned the huge control knob to off and let the last of the water run off his body. He slid back the cubicle door and the steam billowed out into the bathroom. He grabbed a huge fluffy white towel from the rail and started patting and rubbing himself dry. Then he threw it down on the tiles to dry his feet so he wouldn't trail water across the wooden floor of the hall. This was the nearest thing to freedom he'd felt in a very long time. For a moment he even considered masturbation, but the tingle he was feeling all over wasn't really sexual. Although there was something to be said for the thought of Kneejerk waiting impatiently for him downstairs while he…

Sinclair opened the bathroom and stepped out into the hall.

"Hi Dad. You haven't got any clothes on."

"What are you doing here?" Sinclair disappeared into his bedroom and came back in a pair of boxer shorts. "Shouldn't you be at school?"

"It's only eight o'clock."

"Is it? So it is. I lose track of time sometimes. So how's things?" Sinclair went back into the bathroom where the fog was starting to clear and sprayed two bursts of anti-perspirant under his arms.

"Oh, you know. Okay. It was the final curtain last night. Another full house." He wasn't going to discuss his mother's visit while his dad was in his underpants. "You sounded happy in there. How was Washington?"

"Don't ask."

"So what's with this Warren guy anyway? I don't know why you bother with him. I mean, 'Bunny' Warren, who can take a guy seriously that calls himself Bunny?"

"He only does it at election time. Maybe he hopes it makes him sound cuddly and reassuring."

Joshua's face was distorted into a stage grimace. "Cuddly? The guy's a creep. I don't know how you can be in the same room as him. I'm not the only one who's been selling my soul to the devil in the past few days." A large wet fluffy towel came flying out of the bathroom door and hit him on the side of the head. Sinclair followed close behind and went into his room. When he emerged in a dark blue shirt there were patches of damp across his chest where he'd started to sweat again after the hot shower.

"I might just agree with you more than you'd believe, Josh. But much as I'd like to, I don't think either of us has time to talk about this now."

"Yeah, same old story."

"I know. But I've got a horrible feeling my staff are waiting for me downstairs and the good people at Harvest Hill Comprehensive are certainly waiting to continue your education, if you'd care to join them."

The tie really didn't go with the suit. On any other day Sinclair would have taken the time to find one that did. "Oh, I forgot," he said, disappearing back into his bedroom. He came back out with the letter in his hand. "This came for you before we left."

Joshua unfolded the note and read it quickly before stuffing it in the back pocket of his trousers. His look of cocky defiance had vanished as he turned his face away. "Thanks, Dad. Anyway, I'd better dash or I'll be late for school. Mr Clements is taking the Drama Club to a matinée this afternoon to celebrate the end of our sell-out run. Mum said she thought it was great. She stayed over, but I guess you know that."

"Your mother?"

"Yeah. Your wife. Remember? I've got to go, Dad."

"Josh wait a minute."

"I'll see you later, okay?" And with that he disappeared. Sinclair could hear him thudding down the stairs to the main hallway below.

Danny got out of the car and clicked the remote control to lock the doors. Looking up the slope of grass towards Aston Hall, it was as if he was still in the wilds of Buckinghamshire rather than inner city Birmingham. It wasn't exactly a beautiful building, but its red brick Jacobean architecture exuded a confidence and a defiant Englishness that the urban sprawl around it couldn't even begin to dent. To have driven past without stopping wasn't an option.

It had been Danny's idea to book Aston Hall for the victory party at the end of the leadership campaign. He hadn't told Paul Sinclair who he knew would think it was a sign of over-confidence. But two weeks before the result, Danny had been feeling confident. Both Ruth and Jo Morgan had approved the idea. Joanna in particular thought the Hall would send out a message of reliability and reassurance. She was always the one urging Paul to look the conservative so he could act the radical.

The TV lights had surrounded the mansion at the end of what had proved to be a remarkable campaign. They had all been together eating sandwiches and drinking tea in one of the dark wood panelled dining rooms when the Chancellor, who a few weeks earlier had thought he couldn't lose, called to concede defeat and announce he'd be returning to the backbenches. When Paul put down the phone he told them his rival had sounded dignified but broken. The Sinclair Campaign had succeeded in painting him as part of the past, the Establishment candidate standing in the way of the next generation. Paul Sinclair's alternative vision had been fresher and younger and more optimistic and as the constituencies and trade unions started to ballot their members it became clear this was what the party was looking for. By the time he'd made the booking for Aston Hall, Danny reckoned Paul was going to win by 65% to 35%. He was just two percentage points out.

Danny looked at his watch. Ruth would be ready for him soon. He couldn't bring himself to walk up the long lawn and take another look at the room where Paul and Joanna had appeared hand in hand on stage to claim their inheritance. It was an image that today, of all days, he preferred to forget.

He leant on the roof of the car and dialled the office. The media, he was told, were already asking about the Prime Minister's unscheduled stop on the A40. "You told them what, that he wanted a hamburger? And is that true?" He scrunched up his face. "Of course it matters. Because they'll now go and interview the guy behind the counter and he'll say he never saw the Prime Minister. Once you lie, you're dead. You'll never recover. How many times do I have to tell you? Now call them back and say you were misinformed. He just wanted some fresh air. They can't prove you wrong on that." Danny wished again that he'd had the Media Rule Book that he kept in his head printed and distributed to his staff.

36

"Prime Minister. I hope you're feeling refreshed." The Colonel might as well have just called him a slacker to his face. "I thought you might like a situation update."

"Let's get Helen in here first, shall we?" Sinclair couldn't face another *tête-à-tête* alone with Kneejerk. Leaving the flat and coming downstairs had felt like a sacrifice enough. He called out to Rebecca to find his Chief of Staff and when she appeared clutching a large cardboard cup of coffee he took his usual seat behind his desk and put his feet up on the polished surface. Neilson noticed the Prime Minister's shoes were badly in need of a polish.

Sinclair sighed. "Right, Colonel. What have you got to tell us?"

The Number 10 Security Supremo was starting to wonder if the Prime Minister was fully engaged this morning, but he was prepared to put it down to jetlag. "I think we've all seen the CIA intelligence material?"

"I wish somebody had shown it to Joanna Fucking Morgan." When Helen was tired she lost what little control she had over her tongue.

Sinclair didn't have the energy for one of her eruptions. "Not now, Helen. Yes, we've seen the pictures, Colonel."

"So now we have a clear target and while you were in the air there was more radio traffic. It looks like they may be planning to move the hostages soon. The usual tactic is to stage some kind of press conference with the captives pleading with you to do what the terrorists want. They can't do that in some cave. We should deny them that publicity if possible. My recommendation is to send in the SAS at the earliest opportunity." Helen took a mouthful of coffee and looked to Sinclair for his reaction but he was staring out of the window and seemed to be miles away. Kneejerk's moustache twitched perceptibly. "Everything is in place, Prime Minister."

"Thank you, Colonel," said Sinclair, turning back into the room.

191

"You know the Foreign Secretary's view I take it?"

"Yes, of course."

"To be honest I haven't had time to read the whole of the European report. What do you make of it?"

The Colonel was ready with a crisp denunciation of the contents, which were based he said derisively on Italian intelligence sources. "They say this bit of territory is no longer in the hands of the Eritrean army. That strikes me as immaterial, even if true. We have to act in the same way whoever it is we're up against."

"Maybe." Helen shot him a look as he went on. "Well, until there's some sort of movement we can't do much anyway. It will give me time to consider the options."

There was nothing that got Helen more worked up than feeble and indecisive men and she was starting to think Paul was turning into one. She was no fan of Kneejerk's either, but at least he was talking her language. "The Colonel's right, Paul. This is going to call for a tough response. I don't know what options you think you've got to consider, for Christ's sake."

Far from being stung by her rebuke, he looked as if he hadn't even heard her. "Well, if that's everything...? Helen was about to resume her attack when he caught her eye and shook his head. "We'll talk again in an hour." There was nothing Sinclair wanted more than to go back up to the flat, listen to the radio and forget about being Prime Minister for just a few minutes. Helen had a look of ill disguised contempt on her face as she left the room but the Colonel clearly wasn't finished. "What is it Henry? Can we make it quick?"

He came straight to the point. "Do you have the letter?"

"What letter?"

"The letter to your son that was apprehended by Mr Oliver."

"Oh, I gave it to him."

"To who?"

"To my son. It was addressed to him."

Kneejerk looked at him as if he'd committed an act of gross irresponsibility. "That's unfortunate, Prime Minister. It's important evidence."

"Evidence of what?"

"Stalking is a criminal offence. It seems the author of the letter, a

Miss Schneider, of German descent, has been carrying on an internet liaison with your son. I took the liberty of checking his computer records."

Sinclair suddenly turned and looked the Colonel straight in the eye. He was livid. "Number one, Colonel, I simply cannot believe you are wasting your time with this right now. And number two, you are quite correct. That was a liberty, an unacceptable liberty. And before you tell me that you can't afford to take any risks, let me tell you that I've heard all that once too often. He's my son, he's seventeen years old and he can talk on the internet to whomsoever he damn well likes. Do I make myself clear?" The Colonel was open mouthed. He'd never seen Sinclair like this. He wasn't ready to concede the point, but there was obviously nothing to be gained from continuing to argue now so he said nothing. The Prime Minister was in no mood to be asked what he was doing about his wife's brush with the West Midlands Police either. "Thank you, Henry. That will be all."

Two minutes later he was back in the flat with the door closed firmly behind him. From the bathroom he could hear the radio that he'd forgotten to turn off. He threw himself down into the settee and slammed his fist against the back cushion.

37

Danny Oliver ran his finger along the edge of the knife. It confirmed what he'd long suspected, that Ruth didn't do a lot of cooking for herself. "Do you ever sharpen your knives?"

"Not frequently, I'm afraid. I think there's an electric thing for doing that in the cupboard down there somewhere." Joshua had bought it for her for Christmas when he was fourteen.

Danny got down on his haunches and rummaged around in the back of the cupboard. There was a variety of mixing bowls of different sizes piled up on top of each other, an old green teapot with no lid and a six-sided vegetable grater that looked as if it still had bits of dried carrot down one of its edges. Danny remembered making a grated carrot and mustard seed salad the last time he'd been at the house and wondered if it had been in here unwashed ever since. Behind it was a tangle of wires where three or four electrical blenders and whisks had been shoved together. He pushed the whole lot to one side and pulled out the sharpener, its own lead neatly wrapped around the base of the unit by virtue of the fact that it had never been used.

"We could go out. I rang Subash at the Light of Nepal and he can fit us in." The restaurant had been their regular haunt during the leadership campaign. Subash, who had at first thought from the intensity of their conversation that they were an oddly-matched couple of new lovers, had shown great patience when they often lost track of the time and kept him up well after midnight.

"I'm sure he can, but I'd rather stay in if you don't mind. I don't think I could stomach a curry right now and anyway, I do so enjoy it when we cook meals here together."

Danny tried to remember when the word 'together' had ever applied to getting dinner ready with Ruth. Not that he minded. For him cooking was a pleasure, a way to unwind after a hectic week at Westminster. He and Luke loved to spend their Friday evenings at home in Battersea creating new recipes or revisiting old favourites. To Ruth cooking was a chore, something that distracted her from her reading and writing, especially now that she lived alone. She hated wasting her time, and an hour or more spent preparing a dish that, however delicious, would be consumed in ten minutes struck her as absurd. It amazed her that Danny and his partner managed to find the time to cook when they were both so busy.

"How is your lovely King's Counsel?" she asked. Luke had been making quite a name for himself of late as a prominent criminal barrister.

"He's great. Terribly busy but maybe that's just as well when I'm away so much myself."

Danny had plugged in the sharpener and the noise of grating metal filled the room. "There. Now you possess one knife sharp enough to cut through the skin of a tomato without squashing it." He waved the knife above his head. "Let battle commence."

Ruth was suddenly starting to relish the prospect of so much activity in her little kitchen. "What are we having?"

"Something simple. Pasta bake with roasted vegetables."

"I don't know how many vegetables I've got. She hoped Danny wouldn't open the fridge where she knew there were carrots and courgettes literally turning to water in the bottom drawers which she hadn't had the energy to clear out.

"Don't worry," he indicated the large Waitrose bag by the door, "I stopped on the way."

Ruth was feeling spoilt. She was having more meals bought and cooked for her in a week than she normally enjoyed in six months. She was also feeling thirsty and eyed the bottle of rioja in the window.

Danny caught her look. "You open the wine, Ruth, and I'll start on the vegetables."

She picked up the bottle, but put it back down on the table unopened. "It was good of you to come, Danny. I was wondering if they'd send you."

"I don't know what you mean. Nobody sent me."

"You don't have to spare my feelings. When the Prime Minister's wife is found asleep in her car in a lay-by late at night with too much alcohol in her blood, they have to do something."

Danny put down his knife and put an arm around Ruth's shoulders as she sat down at the kitchen table. "Why don't you tell me about it?" Paul had given him only the bare, officially-recorded details.

"I was at a book launch. A new biography of Montaigne by a very clever woman at the university here. It's good, if you're ever short of something to read. Anyway, the publishers had put on a surprisingly jolly party for a rather academic book that's hardly going to sell in its millions. As ever, though, plenty of booze but not a lot to eat. I'd taken the car and when it came round to nine o'clock I realised I'd drunk a bit too much. I could easily have gone back inside and called a cab, but I didn't. I went about half a mile down the road and then decided I really wasn't in a fit state to drive all the way back here, so I pulled into a lay-by. When I looked for my mobile I couldn't find it. It must have fallen out of my bag at the party. I'm not sure what I thought I was going to do, catch a bus or find a pay phone and call a taxi after all, but before I could even start to decide I dozed off."

Danny took his eyes off the aubergine he was slicing and put down the knife as she continued.

"I was woken up at half past eleven by a policeman tapping on the window. Of course I failed the breathalyser and they took me down to the police station at Edgbaston. It was while I was waiting that one of the Inspectors recognised me. I suppose I should have expected that but I wasn't really thinking straight."

"That's understandable."

"So, anyway, the upshot of it all was that I got a caution and no other action was taken. I told the Inspector that I didn't want any special treatment but he said they weren't obliged to prosecute me even though technically I'd been in charge of the vehicle and so had committed an offence. I wasn't sure if I believed him, but then I thought what was the point of going down on my knees and begging them to take me to court?"

"You'd be a bit stuck here without your driving licence."

"It's not that. I could cope. But it would be a terrible embarrassment for Paul and, whatever people think, I try very hard not to cause him any difficulties."

"And we all appreciate that." She was right, thought Danny, the story would have given the papers just the excuse they were looking for to start prying into the state of the Prime Minister's marriage.

"I knew Paul would hear about it soon enough. I mean that's how it works isn't it? A quiet word in somebody's ear. I should really have phoned him and told him myself but we've rather got out of the habit of talking, you know."

"I know, and it's not doing either of you any good." Danny was about to pick up the knife again and start on the peppers, but instead he opened the bottle of wine and poured them both a glass. This wasn't going to be easy. "Ruth, Paul has told me."

"Told you what?"

"I was going to say everything, but what's everything? Let's just say he told me enough. I insisted, I'm afraid. It was obvious that something very serious was on his mind and I couldn't do my job if I didn't know what was keeping Paul awake at night. I am his Director of Communications."

"You're also his friend. And mine, I hope."

"I hope so, too."

"Quite frankly, Danny, I'm astonished."

"Ruth, I'm sorry."

"No. I'm astonished he didn't tell you three years ago. I assumed he had, but maybe I've been doing too much assuming. You must have been wondering what on earth was going on." She was both surprised and touched to see that he was embarrassed. "So what did he tell you?"

"We don't have to do this."

"Yes we do. I think it'll be good for both of us to have it said out loud."

Danny scraped all the peppers into the pan with the rest of the vegetables and poured some olive oil over the top. It was obvious Ruth's oven hadn't been used for some time, but he ignored the bits of dried pizza topping that were stuck to the wire trays and slid the pan onto the middle shelf. He sat down opposite Ruth across the old farmhouse table and picked up his glass.

"Okay. I'll tell it just as Paul told it to me this morning."

"This morning?"

"Yes, we were an hour out from London. Helen was asleep on the opposite side of the cabin and the secretaries were all dozing or working. I told him if he wanted me to come up here and see you, I had to know what it was all about."

"So he did ask you to come."

"Yes. Yes, he asked me to come. But I wanted to, believe me. I know you well enough by now. You're not the kind of person to find yourself sleeping off the booze in a Birmingham lay-by for no good reason."

"There's a reason for just about everything, Danny. What did he say?"

"Not what I was expecting. I'd sort of assumed that all the pressures of living in Downing Street had got to you. That you'd felt you had to get out but had found you were no happier when you did. It seemed to make sense. But he told me a story that went back thirty years not just three. Back to when you first met." Ruth poured herself a second glass of wine but Danny barely noticed. "I mean, I knew that he was already friends with Helen and with Joanna back then. And I suppose, like a lot of people, I assumed that he and Helen had been more than friends. I always thought I was fairly intuitive about these things, but then he told me that Joanna..." Ruth was sitting rigidly, her glass just a millimetre from her bottom lip. Her eyes were willing him to go on. "That it was Joanna who'd been his dark lady. The older woman who'd come into his life at Oxford and had turned into an obsession." Still she didn't move. "And when he met you at some debating competition suddenly this young, ambitious man who thought he could have whatever he wanted had to make a choice."

Ruth smiled a thin smile. "That's me. Just an old fashioned girl with old fashioned morals."

"Maybe. Paul obviously didn't care. He'd met the woman he wanted to be with for the rest of his life. Joanna had taught him all about passion, but it was you who introduced him to love."

"Love."

"He still loves you, Ruth."

She ran the glass around in her hands. "Finish your story."

"Paul said that whatever else they may have given up, he and Joanna still had a chemistry between them but now their shared passion was for politics. They both worked hard at it and by the mid-nineteen-nineties they were MPs and both junior ministers. Are you sure you want to do this?" She nodded. "He didn't try to excuse what happened, Ruth. Many people in his position would have blamed the late nights and the pressures of the job. Paul's bigger than that. I'm not sure he knows himself why the affair started again or even why it lasted almost three years. It sounded to me as if he'd never talked about it with anyone before. You never guessed?"

"No. No, I never guessed."

"Nor did I, but then why would I? By the time we were all sitting round that table in Spain making plans, it was over. Paul had made the Cabinet and Jo was still his biggest supporter. Maybe she was still in love with him, I don't know. She was certainly the one who started pushing him to consider the leadership. When the time came and he went for it, it made sense for her to run as his deputy. I could sense the chemistry, we all could, and politically it was such an asset. It never occurred to me there might be more to it, but maybe I'm naïve."

"I don't think you're naïve, Danny, but then who am I to talk. I was married to him and I hadn't guessed."

"So Paul becomes Prime Minister with just a year to establish himself before the General Election. He has you and Josh with him in Downing Street. Joanna is his deputy and Foreign Secretary and still his most loyal supporter."

"No, Danny, you're wrong there. That's a position I will never cede to her." She put her glass down hard and spilt red wine on the table. He threw her a cloth but she left it where it fell.

Danny wanted to get the story over with as quickly as he could. "With the election everything changed. Paul had to get the security situation sorted out after the Circle of Death Bombing but Joanna was going ballistic, accusing him of running back to the Americans and abandoning the new foreign policy she'd worked so hard on. When he wouldn't budge she demanded to be made Chancellor of the Exchequer. When he refused that as well the dark lady started making dark threats. He wasn't sure how to react. He knew that if she went public about the affair it would damage her as much as it would him, but he wasn't thinking about the public reaction, he was thinking about you. Apparently Jo had already told Ray about the affair and been forgiven."

"The implication being that I wouldn't be so understanding?"

"Exactly, but he took that risk. Paul decided he couldn't let her have a hold over him like that, so he did what he should have done a long time before. He told you about the affair." He waited a second in case she wanted to give her take on the story but she clearly didn't. "Well, his political position at least was transformed. Joanna knew she'd overplayed her hand and was forced to stay as Foreign Secretary. But from that moment on she seemed determined to destroy him. Maybe she decided that if she couldn't govern hand in hand with him, so to speak, then she was going to take his place. Paul doesn't seem to worry too much about that. He thinks he can handle Jo. What he hates himself for is not being the man you thought he was. You weren't the kind of woman to pretend nothing had happened."

"I couldn't." Her voice was cracking.

"I can understand that, of course I can. And I can understand you feeling you had to get away for a while. But now…well, you must be able to see that it's over for good between them. They can barely be in the same room together."

"That's not the point. Integrity has always mattered more to me than fidelity and when the trust is gone how do you get it back? It doesn't help that Jo is still there, attending his meetings and all the rest of it. I daren't put the telly on in case I see them together."

"Maybe he should have sacked her."

"Maybe. There's not much to be gained from dwelling on maybes."

Danny knew Sinclair hadn't felt strong enough to sack her then, not politically at any rate. He was weaker now, though, and he'd paid a heavy price for missing his chance. The woman sitting opposite him staring into her glass with tears in her eyes was living proof of that.

38

"That was a pretty pathetic performance down there." Helen Griffin hadn't knocked. Most of his senior staff knew the access codes to the flat, but only his Chief of Staff could barge in unannounced.

"Thanks for your support." Sinclair had been laying on the sofa for twenty minutes staring at the ceiling.

"It's not about my support, you know that. It's about the fact that you have a hostage crisis to sort out, a party rebellion that could be about to swallow you up, a key piece of legislation that's likely to be defeated and you're sitting here with your feet up."

"What do you want me to do?"

Helen couldn't believe what she was hearing. "I want you to get off your fat arse and cut the crap. Show the world and your party and Joanna Morgan and the newspapers and Father Fucking Christmas that you're not going to be pushed around."

"Ruth was here, you know? While we were in Washington."

"Is all this about Ruth? Do you think Ruth would be any more impressed than the rest of us by the way you're carrying on? Just remember, Ruth wanted you to have this job because she thought you'd be a great Prime Minister. It's not going to make her feel any better if you end up being a useless one."

"I'm not in the mood for this conversation."

"Well I am. That's exactly the mood I'm in."

"No, Helen. No. Not now."

She was wasting her time. "You'd better snap out of this, Paul. I'm going to go and find out just how deep the shit is. I'll leave you to come up with some ideas for how to get us out of it."

~

PJ Walton sighed. Maybe he just wasn't cut out for success. His article revealing Paul Sinclair's unguarded thoughts on the NHS had been put on the front page, a rare honour for a mere columnist. And his Editor had offered him a sizeable pay increase if he'd sign a contract for another two years. And yet PJ was feeling that his reserves of self-respect were at an all time low. The phone rang and he answered it with a gruff greeting that convinced Ray Morgan it was going to be a difficult call. Ray was an uncomplicated and essentially good man. He'd warned his wife that PJ wouldn't like what she was suggesting he write next and he was quickly proved right.

"I'm sorry, Ray, but no. I just can't use that. Did you really think I would?"

Ray didn't try to argue. "Joanna is very keen that you should," was all he managed by way of a riposte.

"Well I'm surprised at her, in that case." When Ray made no effort to defend her, PJ went on, "I think I must insist on seeing her myself. We really need to talk."

"Of course. I'll see what I can do. She does have a very busy diary, but let me worry about that. I keep telling her that you should see more of each other."

"Thanks, Ray." He put the phone down and wondered if Joanna realised what a decent man she'd married. He was still staring at the notes he'd made when the phone rang again. PJ was ready to be impressed if Ray had got an answer so quickly, but it wasn't him.

"Hello," said a familiar voice.

"Oh. Sorry, I was expecting…"

"Don't sound so surprised. I'm allowed to ring my own son occasionally, I hope."

"Yes, mother. Yes. Of course you are."

"I thought I might pay you a little visit, how would that be?" It sounded less like a thought and more like a decision that he wouldn't be able to change if he wanted to.

~

The division bell had been ringing for three minutes already. Helen stood at the top of the stone steps and looked down at the MPs of all parties scurrying to get to the voting lobbies in time. She rarely came across to the House of Commons except for the weekly ritual of Prime

Minister's Question Time but she needed to get out of Number 10 for a while and calm down.

To Helen, who liked things done quickly and effectively, Parliament was an antiquated talking shop that would be better turned into a museum and opened up to the tourists. For many years the party leadership had been able to all but ignore the place, while denying furiously doing any such thing. The majorities had been so large that very nearly anything decided up the road in Downing Street could be sure of getting through the Commons without too much bother. Then things had got more difficult and managing opinion in parliament became important again. When Sinclair had won his own election, with a decent but not a huge majority, the fact that he was a new leader had saved him too many headaches about whether MPs would pass his bills into law. But all that had changed again now. A lot of things seemed to be changing so far as Helen could make out.

One thing that she knew would never change was the vanity of old, overweight backbenchers with halitosis when approached by any reasonably presentable younger woman. Ernie Harwood, the long serving member for Wakefield Horbury, was a case in point and he was coming towards her now.

"Come on, Ernie, nearly there." She was doing her best to look kindly, which always cost Helen a particular effort. But she didn't want him to rush. The government could scarcely afford a by-election right now.

"Don't you worry about me, Miss Griffin. I've been here for twenty-three years and I haven't missed a vote yet."

Some MPs who fancied themselves as the new modernisers asked why votes in the House of Commons still had to be cast in person. After all, they argued, these days you could vote in everything from the Eurovision Song Contest to a General Election by mobile phone or on the internet. But Ernie Harwood was of the old school and Helen, who could think of nothing else they had in common, agreed. So long as MPs had to turn up to vote in person you could keep track of them.

She took his arm and walked alongside him towards the Members' Lobby. She was careful to take his right side. Harwood was completely deaf in his left ear and got very frustrated when he couldn't hear what was being said to him. He could be a difficult man and had never understood why he'd been passed over for promotion as a minister so many times. He had, even for an MP, a toweringly high opinion of his own talents and an almost touching belief that one day they would be recognised. Ernie Harwood was one of the party's weather vanes which was why Helen had taken the trouble to get to know him. He'd gone which ever way the strongest wind was blowing for a quarter of a century and never failed to detect any change in direction. But his sole remaining ambition was to retire from the House at the next election as Sir Ernest Harwood and the one person who could help him achieve that was now at his side.

The doors stood open, a small huddle of journalists at each one hoping to catch a word with a passing minister or a well placed backbencher. It was some time since they had wasted their breath on the MP for Wakefield Horbury. Helen left him at the door. She may have been the Prime Minister's Chief of Staff but only Honourable Members were allowed inside during a vote. "Come and see me for a cup of tea when you're done, Ernie." He nodded. He may have been vain but he wasn't stupid. He knew what he was good for.

Helen stood watching the party whips steer the MPs, most of whom had little idea what it was they were being asked to approve or reject, towards the correct voting corridor. As the crowds began to thin she spotted Janine Clairmont at the door immediately across the hallowed tiles of the huge square room. To get from one side door to the other via the warren of corridors around the lobby would have taken at least five minutes. Janine was tipping an imaginary glass up to her lips and mouthing the word 'drink'. Helen pointed at her watch and shrugged her shoulders as if it was some elaborate parlour game. Janine uncurled her fingers and held up eight of them. Helen nodded, clenched her fist and stuck out her little finger and thumb. Putting her imaginary phone to her ear she mouthed 'call me'.

"Come along, Miss Griffin." She hadn't seen Harwood come up beside her having done his democratic duty. He looked at his watch. "I've got a committee in twenty minutes. Will it take long?"

Helen was relieved. Any more than a quarter of an hour with this man would be beyond the call of duty. "No, not at all. Just catching up."

"Plods?"

The cafeteria known popularly as Plods was where the many policemen who guarded the Palace of Westminster took their breaks. It was an ideal spot for a private conversation as few politicians used it.

"So, how are you, Ernie?"

"Oh, well, mustn't complain. But difficult times. Difficult times. This health business isn't easy to sell back in the constituency. You might tell the Prime Minister that. Nobody really knows what he's up to."

"I know what it's like, Ernie. It's a constant battle for all of us to remind the troops that reform isn't a one-off business. You have to keep up the momentum or you just go backwards."

"I've got a sizeable group on my General Committee who'd be more than happy to go backwards."

"But I know you do your best."

"Well I do, as a matter of fact."

"You shouldn't think it goes unnoticed, because it doesn't. Paul needs people like you and he appreciates your support."

"It's a pity we don't see more of him, though. He can't just expect us to keep on fighting his battles for him for ever."

"And he doesn't. In fact he asked me just this morning to try to arrange a meeting with some of you. He mentioned you by name."

"He did?" Ernie Harwood's back straightened slightly.

"Oh yes." She was confident Sinclair couldn't have picked him out in an identity parade if all the other suspects had been one legged dwarves. "Now tell me, what's the mood like?"

"Fidgety, I'd say."

"Well you've never been a fidgeter. It's just what Paul said he admired about you most. Your steadfastness under fire. So what do you mean by fidgety exactly?"

"Well there are those among the colleagues, not me of course, who think the plates are shifting."

"In what way?" This was proving harder work than she'd thought.

"It won't come as any surprise to you to learn that some people have more time than the Prime Minister to keep in touch with Members of Parliament."

"Go on."

"There have been a lot of invitations for backbenchers to go to events across the road at…"

"The Foreign Office."

"Quite. Lunches for the trade unions, drinks for regional party organisers, policy briefings, that sort of thing. It's always happened, of course, but there does seem to be a lot more of it just now. It's astonishing how Joanna Morgan finds the time."

"It is, isn't it? But then as Deputy Leader it's her job to keep close to the party. And I'm sure that's all she's doing." Helen held Harwood's eye long enough for him to get the message that she wanted more.

"She's very clever, you know. You need to keep an eye on her."

"Well maybe you can help me with that, Ernie. Anything you can do will be appreciated." It was obvious that Harwood knew more than he was letting on. "Greatly appreciated." This was like drawing teeth. "Very greatly appreciated."

Harwood appeared to have come to a decision. "Very well. You didn't get this from me."

Of course not, thought Helen. She knew a man who was hedging his bets when she saw one. If Joanna Morgan offered him something good he'd be with her in a shot. But she obviously hadn't, not yet. "I believe in protecting my friends. Paul's friends."

"Mrs Morgan is always very discrete. She never says anything that could rebound on her, not when I'm around anyway. But she presses all the right buttons for the party. She knows how to talk their language. And the message is always there below the surface that she would do things differently. The same can't be said for her friends, however."

"What do you mean exactly?" She was itching to tell him to cut the crap and get on with it, but Helen could be patient if she really had to be.

"Even her friends in the Cabinet."

She decided to take a risk. "We know all about Stephen Piggin."

"Well in that case," Harwood looked relieved. "You probably know what he's been up to."

"Oh, I think so." *Tell me you tight-lipped bugger.*

"He's not very subtle, our Mr Piggin. If you ask me, he thinks Paul Sinclair is about to sack him anyway so he's got nothing to lose."

"He might well be right there."

Harwood nodded sagely, thrilled to be trusted with such insider knowledge. He was warming to his theme. "After a couple of pints, and that's not unusual for Piggin even at lunchtime, his tongue gets the better of him. He's been going round virtually offering people jobs in Morgan's first government."

"And some people would be foolish enough to listen to him." People just like you, you two-faced buffoon, she thought.

"Well quite. They think it's the health service that's going to do for Sinclair. If he loses the vote you can expect a spontaneous grassroots campaign from now until Party Conference. So spontaneous that all the Morganites are ready in the big unions and so on to go to work as soon as she gives the word." He looked around him but saw only policemen tucking into piles of fried food. "As I understand it, they think that a defeat on the health bill followed by another big defeat on the conference floor and Paul will be dead wood. The party won't want a contest so close to the Election, so Morgan takes over with enough time to establish herself as PM before she has to go to the country."

"All very neat."

"That's how they see it, I'm not saying I agree with them."

"No of course not."

"People like Piggin are saying that it's now or never. Either Sinclair is gone by the autumn or they're stuck with him for another two years at least. They've done the figures and think they can do it. No wonder weaker men than me are starting to go wobbly."

39

Danny Oliver had pulled the roasted vegetables out and let them stand for a moment. The rising steam briefly obscured his view of Ruth, who had taken off her glasses to wipe them on a napkin. He looked down and realised the bottle of wine was almost empty already. Fortunately he'd little more than a glass himself. He didn't think it would help anyone if he joined her on the files of the West Midlands Police. He checked his pager. No messages. He could afford to relax a little over lunch. The office would manage without him and who could say when he and Ruth would have another opportunity like this.

He served her a large plateful and took a smaller portion himself. Long distance flights always played havoc with his digestion. They were both relieved that the business of serving the meal had forced a pause in their conversation. The subject of Joanna Morgan was an unappetising accompaniment to good food.

"So have you been busy?" It was a lame question but it gave Ruth permission to take the discussion wherever she wanted. He didn't want this to feel like an interrogation.

"I have, as a matter of fact. Busy for me, that is. Nothing compared to what you have to put up with." Danny smiled. He wasn't arguing. "I spent a few days in Brighton with mother. She's really quite ill, but the doctors seem to have some new treatment they want to try." She was tempted to tell Danny about Dr Gill but thought he'd probably heard enough about her complex emotional state. "And I saw Josh's play. He was rather impressive."

"It's good that you manage to see a fair bit of him at least."

"I'm still a mother, even if I'm not a very good one. It's tough enough for him as it is and I know he struggles to understand what's going on. We talked a bit after the play but not about anything serious."

"Do you think it would have been better if you had?"

"I don't know. He's got his exams coming up and I don't want him getting upset or distracted just now."

Danny suddenly remembered the curious woman outside the Downing Street security Vortex. "Actually I think he might be a little distracted already. He's got an admirer."

"Oh really? He didn't say anything to me about that." For some time Ruth had been terrified that her son would follow her own example and stop talking about anything personal. She couldn't bear the thought of finding herself cut off completely from all the important things that were happening with him.

Danny could see the worried look in her eyes. "Don't worry, I shouldn't have mentioned it, it's nothing serious. I don't think they've even met. Just some woman sending him love letters. A good bit older than him too, but then even I can see the attractions of an older woman sometimes." He slid his hand across the table and laid it over hers. "He's a terrific boy. You should be very proud of him. Although God only knows what he must think when he hears all the stuff that gets written about his dad. Still I guess he doesn't have to read as many newspapers as I do."

Talking about Joshua always made Ruth feel stronger. "He was brought up with it remember. I honestly think that for him there are two people, his father and the man they write about in the papers. I don't find it so easy to make the separation. That's probably one reason why I rarely read the newspapers these days. Paul's going to be all right though, isn't he? I mean, he's not going to lose or anything?"

"A year ago, maybe six months, I'd have said he was pretty much a dead cert for the next election. The going's got a lot tougher recently, though, but maybe I'm not the best person to judge. When you get so involved in every little storm that rocks the great ship of state it can be hard to see the wood for the trees."

"Promise me one thing, Danny. If you're going to mix metaphors as outrageously as that, don't become a writer. There was a piece in *The Times* just the other week, saying that people like you should never write novels. I hope you saw it."

"I thought you just said you never read the papers."

"Only the book pages and they make me angry enough." Ruth gathered up the plates and took them over to the old Belfast sink in the corner. Since she had been living alone she'd got out of another habit, that of using the dishwasher. She ran the tap and waited with her fingers under the flow for the hot water to come through.

"Shit. And fiction was going to be my next career move. I guess in that case Paul is just going to have to win the election."

Ruth had just put both hands into the washing up water when the phone in the living room started to ring. She looked over her shoulder, uncertain whether to leave it. Danny, who had to be tied down before he could let a phone go unanswered, threw her a dishcloth. "Go on, you'd better get it. I can finish in here."

He was trying various cupboards looking for coffee cups when she reappeared looking, he thought, slightly flushed. "Anything the matter?"

"No, not at all." Ruth was feeling ready to confide in Danny a little more. He was one of the few people she knew who could begin to understand. "It was Mum's doctor."

"Oh, is she all right?"

"No, I mean yes. It wasn't about my mother. He wants to take me to dinner."

Danny crossed his arms and tilted his head to one side. It was one of his few mannerisms that could be remotely described as camp. "And?"

"And what?" She wasn't going to give it all up that easily.

"Well, for a start, does he have a name?"

"Gill. Donald Gill. He's a cancer specialist and while he isn't Mum's usual doctor he seems to think there's a new trial therapy that might help her. If it can get clearance and the funding, of course."

Danny was disappointed. "So he's trying to use you to lobby Paul, is that all?"

"That's what I thought at first. I was very suspicious when he invited me for lunch."

"Lunch? I thought you said dinner?"

"We've already had lunch."

Danny added a raised eyebrow to his inquiring look. "I'm intrigued."

"In Brighton on the day of Mum's appointment. I was fully expecting him to launch into some tirade about the health reforms or something, but he didn't at all. I think he's very committed to his work. To tell you the truth I found him rather engaging."

"Engaging? That's a very novelist's word. It could cover a multitude of sins." Danny uncrossed his arms. "I'm only teasing, Ruth. If you and your very engaging doctor want to have lunch or dinner, sorry lunch *and* dinner, what business is that of anybody else's?"

"Do you really believe that?"

"In theory. Do you?"

"To be perfectly honest, I don't know what I think any more." She went over to the sink and allowed Danny to put his arms around her waist. He could feel the wet hard line of the ceramic edge press against his back as he pulled her head against his chest.

40

The duty sergeant picked up the two files that had just been placed on his desk and took them into the detectives' room. He scanned the rows of desks with an experienced eye. They always managed to look busy whenever he appeared but he wasn't fooled. Anything that came from the front desk was beneath this lot. It might mean getting their fingernails dirty when they had all those nice clean computers to play with. The sergeant's eye fell on Miles Crayton, just out of Hendon with top marks in every module and a passion for the ordinary hard-working people of London that only an Oxford graduate from the Home Counties could ever have. He was twenty-three and looked about seventeen. To his credit Miles Crayton was the first to admit he still had a lot to learn. It was the least the sergeant could do to help him with his education.

"Crayton?" The young man looked up from his psychological profiling. "If you have a moment. There's somebody out here I think you'd find it interesting to meet."

Miles got up and joined the sergeant by the door. "Bring your jacket, Crayton. We always need to make a good impression in this line of work. Meet me in interview room C."

When he came in, Miles saw only the sergeant resting his behind on the single table in the centre of the room. He took the two files from his outstretched hand.

"Take a quick look at these and I'll go and get her. I'd read the top one first. Might save you a lot of trouble. She's been sitting out there for over an hour. I can't bear looking at her any longer so you'll have to deal with her. If I were you, Crayton, I'd charge her with wasting police time and get her out of here."

At that the sergeant raised himself up and went out to collect Mrs Alma Gundry. When he brought her back into the room the young detective closed the file he was reading and held out his hand.

"Mrs Gundry? I'm Detective Constable Miles Crayton." She took a step forward and shook hands. Behind her head as he left the room the sergeant indicated his professional assessment with a twirling finger at his temple. "How can we help you?"

When she finished her account of how the Castle was threatening the well-being of every law abiding person who chose to walk along Wilson Crescent, she adjusted her scarf and gave a firm little nod as if to say that all remained to be done was to arrest the inhabitants and let justice take its course.

"Vomit, you say Mrs Gundry?"

"It was horrible. It missed me by inches and I haven't got the smell out of my coat yet." She looked as if she might be about to bring the offending article up to Miles' nose for confirmation.

"I'm sure it was very upsetting, Mrs Gundry, but people are allowed to be sick. I'm not quite sure I understand what you expect us to do."

She looked at the young man and kicked herself for not insisting on speaking to the sergeant. Although she could hardly have been more wrong, she was sure the older officer would have appreciated what she was saying. "All I'm asking is that someone helps look after us law-abiding citizens. We have rights too, you know. I want an Anti-Socialist Behaviour Order, that's what I want."

From what Miles Crayton had quickly read in the file on the Castle he thought she was probably nearer the truth than she realised. The place had once been a hotbed of anarchistic subversion, but the intelligence team that had infiltrated every left-wing group in the capital had reported that its occupants were no longer any threat. "We do take anti-so…that sort of thing very seriously, Mrs Gundry. But I see here that the police did actually visit the house in question very recently. They found no evidence of any crimes or misdemeanours. The owner, Mr…"

"Walton. PJ. That's his alias, you should make a note of that. It's him I blame. He owns the building and homeowners should show an example. I try very hard to show an example."

"Your efforts to keep your neighbours up to your standards have been, well, nothing if not persistent." Miles opened the second file. You've lived in Wilson Crescent for how long?"

"Sixty-two years. I've never lived anywhere else."

"And in that time, you've filed complaints, let me see, forty-three different times for everything from playing loud music to keeping unlicensed pigeons. You've accused Mr Walton alone of harbouring asylum seekers, environmental pollution and exhibitionism." This last one made the young detective look more closely at the notes. "Apparently if you stood on a chair in your front bedroom you could see him coming out of his bathroom."

"I was very shocked."

"You may well have been. But in all that time there hasn't been a single successful prosecution. And now you want me to add vomiting with intent to the list?"

"Young man, if I might say so, you're from a different generation. Some of us older people still believe in standards and respectability and such like. And if it means you youngsters can't go gallivanting around with no respect for those what live around you, then I'm sorry. And I may be old fashioned, I probably am, but I think the police should help me with that. I know you've got all these terrorists to look for, though you don't seem to be finding many from where I'm sitting, but it's our freedoms you're supposed to be protecting and I don't know if always you remember that." It was an impressive speech. Mrs Gundry had been waiting to make it for a very long time. Miles Crayton made a note in her file and showed her to the door.

"I hear what you're saying, Mrs Gundry."

"So what does that mean? Nothing, I suppose."

"Let me see what I can do."

The desk sergeant watched her pull her coat around her waist and step out into the chilly sunshine. "You gave her more time than I'd have done, Crayton. Did you send her away with a flea in her ear?"

"People like that are on our side you know, sergeant."

"She might be on your side, but if she's on mine then I'm in the wrong team."

Miles put the files in the tray for collection and refiling. He made a mental note to keep an eye on the Castle for a few days. It was on his way home and it was the least he could do.

41

Paul Sinclair was still in the flat. He'd asked Rebecca to cancel all avoidable engagements and, for once, she hadn't objected. The diary had been kept fairly clear in case the Washington visit over-ran. The phone on the side table rang four times before Sinclair picked it up.

"It's Mr Oliver, Prime Minister. He's in the car."

"Thanks, Switch, put him through." Sinclair could hear the hum of motorway traffic in the background. "How's she handling, Danny?" He knew how much his Communications Director loved his little MG.

"Like a dream. There's still a bit of a knock from the rear suspension. I'll take it in over the weekend."

"Where are you now?"

"Just passing Beaconsfield. What's going on? Anything on the hostages?"

"Not really. The Colonel wants me to send the troops in any time now. How is she, Danny?"

It was obvious that what was going on in Aston was preying more on the Prime Minister's mind than events in the highlands of Eritrea. "Look, I was going to go straight home but maybe I should come in and see you."

The radio was still playing eighties hits in the background. "I'd like that Danny, but I don't want to spoil your evening."

"I've got no great plans. Luke has a big case on and is going to the gym when he gets out of chambers so he won't be home till late. Asshole!"

"Was that a reference to me or your boyfriend?"

"Sorry. Some jerk in a Boxer doing a hundred and fifty." Danny Oliver could get very competitive behind the wheel. "So it's a toss up between a quick run around Sainsbury's and seeing you,"

"A hard call, I'd say."

"Yeah, but you win. I'll see you within the hour." The line clicked dead.

~

Helen Griffin went straight from the House of Commons to her own flat across the river. Ernie Harwood's warnings about Joanna's plotting had only confirmed her suspicions but there was no point trying to talk to Paul about it with the mood he was in. She found Otto's note was laying on the coffee table. It was short and to the point. He hoped they could still be friends, but felt he had to move on. Move out was what he really meant and that's just what he had done while she'd been away. Blah, blah, blah, she'd heard it all before. The only real surprise was that he hadn't done it sooner and that he'd finished the washing up before he went. She took out her mobile and dialled.

"Janine? How are you feeling? Not too knackered? Great, how about a drink?"

~

Mrs Alma Gundry turned into Wilson Crescent and was almost knocked off her feet by a young man on a motorised scooter coming the other way along the pavement. She steadied herself and took a seat on the bench outside the row of shops. She was feeling very alone against the world.

Next to where the Post Office used to be, before it was turned into an internet café, a new florist, Fleurs de Lee, had recently opened. Very classy it was too, she thought. Lots of those tall white lilies that she always used to associate with funerals, but which seemed to be very fashionable these days. And all sorts of exotic blooms in bright oranges and deep purplish blues. She had no idea what they were called but she'd taken a peek at the prices and had been suitably impressed. She could never afford them on her pension, but if the nice young couple who ran the place thought they could charge prices like that then it proved Mrs Gundry right. This part of South London was on the way up and if she had to fight a lonely fight to help it on its way then that was what she would have to do.

The young policeman had been very polite but she was sure he hadn't really understood what she was saying. To Mrs Gundry it was very simple. How could a nice shop like Fleurs de Lee hope to attract a better sort of clientele to the area if people ran the risk of being hit by flying vomit on their way down the street? She would have to think of something. A petition perhaps. But she wasn't sure how many allies she'd find if she started knocking on doors. What was it she'd seen on that programme about the Second World War the other morning? All it takes for evil to triumph is for good people to do nothing. That was it. Well Mrs Alma Gundry was a good person and that cesspool of a house wasn't going to triumph.

PJ Walton was 31 years old. He wondered if the urge to hoover whenever mothers were on their way affected all men, no matter how old they were. Would he still be doing this when he was 41? 51? Probably. Fortunately Pete and Helmut had made a good job of clearing away the malodorous pile of sick in the front garden. So all PJ had to do was to make the interior look half way presentable. He wanted to say that she could take him as she found him, but PJ's mother was no ordinary woman.

It was only at the age of 26 that PJ had decided to see if he could have a mother again. His adoptive parents had given him everything a middle class kid could hope for and hadn't been able to hide their disappointment when straight after university he'd moved to a squat in South London and put his expensive education to the benefit of left-wing politics and *Tribune*, a newspaper that, despite its noble past, was now little more than an irrelevance. They'd never visited the Castle, not even after PJ had bought it from the council, and had died together in a tragic road accident before he'd made his big break into national journalism. They would never have agreed with his politics but they would have been proud of his success. His decision to track down his natural mother had come more out of curiosity than need. But, as so often in these cases, it had proved to be a life changing experience. Tidying the house was only the start of it.

Fortunately she wouldn't get much beyond the living room, kitchen and bathroom. She wasn't very interested in how other people lived their lives, not even her son. The bathroom was the important thing.

It would have to be spotless. Mothers noticed that sort of thing.

All that remained was to ensure that Pete and Helmut were gainfully employed elsewhere. At least after the vomit incident he could be sure they'd be ready to cooperate.

42

Danny opted for the public car park under College Green. Even here he had to get out and let the security man scan both himself and the MG but thanks to Kneejerk Downing Street was now out of bounds to all vehicles except the Prime Minister's Daimler and the support vehicles.

He walked the half mile or so past Parliament Square and into Whitehall. As he came alongside the Foreign Office he wondered, as he always did, what Joanna Morgan was up to. One reason Danny was good at his job was that he found politicians and journalists and the games they played frighteningly easy to understand. With every leak and off-the-record story he read, Danny only had to ask himself one simple question. Who did it benefit? The answer was usually the same. But Joanna was clever. Take the Naked Prophet. His column pushed her view of the world on an almost daily basis but every so often it would feature a story critical of the Foreign Office. Whenever it did she would invariably put on a great show of indignation and demand that Danny find out who the mysterious columnist really was.

Maybe if he could persuade Kneejerk that the Foreign Secretary was herself a threat to national security he could get him to start tapping her phones. Now that would be interesting. But the more he thought about it, the more likely it seemed that the Colonel was already at it. Danny didn't rule out the possibility that his own phone was tapped. It was one reason he always carried a private mobile, the pay-as-you-go kind much favoured by criminals by all accounts. A guy had to have a little privacy, after all.

He showed his pass at the entrance to the Vortex and stepped inside the human scanner. The airlock shut behind him and Danny felt that familiar queasiness in the pit of his stomach. The cameras filmed and the sensors sniffed. One of these days the doors would fail to open on the other side and they'd have to send a rescue party with cutting gear before he ran out of oxygen. The thing always made him feel like a miner trapped miles underground, unseen and forgotten by the outside world.

Paul Sinclair was waiting for him with his feet up on the sofa in the flat, where he'd been for most of the day. He'd taken off his shoes and Danny noticed holes in both of his socks. "Come on in Danny. What can I get you? Tea? Coffee? It's only instant I'm afraid."

Since time immemorial, official catering in Downing Street had been available only for official functions. There was no domestic support provided for the Prime Minister at Number 10. Nobody to cook him meals, mend his socks or buy him a new pair. It must have been easier when Ruth was in residence, but given her talents in the kitchen he wasn't so sure. Did either of them know how to boil an egg?

"Yeah, that would be great. It's been a long drive." He followed Sinclair as he padded into the kitchen and put the kettle on.

"Did you tell her, Danny?" asked Sinclair over his shoulder.

"That I knew about Joanna? Yes, I told her. She assumed I'd known for a long time, which quite frankly I should have done. Tell me one thing. Does Helen know?"

Sinclair was filling the kettle from the sink under the kitchen window. He had to raise his voice a little to be heard above the running water. "She worked it out. She was running my office, if not my life, back then too. I'd have been disappointed in her if she hadn't guessed. So how is Ruth bearing up?"

"She's worried we all think she's falling apart and was at great pains to make it clear she isn't. She's certainly drinking a bit, but she knows she's got to do something about that."

"Did she seem…happy?"

Although they had become genuine friends, or as genuine as it was possible to be in politics, Danny still found it difficult to discuss intimate subjects with the Prime Minister. "I don't know if I could say that. She's working hard on her new book."

"I should go and see her myself. I've been feeling terrible that I even asked you to go. I want her to know that I understand what she must be going through. She doesn't have to live in the middle of all this," he gestured around him vaguely, "and maybe that's a good thing, but she's still Mrs Paul Sinclair. She can hardly live a normal life."

"No, she can't and she doesn't." He hesitated before going on. Ruth had had a few glasses of wine, but she hadn't been drunk when she'd told him about the engaging Dr Gill. She knew Danny had gone all the way to Birmingham at Paul's behest, so wouldn't she expect him to report back on what she'd said? He still wasn't sure whether to say anything until he reminded himself of his own advice. Better to find out from someone you can trust than to find out from the newspapers. "I'm going to put this very carefully, Paul. Not because I want to protect your feelings, but because I don't want to make it sound more dramatic than it is. Ruth is getting some attention from, well, from a man obviously. Her mother's doctor. Please don't read more into it than that. But it's better you should know."

Sinclair stood with a spoonful of coffee hovering over the mug in front of him. It was a possibility he'd considered many times, but that didn't make it any easier to hear it confirmed. Ruth was still a very attractive woman. He couldn't expect her to sit at home with her computer writing about the past all her life. She had a right to a future and he'd forfeited any right of his own to have a say in it. He let the coffee cascade into the mug and poured water from the kettle on top. "Thanks, Danny. I appreciate your telling me." He meant what he said.

The Prime Minister sniffed the milk and frowned.

"It's all right, Paul," said Danny. "I like it black."

~

Half a mile away Joshua emerged, blinking into the daylight of St Martin's Lane. His senses had been fooled by the darkness of the theatre. He'd been expecting it to be dark outside too, but the clocks hadn't yet gone back and there was still some weak late afternoon sunshine.

"Are you coming down the pub, Josh?" Charlie Gauthier was up for a good night out.

"Sweet Mephistopheles, thou pleasest me."

"Give it a rest will you? Is that a yes or a no?"

"I dunno," Joshua hesitated. "The last time we went to a pub in the West End I had to escape to the bogs after that bunch of wankers started taking the piss, remember? It's so boring."

"Oh, come on Josh, we'll go somewhere dark and dingy so you can hide in a corner. Nobody will recognise you. Jim's coming." The Head of Drama, who was less than ten years older than his sixth form pupils, had allowed them the familiarity of calling him by his first name. "He says his girlfriend might pop down later, too. And she's fit."

"O thou bewitching fiend." Joshua looked round to where Jim Clements was rounding up the rest of the group in the foyer. "Okay. I'm gonna pop home and change and I'll meet you there. Which pub are you going to?"

"It's all right for some, living in the centre of London. We'll be in the Trevilley Arms. It's the one just down the road on the right."

"I know it. I'll see you in half an hour or so."

Joshua put his bag over his shoulder and pushed his way through the crowd that had gathered outside the theatre. The truth was, he'd come out without his wallet and he didn't want his mates to think he was some kind of spoiled brat who wouldn't even buy a round. It was only a ten minute walk back down to Downing Street and even allowing for the time it took to get through the Vortex he could be back in the pub in half an hour.

When he opened the flat door Joshua heard the sound of conversation coming from the kitchen. He paused in the hall and listened. It was the voice of Danny Oliver that he heard first.

"If you want my opinion, she has to make up her mind. Either she's got to support you, in which case she needs to do it publicly and wholeheartedly, or she should get out and let you get on with it without her. She can't have it both ways. "

His father interrupted. He sounded weary. "All right, Danny, I hear what you say."

"If you don't believe me talk to Helen. She's probably better at reading women's minds than me anyway."

Sinclair laughed. "You don't seem to be doing too badly, Danny. Considering."

Joshua's mobile phone, zipped into the strap of his bag, emitted a shrill warble as a text message arrived. The voices in the kitchen went quiet. "Hey, Dad," he shouted.

"Hi Josh, come on in. Danny's here." Joshua liked Danny Oliver.

He wasn't too stuffy and boring like most of his father's political colleagues. He even went clubbing occasionally, or at least he used to, and had told him some lurid tales of wild nights out on the gay scene. And he took the trouble to keep in touch with his mother too, something Joshua knew she appreciated. He hoped it wasn't her that Danny had just been referring to.

"Hi Danny, how's it going?" Danny beamed. He enjoyed Joshua's company every bit as much as Joshua enjoyed his. Left alone together they could easily fall into the kind of camaraderie that took both of them far away from the surreal world in which they lived. Danny was tempted to reach out and give the boy a hug but he hesitated. This was just the kind of occasion, very rare but intensely annoying nevertheless, when he felt constrained by his sexuality. He hadn't the slightest interest in guys of Joshua's age and he was sure Joshua knew that. But Paul? He felt himself holding himself back from expressing any kind of affection in case Paul misinterpreted it and he kicked himself for it. In that moment of awkwardness he forgot about his tirade against Joanna Morgan. "I'm great, Josh, what about you?"

"Yeah, not bad. I was about to go down the pub, if you fancy it."

"Not this time, I need to be getting home." Luke would be back from the gym soon. Danny picked up his car keys and mobile phone. "Let me know as soon as you hear anything on the hostages. I can be back here in half an hour. And, honestly," he put a hand on the Prime Minister's shoulder as he left, "it's going to be all right."

Paul Sinclair nodded. He would speak to Ruth himself and try to find a way of helping her through all this, if she would let him. But how much more was going on inside his family that he knew nothing about? He realised he barely knew what his son was up to half the time.

"Who are you meeting in the pub?" Then, worried that he might be accused of prying, "not that it's any of my business."

"Just the guys from the Drama Club. Mr Clements will be there too. Maybe you should come along."

"Maybe I should. God, if you only knew how tempting that sounds right now."

Joshua could see the longing in his father's face. "Even you deserve a life, Dad."

"Thank you, that's very sweet of you. I wish everyone could see it like that. Josh…"

"Huh?"

"I think we should all, you know, maybe talk a bit more."

"Oh here we go. I was waiting for this. I suppose you want to ask me about the letter?"

"Actually I wasn't thinking about that."

"Well you're going to have to know about it sometime." Joshua could see the hand of Kneejerk behind all this somewhere and the last thing he wanted was the man on his back any more than he was already. Much better to clear the air now.

"It's none of my business."

"No, you're right, it's not. But since you've seen it."

"Colonel Neilson thinks you're being stalked. He may have the woman in the Tower already, I should warn you."

So he was right. That uptight Scottish bastard. "I hope not, Dad. She hasn't done anything wrong." Joshua pulled up the other stool and sat next to his father. "Her name's Evie. I met her on the internet." Sinclair let his son continue without admitting that the Colonel had told him that much already. "It's nothing seedy or anything, you don't have to worry. It's just, I don't know, you've no idea what it's like for me. The girls at school always see me as the Prime Minister's son first and Josh Sinclair a distant second. They either get all haughty and snotty or giggly and girly. I can't win. I mean they're such a bunch of kids anyway, not really my type."

"So Evie is…"

"Older, yeah. Twenty-eight she said, but on the net you can never be too sure. She looked fit though, from her picture."

"So you've never met her?"

"No. Never. If you really want to know, Dad, I messed up. I thought she might be different. It started off all anonymous like it always does." He smiled, and thought what the hell, he'd come this far. "She was Heidi Hounslow and I was," he sighed, "Premiership Lad"

Paul Sinclair laughed at the allusion. "Nice one, Josh. Go on."

"Well we chatted for what seemed like weeks. She was very into theatre, she'd travelled a lot. She didn't treat me like a kid or like some kind of freak either. She seemed really into me for just being me. So, anyway, she sent me a photo and I really fancied her. She's a good looking woman. She kept asking for one of me and eventually I gave in. I didn't want her to get bored and go after someone else, I suppose. It was quite a distant shot, in my football kit, all muddy and that. I didn't think she'd recognise me, but of course she did. And then she started getting really pushy, wanting to meet up and everything. I guess I got cold feet, or else something just felt wrong all of a sudden. Anyway, I stopped answering her messages and I logged off whenever I saw she'd come on line. But by then it was too late, she knew where to find me. Sorry, it was a bit stupid I know."

Sinclair put an arm round his son's shoulder and he wasn't rebuffed. "I'm not going to say I know how you feel, but I understand better than you think."

"I mean, I know you and Mum don't see much of each other." That was another conversation Sinclair was going to have with his son. "But at least she's there. What am I supposed to do? Go out on the pull and bring someone back here? Kneejerk would frisk her at the door."

"I can understand that."

"The net gives me some freedom and some privacy. Until I blow my own cover, of course. But it's not exactly the real thing is it?"

Sinclair looked at him and wondered how much he knew about the real thing. He'd assumed that at seventeen Joshua was probably sexually active by now, but they'd never discussed it except obliquely, by way of a joke.

"And now to think that Colonel Bloody Kneejerk knows all about it." Joshua's embarrassment was giving way to anger.

"I've already told him that this is none of his business."

"He thinks everything is his business."

"I know he does, but he's going to have to learn. Leave him to me." He laughed. "Premiership Lad, huh?"

"I thought it was the only way I was ever going to score." Joshua cringed at his own joke.

"That was awful."

"Yeah I know, sorry." They were both laughing now. "Maybe I'd better find myself a new handle."

"Forget about the internet for an evening. Just go out and enjoy yourself with some real people. You shouldn't have to hide behind some alias. Go on, go out and have a good time." He handed his son a twenty euro note. "And have one on me, I really wish I could join you."

Joshua took the money and slipped it into his jeans. He was feeling a lot better and remembered the Drama Group waiting for him in the pub. "Let me have a wife, the fairest maid in Germany, for I am wanton and lascivious and cannot live without a wife."

"Well let's not rush into things, shall we?" But Joshua was already rooting out his favourite shirt. Suddenly, something clicked in the Prime Minister's mind. A connection that simply hadn't occurred to him before. "Just one thing. Where did you send your e-mails from?"

"Well not the school computers, that's for sure. There are no secrets on those things. I used the laptop in the study. I thought it would be more secure. I mean," he laughed "Kneejerk is always telling me that I have to think about security." His father was laughing too by the time Joshua clattered out of the flat's front door and down the stairs.

43

It was still early evening and the café bar where Helen and Janine were sitting was quiet. It was one of those places that made most of its money at lunchtimes serving expensive meals to city people and PR executives on expense accounts. The view out over Tower Bridge was one of the best along this stretch of the Thames. They had both ordered the pasta special, something with lots of vegetables that they had convinced themselves must be healthy. Janine was sipping a glass of white wine and Helen had already downed her Bloody Mary and was waiting for the second. The only other customers were a group of already slightly drunk young men in rugby shirts at a table on the other side of the room. Janine had scanned them with an expert eye as soon as they arrived.

"What do you think of the one in the blue top?" she asked.

Helen didn't even look round. "I'm really not in the mood."

"What's this? Has Lady Diamond finally discovered she's not so resilient after all? Your builder..."

"Architect."

"Your architect was a bit of a catch. I'm sure it's not too late, you know, for a rear guard action." Janine was watching the muscular behind of the rugby player in the blue shirt as he went towards the toilets.

"I don't have time for all that, darling. It's crap cutting time."

"You only got back from Washington this morning. Surely you can relax for an evening."

"I wish, darling. I really shouldn't be here at all. Things are getting pretty serious back at the ranch. This hostage thing could turn nasty at any minute. It's the last thing we need right now. Paul's little bit of straight talking on the NHS has given the useless wimps on our backbenches all the excuse they need to rebel tomorrow. Half of them are already panicking about the next election. Joanna Morgan's wagons are getting ready to circle, and Paul Nice Guy Sinclair doesn't seem to know what's about to hit him. So it's not the best time to go chasing around London after the lovely Otto. Although, you're right, he was lovely. What's your reading of it all? You're a political correspondent."

"I'm glad you spotted that at last. And in case you've forgotten, I'm also the author of a soon-to-be best selling biography of your Mr Nice Guy. Remember? The book you're supposed to be helping me with, despite all the evidence to the contrary."

"This is important. I'm talking about the here and now, Janine. Unless you want to be writing the biography of a has-been."

"Nice try. I'll do you a deal."

"Deal?" Helen didn't like the sound of that.

"I'll tell you just how deep I think the shit is."

"That's what I was hoping."

"And in return you'll tell me all about life as Paul Sinclair's dark lady. And I mean all."

Helen pretended to look unsure. It was the best deal she'd been offered for a very long time. "You've got it," she said as if the concession had been wrung out of her.

"You're right. Joanna Morgan and her cronies are on the move. I've never seen them so confident. For the past couple of years or so all they've done is give stories to their friends on the *Guardian* and to the Naked Prophet on the *Mirror*, of course. Now they're talking to just about anyone who'll listen. Not Joanna herself, she's too clever. But people who count. If they're going to do something they want to be sure the press is going to fall in behind her at the critical time. And they way things are right now, I think they will. Paul's looking weak all of a sudden and when the press get the smell of weakness they can be pretty ruthless."

"You're beginning to sound just like Danny."

"Well, he knows what he's talking about. You should listen to him. I mean what was all that bollocks about Sinclair stopping for a hamburger on the way back from the airport and then no, it wasn't a burger it was for a breath of fresh air? Little things like that count for a lot when the mood has shifted against you. If he loses tomorrow, well, I wouldn't like to be in your shoes."

"We're not beaten yet, darling, I for one am not about to be the

Chief of Staff who watches her party or her Prime Minister go crashing to defeat. He's stronger than you give him credit for. He's not going to give up and nor am I." She hoped to God she was right.

"Lady Diamond lives, okay, I get it. So, come on it's your turn. You've seen mine now show me yours."

"That's easy, Janine. And this is on the record. I am not and never have been Paul Sinclair's so-called dark lady. You're on the wrong track."

"Oh, come on, Helen."

"Don't you 'come on' me. It's true that I quite fancied him when I first met him. You should have seen him in those days."

"He's still in pretty good shape now."

Helen wrinkled her nose. "Well maybe. I'm too close to tell any more. But his judgement isn't always what it could be and the feelings were not mutual. I never got a sniff."

"You expect me to believe that?"

"Yes, I do. Because it happens to be true."

"So why have you never denied it when it's been in the gossip columns?"

"Danny says if you deny everything then the press just keep on guessing until they get it right. Sometimes it's better to just let things sit there."

Janine had seen Helen's deadly earnest look enough times to know not to argue. "So long as people assumed it was you they never bothered looking for the real dark lady?"

"Your words not mine, darling."

"Well, for once you're being more helpful than you think."

"That's what I was afraid of."

Janine looked around the bar and back at her friend. She shook her head slowly. "Well bugger me. And I had visions of you two consoling each other after a long day dismantling the NHS. I thought maybe that's why you weren't too bothered when the latest little Otto or whoever packed up his toothbrush and left."

"Yeah well, we can't have everything." The bar was starting to fill up and the table of rugby players had been joined by another half dozen men. It looked like the beginning of a pub crawl. The very thought of it made Helen weary. "I think I might go back to married men, though, they're so much less demanding."

"I know what you mean. But let's face it, we've both been there. Married men never keep themselves in such good shape as the single ones. Men are just naturally lazy. They only make sure they're looking good if they have to. Never let them get too comfortable, that's what I say."

"Yes, darling, you're right of course. But what I need is somebody who's there for a bit of good sex and a laugh and the odd night out. Without all these hang-ups and demands and sulks and everything else. Is that too much to ask?"

"But only on your terms, right? When it fits in with your schedule?"

Helen sighed. She knew her friend was right, she was asking for too much.

"There are alternatives, you know." Janine had a glint in her eye. At the same time she had caught the eye of the man in the blue shirt, who'd taken it as a sign of encouragement and looked as if he might come over.

"No, darling, I tried that. Too cold and the batteries kept going flat."

"I didn't mean that. Here." Janine took a card out of her purse and pushed it across the table. "I've used them occasionally, they're very discreet."

Helen read the words on the card and looked up at her friend. "Angels and Demons?"

"Yeah, you sort of get to choose. I usually went for the demons. There's even a web site so you can see what you're getting. They're not especially cheap, but when needs must..."

"And have you really...?"

"My mates and I was wondering if you'd like to join us for a drink ladies?" It was the man in blue. Helen quickly put the card in her pocket and glared at Janine. She took the message.

"Not just now, but thanks for asking. Maybe later." She gave him the merest hint of a wink as he made his way a little unsteadily back to his friends' table.

"Honestly, Janine."

"Don't you 'honestly' me. You wouldn't have hesitated not that long ago and you know it. If young Scott Bolton wasn't waiting for me…"

"The boy from the newsroom?"

"Hmmm. I'd say an angel with definite demon tendencies. He's becoming a bit of a star in his own right, actually. His bloody Neighbours From Hell feature gets ten times more viewers than my stuff on politics, but are we surprised? I just hope he doesn't get too big for his boots. Mind you," she grinned, "he does have very big boots. Anyway, think about what I've said. What have you got to lose? A lot of women who can't afford to get caught out for one reason or another use them. That's one reason why they're a little more expensive."

They were interrupted by a loud cough. "Excuse me, ladies."

"Now look…" Helen swivelled round in her chair ready to give whichever of the rugby team had decided to chance his luck a ruder brush off this time. But whoever these two were they weren't members of the 1st XV, nor the second or third either. The short fat one looked as if he couldn't run more than twenty metres without needing to sit down for a rest. As for the tall one with the long dangling arms, while he might have something to offer on a basketball court, he didn't look like the sporty type either.

Helmut and Pete weren't sure if they were still being punished for the vomit incident, or if PJ just wanted them out of the way while his mum paid a visit. Probably the latter as he'd given them fifty euros to enjoy themselves once they'd done their duty. In a bag over Pete's shoulder were two hundred leaflets calling on the good people of South London to rise up against the destruction of their health service. Helmut said it would be bad for business if he showed up handing out flyers in any of his usual haunts, especially as he had nothing more interesting to offer his clients after the disaster of his latest recipe. So Pete had suggested walking the mile or so up to the fancy pubs by the river where nobody would know them.

"Excuse me, ladies."

The woman with her back to them had swivelled round in her chair so fast and so aggressively that Pete took a step back in surprise. He handed her a leaflet.

"Demonstration against the health cuts," he blurted out.

"They're not cuts, they're reforms," snapped Helen in reply. Janine put a hand on her friend's arm to warn her this wasn't the time.

231

"Paul Sinclair wants to sell off the NHS," went on Pete, "he's said so himself. We have to fight for it or we'll lose it." He'd learnt his lines well. "You can write to your MP too."

Helen thought that if her MP even considered voting No his life wouldn't be worth living, but she just looked at this funny elongated man and his fat little friend. Was this really all they were up against?

"It's a class issue," said Helmut. Pete looked down at him in surprise. It was the longest sentence he'd uttered all day.

"Is it now?" said Janine, taking a leaflet. "That's very interesting. We'll give it some thought." The lanky one was obviously a fool, but there was something she couldn't put her finger on about the overweight one. Something almost sexy. She watched them go over to the men at the other table who now looked even more drunk.

"How would it be if I solved a problem for you, instead of just creating them all the time?" Sinclair had called Danny at home just as he and Luke were about to settle down for dinner and a decent bottle of wine. Fresh from the gym, Luke still had a glow about him that made him look even more attractive than usual. Despite his jet-lag Danny had been about to suggest putting the meal in the oven to keep warm for half an hour. There were times when even a call from the Prime Minister was unwelcome.

"That would make a nice change. Tell me more."

"To be honest, we've both been a bit stupid. We probably should have worked this out days ago. It's about my secret lover."

Knowing that Luke was listening, Danny repeated what he'd heard out loud. "Oh yes, Prime Minister. Your secret lover. Are you going to tell me who she is?"

"You already know, Danny. You've met her."

Danny took Luke's hand as he played out the game. "I've met her? Not Rebecca, your ever-faithful Diary Secretary? Or, don't tell me, the woman who brings us coffee in the mornings? I thought there was always a twinkle in her eye."

All three of them were laughing by now. "Seriously," said Paul, "you can ring Alastair and tell him to forget it. I've been carrying a letter from the woman around with me for the past two days too. I think you'll find the woman who's husband is so hot under the collar has an infatuation for my son, not me. Joshua was using the laptop here in the study and the computers are all networked together. So it could easily have looked as if it came from me."

Danny was looking more serious now. "Well done Sherlock Holmes. So you want me to ring the *Daily Mirror* and tell them your son has been chatting up older women on the internet and using a Number 10 computer to do it. You don't think that might just make a story?"

"I hadn't thought of that. No, keep Josh out of it. Damn." He no longer felt so pleased with himself. "Sorry I disturbed your evening, Danny. Maybe I'd better just leave media strategy up to you."

"That's probably not such a bad idea." The Communications Director put down the phone and picked up his fork. He was suddenly feeling more tired than he'd realised.

44

Detective Constable Miles Crayton had walked past the Castle many times on his way home but had never really looked at the building properly. It was true that the derelict site next door where the end of terrace house had collapsed was a bit of a mess, but the Castle itself didn't seem that much worse than many of the older properties around here. He felt he knew the inside of the house already. The Special Branch infiltration team had left a detailed account of it in the file. It couldn't have changed much in the three years since they'd declared the occupants no longer a threat to the state.

Now all the Castle threatened, it seemed, was the peace of mind of Mrs Alma Gundry. Miles looked at her admittedly much neater terraced house across the street. He saw the curtain in the front window twitch and was neither surprised nor concerned. It couldn't do any harm if she knew he was checking out her complaint in person.

The privet hedge in front of the Castle was threadbare and looked as if it had been attacked by some disease. Miles stepped on to the short path that led up to the front door. He knew he was still well within his rights when investigating a complaint from the public. There was certainly a funny smell in the small front garden, but he couldn't immediately identify it as vomit. It was more like something that had recently died. He followed his nose along the edge of the privet and then stopped when he heard a sound from inside the house. Through the net curtaining on the dirty front window he could see the shape of a man busy with a vacuum cleaner in the hallway. This didn't exactly accord with Mrs Gundry's account of a hovel that hadn't been cleaned in years. The light was on inside and Miles was fairly confident he couldn't be seen in the early evening shadow, but he didn't want to have to explain his presence if he could help it so he crouched down waiting for the man to disappear.

When a car pulled up outside, Miles cursed his bad timing. The figure in the hallway had vanished but he still couldn't move. He heard a woman's voice telling the driver to wait for her around the corner. The car door slammed and the woman stepped onto the path. As she did so there was a scurrying noise behind him and a large white cat appeared from beneath the hedge. It had a dead vole in its mouth. The woman turned to face the noise and saw Miles still crouching down with a look of panic in his eyes. The look turned to astonishment as he straightened his back and took two steps forward.

"And who might you be, young man?"

"Detective Constable Miles Crayton. I'm sorry Foreign Secretary, I…"

Joanna Morgan didn't give him a chance to finish. "This is most unsatisfactory. I gave very clear instructions that I wanted no security back up."

Miles' brain was working overtime but getting nowhere. This wasn't something they prepared you for at Hendon Police Academy. "Just routine surveillance, Foreign Secretary. We've had complaints about this house. We…I thought I should monitor it for…irregularities."

She fixed him with her most intimidating stare, one that had tamed many a stronger adversary than Miles Crayton. "Detective. Do you think that any house where I was paying a visit would be subject to irregularities, as you so quaintly put it?"

"No, of course not."

"Exactly. Of course not. You may take it from me that this house requires no surveillance, routine or otherwise. Do I make myself clear?"

"Perfectly."

"And Detective. Detective Constable Miles Crayton." She made quite sure he knew she had his name. "As this house requires no surveillance, all you have to do is go back to the station and make sure that's on file. No need to make any report on your little clandestine operation here tonight. I'm sure we understand each other." Miles didn't understand at all, but he had a strong suspicion that crossing the Foreign Secretary wasn't going to be a good career move. "That will be all, Detective."

He darted out onto the pavement and around the corner. Ray Morgan, who had the heater on and was listening to the Thursday Night Concert had his eyes closed as Miles passed by.

Ruth handed her coat and bag in at the cloakroom and went over to the woman with the large reservations book propped up on a wooden lectern.

"I'm meeting Dr Gill."

"Yes, madam, he's waiting for you at the table. Shall I take you over?"

"No, I think I'll just pop to the ladies, if you'll excuse me."

With her compact in one hand Ruth looked at herself in the bathroom mirror. She had very nearly phoned to cancel the appointment from the taxi, but had decided that her uncertainty about what she was doing was no excuse for bad manners. She didn't begin to understand this man's motives, a man she barely knew, and yet a man who had somehow left her feeling like an awkward teenager on a first date. She told herself she was far too old to be impressed by his looks and his charm. He aroused her curiosity, but there was nothing wrong with that, and he seemed to care as deeply about his work as she did about her mother's health. Put like that she had every good reason to be here.

She took a deep breath and reached into her bag for her bottle of perfume.

PJ ran to the door as soon as he heard the knock. He had a feeling his mother wouldn't want to be left standing on the doorstep for too long.

"How nice to see you," he said. "It's been too long."

"It has and it's my fault, I know that. What can I say?" She stepped inside and looked around. Nothing seemed to have changed since her last visit over three years before. On that occasion she had been the nervous one. Joanna Morgan didn't like to be in situations that she couldn't completely control. Inevitably the shock of having the son she'd given up for adoption track her down had been tempered by the knowledge that it had been almost certain to happen at some time, but no amount of intellectual preparation had readied her for the emotional impact of seeing him. On that first occasion her eyes had instantly searched his face for traces of his father's likeness and she had been pleased to find enough but not too many.

Not for the first time or the last she was thankful to have found a man as loyal and trusting as Ray with whom to share her life. He'd taken to PJ immediately, and accepted him into their lives. He wasn't the kind of man to make demands. There was no reason why the events of over thirty years ago should upset the delicate balance of their lives together now. He had accepted that if she couldn't say who the father had been, then so be it.

It was PJ himself who'd had the most difficulty in adjusting. Nothing had prepared him for the discovery that the mother he'd so often fantasised about was a woman he'd seen a thousand times already on the television. And he quickly learned that she had only one way of relating to anybody and that was on her own terms. At first, when she'd said she didn't want their relationship to be a part of the soap opera of politics, he'd admired her. Then, when he realised it would mean only occasional meetings over lunch or dinner in restaurants away from Westminster or being entered in her diary as official business, he was less sure. There was no father's name on his original birth certificate and when, in answer to his questions on the subject, she'd said she couldn't tell him he hadn't been listening for a politician's double speak. He thought she didn't know herself.

Even after three years their relationship could hardly be described as warm. He saw and spoke to Ray more often than he did to his own mother. And what her husband made of being the go-between for mother and son as well as politician and journalist nobody knew because nobody bothered to ask.

"Come in." PJ took a deep breath and felt the constriction in his windpipe. He couldn't stop himself feeling let down. He should have been able to look forward to welcoming her to his home again, but she hadn't made that easy.

"Doesn't your mother deserve a kiss?"

He leant forward and kissed her on both cheeks, which felt very unemotional. "It's good to see you. Are you on your own?"

"Yes, Ray's happy to wait in the car."

"Can I get you anything?"

"Maybe a cup of coffee. Where shall we go?" She could see that the living room had been tidied and cleaned but it still had no proper curtains and being spotted and recognised once tonight had been once too often. "How about the kitchen? I seem to remember it's very cosy in there."

She sat at the table as PJ fiddled with the cafetière. "It's funny, isn't it?" he said over his shoulder. "I'd sort of imagined finding a mother who'd take me for tea at Fortnum and Mason's. Although a rum and coke at the pub at the end of her road would have done just as well. For some reason, making coffee for the Foreign Secretary in my own back kitchen in Bermondsey just hadn't occurred to me."

She looked carefully at the tablecloth before deciding it was clean enough to rest her arms on. "I know, I'm sorry. By the time we met it was a bit late for all that. It's always a pleasure to see you, though. I only wish we could do this more often. I do hope you understand why we can't."

"I try to." It was the best he could manage. He'd realised some time ago that keeping their relationship private had little to do with protecting him from the glare of the media. At first her help with his career had seemed like the best gift she'd been able to give him. Now, however, her regular drip-feed of political inside information had become something of a drug on which they were both dependent. It no longer felt healthy at all. He picked up the carton of milk and turned to the table. "You know, I think I might start supporting the opposition."

"I'm sorry? Your conversation can be very hard to follow sometimes, you know. Are you all right?"

"It's just that maybe if you lost office we'd have the time to get to know each other properly at last." He sounded as uncertain as he felt. He had a real fear that the more he got to know his mother the less he might like her.

She laughed again as if to convince herself he was joking. "I don't think we need to go in for quite such drastic measures, do you? We were apart a very long time. It won't do any harm to take a little while to get to know each other. And, besides, I'm here now aren't I?"

He nodded and sat down opposite her. "And why is that? I've been nagging Ray to arrange something for months. Are you sure it doesn't have something to do with the fact that I've refused to run with one of your stories for once?"

She was eyeing the pile of newspapers waiting for recycling beside the waste bin. "I thought it was the sort of thing you liked. You've been making quite a name for yourself with your articles on the health issue. I don't see what was so different about this one."

"Really?"

"Absolutely."

"You can't see any difference between a story about Paul Sinclair's declared views on the NHS and one about the private medical details of his mother-in-law? Nothing at all?"

"Of course there's a difference. But if it helps her get the treatment she needs, isn't that a morally good thing to have done? The NHS that I came into public life to defend should be there for people like her."

"And that's a very laudable sentiment. I just find it hard to accept that the Deputy Leader of the Labour Party can't win a political argument like that without leaking the confidential health records of a sick old lady."

Joanna Morgan looked pained. "I'm sorry you feel like that. I really was trying to do what I thought was best. Believe me. But I can see you feel very strongly about this and I respect that. Let's not let it spoil our evening, shall we? Do you think I might have some of that coffee now?"

45

As they all clambered on to the top deck of the bus, Pete looked for a spare seat and sat down with his long legs sticking out into the aisle. It had been a long time since anyone had so much as invited him out for a drink, never mind a pub crawl. The rugby players seemed a nice enough bunch, although he'd have to do a bit of catching up on the alcohol front. He fingered the 50 euro note in his pocket and wondered how much a round would cost. Helmut took the seat in front of him and spread himself out so there was no possibility of anybody sitting next to him. He could think of no good reason why they were on a bus heading for the West End but recognised that his options were limited. His girlfriend was at work and he was banned from her house when she wasn't there, he had no drugs to offload on the space cadets of South London and PJ had made it very clear he wasn't welcome at the Castle tonight. He consoled himself with the solitary thought that, compared to the dubious company in the last bar Pete had dragged him into, at least these men were probably heterosexual and might keep their clothes on.

By the time they reached the Trevilley Arms, by way of two pubs in the Strand, the sportsmen were getting rowdy. The barmen eyed them warily but judged it prudent not to try to evict all fifteen of them on his own.

Joshua looked over Charlie Gauthier's shoulder as they came in. He'd been hoping the pub would stay quiet but at least these guys looked too pissed and too involved in their own banter to take much notice of anybody else. Jim Clements was in good form, nothing like a teacher really, although his girlfriend had failed to show up so far. Maybe his stories of undergraduate sexual adventures would have been less interesting if she had.

"I can't wait to get to college," Joshua said to no-one in particular. "Free at last, free at last!"

Charlie reached under the table and grabbed both Joshua's knees. He was a good enough mate not to embarrass him in front of their friends. He leant over and whispered in his ear. "Going to lose that precious virginity at last are we, you naughty boy?"

"Lose it? I'll be ready to give it away on street corners. Anyway," he said, pushing Charlie back into his seat, "where's all the talent you promised me, eh? I thought you knew how to show a boy a good time?"

"Patience, my man. The night is young. Your time will come."

"Yeah, well I'm going for a piss." He got up and went over to the far side of the bar where he'd spotted the Gents on the way in. One of the rugby team passed him on his way out but didn't even look at him. The cubicles were all occupied so he went over to the stainless steel urinals against the back wall. Like most teenagers, Joshua had done his fair share of secretly comparing sizes in the showers after games and had seen enough appendages to feel confident that if his time ever did come he wasn't going to feel inadequate. If he hadn't noticed out of the corner of his eye that the guy standing beside him was so tall, Joshua might not have looked his way and seen him tuck a longer penis than he'd imagined possible back into his trousers. Suddenly embarrassed that his stare might have been misunderstood he focused on the man's lapel badge which was level with Joshua's face.

"Sweet F.A. What's that all about then?"

Pete was feeling a little sore that his new found friends out in the bar were ignoring him. While Helmut had surprised him yet again with a hitherto hidden knowledge of rugby, Pete had been left on the margins of the group with nobody to talk to. "You really want to know?"

"Sure." Joshua was conscious of being pee shy and really just wanted the man to leave him alone for a minute.

"Come on then, I'll buy you a drink and tell you all about it. What will you have?"

"A pint of John Smith's. Thank you very much."

Janine dropped Helen off outside her front door and apologised again at having to leave her. "Young Scott is here there and everywhere filming his Neighbours from Hell, so while he's here I feel I have to make the most of him."

"That's okay, darling. Enjoy yourself. And I don't want to hear all about, got it?"

Janine pulled out into the flow of traffic and stalled. The van coming up behind her had to swerve to avoid a collision and the driver leant hard on his horn. Through the rear window, Helen could see her friend offering him a small apologetic wave. She unlocked the front door and went upstairs into the cold flat. She switched on the heating and thought about pouring herself a drink. Her first call was to Downing Street to make sure there were no developments in the hostage crisis. For her second, she needed a large gin and tonic.

"As soon as possible, to be quite honest." She took a long slug and felt a comforting tingle as the gin hit her stomach. "Oh, I don't know. I think I'll start with an Angel."

By the time he'd finished, Pete, who was more than a little drunk, had made the Freedom Alliance sound like a tantalising mix of liberation movement, anti-establishment crusade and campaign group for free love. He wasn't used to people taking such an interest in what he had to say and he didn't want to disappoint the boy. Joshua already had a leaflet in his pocket and Pete's own 'Sweet F.A.' badge on his shirt. He saw Pete Morley as everything Kneejerk would despise and that made him a very attractive proposition.

"It's open house, so drop in whenever you like. We're always looking for new recruits to the cause." Pete was getting carried away and starting to believe his own fantasy. That the South London Freedom Alliance hadn't met for over three years and now existed as little more than a name and a logo on the posters that very occasionally emerged from the Castle workshop seemed to have slipped his memory.

"Cheers. Well I'd better go and join my friends." Charlie Gauthier had been giving him quizzical looks for the past ten minutes.

"Yeah right, me too. Good to meet you. I'm Pete, by the way." He held out his enormous palm.

"Thanks. I'm...er...really pleased to have bumped into you."

Pete sat alone at the bar feeling at a loss for what to do. The rugby crowd were getting noisy and boisterous. Somebody was singing about a Zulu Warrior and it looked as though another of them was about to drop his trousers. The barman was pacing up and down, unsure how to react, and at the sight of two very hairy buttocks Helmut quickly separated himself from the group and came over to where Pete was sitting.

"What is it with you British?" He looked perplexed. "In Germany if we want to be naked we are just naked. Here you always seem to make a dance and a song about it."

Pete was still trying to think of an answer to that one when the first punch was thrown. What had been drunken good humour had turned nasty in a flash.

"What the fuck is all this about?" The barman swung open the counter top and came out into the lounge, but it was obvious he had no idea what he was going to do next. Six of the hefty men were now tearing at each other's clothes and throwing punches wildly. Everybody else seemed to be cheering them on.

Joshua had only just sat down to start telling Charlie about the forbidden fruit tree that was the South London Freedom Alliance when the commotion started. He was quickly on his feet again to get a better view. He'd never seen a bar room fight before and was struggling to work out who was fighting who. Jim Clements looked over at the only door out onto the street. It was too close to the brawling mass of bodies for comfort so he decided it would be safer to keep his charges where they were.

"Sit down all of you. You too, Sinclair."

Pete and Helmut, who were feeling dangerously exposed alone at the bar, came over to join them. Joshua was on the point of attempting some sort of introductions when the first blue lights appeared through the frosted glass windows.

Helmut had one hand in his trouser pocket where he was gripping a small plastic bag between his thumb and forefinger. He hadn't intended bringing any of his wares with him but it was too late to chide himself for being so careless.

"Peter, I think it is time for us to go."

"What's the hurry, Helmut?" Pete was rather enjoying the excitement. "Hey maybe the people are rising up."

"No, I think they're falling down Peter." The fighting seemed to be subsiding a little but the lights of the police vans were now clearly visible through the pub doors. "Come on, let's go."

"Go where?"

Once again Helmut's agility in a crisis came as a surprise to his friend. He was already half way to the Gents, without so much as a goodbye. Pete shrugged his shoulders. "Better go, guys. He can be a bit funny sometimes."

Pete's lanky frame disappeared into the toilet just as a group of six policemen in helmets crashed through the doors. The sight of their batons and shields struck the brawling rugby players like an electric shock. They hurriedly tried to disengage themselves from the mêlée, bracing themselves for what was to come, but the policemen pushed past them with barely a glance at the tangle of bodies. When they got to the table that Pete and Helmut had left just seconds before, they turned to face out into the bar and set up a wall of riot shields around the drama teacher and his pupils.

"Mr Sinclair? Come with us if you wouldn't mind." With that Joshua was lifted up by the arms and escorted out into the street.

Helmut pushed his broad body through the lavatory window with relative ease and waited for Pete to slide all six foot eight of himself in the same direction. Out on the pavement they saw no fewer than six police vehicles blocking the street to traffic. Doing all they could to look inconspicuous Pete and Helmut crossed the road and started walking down towards Trafalgar Square. When they heard the vans approaching from behind they stopped and pretended to be taking a keen interest in the timetable attached to the nearest bus stop. The flashing blue lights finally disappeared and Pete leant his body against the plate glass window of the shop behind them. He could see that Helmut, still standing bolt upright, was shaking and there was sweat gathering at the back of his neck. Pete found himself thinking about Mrs Alma Gundry and just how impressed she'd have been by such an effective show of force.

"It's a fine view." Sacha had a glass of wine in his hand and was looking out at the park on the other side of the street. He turned and saw that his new client was sitting on the leather sofa watching him intently. She had been taking in the shape of his buttocks in his leather jeans.

"Yes, Sacha, it certainly is. Is that your real name by the way?"

"Actually, yes." His diction was perfect but with the tantalising edge of a mild French accent.

"Well, Sacha, what do you normally do in these circumstances?"

"That depends very much on who am I with and what she wants. The most important thing for me now is that you should be feeling comfortable with me."

Helen smiled. She had expected to be feeling nervous, or foolish, or maybe both, but she felt nothing of the sort. She felt very much in control. "You don't need to worry about that, darling. Now why don't you come over here and show me just what it is that's worth a hundred and fifty euros an hour."

Sitting in the back of the police van, Joshua was too shocked and disorientated to say anything. The young constable sitting opposite him muttered a brief apology, something about his own protection and not being able to take any chances, but hadn't pursued the matter when the Prime Minister's son had replied with a glare of incomprehension. In the ten minutes it took them to reach Downing Street, his mood had built up to a simmering fury. He thought of getting up, opening the back doors and walking away as the van was held in the Vortex for several minutes and checked over by the electronic sniffers and cameras. Were even the cops suspect in Kneejerk's crazy world?

He was hoping his father's Security Supremo would be lurking as usual in the Entrance Hall. Joshua had the speech of his life ready to deliver, one that would have put the shits up Lucifer himself. But this wasn't a night for just desserts. Sergeant Terry Woods whispered to him that the coast was clear and the doorman admitted him to an empty vestibule. Cheated, he was left with no choice but to stomp up to the flat.

Joshua slammed the door behind him and saw the light was on in his father's study. He went in without knocking. Paul Sinclair was sitting alone on the sofa with a glass of whisky in his hand. He looked up at his son with a mixture of apology and remorse. "I wasn't asked about it, Josh. The Colonel only told me a few minutes ago."

"Is that supposed to make it all right? I can't believe you, really I can't. You sit here all warm and cosy inside this, this fortress while that Scottish git runs some kind of police state in your name."

"Hang on a minute, Josh."

"No, you hang on a minute. Just for once. How much of his bullshit do I have to put up with? He opens my letters, he reads my e-mails, and now when I go out for a night with friends he has me followed and spied on. Most of the time I just take it because I don't know what else I'm supposed to do. I hope that if I ignore the bastard he'll leave me alone. Well this time I've taken more than my fill. I can't go on like this, Dad, it's just not fair."

"There was a report of a violent disturbance. I don't know what it was all about. You tell me, I wasn't there, but how was he to know you weren't at risk?"

"Right. You weren't there and nor was Colonel Bloody Kneejerk. Unless he's got me wired for sound, has he?" Joshua started pulling wildly at his clothes and then brought his hands up to his face. "You might be happy to live like this Dad, but I don't know if I can do it any more. What do you suppose my friends made of that little performance by Kneejerk's stormtoopers?"

"Calm down. Let's talk about this properly. I know how you must be feeling."

"Oh Christ, not again. Listen to yourself. Change the track will you? I know how you must be feeling. If you knew how I was feeling you wouldn't be asking me to calm down. You'd be as mad as I am. It's just another issue for you, isn't it? Just one more thing you have to sort out. Well you might think you can treat Mum like some unresolved problem in your in-box but this is my life." He could see his father wanted to interrupt, but he was having none of it. "I'm seventeen and I won't ever be seventeen again. So don't ask me to calm down because if I calm down nothing is going to change. There's no point talking to you. I'm going to bed."

Sinclair was too stunned by the barrage to argue. He wanted to tell him he was wrong about Ruth and wrong about himself but he wasn't sure what he could say that wouldn't sound as if he was trying to talk himself out of trouble like any other politician. He took a long sip of his drink and watched his son's back disappear through the door.

46

Sacha swung his legs over the side of the bed and stood up. Helen, who was generally very bad at doing nothing, just lay there and watched him. Sacha had been the one to suggest staying on top of the duvet. Good sex should never be hidden away, he said, and it had certainly been that. His legs looked strong and were quite hairy but she'd been relieved to see that his buttocks were completely smooth. It had occurred to her that escorts might even shave their arses, but she was an expert on getting rid of body hair and her fingers had reassured her that his was naturally hairless.

He turned and looked down at her. There was reassuring evidence that his passion had been at least partly genuine. The woman on the phone had said that all Angels and Demons staff were stimulant free and she assumed that meant no erections courtesy of the pharmaceutical industry. "I must pee," he said.

He strode off in the direction of the bathroom and Helen propped herself up on one elbow to make the most of the view. She was just weighing up whether the extortionate sounding overnight rate might not be good value after all when her mobile rang. It was the first time in years that she had even considered not answering it. It was Switch. "What's happened?" She looked at the bedside clock. It was 12.30am. "Okay. I can be there in fifteen."

Sacha was standing in the doorway. "Is there a problem?"

"Yes, I'm sorry. Work, I'm afraid. I have to go."

"At this time?"

"Yeah, well, you know…"

Sacha didn't ask any more questions. She wouldn't have been the first client to arrange to be telephoned to give herself a get out if she needed one. "That's fine. I should be going. Maybe we can share a cab or something?"

"Um, no. I don't think that's such a good idea." Could his look of disappointment really be as genuine as his hairless backside? "Look, if you're free, um, maybe we could pick up where we left off tomorrow?"

"Why of course. I am here for your pleasure after all." She was glad she'd gone for an Angel. "What time?"

"How about nine? If there's any problem, do I just call the Angels and Demons office?"

"Yes, that's probably best." He pulled on his leather trousers and sat on the bed to put on his boots. Helen lent forward and kissed his neck. He turned around to meet her lips, but she stood up at the same instant and his nose collided with an unexpected breast. They both laughed as she scrabbled about trying to find her discarded clothes.

On the pavement, he let her take the first cab. "Good night and, well, à demain." Even the accent sounded too good to be true.

~

Paul Sinclair liked to be in bed before midnight. He'd read about previous Prime Ministers who could get by on four or five hours sleep a night and wondered if this had been part of their own myth-making. He needed a good seven hours if he was going to be at his best. But tonight he knew he wouldn't get off easily. A second whisky was tempting, but that would only make him feel worse in the morning. He'd been sitting nursing his empty glass, staring at the ceiling and thinking about going up to bed when the Colonel's phone call had come through. "I think you'd better come down, Sir, if you don't mind."

~

At home in Battersea Danny and Luke had been sound asleep and tied up in the kind of bodily knots that only serious exhaustion will permit when the phone rang again. Luke had groaned, disentangled himself and rolled over, tugging the duvet with him. Danny, feeling the sudden cold of the night air as he was deprived of any cover, had clutched at the disappearing duvet with one hand while he picked up the phone with the other. He'd half expected an insomniac Paul Sinclair and was taken aback by Kneejerk's insistence that he come back into the office.

The little MG was turning into Whitehall as Helen's taxi pulled up outside the Vortex. Danny knew it must be serious. Kneejerk had given special permission for him to bring his car into Downing Street itself. When they knocked on the door to the Den and went inside the Colonel was already sitting with Sinclair pointing to a set of photographs on the table between them.

"What's going on?" Helen was the first to speak. "The hostages?"

"Yes." Sinclair was looking desperately tired. "These images have just come through. It looks like Warren was right. They've been using the cover of darkness to bring them into the camp."

The pictures were grainier than the earlier ones, presumably because they were taken after sundown. But there was no mistaking the groups of men with what looked like rifles or machine guns over their shoulders. "Can you see the hostages? Are they all right?" asked Danny.

"Impossible to say," said Sinclair. "But I've seen the transcripts of the radio intercepts and it seems the Colonel's prediction was right. They're planning to stage some kind of press conference."

Of course the prediction had been right, thought Kneejerk. At least somebody in the room knew exactly what was going on. "If I might say so, I think it's time to act. If we move now our forces will be in situ before first light. It's the perfect time to catch them off guard and effect a rescue. We're not going to get a better opportunity than this."

Sinclair got to his feet and went over to the window. The infra-red security lights cast a mournful glow over the garden. Helen looked at his back hoping for some sign that the crisis would break him out of his indecision. When he said nothing she turned to the Colonel. "What are the risks?"

"No military action is ever free of risk, Miss Griffin. But we have some experience of this sort of thing. Provided we act quickly and with total secrecy."

"What's the Foreign Office advice?" asked Danny.

The Colonel looked confused. "The Foreign Office? We want secrecy, Mr Oliver. I thought I just said that."

The phone rang on Sinclair's desk but he still didn't move. Helen went over and picked it up. She held out the receiver. "It's the President."

Sinclair took it from her. "John." As the Prime Minister listened his fingers ran back and forth across his forehead. Three pairs of eyes watched his face as he took in what the President was telling him, but it gave nothing away. "Yes, of course, I've got the pictures here. What I have to consider is whether they justify putting British servicemen at risk."

Helen was cursing herself for not having gone into the outer office where she could have listened in to the call. Sinclair was nodding now. He'd picked up a pen and was doodling with short, sharp strokes on a piece of paper in front of him. "I can't promise that, John. I need to talk to my people and I need to think. When's your next window? Okay. I'll call you then." He put down the receiver and looked at his jottings. "The President believes there is an overwhelming case for a raid. In fact he seemed a little concerned that we hadn't already ordered one. I must say he's taking a great deal of interest in this, considering there are no American citizens being held."

"We should be grateful to have such a reliable ally." The Colonel never missed a chance.

The Prime Minister knew where his Security Supremo and Chief of Staff stood on the issue. His Communications Director, on the other hand, was usually less gung-ho. "Danny? What do you think?"

"Not my call. You make the decisions, I convey them to the media. That's the way it works. All I would say is that Washington is a very leaky place. If you want to have the benefit of surprise, I'd do it before somebody over there starts talking to the media. We don't have to say anything here until the operation is over."

The Colonel cut in quickly. "Speed is of the essence, Prime Minister. If these guys get wind of something and disappear back into the hills, we may never get a fix on them again."

Paul Sinclair had been Prime Minister for over four years and, to his relief, he had never yet had to send troops into action. He'd thought about it often but now the time had come he found himself asking if he could have anyone's death on his conscience. Every soldier, even in the SAS, was somebody's son, somebody's loved one. And something more fundamental was nagging him. He liked to have all the facts at his fingertips when making big decisions and facts seemed to be a commodity in dangerously short supply. "When can we expect any more pictures? These really don't show us much."

"Not until tomorrow and by then it may be too late. If we don't act now those hostages' lives are in real danger. You have to be seen to mean business."

Sinclair looked up at the ceiling and then out once more into the darkness of the garden. Anywhere to avoid meeting the eyes of the others in the room. "I don't care how I'm seen."

This wasn't the reaction the Colonel had anticipated. Something had happened to the Prime Minister to weaken his resolve and he had no idea what it could be. "I cannot make my point too strongly. Not to respond now would be an act of unspeakable irresponsibility. Not to say weakness."

Helen couldn't hold herself back any longer. "He's right, Paul."

"You're saying I've got no choice?"

"No, I don't think you have. Come on, Paul. If you could have authorised the use of lethal force to bring to justice those bastards who put nerve gas in the underground, you'd have done it. Am I right?"

He couldn't deny it. "Yes, I suppose I would."

"Well remember how you felt then." For Helen it had been Paul Sinclair's moment of greatest strength. "It's no different now."

The silence lasted almost a minute and felt like an hour. Sinclair was facing the window again when he gave the order. The darkness reflected his face back into the room. His eyes were tightly closed. "I hope to God we're doing the right thing." He opened his eyes and looked straight at the Colonel for the first time. "Go ahead, Colonel. Please issue the necessary instructions."

47

Mrs Alma Gundry hadn't slept soundly since her husband died. The noise of Pete and Helmut arriving home in different stages of drunkenness had woken her some time after midnight. She'd gone to her bedroom window on the off-chance she might see something she could report to young Detective Constable Crayton. She couldn't be sure but it had looked very much like the tall, thin one, Peter he'd said his name was, had been relieving himself behind the privet hedge. Smells like that could linger, she thought, but the police were bound to say there was no law against it. Mrs Gundry was coming to the view that she would have to find other means of dealing with the Castle.

By seven o'clock she was awake again and went downstairs to put the kettle on. She turned on the little television beside the microwave as she did every morning. Mrs Gundry was an avid fan of AM-TV. She especially liked the features on house and garden makeovers. They reassured her that other people were trying as hard as she was to improve their neighbourhoods. And while she usually found the news bulletins a bit depressing she felt it was her civic duty to keep up with current events.

Across the street PJ Walton was also awake. If Pete had been trying to be considerate by peeing outside so as not to wake him, he needn't have bothered. After his mother had left PJ had paced his study doing his best to salvage any filial affection that he could find inside himself. It was meagre pickings. By two in the morning he had decided to give up his column. The price was too high. At six, after a few hours troubled sleep, he remembered the mortgage and started going through it all in his mind again. At seven, he too was in his kitchen in front of the TV. Janine Clairmont was standing at the end of Downing Street.

"This could be the most critical day in Paul Sinclair's premiership. This afternoon MPs vote on the controversial Health Bill. And my sources tell me the Prime Minister is also weighing up whether there's a military solution to the hostage crisis. And the big question behind both is how will the Deputy Prime Minister respond? Sources close to Joanna Morgan have revealed she has her own doubts about the health reforms and we've heard from her own mouth that she's against the use of force in Eritrea." PJ turned the set off and put his hands on the back of the seat Joanna Morgan had been sitting in less than twelve hours before. He had no more idea than Janine Clairmont what his mother might do next.

Mrs Gundry was waiting for the toaster to pop up. She rather liked the woman on the TV. She was always very nicely turned out. When her report finished the camera stayed on her longer than it should have done for some reason and Mrs Gundry was sure she saw her smile when the next feature was announced. Scott Bolton was in Saffron Walden in what looked like a smart, respectable street of the kind Alma Gundry approved of. "Don't be fooled by the big houses and the BMWs," he said, "in every corner of Britain there are Neighbours from Hell." Mrs Gundry didn't hear the toaster pop. She was too engrossed in a story involving a very large snake and not one but two missing kittens.

COBRA. It stood for nothing more dramatic than Cabinet Office Briefing Room A, but it held out a world of promise to the Colonel. It was here that the Army, Navy and Air Force Chiefs, the heads of the intelligence services, even the Defence Secretary, bless his ineffectual cashmere socks, were meeting to coordinate the military action. For the first time in the three years he'd been at Number 10, it was finally in session. And yet only because he and Helen Griffin had had the foresight to organise it. Immediately after giving the order last night, the Prime Minister had gone back up to the flat.

The Security Supremo was in his little office under the stairs. He'd spent the night on the fold away bed that he'd had installed for just such an eventuality. The light above his console showed that Britain was on security alert beta. He sat in his chair, feeling in control at last. The monitors flicked between the various cameras around the Downing Street cordon. There was already a handful of demonstrators in the Compound and he was sure their numbers would swell. He counted two 'Save the NHS' banners and one hurriedly put together to read 'Hands off Eritrea'. Ordinary Decent Malcontents, each and every one of them. He felt almost charitable towards them. At least they'd got themselves out of bed this morning. And for once since he'd taken over this job Colonel Neilson's enemies carried guns and had a grid reference. What's more they might very well be dead. He sat back in his chair and took a deep, highly satisfied, breath. Through the intercom on his desk, Rebecca informed him that the Prime Minister had arrived.

The Colonel was pleased to see that the Chief of Staff and Communications Director were already on duty. It was clear that Danny had had no sleep at all, but Helen Griffin looked on the ball as ever. As for the Prime Minister, it was impossible to tell.

"Mrs Sinclair?"

Ruth was still in bed. Not quite awake but not asleep either, she'd been letting her mind run over last night's dinner with Dr Donald Gill. If it hadn't been for the half bottle of rioja she'd polished off after he'd dropped her home her memory might have been clearer. She didn't recognise the voice. "Who's speaking?"

"I'm sorry to trouble you, Mrs Sinclair. I hope I haven't rung too early? Only I didn't want to miss you."

The warm, comfortable feeling that had accompanied her half-conscious rememberings was ebbing away as Ruth became more awake. She was already resenting the intrusion and it showed in her voice. "Who is this please?"

"My name is Neville Standen." The name meant nothing to her.

"Yes, Mr Standen, how can I help you?"

"I'm calling from the *News of the World*."

Ruth took a deep breath and closed her eyes. "Are you now?" There was a pause at the other end of the line. "Well, if you've got something to say you'd better say it."

Paul Sinclair looked at his watch. The raid would now be underway. It was still dark over the Horn of Africa, but if all went well they should get news within the hour. Danny had prepared statements for the press for all eventualities, but had decided to hold back the one that would try to excuse a failed rescue and the death of any of the hostages. With luck the Prime Minister would never know he'd even written it. Helen, always the best strategic thinker amongst them, was trying to get Sinclair to focus for a moment on the Health Bill. The boys could play with their toys, but she knew where the real threat lay. "If we don't win this vote today it's going to take a lot more than a few brave men risking their lives to get your credibility back."

"Let me say something to all of you." Until now Sinclair had been virtually silent. "People's lives are at risk while we sit here in our comfortable chairs. I don't want any of you to forget that." Danny nodded his approval while Helen and Kneejerk exchanged the briefest of looks.

Helen cleared her throat. "Of course we're all with you on this, Paul. You're right, but there's nothing left for us to do that might help them. Maybe we should all just concentrate on what we can influence. When are you going to brief the Foreign Secretary? If she goes off the rails over this and pulls out her people to punish you this afternoon she'll probably succeed in defeating the bill."

Sinclair knew she was right. He'd already decided for his own reasons that he needed to talk to his deputy. "As it happens I called the Foreign Secretary an hour ago. She's next door in the Cabinet Room. So, if you'll excuse me, I think I've kept her waiting long enough."

The Colonel knew a dismissal when he heard one and quickly left the room to check on the latest intelligence. Helen waited for something more by way of an explanation but Sinclair opened the large double doors through to the Cabinet Room without another word. They closed behind him with a thud.

"What is he playing at this morning?"

"He's a good man. I thought he was dead right, if you want my opinion," said Danny.

"Maybe, I don't know. I don't really do all this conscience stuff, like you sensitive men. I have enough on my plate keeping this government from disappearing beneath the shit. So my concern right now is what the hell he's talking to the shit-stirrer-in-chief about."

On the other side of the double doors Joanna Morgan was alone at the huge oval table. She was sitting in her usual chair, two seats down from his own, with her back to the grey marble fireplace. She didn't look up. Joanna was not the kind of woman who responded well to a summons. And yet it was either a very good act or here was a woman calmly in control of herself and confident of what she was doing. He found it strangely impressive. He always had. Nobody could deny that she had that inner strength that leadership demanded, perhaps more so than he did himself. He was less than two metres from her when she finally turned her head and locked her shockingly blue eyes with his. He was sure if he came any closer she'd be able to smell the uncertainty in his pores. Her face was utterly impassive.

Sinclair stopped and for a full ten seconds they looked into each other's eyes. Neither one blinked. By the time he broke her stare and took his own seat Paul Sinclair had made up his mind. Faced with so overt, so uncompromising a challenge, he knew he had just a few seconds left to either fold or fight.

Out in the corridor Helen and Danny were making no secret of their efforts to overhear what was going on. They were expecting, in Helen's case hoping for, fireworks. When all they heard was the low murmur of quiet conversation they couldn't even tell who was speaking. Helen was beside herself with frustration.

"He should be tearing her limb from limb," she hissed to Danny. "I don't know what the fuck he's up to any more."

Suddenly the door burst open. Helen was so close to it that the rush of air into the room almost dragged her with it. They had no time to compose themselves and looked like a couple of naughty children caught listening on the stairs after being told to go to bed during a grown ups party. The Foreign Secretary emerged, her skin pale and her features drawn tight on her narrow face. She didn't acknowledge them but walked straight for the front door and out into the street. Helen went in to where Sinclair was still in his chair.

"Well?"

"She may be sitting in this seat by the end of the week, but for now at least I think Joanna knows what the stakes are."

Helen had never doubted that. The only question was which of them had the balls to outplay the other. "What did you say to her?"

"Close the door, Danny. Thanks." These were his two closest

advisers and they were both, in their different ways, his friends. "Not surprisingly, she thought that launching military action without informing the Foreign Secretary was a betrayal of trust."

"If we had trusted her we would have told her, she can't have missed that surely?" said Helen.

"She threatened to resign, of course, but I expected that. Who knows, maybe she will this time but I doubt it. Anyway, I told her that she can have my job if she wants it so badly." Helen wasn't sure what she was hearing but she was pretty sure she didn't like it. "But in that case she'd have to come out and say so honestly. I'm not having her cut away at me slice by slice like a piece of salami. If the party or the country would prefer her to take over then that's fine by me. I thought it was rather a fair offer."

"So what do you think she's going to do?" asked Danny.

"I don't know, to be honest." It almost sounded as if he didn't care.

"Paul, you're scaring me, you really are," said Helen. "If I had to put money on which of you really had the stomach for a fight right now, I'm not sure I'd be backing you."

There was the briefest of lulls as Helen drew breath and prepared to go on. "Is winning always that important, Helen?"

"Actually yes. Yes, it is. I only wish I wasn't the only person in this building who thought so. I've got work to do if nobody else around here has." She went out and pulled the door hard shut behind her. Sinclair looked to Danny for some sign that he understood.

"Sorry, Paul, but she may have a point," he said eventually. "If you want out for any reason, for Ruth, for Josh, for yourself even, this isn't the way to go about it."

"Who says I want out?"

"Don't you?"

He paused for no more than a fraction of a second. "See if you can talk to Helen, will you? Calm her down."

"That's not an answer to my question."

"I'll give you an answer as soon as I have one, Danny. I can't do any better than that."

48

PJ was just locking the front door when the sound of Mrs Gundry's sensible shoes crossing the road made him brace himself. They hadn't spoken since the day of the vomit but if she was hoping to complain to him now about the behaviour of his tenants she had chosen the wrong morning. PJ swung round on his heels.

"Mrs Gundry, I know what you're going to say so you can spare your breath. Peter and Helmut have told me what happened and I'm sure it wasn't at all pleasant for you. But it wasn't very nice for them either. Sickness can come upon any us at any time, Mrs Gundry, and I'm told they cleared up the mess as soon as they could."

"But…"

"I'm sorry, Mrs Gundry, but I've had just about all I can take. I've given my lodgers enough lectures on your behalf about not dropping litter or making too much noise late at night. I'm not about to tell them that they can't get ill either. I'm all for good neighbourliness, I really am Mrs Gundry, but I'm afraid this needs saying. We can't all live by the same rules and while there may well be plenty of things about our lifestyle that you don't approve of, you're just going to have to learn to look the other way occasionally. It's bad enough that we have to live in a virtual police state with cameras on every street corner, but we don't have to put up with you peering through your net curtains every waking moment. I'm sorry to have to be so blunt, but that's the way it is. Now if you don't mind I'll just go about my business and let you go about yours. Thank you, Mrs Gundry."

Alma Gundry was left standing open mouthed as PJ went off in the direction of the newsagents. She felt her cheeks tingling with anger and embarrassment. What a very, very rude young man.

Ruth had been sitting in her chair without moving a muscle for more

258

than half an hour. The loud click of the central heating system as it fired up the boiler, something she never normally noticed at all, startled her out of her trance. She went back over the telephone conversation in her head, trying to remember every detail. He said they had photographs, but how could they? It was dark when she and Donald had left the restaurant. Yes, he'd kissed her, they were right about that, but not in a way that anyone who'd seen it could have considered improper. Although she'd been married to a politician long enough to know that a photograph was quite capable of making the most innocent human gesture take on a wholly different complexion. But that man, what had he called himself, Neville something, he knew the name of the restaurant all right, and even knew which table they'd been sitting at. At least she had the foresight not to confirm or deny anything. Danny had taught her that. Danny. Danny would know what to do. She picked up the phone again and dialled his private mobile number.

"Hi this is Danny. Please leave a message after the tone."

"Danny, it's Ruth. I'm sorry to trouble you. It may not be anything important, but could you call me back? Thank you very much."

She replaced the receiver once more and went into the kitchen. She pulled her warm, padded coat off the back of the chair and picked her car keys up from where she'd thrown them on the table. Something made her look out of the hall window before opening the door. The photographer at the end of her drive was making no attempt to hide.

~

Alone in the Den, Paul Sinclair could hear the military bands practising just a few hundred yards away on Horseguards Parade. The sound was so familiar he usually didn't register it at all, but this morning he wanted to go out there personally and ask them to be quiet. Instead he did his best to remember the advice Ruth had always given him. When the problems mount up just concentrate on those you can do something about.

"Rebecca. Could you get me Jim Clements at Harvest Hill Comprehensive? He's the Head of Drama."

Jim was on the line in a matter of seconds.

"Jim, I just wanted to thank you for last night. Well, to apologise really. It must have been quite a shock for you and especially for the kids. I'd like you to know that it wasn't what I'd have wanted. In fact as I tried to explain to Josh, I wasn't even consulted. He seems to think that nothing happens without my say so, but that's not always how it is. Well, anyway, I wish it hadn't turned out the way it did."

"It's good of you to call, Prime Minister."

"Paul. I've told you, I'd much rather you called me Paul."

"Paul. In fact I wanted to ring you, but I wasn't sure I'd ever get through. Is Joshua all right?"

"To be honest, he was still asleep when I came down this morning." He looked at his watch. "I guess he's at school by now."

"Well that's the point. He hasn't appeared. I felt certain there was some good reason but I wasn't sure how to check."

"I see. Well, look Jim, give me five minutes to pop up to the flat. I suppose he might have overslept but that's not like him. I'll call you back. You might just make sure that he hasn't slipped into class in the meantime."

The flat was empty. The clothes Joshua had discarded the night before were laying in a pile at the foot of his bed. Despite feeling that he was breaking his own rules, Paul pulled out the piece of paper that was sticking out of the pocket of his son's jeans. Sweet F.A., The South London Freedom Alliance. It was a new one on him.

Ray Morgan had never seen his wife so tense. All the poise and authority, the rather intimidating self-assurance that made him admire her so, had gone as she paced between the bedroom and the living room of her official residence. She'd barely spoken a word since getting back from Downing Street other than to send her Private Secretary packing when he'd come to remind her about the next meeting.

"What is it, my love?" In their many years together, she had never ignored her husband. It was part of the exaggerated civility that made their marriage the success that it was. So when she said nothing he knew it must be very serious indeed.

Joanna Morgan was a woman who liked to take her time, to plan and to prepare. She liked the control that came from careful deliberation. She was not the kind of woman who took kindly to being forced into a corner. Decisions made in haste were almost always bad ones, according to her way of thinking. And actions prompted by emotion rather than intellect were very dangerous indeed. As if to test her theory she went over to the mantelpiece and swept all the silver framed photographs onto the marble hearth. She looked down at Nelson Mandela and the picture of herself and Paul Sinclair with their hands held high in victory. Shards of glass had torn the paper. It was the first impetuous thing she had done for a very, very long time and it hadn't made her feel the slightest bit better.

"Ray. The outfit is wrong."

"The blue suit, my love?"

"No, Ray. I think the red one. And can you get hold of the Health Secretary for me? Stephen Piggin and I need to have a talk."

After poking his head into several of the offices in the labyrinthine corridors of Number 10, Danny Oliver finally tracked Helen Griffin down in the Cabinet Office canteen. The Chief of Staff had a strong cup of black coffee in front of her. He sat down opposite her and leant forward, all too aware that their presence together would have been noted by the small group of civil servants, trained observers each of them, having breakfast on the neighbouring tables.

"Don't worry, Helen. He's got a lot on his plate."

She was in no mood to be understanding. "He's always got a lot on his plate. But he's been behaving like he just doesn't care any more. He's going to have to get a grip on himself and fast."

Danny kept his voice barely above a whisper, all too aware that a dozen pairs of ears would be straining to overhear their conversation. "He's very worried about Ruth, and about Josh too, I think. We knew we'd have to support him once she left. I'm surprised we haven't had to do it more often, quite honestly."

"Well he picks his moments."

"I know. I think it's just hit him that they're both having a pretty tough time. There's the drinking, of course." Helen nodded. She'd read the reports. "He's convinced himself that she's only going to be happy if he does something to make it easier for her. I don't want to get too melodramatic, but I think he's even considered making their

261

separation more... permanent." For once, Helen looked genuinely surprised. "There might be somebody else in her life, I'm not sure. And Josh is finding it all pretty tough going too. Wouldn't you, stuck in there at the age of seventeen?"

"I don't remember ever being seventeen. But, hang on. Do you mean divorce? Are you serious? Why hasn't he talked to me about it?"

"Maybe he just wants to be sure first. He hasn't said so in as many words. I'm guessing. I may be wrong. But we're not going to get him back firing on all cylinders until he sorts the personal stuff out. We have to give him a little space to do that." She didn't look convinced. "Look, Helen. We've got a matter of hours before the vote. What do you say we give him the benefit of the doubt for that long at least and just see if we can't win it for him."

For once Helen didn't argue. "Okay, Danny, but on one condition. He has to know that even if we pull off some miracle and rescue his arse for him he can't expect us to keep on doing it for him indefinitely."

"I think he knows."

"So what's it going to be then? The usual routine? I chew balls and you lick arse?"

He gave her a boyish grin. "Funny how we both get the jobs we're best suited for." The small huddle of civil servants at the neighbouring table went back to their newspapers and breakfasts as Helen and Danny stood up and made for the door.

~

The piece of paper contained only seventeen words. Sinclair read it over twice before looking up. If the Colonel had been expecting to be congratulated or even thanked he was disappointed. "Has anybody else seen this?"

"I brought it straight to you from COBRA, Prime Minister."

Operation complete. All service personnel returned safely. Light injuries only. No civilian casualties. Control Room, *HMS Achilles*.

"Ask Rebecca to find Danny and get him in here would you?"

Kneejerk hesitated. "I think you should inform the President, Sir."

Sinclair was getting irritated and he knew it was unfair. It had been a long time since the Colonel had been able to report anything that could be described as a success for his security policy, but he wished he wouldn't go on about the President quite so much. Anybody would think he was employed by Warren not the British government. "I'll speak to him later. It's the middle of the night over there, in case you hadn't noticed."

He felt no hint of triumph, only a profound sense of relief. When Danny appeared he told him to put out a factual statement that the hostages had been freed and nothing else. He would need more than seventeen words before he started claiming any credit.

49

The Prime Minister was on the phone when Danny returned. He waved for him to come in while continuing his conversation. "No, Jim, no sign. It sounds rather pathetic to have to ask this, but do you have any idea where he might be?" Jim Clements said he'd see what he could find out and would call back. "If you could. I'll tell Rebecca to put you straight through."

He held the receiver in his hand and turned to face Danny. "Josh didn't turn up at school this morning."

"Well, I wouldn't start worrying yet. He's got a mobile hasn't he? Give him a call."

"The mood he was in last night, I'm not sure he'll want to talk to me."

"There's only one way to find out."

Sinclair clicked a button on the phone to get himself a new line. "Switch, do you have my son's mobile telephone number? Could you put me through to it please?"

The two men waited in silence. Sinclair's cheeks were drawn in tight against his jaw line. He stared into the middle distance and ran his finger down the ridge of his long nose. The operator came back on and he nodded.

"Thanks, Switch." Then to Danny: "No answer. Maybe I should have left a message?"

"Well if he's got it turned on then I'm sure Kneejerk's electronic wizardry could have a fix on him in a few seconds."

"I daresay it could, but in the circumstances I'm not sure that would be such a good idea."

"You could always try texting him." Sinclair looked as if he were being asked to speak in Chinese. "Here I'll show you. You need another mobile really. Use mine. It's only programmed to recognise my voice, so you'll have to type it in."

Danny realised he hadn't had his private phone switched on. It glowed into life and told him he had a message. He listened to it but something in the tone of Ruth's voice warned him against telling her husband until he knew what it was about.

Even with Danny explaining the procedure it took Sinclair five minutes to key in the simple message: *Josh its Dad. We need to talk. Please ring me.*

"Now you just press send. I can't believe you've never done this before."

"Danny, after a while you start to think that lifts go up and down by themselves and car doors open automatically."

"But we were texting each other all the time during the leadership campaign."

"Helen was doing it all for me, I'm afraid."

"We're going to have to keep you in office. I'm not sure you'd survive in the outside world. I suppose Josh has video messaging?"

"Don't ask me, Danny. Probably. You know what kids are like. Do you have it?"

"Yes, but I never use it. At least with old fashioned texts nobody knows where you are or whether you've shaved."

"I've never seen you unshaven."

"That's not really the point. Anyway, I don't think it would be a good idea for the Prime Minister to start sending video messages across London. They're very easy to intercept if you have the right equipment. Remember what happened to the Prince of Wales. You really don't want to go there." He could just imagine the headlines.

"This is so unlike him. As a kid he would throw some pretty dramatic tantrums, it's true. He was quite theatrical even then. But he never tried to run away. I've never known him walk out on an argument in his life. And yet last night behind all his fury I could see that he just felt impotent. I think we both knew that however ghastly it all seemed, there was nothing either of us could do about it. There was this look of utter frustration on his face. You know, like when your children want something and ball their heads off and when that doesn't work they look fit to explode? They just don't know what else to do. They've fired their best shots."

"Not from personal experience, no."

"No, of course, Danny. But you know what I mean?"

"Yes, I know what you mean." Danny's mobile gave a shrill beep. "Well, it looks like he got the message. Now just press OK." Sinclair looked dejectedly at the tiny machine. "Oh, give it here." He brought up the message and tilted it towards Sinclair's face. *If u want 2 talk, come and find me. Cant talk there.*

"What's that supposed to mean?"

"It sounds pretty clear to me."

"Find him where?"

"Ask him."

Where are you? Sinclair completed his second message in less than half the time. But no answer came back.

"It looks like he's said all he's got to say."

"Well, thanks anyway." Sinclair offered Danny the phone.

"No, you keep it. He might change his mind. It's my personal one anyway." Sinclair raised an eyebrow. "I keep one for personal calls and one for work. I won't need it. Luke's in court all day and he never calls me from the office anyway. I'll drop by and pick it up later." Danny met Rebecca at the door as he was leaving.

"Prime Minister," she said, "Colonel Neilson was hoping for a word."

"Tell him I'll be with him as soon as I can."

Five minutes later Sinclair was still standing looking out of the window at the garden and the tall security fence behind it. He'd never felt more helpless or more trapped. When the phone rang it was Jim Clements asking if Joshua had returned home. "No, but he has sent me a message asking me to go and find him. I don't know what I'm supposed to do now."

"Just a second." Paul could hear the teacher in the background telling someone that it was time to stop playing games. He couldn't make out the reply but Clements said, "I've got Charles Gauthier here. You may remember him as Mephistopheles and I'm starting to wonder if he was typecast. He was very reluctant to tell me anything, schoolboy *omerta*, but he's spoken to your son this morning."

"And?"

"He says Josh met someone last night, some radical lefty who told to him to drop round whenever he felt like it. Somewhere across the river, although my informant here says he doesn't know where exactly. I think Josh was quite taken by the idea, so my guess is that's where he's heading."

Sinclair took out the piece of paper he'd found in Joshua's jeans. "The South London Freedom Alliance?"

There was more discussion at the other end of the phone. "Sweet F.A. according to Mr Gauthier here."

"Yes, that's it." He turned the paper over. "Well there's an address here. Printed and published by the South London Freedom Alliance, Castle Terrace, Wilson Crescent, SE1." He thought for a second. "Jim, can you take me there?"

"Are you serious?"

"Yes. I'm serious."

Paul heard Clements send the boy out of the room. "My car is in for a service, but I can probably borrow the school mini-bus. Let me see, I've got one lesson before lunch but I should be able to call in a favour and get cover for that. I can be with you in twenty minutes." The Prime Minister told the Head of Drama at Harvest Hill Comprehensive where he wanted to be collected and hung up.

PJ Walton was back with the newspapers in fifteen minutes. His lecture appeared to have done the trick. For once there was no sign of life from Mrs Gundry across the road. Maybe he could get a little peace at last, although the row had left him in a bad mood and he doubted whether he'd be able to get on with anything very productive. When he went into the kitchen Pete was sitting at the table in a leather jacket and knitted cap. The demonstration outfit. "What's up with you? Taking to the streets again already?"

Even Pete, not the most intuitive of people at the best of times, could sense his irritability. "Well that was the idea." Pete had woken up in a very buoyant frame of mind, with his enthusiasm for direct action rekindled. He thought of the young man in the pub and what a good impression he's made on him with all his talk about fighting for the freedom of the masses. Pete had appreciated that look of admiration verging on awe. It wasn't an effect he had on people often. He decided it was time to put some purpose back into his life. Maybe the boy wouldn't be the only one to be impressed.

Unfortunately the one person who had been decidedly unimpressed was Helmut Feldhofer. He reminded Pete that the masses had had far better opportunities than this to stand up for their rights and had utterly failed to do so. He, for one, had no intention of spending the day standing around in the Compound.

"So have you changed your mind then?" PJ was used to Pete's vacillation.

"Well Helmut's not really up for it."

"You could go without him, you know." But before there was time to assess such a radical suggestion there was a tentative knock on the front door. PJ pulled a face as if to say he wasn't expecting anybody and Pete got the message that he should go to answer it.

Joshua looked a little sheepish. "You did say it would be all right, didn't you?"

"Yes, yes of course. Come in." He briefly considered introducing his new disciple to PJ, but given the mood his landlord was in he thought better of it. "You'd better come right on upstairs."

~

The doorman in the Entrance Hall saw Paul Sinclair walking purposefully towards him and assumed he would turn right at the last minute as he usually did and go up to the flat. When he didn't, there was only a second to spare. Normally the front door security position was given warning when the Prime Minister was going out. But if he hadn't released the lock and opened the door as quickly as he had the doorman was convinced Sinclair would have walked straight into it. On the monitor sitting on the side table he watched him stride down towards the Vortex. He picked up the phone to warn the policeman on duty at the far end of the street.

Sergeant Terry Woods had only a few seconds himself to rack his brains for the correct procedure. He wasn't sure there was one as the Prime Minister never left the building unaccompanied. But as his car was the only vehicle allowed through the Vortex without screening, it must follow that he was allowed out through the pedestrian gate if that's what he wanted to do. It would be a brave policeman who told him he couldn't.

Outside in the street the small group of demonstrators in the Compound were too preoccupied even to notice. A group of Japanese tourists thought he might be famous so took his photograph just in case before he crossed the street and disappeared into the crowd on the other side. Colonel Henry Neilson would later study those pictures in silent, numb incomprehension. They were the last anybody in Whitehall saw of the Prime Minister for a very long time.

50

Helen Griffin let the door swing behind her as she left the corridor that housed the Prime Minister's Commons office. Things were not going well. She had just been talking to two senior backbench MPs who ought to have known what the stakes were and they had refused to guarantee their support until they'd spoken to Paul Sinclair himself. The vanity of these people. She knew they'd fold. They knew they'd fold. So why waste her valuable time, let alone his? As if he wasn't perfectly capable of wasting it himself. Just so they could go back and tell their precious constituency parties they'd demanded a meeting with the Prime Minister in person and had received the assurances they needed. Pure vanity.

Still seething, she read the name plates on the doors as she passed. Every member of the Cabinet had a room here, the size of each reflecting their relative importance in the political pecking order. Yet more vanity. How many of them, she wondered, would be there for Sinclair if it came to the crunch? Half? A little over? She'd probably never know the true number.

Out of the corner of her eye she saw the unmistakable rotund back of the Health Secretary, Stephen Piggin, disappearing towards the Chamber. She spat out the word 'gutless' under her breath. She didn't need to guess who he'd been in to see. She strode up to the Foreign Secretary's door and opened it without knocking. Joanna Morgan was sitting at her desk. Clearly Paul had been right, the woman didn't have the guts to resign no matter what humiliation she suffered.

"We need to talk, Jo. Don't worry, I'm not here to rub your nose in it over the hostages. You were wrong and you know it…"

Joanna Morgan, who believed good manners could be upheld even in the most difficult of circumstances, was taken aback. "Hang on a second, Helen."

"No, you hang on. Paul made his point back there, you have to put up or shut up. I see you're still sitting here so it looks like shutting up is what it's going to be. You've had your little game and you lost. Now it's time to pull your finger out and behave like the Deputy Prime Minister for once, if that's what you want to be. We have a vote to win and you'd better be out there helping us do it or I'll have you and your precious principles strung out to dry before the day is over."

"Oh come on, Helen, if we're going to talk let's be sensible about it."

"I saw Piggin leaving just now. I'm surprised either of you have the time to be enjoying little chats. If you cared two cents for the government you're both a part of you'd be out there making sure your pathetic little band of supporters get it into their thick heads that they owe everything they've got to Paul Sinclair. If it hadn't been for him they'd be in opposition by now and so would you. Instead you're sitting there enjoying one of the great offices of state while conniving and conspiring to bring down the man who put you into it. There's only one word for people like you. Pathetic." Helen wiped a line of spittle from the edge of her mouth with the back of her hand.

The Foreign Secretary's eyes narrowed. She got up from behind her desk and came round to stand directly in front of Helen. The two women were almost exactly the same height, but there the similarities ended. Joanna Morgan was, as ever, perfectly turned out. Her red suit looked as if it had been pressed that morning. Her make-up was subtle and expertly applied. There was a small gold cross on a chain around her neck and a wedding ring on her finger but otherwise she wore no jewellery. Helen's make up was a little too bold for a woman of her age and her blouse appeared not to have seen an iron for some time. She looked like a woman who'd been dragged out of bed in the early hours of the morning and hadn't had the time to repair the damage since. Which is exactly what she was.

"I hope you feel better for getting that off your chest, Helen." Joanna's voice was almost unnaturally quiet. "Your loyalty is touching but I fear the Prime Minister may come to regret having a Chief of Staff with such poor judgement."

The sound of Helen's pager going off cut into the room with such force that both women's eyes were drawn to its illuminated screen. From where she was standing, just inches from Helen's face, Joanna could read the message clearly. "It looks like you're wanted back at Number 10. Well run along and perhaps, when you've calmed down and feel ready to apologise for your little tantrum, we can renew our discussion in a more civilised fashion."

Helen could smell a faint trace of peppermint on the other woman's breath. She turned and took two steps towards the door. With her fingers on the handle she turned. "Go fuck yourself, Joanna."

It was only right that the Security Supremo should have been the first to hear that the Prime Minister was no longer in the building. The manner of his departure was highly unorthodox but even Kneejerk had had to check with Danny Oliver that it hadn't been in response to some last minute summons to the House of Commons.

When Helen reached the Den she looked around for him and met only Danny's troubled face. "Now what? I get hauled back over here and the guy's not even around. Has he had to go and have a little lie down after all the exertions of the morning?"

"He's not here."

"Thank you, Danny, I can see that."

"No. I mean, he's not anywhere."

"I think you'll find that everybody's got to be somewhere."

Colonel Neilson was starting to think their little banter was never going to end. "Miss Griffin, the Prime Minister has left the building. Unless you know where he is, I'm afraid we may have a serious situation on our hands."

She looked at each of them in turn and could see they were serious. "For fuck's sake! Left the building? Who was the last person to see him."

"He told Rebecca that he'd be back soon but didn't say where he was going. This is most irregular."

"You can say that again. Who was in here with him last?"

"I suppose I was," said Danny.

"So? Think. He must have said something about where he was going."

Danny Oliver was chewing the flesh on the inside of his lower lip. "When I left him he was on his own in here." Better to tell the truth

272

and nothing but the truth. The whole truth might have to wait. "He hasn't been gone long. Give the guy a break, can't you?"

Helen was now pacing the room but still held Danny firmly in her sight. "No, Danny, he's had enough breaks. I don't mind him sulking in the flat occasionally if he has to, so long as I know where he is. This is different. He knows full well that being Prime Minister means becoming public property, it means never being off-duty, it means having it minuted every time you go for a shit. It does not mean walking down Downing Street and out into fuck knows where without telling anybody."

Once again the Colonel found himself in alliance with the Chief of Staff. "Britain cannot be without a Prime Minister, even for an hour. I really should inform the Deputy Prime Minister that she may be required."

"Don't," Danny startled himself with his vehemence and then over-compensated by going on in a whisper. "Don't do that, Colonel. I'm sure we can give him a few minutes more."

Kneejerk looked at his watch "There should be another dispatch from the *Achilles*. The Prime Minister asked to be kept informed on the latest developments."

"In that case I'm sure he won't be gone long," said Danny, who was sure of nothing of the kind.

It took a great deal these days to surprise Helmut Feldhofer. This morning, however, he was beyond surprised, he was rendered almost speechless. Not that Pete had noticed much difference. In the first place, it had dawned on Helmut that his friend had spent fifteen minutes talking to the Prime Minister's son the night before without having the slightest idea who he was. And now that very same young man was sitting in the workshop at the Castle listening intently as Pete, still none the wiser, explained how direct action against Paul Sinclair's government could be put into effect at the press of a button. So far Pete had omitted to mention that the buttons hadn't been pressed in earnest for some time. He was obviously enjoying the attention.

"So, you see, we store all the templates on disc and then let's say the Prime Minister announces he's going to sell the education department to WHSmith, well," Pete typed a few words onto the computer keyboard, "Save The NHS becomes Save Our Schools. We can download the latest picture of him and maybe doctor it a bit, add a pair of horns maybe and turn out a thousand posters an hour."

This was just great, thought Joshua, the lamentation of Kneejerk being produced in a back bedroom in Bermondsey on some cheap computer equipment from PC World. He had visions of getting his own back against that Scottish megalomaniac. He could become a mole. It would be so easy to find out what was bugging Kneejerk most on any particular day, give Pete a ring and there could be a demonstration about it on his precious little CCTV monitors from the end of Downing Street in a couple of hours. Perfection.

"Of course, PJ comes up with most of the ideas," Pete continued. "He's the one most plugged in to what's going on, what with his column and everything." He'd already explained to Joshua that the Castle was owned by none other than The Naked Prophet, Paul Sinclair's sternest critic in the popular press. The news had produced in Joshua another tingle of exhilaration in what was already proving to be a very satisfying morning.

"And of course with the internet," Pete went on, "we can tell our brothers and sisters about a demo in seconds. I tell you, modern technology makes taking on the forces of reaction a whole lot easier."

"Go on then, this is great. Show me more."

Pete sat at the keyboard and typed in a web address. "This is the best one. Everything you need to bring the State to its knees." Even Pete, who took almost everything at face value and was the kind of gullible consumer that advertising executives only dream about, knew that couldn't be quite true. The State's knees were as well locked as a horse's so it could sleep standing up. Not that Joshua was too bothered. He'd be happy just to give it pins and needles.

"I don't suppose it tells you how to dismantle the Vortex?"

"Near enough." Pete clicked on a couple of links and a host of detailed diagrams appeared. "Those things have been around in the States for a while and although our American comrades are a bit thin on the ground, they're very clever. Old brains over there," he nodded at Helmut who'd been listening with the benign indulgence of a lapsed Catholic who no longer believed in the power of prayer, "reckons he

274

could disable one of these if he ever had a decent look inside."

Joshua thought of Kneejerk in his little office surrounded by his cameras and sniffers and computers and satellites. He didn't want to burst the bubble of Pete's enthusiasm by telling him the odds were still stacked against them.

51

Colonel Henry Neilson played and replayed the short sequences from the surveillance cameras like a teenager addicted to a video game. His eyes bore into the screen in the hope of seeing something he'd missed in the first two dozen viewings. The Prime Minister could be seen clearly leaving the Vortex and crossing Whitehall. There was a brief glimpse of him on the camera monitoring the yard in front of the Health Department and then he disappeared. The street didn't appear to have been any busier than usual this morning but somehow he'd vanished into what crowds there were. He couldn't have gone north. The Ministry of Defence had almost as many cameras around it as Downing Street and he was nowhere to be seen on any of them. If he'd gone the other way towards the House of Commons he should have been detected by the cameras on the corner of Parliament Square.

The Colonel had already asked the managers of Boots and the Churchill Café to bring in their security tapes. Even the barman at the Red Lion had received the same request although the pub wouldn't open for another two hours. But they'd all had similar phone calls from Neilson in the past during his many drills and exercises so they thought little of it.

Rebecca could see that the Colonel's collar was wet with perspiration. "The Chief of Staff would like you to join her in the Den."

"Yes, of course," his voice was no less clipped than usual but was noticeably more hoarse.

"Ah, Colonel, good of you to spare the time." Helen was speaking through pursed lips. Danny started to breathe a little more normally as her attention shifted to the Security Supremo. "Perhaps you could tell us where the Prime Minister is just at this moment."

"I would like to do that Miss Griffin."

"And we would all very much like you to, Colonel."

"But I'm afraid I'm unable to."

"That's a shame, Colonel, that really is a shame. You see, we're quite keen to get the Prime Minister back. I see quite enough of him as it is, although I think even I would be sorry to lose him completely. But Danny here is a little worried that the press might start to take an interest in his absence. Wouldn't you say, Colonel, that losing the Prime Minister was a bit of a lapse of security?"

"Well...."

"You are the Security Supremo, I believe?"

"Might I suggest Miss Griffin that this is a time for action rather than sarcasm? I do have a plan. I suggest a London-wide alert. Notify all officers, get a message to every taxi driver. There's a procedure."

"Oh I'm sure there's a procedure, Colonel. But do we really want to advertise that we've lost the Prime Minister? Might that not make us a little," she paused. "Vulnerable?"

Rebecca put her head around the door. "The Foreign Secretary is on the line. She says she wants to speak to the Prime Minister immediately. A matter of considerable importance, she said."

"Tell her he's busy. He'll get back to her as soon as he can," said Helen

"I don't think she's going to like it."

"I don't suppose she will, but that's the message." Helen turned to the others. "Now what?"

"Miss...Helen's right," The Colonel rarely called her by her first name but he was keen to bind her in as best he could. They were all in this together and he'd been thinking carefully about what she had said. "We cannot afford to admit to any vulnerability. I can order a Grade B alert, London wide, without having to specify what we're looking for. I think if the PM were to show up somebody would let us know. SIS can run surveillance sweeps on all their principal targets on the same basis. There's a lot we can do without letting the balloon go up."

"Are you sure we're not over-reacting?" asked Danny. With his own mobile phone in the Prime Minister's pocket, he knew they could track him down if they had to. And if Paul Sinclair wanted to put his family first for an hour or so then the rest of them would just have to cope. "He could be stuck in a superloo somewhere or something."

"We have cameras in those too, Sir."

"Do you?" Danny looked aghast.

"Go ahead, Colonel." Helen had instinctively taken charge and nobody was arguing. After Neilson left to set things in motion, she turned to Danny. "If there's anything you're not telling me I'm going to have your big black balls on toast."

"What a charming turn of phrase you have sometimes. I'm just going to pop to the loo, so I'll bear that in mind. I won't be a tick. Stay here."

Danny went out into the corridor and tried to think where he might find an empty office. He took a risk by slipping into Helen's and picking up the phone. He dialled his own mobile number and waited. There was no reply.

"Is this yours?" Helen asked him as he came back into the Den. "It was ringing and I found it down the back of the sofa. I didn't like to answer it."

"Oh. Yeah, thanks." Danny took his phone and put it into his pocket. "I wondered what I'd done with that."

Rebecca had followed him into the room. "It's the Foreign Secretary again. She says if she can't speak to the Prime Minister she wants to speak to his Chief of Staff."

"Okay, I'm coming." Helen looked grim as she went out of the door. Danny was still in the process of dialling the home number in Aston when she came back in. It was a very rare event, in his experience, for the Chief of Staff to look shocked and Helen Griffin looked very shocked indeed. It was serious news and she knew she might have played some part in bringing it about. "Whoever you're calling, they're just going to have to wait. Do you have a copy of the Rules of Procedure anywhere?" Danny frowned and shook his head. "Joanna Morgan has just handed in her resignation. It seems we've not only lost the Prime Minister but we no longer have a Deputy Prime Minister either."

Joshua was taking advantage of the Castle's old computer to check his e-mails. Seven from Heidi Hounslow, all of which he deleted without reading them, and one from Charlie Gauthier warning him that Jim Clements had been asking a lot of questions. Joshua wasn't surprised, it was pretty much what he'd expected. He'd never had any doubt that his father would be able to find him if he wanted to. He should probably go before Kneejerk's battle squadrons were dispatched.

Although he was concentrating on the screen, Joshua could sense that he was being stared at intently from the other side of the room. Pete was looking at him quizzically. It was a look Joshua had seen many times in the past. The media rules on the privacy of minors meant his picture rarely appeared in the papers or on the TV, so people were always looking at him, trying to work out if they'd met him somewhere before.

"I've been thinking," said Pete. Helmut, who was staring out of the window, waited to hear the results of this rare bit of cerebral activity. "I was sure I recognised you from somewhere." Helmut listened for the sound of a penny dropping very slowly from a considerable height. "But I know what it is. You look a bit like our PJ, you know that?" Of course he didn't know that, thought Helmut, the two of them had never met. "Must be the nose I think." Helmut went back to staring at Mrs Alma Gundry's neatly tended flower boxes.

~

The crowd of Ordinary Decent Malcontents in the Compound grew little by little each time Kneejerk looked at his screens, but he didn't notice them. He wasn't a particularly religious man despite his Calvinist upbringing, but the Colonel was silently praying that the one face he wanted to see would miraculously appear. So far the sweep had turned up no suspicious vehicles in the vicinity of Downing Street in the past two hours and no reports of unaccompanied Prime Ministers wandering the streets of London.

The light on his secure line began to flash. It was a sight that usually gave him an unambiguously proud feeling. He liked the idea that he was a key link in the chain that kept the world a safer place. This morning, however, it seemed unlikely to be the conduit for anything that might help him out of his current predicament.

"Colonel, it's Kapolski. Wanna put me on the screen?"

"Not today, if that's all right with you." There was no telling who might burst in the way things were going and he wasn't sure the situation would be improved if he was caught in conversation with the CIA.

"That's a shame, Colonel. I wanted you to see the broad smile on my face. We're happy people over here, you should know that. And we have you to thank. When the President wakes up he's going to be in a very good mood indeed and that makes life for the rest of us a lot more pleasant."

"I'm very pleased to hear that." Kneejerk wasn't sure how happy they would be if he couldn't deliver the last element in their carefully choreographed plan.

"Yup. You can tell your man that by a fortuitous," he seemed to almost chew on the word as he savoured it, "a highly fortuitous chance, the British military have destroyed a key training base in the international network of terror. That place was not just home to hostage takers but to some really nasty guys. Coupla Somali warlords who we've been after for years, for a start. The President is going to praise your guy to the heavens in a big speech in a few hours. Of course, he does have an election to win, so he may take just a little bit of the credit. A successful counter-terrorist operation made possible by the direct intervention of our own President John 'Bunny' Warren."

Kneejerk didn't need to be told. It had all been planned long in advance and written into the grid. If the Americans hadn't had so many foreign policy disasters in Africa in recent years they'd have launched the raid themselves. But failure was too high a risk in the middle of an election campaign. If it went wrong, the Brits would take the blame. If, as it had turned out, it was a success they could share the glory.

Kapolski was still in full stride. "So all we need now is for your Sinclair to call the President in the next couple of hours and agree the line. The...," he chuckled, "the hostages are all safe, I hear." Of course they were safe. They'd never been held captive. Poverty Action, a CIA front organisation, had made sure five suitably dishevelled people in chains were there for the SAS to 'rescue'. Nobody need know that they'd been driven to the site only minutes before the first rescue helicopter arrived. And if any of the surviving terrorists claimed never to have seen them before, nobody would believe them. "I think you should tell the Prime Minister the good news right away, Colonel."

"So do I, and believe me I will. Just as soon as I can." Kneejerk heard footsteps in the corridor outside his room and quickly cut short the call. He'd barely replaced the receiver when the door opened and Helen came in demanding to know if by any chance he'd found the Prime Minister. Danny Oliver stood in the doorway looking uncomfortable. It was beginning to sound as if Helen thought Paul Sinclair's decision to walk off the job was entirely the Colonel's fault. She took his silence as the only answer she needed.

"The way I read it," she said, "we have no choice. The world, his wife and his whole extended family have to believe that Paul Sinclair is still here. Danny and I are going over to the House of Commons. If you can't find him for us, can you at least make sure that no word of his absence leaks out? Lock people up if you have to, you'll enjoy that." The Colonel looked as if he was giving the idea some serious consideration.

She turned to Danny. "You'd better tell the press straight away about Morgan's resignation. She's probably told them herself by now anyway. If they ask for Sinclair's reaction just say he's tied up on other business. The fact that we have no idea what it is needn't concern them. And put it about that Paul is thinking of using the resignation for a wide-scale reshuffle. There's nothing like the vague hope of promotion for keeping those spineless wankers in line, and the more people we can keep dancing to our tune for as long as possible, the better."

"And how long is that, do you think?" asked Danny.

"Do you mean, how long can we make out that it's business as usual when the Prime Minister has vanished off the face of the earth? I have no idea, but maybe we're about to find out. Anyway, we still have a vote to win and we're not going to do it by sitting on our arses over here." She saved her last word for the Colonel. "And if you should find him, do let us know. There's a good chap."

52

Mrs Alma Gundry was on the telephone when she heard the school mini-bus draw up in the street outside. Without interrupting the flow of her conversation she pulled back the net curtain to get a better view. The vehicle was slightly obscuring her vision, but through its side window she could see a figure standing on the doorstep of the Castle opposite. Another relatively well dressed young man was locking the driver's door. The name of Harvest Hill Comprehensive School painted down the side meant nothing to her.

"Sometimes there are people coming and going all day. If you were here now you could see for yourself. And there's no telling what they get up to in there," she said into the phone. Mrs Gundry was feeling a lot better now she had decided on a course of action and had found somebody who seemed to sympathise with her plight at last. "Now, I've told you about the litter, dear, haven't I? Have I told you about the vomit?"

Neville Standen had left three messages for Danny Oliver already that morning and was starting to give up any hope of being able to speak to him. Sunday journalists are peculiar creatures with a life-cycle that repeats itself on a weekly basis with more highs and lows than a mountain range. Fridays were always the worst. Anxiety levels were at their peak and even Neville Standen with ten years on the *News of the World* under his belt wasn't immune. If he didn't have a scoop for that week's paper then time was running out fast. If he did, and this week he thought he did, there was the constant risk of it falling into the hands of another journalist before that magic word EXCLUSIVE could be set in large type beside his by-line. And to make matters worse, people like Danny Oliver who could make or break his stories never seemed to appreciate the importance of returning his calls.

A conversation with the man from the *News of the World* was the last thing Danny had time for, but Neville Standen caught him in the narrow stairwell that led up to the warren of little offices where the Westminster press pack worked. "Does the name Dr Donald Gill mean anything to you?" He spoke in little more than a whisper, in case he was overheard.

"Carry on, Neville, I'm listening."

"I'll take that as a yes, then." By the time he'd finished, Danny was cursing himself for not returning Ruth's call earlier. "I'll need a statement."

"Well you'll just have to wait."

"I don't have long, Danny, and I do have pictures. Remember that."

"Don't try to bully me, Neville, I'm not in the mood. You'll get your statement by the end of the day. Now, if you'll excuse me, I have more pressing things to attend to." He pushed past the objectionable little man and went into the Gents at the top of the stairs. Once he was sure the room was empty he called Ruth and told her to stay indoors, draw the curtains and to try to get hold of Donald Gill and tell him to say nothing. He looked at his watch. The debate was due to start in less than an hour.

~

At least the MP for Wakefield Horbury wouldn't need a word with the Prime Minister to persuade him to vote the right way. Helen came up beside him, careful to avoid his deaf ear. "Well, Ernie, you were right."

She'd startled him but he quickly regained his composure. "I was?"

"About Joanna Morgan. You know she's resigned?" She had no doubt that he did. By virtue of the fact that he had little else to do with his time, Ernie Harwood was the best gossip in the House.

"Ah yes. Well, as I told you, she's clever."

"So what's she doing?"

"Playing her cards pretty close to her chest as usual. She won't say anything until after the vote. If she's going to be leader she doesn't want to be seen encouraging a government defeat."

"And Piggin?"

"The Health Secretary is too much of a coward to resign, even if she wanted him to, which she doesn't. No, he'll go out there in a little while and make the best case he can having already told half the parliamentary party, in the strictest confidence of course, why they should be voting against him."

"So come on, Ernie, if any one knows the answer to this question you do. Are we going to win?"

"You know I wouldn't soft soap you, Miss Griffin. I don't think you are. Not unless Paul can turn things around at the very last moment. I'm sure he's doing his best."

"Oh yes, Ernie, you know Paul Sinclair. He's always on the case."

~

Helmut watched the mini-bus draw up and had to lean forward a little to see who was getting out of the passenger door. He called Joshua over to join him at the window and pointed down into the street. "Correct me if I am wrong, but is not that your father?"

The last time Joshua's heart had pounded so fast he'd been about to step out on stage in a false beard and half an inch of make-up. "I think perhaps you should go down and welcome him."

PJ was just opening the door as Joshua got to the foot of the stairs. He looked at the boy. "Aren't you...?" He turned as the door opened fully. "And you're…" When it was obvious that neither sentence was going to be finished in a hurry, Paul Sinclair stepped forward.

"May I come in? It's rather chilly out here."

PJ stood back and made a feeble gesture of welcome. Joshua pushed past his father and saw Jim Clements coming up the path. A quick glance in either direction revealed no large Daimler and, so far as he could see, no security back up either. Upstairs in the workshop Helmut had come to the same conclusion. It was a mark of how far he'd come from radical revolutionary to purveyor of freedom pills that the first thing he did was check his pockets for anything incriminating. He thought of the hole in the Castle roof but another escape in that direction was more than he could cope with. He'd just have to hope that if, when, the police arrived it wouldn't be him they were interested in. Pete looked dazed, his control of the situation having slipped away with extraordinary speed. The two friends went to the top of the stairs, leant over the banister and listened.

"I'm sorry, Mr…"

"Walton. PJ."

"I knew my son had slipped out of my house without an explanation, but I hadn't expected him to smuggle himself into yours in the same way."

"I'm sure there's an explanation, Prime Minister. I think it must have something to do with my lodgers." He looked up and saw Pete's head disappear quickly from view. "Peter, Helmut, could you come down here a moment?"

"I think if you don't mind," said Sinclair, "I'd just like a few minutes alone with my son."

That sounded to PJ like a very good idea. It might give him time to work out what on earth was going on. "Yes, of course. Let me show you my study. You can talk in there."

"That's kind of you. I'll try not to be too long." He put an arm around Joshua's shoulder and turned back to his teacher. "Jim, maybe you could help put Mr Walton's mind at rest that this is not an official visit."

PJ closed the study door and joined the other three men in the kitchen. Pete was the first to break the silence. "You know what? That bloke doesn't half look like the Prime Minister."

Danny Oliver had had to fight to get through the scrum of journalists outside the door to the viewing gallery that looked down onto the Chamber. Their excited demands for Sinclair's reaction to the resignation of his deputy had gone unanswered. Danny had stonewalled, telling them they'd have to wait. A replacement as Foreign Secretary would be appointed in due course. He knew he couldn't get away with it for very much longer, but for now the hacks were as keen as he was to see what was going to happen on the floor of the House.

He took the seat reserved for the Number 10 Director of Communications just to the side of the journalists' own banks of seats. Down below him he could see Stephen Piggin waiting to begin the debate. The Commons was in an excitable mood. There's nothing MPs relish more than an unfolding drama and it's not every day that the second most important person in the government resigns on the day of a knife-edge vote. Tradition has it that at times of trouble, the Prime Minister takes his own seat on the front bench to show his support for whichever of his colleagues is taking the flak. Piggin looked round nervously and, sensing his discomfort, the opposition started pointing their fingers and demanding "Where is he?" Janine Clairmont who, with the rest of the TV journalists, had a seat near the front, caught Danny's eye and mouthed the same question.

53

"Well, here we are then." Sinclair's voice was calm and measured, but this was uncharted territory for both of them.

"Here we are. Who'd have guessed it." Joshua looked over at the closed door. He still couldn't quite believe that his dad had come at all, never mind without his police protection. He was beginning to feel as if he'd started something that was going to be a lot harder to finish. But his face suddenly broke out into a broad, toothy grin. "Jesus, Dad, I didn't really expect you to come. I thought you had a country to run?"

"I do, although I don't suppose it will fall apart without me. I had to come. I mean I wanted to. Not coming just wasn't an option." He went over to his son and ruffled his hair.

"Hey, don't do that. You know I hate it." He tried to look angry with his father, but it didn't come easily.

"So, now what?"

Joshua shrugged. "I don't know. I was so wound up this morning, I could have hit you if you'd been there. Maybe it's just as well you weren't. I felt like I'd been convicted of something terrible that I couldn't even remember doing and nobody would tell me how long the sentence was. So I jumped bail. Talking of which, does Kneejerk know you're here?"

"No, he doesn't. At least I don't think he does. I'm never quite sure, but I'm starting to wonder if he doesn't know rather less than he likes to claim."

"That is so awesome. He must be having kittens."

"Probably. You're not overly fond of the Colonel are you?"

"Oh, is it that obvious? I was hoping nobody had noticed. He's awful, you must be able to see that. I can't walk around that place without the feeling that he's about to pounce out at me from somewhere. That was what was so horrible about last night, knowing that wherever I went he was still there looking over my shoulder. I mean, I thought he was supposed to be catching international terrorists or something, not having me followed round the West End. It was so embarrassing."

"I know you won't let me get away with saying I know how you feel. But I can see where you're coming from. Having said that…"

"Oh, here we go."

"No, Josh, this is serious. Do you think I'd be here if I didn't agree with you? Whatever happens, when I go back things are going to be different, I can assure you of that. I may not even be Prime Minister tomorrow, and that's just fine. But if I am there's only so much I can promise. You're entitled to your privacy, your nights out, your Heidi Hounslows…"

"Thanks, Dad, I didn't need reminding of that."

"Okay, well as I was saying, you're entitled to your privacy but I'm entitled to want to keep my son safe. Any father has that right. Except I couldn't be just any father, even if I'd wanted to be."

"Did you? I mean did you ever want to be just an ordinary dad?"

Sinclair knew he didn't have all the answers to his son's questions, but he was going to be as frank as he could be. "I suppose not. Today, though, it's all that matters to me. Tomorrow will have to take care of itself. Just remember that there are plenty of people who'd be more than happy to use you to get at me and I'm not prepared to let you get hurt on my account. So for as long as I've got left in this job, things have to be a bit different for you too."

"I know. I understand that, I always have. It's just that it's not always easy and Kneejerk has a way of making it feel a hell of a lot harder." Joshua puts his arms around his father for the first time in many months and hugged him tight. They held each other without moving for what felt like several minutes. "You came, Dad, I can't believe it," Joshua spoke into Sinclair's neck.

There was no more they needed to say to each other, so Sinclair eased his son away. "Why don't you pop down and see if you and Jim can do something about getting some food? I don't know about you, but I've been up since God knows when and I'm starving. I'd better talk to Mr Walton for a minute Josh. He must be a bit bemused by all this. Do you know anything about him?"

"Not really. Pete said he was a journalist or something. I don't think he's one of your biggest fans."

"Find me a journalist who is these days. So you've lured me into the den of a journalist. Great. He's probably filing the story of how the Prime Minister came to visit as we speak. Ask him if he'd mind popping up here, can you?" A journalist. If there was anything left of him by the time Helen had finished, Danny was going to kill him too.

Joshua nodded. "Yeah okay. I'll organise some pizzas or something, if Kneejerk hasn't got the place staked out already."

Alone in the room, Sinclair looked at his watch. A part of him, that small part that was still more Prime Minister than father, was alarmed he'd managed to spend so long here undisturbed already. He knew he'd have to check back in soon, but curled around his anxiety like the helix of Kneejerk's precious DNA was the intoxicating buzz of feeling like a naughty school-boy himself.

Stephen Piggin sat down, red in the face and deflated. His bulky body slumped back into his seat and the merest murmur of assent reached him from the rows of benches behind him. He wasn't a clever man but he'd been in the House of Commons jungle long enough to be able to hear the distant flap of circling vultures. MPs could smell defeat like animals smelt death and fear. Across the despatch box his opponent was ready to pounce and Piggin's only consolation was that he knew already exactly what was coming.

Upstairs in the gallery Danny fiddled with his pager but it carried no news. He thought of going back to the office but something made him stay and listen to what the opposition spokesman had to say. Helen too had slipped into the officials' box to the side of the Chamber.

"The Right Honourable Gentleman has my deepest sympathy." The mauling had begun. "First the Prime Minister pulls the rug out from beneath him and then he doesn't even have the courtesy to be here to watch him fall on his," he looked at the Speaker's chair, "on his ample behind. If I might remind the House, it was Paul Sinclair himself who said, and I quote, that the National Health Service should be left to those people who know what they're doing. And isn't that an admission, Madam Speaker, from the Prime Minister's own lips that he and his government have no idea what they are doing?"

PJ went over to the bread bin to find the pile of take away menus that were always stuffed behind it. For reasons that he still didn't fully understand, the Prime Minister was currently sitting in his study waiting for him. In the circumstances, the fact that he was also hungry seemed perfectly natural.

Jim Clements took the pile from him. "Leave it to me, I'll get them. I feel a bit redundant around here as it is. Josh, what does your father like? Nothing too bland I hope, that really would disappoint me. How about an American Hot? What about you, PJ?"

"You know, I'm really not hungry." He knew the Downing Street Press Office would never have granted him an interview with the Prime Minister, which is why he'd never asked for one. Now Paul Sinclair was asking to see him and he hadn't a clue what he was going to say.

Sinclair was leaning over his desk when he entered the study. Several of his own articles were scattered around, along with notes scribbled on random pieces of paper. PJ Walton didn't keep a very tidy desk, but then for some reason it had never occurred to him that the man he spent so much of his time attacking would ever see it.

"You're an avid fan of the Naked Prophet, I see." Sinclair was smiling. "I try not to read him myself, but I dare say you agree with every word he writes."

"Actually, it's funny you should say that. I'm not altogether sure that I do."

The Chamber was suddenly electrified as Joanna Morgan came in through the big double doors and walked towards the despatch box. Her flame red suit showed her remarkably good legs off to great effect as she turned away from the front bench where she would normally have sat and climbed up to the backbenches. There was a lot of shuffling around her as MPs reacted with either pride or panic at the thought that she might sit beside them. She chose a place close to the steps where she knew the TV cameras would get a good shot.

The opposition spokesman had paused to allow this little piece of theatre to be played out. "May I welcome the Right Honourable

Lady to the Chamber? We look forward to her resignation statement with great interest. But is it not clear, Madam Speaker, that the Prime Minister's own deputy has lost confidence in him? How then can this House or indeed the country avoid coming to the same conclusion?" From his perch up in the gallery, Danny saw Helen Griffin get to her feet in the box reserved for officials. He thought for one moment she was going to break all the rules and go into the Chamber itself to tell Joanna Morgan just what she thought. He breathed again when he saw her turn on her heels and leave.

"Perhaps the Right Honourable Lady will tell us if she intends to support the government in the voting lobbies today." Joanna Morgan sat impassive, soaking up the attention. "If she decides to vote with us, however, she will be on the side not just of common sense but also of the poor and vulnerable who so depend on the NHS in their everyday lives. Let me give the House just one example. Mrs Olive Reynolds is a pensioner living in Brighton. She has a serious brain condition but one that could be helped, possibly even cured, if only this government would release the funds for the treatment she needs. Madam Speaker, I'm sorry the Prime Minister can't be with us to hear about the case of Mrs Reynolds. It ought to be a matter close to his heart. Because Mrs Olive Reynolds, that old lady still waiting to hear if this callous government will help her or abandon her, is none other than his own mother-in-law." The Chamber fell silent for a second and then erupted into cheers from one side and shouts of "shame" from the other. The former Foreign Secretary didn't move a muscle.

Danny was out of his seat and through the exit doors before any of the journalists had time to catch him. In a matter of minutes he was back in the relative safety of Number 10.

"Where the fuck did he get that from?" Helen was marching up and down the Den punching the furniture.

"Calm down. Let me see what I can find out." Danny dialled Ruth's number but it was engaged. He pressed the redial and on the third attempt it rang and she answered immediately. She listened as Danny told her what had happened and urged her to get somebody to her mother's house before the media arrived.

"I've already thought of that. I'll ask Sandra. My agent. She lives not far away and she'll know what to do."

"So you saw it?"

"No."

"So how…?"

"Donald just called me. He was watching it in his office."

"The doctor?"

"Yes. Yes, the doctor. I know what you're probably thinking and I'll be honest, Danny, I don't know if Donald Gill could have done this. But he just told me he didn't and while I don't know him well, my feeling is that he was telling the truth."

"Well the opposition found out somehow."

"Donald says he did just what I advised him to do."

"Which is?"

"He called Stephen Piggin's office. When he seemed to want me to help, I just told him to speak to the Health Secretary."

"Thank you, that's very helpful. Very helpful indeed. Ruth, I know this isn't a good time, but there's something else you should know." She looked at the open bottle on the table beside the phone, relieved that she hadn't touched it, as Danny explained that, while he didn't think she should worry, both her son and her husband had disappeared.

54

In the blimey-who'd-have-guessed-it stakes PJ and Sinclair were now just about even.

"So the Naked Prophet is unmasked at last," Sinclair laughed. "Well your secret is safe with me. Mind you, you've given me my fair share of headaches. Weren't you the guy that dredged up all that stuff about the Health Service? I'd love to know where you get all your information from." He looked at his watch. Whatever else he did, he had to be back in time to vote.

"I bet you would, although I don't know if you'd believe me. How long have we got?"

"I haven't a clue. Normally I have people to tell me how long my meetings are, but this is slightly different, I'm pleased to say. I hope I'm not keeping you from anything important." The absurdity of the comment made them both smile.

"Not at all. I don't have to do tomorrow's column until a bit later. Maybe you can give me some suggestions."

"Now that's too good an offer to refuse. I wonder what your readers will make of this little encounter?"

"They don't have to make anything of it."

Sinclair looked amazed. "Don't they?"

"How about we agree that everything said in here is just between you and me? Off the record."

"My Communications Director tells me that everything is on the record in the end."

"Well, maybe, but you can save it for your memoirs if you want to."

He hadn't given much thought to his memoirs, but Sinclair could tell that this particular chapter was one a lot of people would find hard to believe. "That's a very generous offer, PJ. I'm not sure I have any right to be treated so lightly."

"Perhaps I'm not such a great journalist after all. I'd rather have a conversation that's worth having than one I can write about in the morning. I mean, it's not every day the Prime Minister of Great Britain…"

"And Northern Ireland."

"I was coming to that. It's not every day that the Prime Minister of Great Britain and Northern Ireland pops in for a chat."

Sinclair was pacing about the room as he talked. The sunlight from the window caught the dust on the piles of books and newspapers stacked against the wall. "You are looking after my son, remember. I wouldn't be here otherwise."

"I don't think I can take much credit for that. It's not the first time strangers have been invited into my house without me being asked. But while I can just about accept that you're here because of him, I still don't know why he's here at all."

"The best answer I have to that one is that he's seventeen, he thinks I lock him up in some kind of fortress and signing up to your Freedom Alliance or whatever it is struck him as a good way of letting me know."

"Well he's in for a bit of a disappointment on that front. We gave up on overthrowing the State in this house a while back."

Sinclair settled finally on the arm of a chair by the window. The light cast one side of his face into shadow. "I'm pleased to hear that, I must say. But Josh has a point. Downing Street is no place for a teenager really." How old was PJ? Thirty, maybe slightly older. Sinclair felt strangely comfortable in his presence. There was something in his appearance and manner that connected with him at a deeper, more instinctive level than he was able to explain. He felt sure he was in the company of a man he could trust. "And to make it worse, his mother isn't there very much. Children need their mothers."

PJ still had one surprise up his sleeve, which is where he decided to leave it for now. "I was adopted. I don't really know my birth mother all that well."

"Josh doesn't see his as often as he should. And I feel responsible for that. Who am I to impose such a crazy life on them? I look forward to the day when we can all get back to some kind of normality."

"Would that make such a big difference? I thought ex-Prime

Ministers got just as much security as serving ones these days."

"It would be better. But, you're right in a sense. It's a dangerous world."

"Well nobody could ever accuse you of letting us forget that."

"Don't get me wrong. I'm not apologising for wanting to keep people safe. I told Josh as much just now. I suppose the Naked Prophet thinks I just do it for the fun of it."

PJ shook his head. "No, the Naked Prophet, if I remember rightly, accuses you of trampling on civil liberties in order to let the security industry and their friends in America take over the running of the country. Something like that. Quite a lot of people would agree with him."

"Maybe. But he does have a habit of forgetting that the measures we brought in were for a very good reason and had wide public support."

"The reason being the Circle of Death?"

"That and everything that went before. Is that so outrageous?" He stood up again and resumed his pacing. "You can't have madmen on the loose trying to poison the entire London Underground."

"And yet you've never caught them, have you? Despite holding just about everybody in Britain with an Arab name in custody at one time or another. Despite all your DNA biometric ID cards and your Vortex scanning machines and whatever else. Have you ever wondered why not?"

"I think about it all the time. But there hasn't been a repeat attack. We haven't caught them but we might have stopped them doing it again."

"Possibly."

"It sounds to me like you know more than you're letting on."

The two men looked at one another. There was an unspoken agreement that while both of them might have to reserve something, they each had a powerful interest of their own in continuing. "Do you mind if we talk in hypotheticals, Paul?"

"Oh I don't know about that," Sinclair smiled, "you know how we politicians hate hypotheticals."

"I didn't say you were going to like them. Look, I don't know exactly what lay behind a McDonalds bag full of chemicals ending up where it did." Sinclair was looking more serious all of a sudden. They both knew that the brand name on the bag had never been made public. "But I think I have a better idea than some of the people you've been putting your faith in so far."

"That wouldn't surprise me."

"Paul, I want to help you because it's important. But I'm not about to hand you any scalps."

The Prime Minister nodded his acceptance. "You don't have to go on if you don't want to."

"Let's just suppose for a minute that it had nothing to do with Al Qaeda or international terrorism or anything like that."

"I find that a little hard to believe, but I'm listening."

"Just bear with me for a while. Take it from me that the people behind the attack, or whatever it was, didn't learn their politics in the foothills of Afghanistan or at the feet of some radical Imam."

"Go on. Maybe you're going to tell me it was the South London Freedom Alliance all along. Although whatever their failings I think the security services managed to rule out all the home grown extremist groups. They'd all been well infiltrated. Sorry, PJ."

PJ shrugged and continued. "But what if there was no bomb?"

"No bomb? What are you talking about? I thought you were being serious."

"I am Paul, I promise you. What if the chemicals they found in that bag were never intended for anything more sinister than some rather nasty designer drug? Do you know what young people take into their systems these days for the fun of it? Ask Joshua."

Sinclair's frown deepened. "I very much hope he doesn't know."

PJ looked dubious but went on. "They've been using things like bleach and heavy duty solvents for years to mix up some of those party drugs. It was only a matter of time before they started experimenting with more and more dangerous chemicals. The kids on the dance floors are so loaded by the time they go out they don't ask for a list of ingredients." The Prime Minister was shaking his head. "Stick with me Paul, just for a minute. I said we were talking hypotheticals. Let's say your guys, in all good faith, thought they had come across what they'd feared for so long. A chemical weapon. The alert goes up, you give your orders, the whole country is terrified. Can you blame them if, when later on they discover how wrong they were, they keep quiet about it? There have been some unintended benefits from their point of view. The scare stiffened your resolve. Brought you back from your plans to reverse some of your predecessor's more draconian measures. And besides, they'd have been a laughing stock if they'd turned round and said, whoops, it was just some nasty ingredients for a party drug that had been stashed out of the way when someone thought the police were following him."

Sinclair still didn't find the story credible, but at least it had a consistency to it. "Do you really believe they could be that cynical?"

"For a while I thought you were in on it. That you'd seen how the tough new measures were popular and agreed to stay quiet when they told you the truth. You've got to admit, it did wonders for you politically."

"For a while? You thought that for a while? What did I do to change your mind."

"Nothing specific to be honest. I just came to the conclusion you weren't that kind of a guy."

"Well thank you for that at least. Let me assure you, I don't maintain all this security just for the fun of it. And certainly not for the sake of looking tough."

"No, I don't believe you do. But you can see why it might be in the interests of people less principled than you to keep the truth under wraps. It's not even as if the public objects to what's happened as a consequence. The Naked Prophet may go on about you crushing civil liberties, but the truth is that when you crack down the masses applaud and just ask for more chains." He beckoned the Prime Minister over to the window. "There's a woman over there in the house across the street who thinks you're soft for not having put armed police on every street corner."

Sinclair looked out to where PJ was pointing. Mrs Alma Gundry was by her gate talking to a young man in a leather jacket. He had a notebook in his hand and, though neither the Prime Minister nor the Naked Prophet could hear her, she was just getting into her stride on the subject of vomit. Paul Sinclair perched on the window sill and said over his shoulder, "I'm sorry, PJ, I just don't buy it. My wife writes better fiction than that."

"As you like. Did you ever see exactly what was found in that bag?"

The Prime Minister turned away from the window and shook his head. "No, but I had a full report. I saw the chemical breakdown, not that it meant much to me. All the scientific experts agreed on the potential death toll if it had gone off properly."

"Hold on just a second. Do you mind?" PJ went out onto the landing and down the flight of stairs to the kitchen. Helmut and Joshua were sitting watching the coverage from the House of Commons on the TV in the corner. When he heard what his landlord wanted him to do, Helmut was horrified. He started to argue but PJ waved to him to be quiet as the announcer delivered the news of the upset in the Commons, the latest twist to the crisis facing the government of the Right Honourable Paul Sinclair. When PJ uttered a barely audible 'Oh mother' the others didn't hear and wouldn't have understood if they had.

55

The Presidential motorcade was surging through the narrow streets like blood through veins, and so far as John Warren was concerned its presence was no less vital. On the seat beside him, Tracey Warren was looking through her notes. These towns in Middle America all looked exactly the same to her and she wanted to check which Hicksville this was supposed to be. From the blue gingham dress the wardrobe assistant had given her, she had her money on Tennessee.

The big speech would be made to an adoring crowd of defence workers. 'Bunny' Warren was feeling good. He'd made the same stump speech a thousand times already in this campaign, and he was looking forward to having something new to say for a change. He was sure Paul Sinclair would play the game. He was a politician too, for God's sake, and he knew about winning elections. He might be a bit sore at the deceit, but he'd soon realise there was nothing he could do about it now so he might just as well share in the glory. The car's mobile communications unit had just connected the President to Number 10 Downing Street.

"Helen, it's good to talk with you but, you know, I think I should be speaking to the Prime Minister if you really don't mind."

"Mr President, Paul would love to speak to you too. It's just that things are a little up in the air over here at the moment."

"I heard that your Foreign Secretary quit, yeah. It's been on the radio. Sounded pretty weird to me when the operation was such a success. She's the woman who kept on shooting her mouth off on television right? I'd have thought you'd have the champagne open by now."

"Well things aren't always as simple as they seem."

"I guess so. Paul said it was something about Parliamentary Democracy. Beats me. I thought you guys got to do pretty much whatever you wanted over there. Anyway get him to call me quick.

299

I've got this speech to make and he'd probably want to know what I'm going to say about you brave little Brits."

The alarm bells were starting to ring. "It might be quicker if I just passed on a message, Mr President."

"I don't know about that. I should be telling this to the Prime Minister. No disrespect, ma'am."

"None taken, Mr President, but believe me the fastest way of getting this information to him is to tell me. Paul trusts me with everything, as you know."

"Protocol normally dictates that we make time for each other, whatever else is going on."

"I know that Mr President."

Warren waved to his wife and mouthed the word 'speech'. She found it in the briefing pack and passed it over to him. When he read over the passage about how, with the United Kingdom's help, notorious Godfathers of terror had been killed, Helen interrupted him. "Who exactly do you mean, Mr President?"

"Eh? The Somalis and other guys who were hanging out at that training base your brave SAS men just raided, of course. I thought you were supposed to be the Chief of Staff. Don't your people tell you anything? I think you should get this to Paul just as soon as you can."

"I think I should too, Mr President. I think I should too."

"All right, well thank you Helen. I hope you sort out whatever's getting to you guys just as quick as possible."

Helen placed the receiver back in its cradle as if it were a tiny baby that might wake up and start screaming the place down again at any moment. She took a deep breath and called through the open door. "Rebecca, can you get me the Poverty Action office in Cambridge on the line?"

PJ Walton handed the Prime Minister a piece of paper. Sinclair looked at the rough scribble. "What's this?"

"A formula. Have somebody you trust take a look at what you have on file and see if they match. If they do, maybe you'll think carefully about what I've been telling you."

Sinclair put it in his trouser pocket. "That sounds reasonable enough. Just one thing more, PJ. Have you told anybody else about this?"

PJ looked around the room and back at the Prime Minister. "Only one person. My mother. Unfortunately, I have a very unusual mother. I caught a bit of the news while I was downstairs. Have you any idea at all what's been going on while you've been away?"

Sinclair wasn't sure if there was supposed to be any common thread to what he'd just been told. "None at all. Am I starting to wonder? Yes, of course I am. Should I be there sorting out whatever the latest mess is? Yes, I should. But do I regret coming here to find Josh with the unexpected bonus of finally meeting the Naked Prophet? Not for a moment. So. Is there something I should know?"

As soon as he'd heard on the television that the story he'd refused to break was now in the hands of the opposition PJ Walton knew he'd been taken for a fool for a very long time. He wanted Sinclair to know exactly what he believed she had done, but first there was a story to tell. About a son given up for adoption who reappears and threatens to cast a shadow over a carefully crafted political image but who quickly proves to be a useful tool for an ambitious woman. And about a son who today felt he was about to be orphaned for a second time, with no father he could put a name to and a mother he could no longer respect. By the time PJ had finished the Prime Minister was unable to put his own thoughts into words. Knowing he wouldn't be able to articulate even a fraction of what was going through his mind, he took the younger man by the shoulders and pulled him close. "Thank you." They both heard the front door slam but neither moved to break the embrace.

Joshua came into the room first with Jim Clements close behind. A smell of pizza spiralled up the stairs from the kitchen. On a day like today, seeing your father in the arms of another man didn't seem anything out of the ordinary.

"I think you should move away from the window." Jim was already pulling the curtains.

"What's the matter?" asked Sinclair.

"You hadn't spotted there was a television crew outside in the street?" There was silence. "I thought not. I've just been asked if I was delivering pizza for the Prime Minister."

"Danny. Situation report. You go first." Somebody had to take charge of a situation that was getting more bizarre by the minute and Helen was more than ready to oblige.

From the start, Danny had been the one with the least confidence that the disappearance of a Prime Minister could be kept under wraps. The Danny Oliver Media Rule Book stated quite clearly that there was an inverse relationship between how bad a piece of news was and how quickly it would leak out. So nobody was more surprised than him that he was able to report that in public at least things weren't looking so bad. The media had been so absorbed by the Foreign Secretary's resignation and the dramas in the House that they simply assumed Sinclair was at his desk keeping his head down. Sandra, Ruth's agent, had quickly grasped the seriousness of the situation and Mrs Olive Reynolds was currently enjoying tea at the Grand quite unaware that she was at the centre of a political storm. Neville Standen of the *News of the World* was paging him every half an hour but Helen didn't need to know about that just yet. What excited the Chief of Staff most, however, was what Ruth had passed on from Dr Donald Gill.

"It's just what we needed to know. Trust me, Danny, we're back in the game. As soon as we're done here I want the word spread around that we've discovered a trail that leads from Joanna Morgan and Stephen Piggin to the opposition front bench. Our people may not love us very much right now, but there's nothing they hate more than a traitor."

"Shouldn't we ask Paul before we hang his Health Secretary out to dry?"

"Oh Danny, what a clever boy you are. Why don't we do exactly that?" She put her hands on her hips and swayed from side to side as she looked at each corner of the room in turn like a pantomime dame. "Oh dearie me. He doesn't seem to be here. I wonder where he can have got to?" Her voice switched in a the blinking of an over made-up eye. "Colonel?" she growled, "Over to you."

Neilson was in no mood for Helen's mockery, indeed he was starting to feel distinctly nauseous. His military training told him to hold fast and get the situation under control as quickly as possible, but he was starting to wonder if that could be done. He should have been having a private talk with the Prime Minister right now, persuading him that having taken out a terrorist training camp, albeit unintentionally, was something to be proud of. He had a feeling Helen Griffin would be harder to convince. "We've run checks at all hospitals and doctors' surgeries in London," he offered feebly, "as well as taxi firms and minicab companies. CCTV pictures from every underground station and bus stop are being analysed as we speak, but so far nothing. I think we have to consider the possibility that he's being held somewhere against his will."

"So what do you suggest?"

"Some old fashioned police work. I can get Scotland Yard to start talking to their touts, that sort of thing."

"When this is all over, Colonel, I'd be very interested to see the figures for the cost of all your cameras and listening devices and whatever else it is you've been bragging to us about these past few years. It might make for an interesting cost-benefit analysis."

Kneejerk was hunched in his chair, unable to meet Helen's eye. It was Danny who came to his rescue. "Come on Helen, we have to stick together. This may be the most incredible high wire act that ever there was but, so far, it seems we haven't fallen off. If we start taking swings at each other, we're going to lose our balance and it won't be pretty."

Helen looked at her watch. "So are we saying that Paul Sinclair has been on Planet Zog for over four hours now and nobody, with the possible exception of the President of the United States, has noticed anything unusual? Christ, if we ever get him back we'd better not tell him. It'll make him feel even more useless than he actually is. It might be time to try the psychiatric wards. Maybe he's been found wandering the streets somewhere claiming to be the Prime Minister."

Nobody laughed. "Now, Colonel, while I'm on the subject of the President, I just got off the phone to him. It was a very interesting conversation. And when I'd finished I rang my friend at Poverty Action and told her the President had personally filled me in. She was obviously impressed and very forthcoming too. When were you planning to tell us that you and your cohorts in the CIA had tricked us into sending the SAS to attack a heavily guarded terrorist camp on behalf of your friend Bunny Warren?"

Kneejerk had a handkerchief to his mouth and was dangerously close to being physically sick. Helen's contemptuous glare was distracted by the mobile ringing in her bag. She fished it out and saw Janine Clairmont's number on the screen. She thought about it for a second and then pressed the green button.

"Janine."

"Helen. Don't bullshit me."

"I haven't said a word. Apart from your name."

"Well don't bullshit me now. Just answer me straight. Is Paul Sinclair sitting right now in a house in Bermondsey eating a pizza or is he not?"

"Janine, I don't know what you're talking about."

"I said don't bullshit me."

"What are you trying to say, darling?"

"I just had a call from Scott."

"Scott?"

"You know, the boy who's taken a bit of a shine to me. He does those Neighbours From Hell features in the mornings. Anyway, it doesn't matter. He was getting ready to film at this place in South London somewhere and swears he saw Sinclair at the window of some slum."

"How likely is that?" Helen was buying time.

"Come on, Helen. Scott's not just a cock on legs. He's a smart kid. I think he knows what the Prime Minister looks like. And he also has film of the Harvest Hill Comprehensive School minibus which is parked outside. Forgive me if I've gone mad but isn't that young Joshua's school? So is Sinclair there or not?"

"Janine. Listen to me. Carefully. Just give me the address and tell you're boyfriend that he mustn't move. The same goes for the camera crew. Understand?"

"Not this time, Helen. I've done you too many favours. If we've got exclusive pictures of the Prime Minister on some secret rendezvous then we have to use them. There's a woman involved isn't there? Is he shagging the sports mistress or something?"

"Oh, don't be ridiculous, Janine."

"I'm being ridiculous, am I? Okay, well if he's not there, where is he? Maybe we could have an interview with him about the resignation of the Deputy Prime Minister. He's been pretty quiet on that front so far. If he's not too busy, of course."

"Janine, this is my final offer. Tell Scott or whatever the fuck you call him to wait for you and do nothing until he sees you. I'll meet you there. Just give me the address."

"You're not in any position to make offers."

"Janine. The address."

56

PJ Walton's story had affected the Prime Minister on many levels. There was a lot he was going to have to think about very deeply, but for now it had helped Sinclair to refocus and start to regain his capacity for action. For several hours he had been content to let events take their course, unsure that he any longer had the power or the will to steer them. Now he knew he had to try. "PJ, we will have to talk further about all this and soon. But right now I need to use your phone. I think it might be time I reported back for duty."

"Yes, of course." PJ Walton studied Sinclair's face but he wasn't yet enough of an intimate to be able to read it. "It's over there."

Joshua's stomach was churning as he stared at the curtains pulled tight across the window. He'd been so proud of his father for coming, so pleased with himself for having got him here, but suddenly he felt selfish and childish and stupid. "This wasn't in the script, was it?" he said without raising his head.

Helen was still holding the phone in her hand but she dropped it down by her side.

"That sounded interesting," said Danny.

"Very." She stared hard at Kneejerk. "Friends, Colonel, you should get a few. Real ones, I mean. They're a lot more useful than you might think. The Prime Minister is at least looking after his stomach. If my information is correct, he's currently enjoying a takeaway pizza."

It was the turn of Danny's phone to ring before Helen could explain. He listened for a few seconds before cutting in. "Just tell me one thing. Are you eating pizza?" Danny shook his head. "Hang on you'd better speak to Helen." He held out the phone. "Apparently the food is going cold."

"What the fuck are you up to?" she spat.

"Helen, it's nice to talk to you too. But I don't think this is the time for one of your lectures."

"Don't worry, I wasn't going to waste my breath. Where are you?" She heard him ask somebody in the room and when he came back on the phone with the information she looked down at the address Janine had given her. "Well just stay where you are."

"I think you should know…"

"That there's a TV crew in the street? Yeah I know. I'm doing what I can to handle that, which is why you must stay put. Do you think you can manage that? We'll be with you as soon as we can." She rang off and turned to Danny. "Where's that sexy little sports car of yours?"

Kneejerk slipped back into his office. He hadn't been invited to join them. But this time if anybody was going anywhere he meant to know exactly where it was. The details of Danny Oliver's silver MG were swiftly programmed into all the surveillance equipment at his command and the onboard computers of every police helicopter over London. Danny wouldn't be able to look in his rear view mirror without the Downing Street Security Supremo knowing about it.

Being told to do nothing was a new experience for Paul Sinclair. He could barely think of a single time in the past thirty years when it had even been an option. His mind was racing hither and thither over everything that PJ had told him and reaching some extraordinary conclusions. If he was right then the contours of his world had been redrawn in just about every direction he cared to look. Nobody in the room at that particular moment could help him make sense of it, so rather than torture himself any further he tried to distract himself with more mundane tasks. He began by learning that microwave ovens are not the best way to reheat pizza. And that his son appeared to know his way around a kitchen rather better than he did.

"Here, Dad. If you microwave it the base goes all soft. You have to preheat the oven and put them in for a couple of minutes. Any longer and they get too dry and crispy."

With a slice in each hand Pete announced he was going back up to the workshop where Helmut had been lurking, very frightened indeed since handing over the formula. Pete hadn't been able to fathom what was going on, but he was used to that. He hoped a piece of reheated pizza might at least cheer his friend up.

"Do you want to show me what else you can do with that computer?" Joshua, still dreaming of Kneejerk's Revenge, followed him out.

Across the road, Mrs Alma Gundry was getting a little frustrated. The young man had sounded very polite on the telephone and she'd been delighted when he said he could be in Wilson Crescent so soon. He'd made lots of notes and had complimented her on her Bakewell tart and asked about her china figures before she told him the long history of the Castle and its inhabitants. The cameraman had been a little gruff, it was true, and had trailed dirt into her sitting room, but he'd taken lots of film which he said would show what a responsible neighbour she was. But when she'd come out with the second pot of tea, they seemed to have lost all interest in her and what she had to say. The young man kept pointing at the windows of the house opposite and waving his arms around. He appeared to be having an argument with somebody on his mobile phone who he'd called darling and then, when he'd put the phone down, bitch. When Mrs Gundry had offered him another slice of tart he'd told her to be quiet, which she thought was quite unnecessary.

The cameraman was trying to offer a window cleaner fifty euros for his ladders when Danny Oliver parked his little MG at the end of the street.

At first sight, Danny's assessment of the Castle would have been music to Mrs Gundry's ears. "What a dump. Are you sure he's in there?" The lime green vinyl wallpaper that clung relentlessly to the side wall was clearly visible from fifty yards. Gusts of wind caused the edges of the fly-posters pasted beneath it to flap. The roof was obviously in bad repair, with several tiles missing and the hedge along the front of the building looked as if it hadn't been cut in years.

Helen Griffin tucked her phone under her chin and looked at the piece of paper with the address on it. "Yup, that's it." She had a vague feeling she was not so very far away from the rather smart wine bar where she'd been drinking with Janine only the night before. The Political Editor of AM-TV herself was at that moment in a black cab, turning into the other end of Wilson Crescent. She had been cutting between two conversations, trying to persuade Scott Bolton not to tell the newsroom about his scoop before she got there and to convince Helen that this time friendship alone wouldn't be enough to make her bend to her will.

Helen didn't need to be told that her powers of persuasion were reaching their limit. It was time to clutch at straws. "Janine, your programme doesn't go on the air until six o'clock tomorrow morning, am I right?" She was. "Well in that case, if I don't make it up to you by giving you something," she turned to Danny and shrugged. She hadn't the slightest idea what that something might be, "something even more tantalising than what you may think you have right now, then you can do whatever you like. All bets will be off. But first of all you have to get that camera out of the fucking street, okay?"

Janine kept talking as she paid the cab and barged into Mrs Gundry's hall where Scott was waiting for her. She put her friend on hold while he confirmed that the cameraman had so far failed to get a shot of the Prime Minister at the window. Helen didn't know it, but they had nothing to prove Paul Sinclair was in there. She was certain nobody would be coming out of that house, certainly nobody her viewers would recognise, as long as the camera was still in the middle of the road. And at the back of her mind was every journalist's fear that the jungle drums were already beating calling her competitors to this unlikely corner of South London. She made sure Helen could hear her as she told Scott to call the cameraman into the house.

"What the fuck…?" Scott, who'd never come within a mile of a scoop before in his brief career in television, was horrified.

"Just do as I tell you. I know what I'm doing." Scott didn't move. "I'm waiting. I said get your cute little arse out there and bring the camera inside."

~

From the upstairs window of the Castle where he was carefully hidden behind the dingy curtain, Pete watched as the cameraman picked up his tripod and followed the younger man back into Mrs Gundry's hallway. At the end of the street Danny and Helen saw the same reluctant retreat and clenched their fists in a simultaneous sign of victory.

309

"Thanks, Janine, you won't regret this," said Helen.

"I wish I could be sure of that." Janine waved away Mrs Gundry's offer of a cup of tea and a slice of Bakewell tart.

"Now what?" asked Danny.

"The Prime Minister is waiting for us. He may be a total waste of space but we'd better get him out of there. Can you move the car up a bit closer?"

Pete now watched the little silver MG edge along the street towards the Castle. Then he turned his head a fraction to look back at Mrs Gundry's house across the street. The sun glinted off something in an upstairs window.

"Come on Helmut."

"Come on where exactly, Peter?"

"Just follow me."

On the pavement Helen and Danny stood and stared for a moment at the front of the Castle, at the peeling paint on the front door and the dirty net curtains that hung in the windows on either side. Without even thinking about it Danny pressed the remote control in his pocket and the car doors clicked into the locked position. By the time Helen had reached the gate with Danny two steps behind, Pete had pushed a protesting Helmut up through the plastic covered hole in the roof and was pulling him by the arm towards the far end of the terrace.

Helen was about to knock on the door when she heard the sound of engines being driven at high speed. She turned and saw two police vans coming towards them. "Shit," she said, swivelling round to see two more of the same coming in the opposite direction. The noise of the rotor blades made them both look up and as they did so they missed seeing Pete and Helmut dash across the road in front of the oncoming vehicles.

In Mrs Gundry's front bedroom Scott Bolton also heard the helicopter and looked up. His cameraman tilted the lens upwards to get a better shot. With his eye stuck to the side of the camera, he failed to notice Helmut's stocky figure appear as if from nowhere at the first floor window.

"Hurry up, mate, I can't hold you for long." Pete was stretching his full six foot eight inches up the front of Mrs Gundry's house. In each of his broad hands he held one of Helmut's feet. He steadied himself as his friend leaned in through the open side window and grabbed at the tripod. The cameraman fell over backwards, knocking Scott onto the pink tasselled eiderdown. By the time they had picked themselves up, tripod and camera and disappeared.

"Excuse me, Madam." The first of the police officers pushed past Helen and went to apply his strong shoulder to the door of the Castle. Mrs Gundry, who was watching from her living room, muttered something to the effect that he wouldn't need to push too hard when the door gave way easily and the policeman tumbled into the hall. There were now men in uniform at the back of the house too, and others were being lowered onto the roof on long ropes. Seconds later the Prime Minister and his son were whisked out of the door and escorted into the first of the waiting vans. Shortly afterwards PJ Walton and Jim Clements were dragged with much greater force into the back of the second vehicle. Helmut was still clutching the TV camera to his chest looking for a way to escape when a strong hand gripped him by the arm and pushed him in too. Pete cracked his head on the door frame as he was shoved in behind. Less than two minutes after she had first seen the police drive up Mrs Alma Gundry was looking out on an empty street. She heard a strangled cry of anguish and saw that the woman from the television was on her knees pounding her fists on the floor of the sitting room.

57

Cornwall. Mrs Woods would like the idea as she could be close to her mother and her myriad of aunts, most of whom seemed to be called Betty. Sergeant Terry Woods could see himself growing broccoli and making a bit of extra money from market gardening. He'd been on duty at the Vortex since early morning, but was as sure as he could be that Kneejerk would have him out of the force by the end of the day. He imagined the Colonel breaking the news like some bristling moustachioed Lady Bracknell. To lose the Prime Minister once may be regarded as a misfortune; to lose him twice looks like carelessness. If he went quietly and kept his pension, he and Mrs Woods could probably afford to live comfortably enough. Terry was surprised that he'd been left at his post at all. His best hope was that with Paul Sinclair still missing, the Colonel had simply forgotten about him.

Colonel Henry Neilson was studying the cameras in his little office, waiting for the vans to come into view, and doing his best to weigh up his own prospects. Surely nobody could blame him for the crass stupidity of a Prime Minister who had walked off the job without so much as a by your leave. Sinclair should really be grateful to him for executing a rescue with the minimum of force and disruption. So long as he ate a bit of humble pie and acknowledged the valuable intelligence provided by Helen Griffin's contact, things might yet get back to an even keel.

He looked at his watch and tried to remember exactly what time the President was due to make his speech. If he could get the Prime Minister safely back in the precincts of Downing Street fairly soon it should still be possible to persuade him to turn the hostages situation to his, and everybody else's, advantage. He was a politician, after all. And the Chief of Staff was a hard-headed woman who would take a pragmatic views of things as well, once she had calmed down.

Yes, he should be justifiably pleased with his achievements. Two security operations, one at home and one abroad, in which nobody had been harmed, the captives had been rescued and the perpetrators were dead or detained. It was a day's work he could be proud of. The fact that it was the boy, Joshua, who had provoked the domestic crisis and who would now have to be reined in at last, was just the icing on the cake.

Word came through that the Prime Minister had asked to be taken straight to the House of Commons to enable him to vote. The armour-plated Daimler was despatched to pick him up and it was another twenty minutes before the Colonel could see it turning into the Vortex. He put on his jacket and checked his shoulders for dandruff. He would go to the Entrance Hall and prepare to receive in all modesty the congratulations that would surely be coming his way.

~

"Colonel, I'd like to see you in my office in about half an hour." It wasn't quite the welcome he'd been expecting, but it was understandable if the Prime Minister wanted to express his gratitude in private. "And please have the final report into the Circle of Death sent up to the flat straight away. The one with the technical appendices."

"Prime Minister?"

"Thank you, Colonel. I'll see you in thirty minutes."

Danny and Helen had driven back from Bermondsey in the little silver MG as fast as they could without the benefit of a police escort and had arrived just in time to meet him and Joshua in the Entrance Hall. Danny had the few seconds it took to climb the two flights of stairs to the flat in which to tell Sinclair that the media had been so preoccupied with other events that they appeared happy to believe the Prime Minister had been at his desk all day.

Sinclair had only one question. "How's Ruth?"

"As well as can be expected, I think. Her mother is out of harm's way at least. But there is something else you need to know. The *News of the World* seem to think they have a story about her and her doctor friend."

Sinclair just nodded. Once inside he went straight into the kitchen and put the kettle on. The others huddled in the doorway unsure whether to interrupt him as he bustled about gathering mugs, spoons, milk and a packet of chocolate digestives. When he had a full tray of drinks ready he led them into the study. "Helen, would you ask Switch to hold all calls until I tell them otherwise?"

Paul Sinclair appeared once again to be a man very much in charge and that was the way Helen liked him. But he was also showing signs of having made his mind up about something and, as she didn't know what that was, it put her seriously on edge. Part of the job of being Chief of Staff was to know what the Prime Minister was thinking even before he thought it. "Are we going to talk about this, Paul?" she asked when he finally put the tray down and sat on the sofa.

"Actually, yes, we are. I just want to make sure I have all the facts I need. You and Danny will be party to everything, so try to relax. I can't promise that you'll like it, but at least this time you'll be able to tell me so first."

Helen was only marginally reassured. "Well maybe you can start by telling us where you've been all day."

"I'm not sure you'd believe me if I did."

"Try me."

"All in good time. Danny seems to think that as yet nobody has noticed my absence, is that right?"

"With the possible exception of the President of the United States, yes," said Helen.

"So I've got a bit of time to play with?"

"Now look…" But before she could go any further there was a knock at the door and the face of Colonel Henry Neilson appeared quickly followed by the rest of him. The room fell silent and the Colonel followed Helen's gaze up to the ceiling where she seemed to be taking an unusual interest in the chandelier.

"Henry, come in. Do you have the report?"

"Yes, of course." He put a beige folder down on the study table. No evidence yet of any Prime Ministerial gratitude. "If I might say so Sir, I do think there are more pressing matters to attend to."

"Like?"

"The President…"

"I'll speak to him. Anything else?"

"Well, the detainees."

"What detainees?"

"Your captors. We have the power to hold them for seven days initially but we must start the interrogation process soon. We can't be sure there weren't any co-conspirators. So I really need to get some details from you about your period of captivity."

"If you'd like a discussion about conspiracies and conspirators, Colonel, I'm happy to have one, but I'm not sure you'd find it all that comfortable." Kneejerk was now looking at his shoes. "For the moment, however, I think we can agree that you have been part of a conspiracy to keep my absence from this building a secret. And with some success. Am I right?"

"That is correct, Prime Minister." Kneejerk felt a little better already. "But it was a team effort. I have to say that Helen and Mr Oliver were magnificent. I couldn't possibly take all the credit."

"I wouldn't worry too much about that, Colonel. But if I haven't been away then I couldn't have been held captive surely?"

"That's hardly the point, Prime Minister."

"Oh, I beg to differ, I think it's very much the point. There are no captors because there was no captivity. Let them go, Colonel."

"But "

"Let them go. Helen, can you make sure we get them looked after until I've had a chance to check a few things out? I may need to speak to them again this evening. Now, Colonel, if you'll excuse us."

Joshua, who had been curled up all but unnoticed in a chair in the corner, took another gulp of tea and grinned.

Helen watched the door close and took a deep breath. "I hope you know what you're doing, Paul."

"So do I, but I'm sure you'll be here to tell me if I'm wrong."

"Have I ever let you down on that front?"

"Not that I can remember." He put a hand on her arm and she didn't pull away. "We've known each other a very long time and we've come a hell of a distance together. Now maybe we've reached the end of the road, I don't know for sure. I've learned a lot today, not least about the power that goes with being Prime Minister, or its limits. But I don't have all the answers I need yet and so long as I've got some of that power I mean to get them. "

Joshua raised an eyebrow as if to ask if it was all right for him to stay and was rewarded with a nod as his father started to explain how leaving Downing Street to make sure his son was all right had brought him face to face with the Naked Prophet and his curious lodgers. He didn't give away everything he'd learned but Sinclair quickly related PJ Walton's hypothesis about the chemical attack on the underground that never was. "I've heard a few tall tales in my time, but none quite like this. If the Naked Prophet is to be believed, the whole thing was nothing like what it seemed at the time. That massive alert was caused by some dodgy drug dealers getting rid of their stash. It sounds preposterous I know but maybe, just maybe, there was no Circle of Death."

Helen looked at him dismayed. She had thought he was back in control whereas now it looked like he'd lost touch with reality entirely. "Paul…"

"Hang on, Helen. All I know for sure is that it's a theory the Naked Prophet passed on to Joanna a long time ago. He seemed to think she was ready to believe it at least."

Helen spun around. "It sounds utter bollocks to me, but it may explain something. It's the Big One, it must be. If she thinks she can reveal that you were duped into all the State Security Act stuff then that's dynamite and she knows it. A lot of people would think it meant you weren't fit to be Prime Minister. This is the secret weapon Piggin was blabbing about, I bet you."

"It gets worse," said Paul. "If what I've been told is right the security services realised their mistake but never told the rest of us. They were afraid we'd take away all their new toys."

Helen was suddenly starting to find the story a little more credible. "I've learned a thing or two while you've been away that sort of fits in with what you're saying. Don't get me wrong, I'm not buying into this fantasy, but I know for a fact that Kneejerk and his American friends haven't been playing straight with us."

"PJ Walton, that's the Naked Prophet to you and me, gave me this." Sinclair fished out the piece of paper from his pocket. "If this formula matches whatever's in the dossier that the Colonel has so promptly provided then it's true, I have been the biggest fool ever to hold this office. Do we have anyone who could check it out?"

Helen shrugged but Danny stepped forward to take the paper. "Luke might be able to help. Like every good barrister he's got contacts in the Forensic Science department who owe him a few favours. Shall I see what I can do?"

"That would be very helpful."

"But presumably they'd need to see the stuff in the dossier too and that's all classified," said Danny. "We'd need some kind of clearance."

"I don't know about that. Unless I'm much mistaken, I'm still the ultimate head of the intelligence services. If anybody can give clearance, I can. Helen, what do you think?"

"Oh I think you're absolutely right. I don't know what Kneejerk would say about you giving classified information to Danny's boyfriend but frankly I don't really care. He's probably more reliable that some people I could mention. Like 'Bunny' Warren, for example." Sinclair listened intently while Helen gave her take on what the President had been doing to help further his own re-election campaign.

The longer they talked the more they all saw the pieces slotting together. A much bigger picture was starting to emerge. If Colonel 'Kneejerk' Neilson, the ex-MI6 man brought in to sort out the security situation, had kept the Prime Minister in the dark once, he probably thought he'd have no trouble doing it again. "You realise what this means?" said Sinclair finally. "Joanna was right all along. Right to say we couldn't trust the Americans, right to say the situation in Eritrea wasn't what it seemed. Right about the Colonel and his Vortex for that matter."

"She's still a conniving bitch," said Helen. "And even if she was right, which I'm not sure I'm ready to concede, she was right for the wrong reasons."

"She was sufficiently sure of herself to resign over it. That takes guts. And what if any of our servicemen had been killed in that raid, how do you think I'd be feeling now?"

"Oh come off it. She didn't resign out of some high-minded principle, you know that. She resigned because you were in the shit and she didn't want to miss her chance. Take it from me, unless we deal with Joanna Morgan pretty goddamn fast, she and her precious Ray are going to be moving in here before we know it."

Sinclair's eyes narrowed. "And would that be so terrible? Maybe she's more cut out for this job than I am. Maybe she's even got better judgement."

The next person to speak did so with quiet conviction. "You cannot believe that." Nobody had heard Ruth Sinclair let herself into the flat, but her words silenced them all immediately. Joshua was the first to move, jumping out of his chair to put his arms around his mother's waist.

"Hey, Mum. Welcome back to the mad house."

"Well I have to say that's just what it sounds like to me." She looked around the room at the familiar faces and settled on that of her husband. "So you haven't disappeared off the face of the earth after all. Well that's a relief. Perhaps you could make me a cup of tea and tell me what's going on."

58

The Foreign Secretary's residence at Carlton Gardens was waist deep in packing cases and cardboard boxes. Ministerial resignations are high on the list of those unpredictable events for which the civil service is nonetheless always prepared. All personal belongings have to be gathered up and out of the door in time for the new Minister to move in. Except, so far today, there had been no news from Downing Street about a replacement and, until that happened, Joanna Morgan was free to stay.

Ray followed her from room to room like an obedient old dog afraid of being left behind. He'd never disagreed with a single decision his wife had made in their time together and he wasn't going to start now. Although from the way she was behaving he couldn't be sure she wasn't already regretting it.

"Bastards." Joanna Morgan wasn't a woman given to swearing but things were going seriously awry with her carefully planned strategy. It was bad enough that Sinclair had won his vote by a comfortable margin. Far more serious was the reason why. Rumours had swept the Commons that the former Foreign Secretary had been colluding with the opposition to further her own ends. It was enough to drive many of the potential rebels back into voting for the government. So far she hadn't deigned to respond to such scurrilous nonsense. Everybody knew she was a woman of principle. And yet, to her horror, the rumours were fast hardening into accepted fact. "The bastards."

"Who exactly do you mean, my love?" She gave him a withering look and he cowered visibly. Ray was unused to having his wife's anger directed at himself.

"I think it may be time to reconsider our options," she said tersely. She looked down at her flame red outfit, the one she always wore when she wanted to remind the troops what a good socialist she was at heart.

"A new suit, I think Ray. See if you can remember where we packed the grey one."

With the door closed behind him, Kneejerk watched on the internal cameras as the Chief of Staff and Communications Director emerged from the flat and went to their respective offices. The boy, Joshua, was trailing along behind Helen Griffin with a mischievous look on his face and the Colonel could see the file he'd given the Prime Minister a few minutes before now tucked under Danny Oliver's arm. He'd already seen Mrs Sinclair arrive and go upstairs so he calculated they must now be alone together. With the hotline from Kapolski flashing incessantly he needed to speak to Sinclair himself very badly indeed. He decided to take the risk of disturbing him, only to be told by Switch that no calls were being put through to the flat.

Helmut Feldhofer was feeling disorientated and more than a little disappointed. His period as a political prisoner had been laughably short. They hadn't been at Paddington Green police station more than an hour before a rather attractive young WPC had come to the interview room to tell them they were no longer in detention. Not so very long ago Helmut had rather looked forward to the prospect of going to jail for his beliefs. Admittedly his political fervour had subsided somewhat in the past few years, but common vagrants were held for longer than they had been. Had the British State that he'd once put so much effort into opposing been able to discover he was no threat to it quite so quickly? It was almost humiliating.

In any event, the circumstances of their arrest weren't exactly what Helmut in his more radical days had ever envisaged. He was now facing up to the fact that he'd been taken into custody while in the process of defending the Prime Minister, whatever the police might have thought at the time. The world really was a confusing place. If he was honest with himself, and Helmut always tried to be that, he was no longer sure whose side he was supposed to be on, never mind why.

For his part, Pete too was a little disorientated, although he put it down more to the crack on the head he'd received while being pushed into the police van. It had certainly been quite an eventful few hours and he thought he'd played his part with distinction for once. It wasn't every day you shared a take-away with the Prime Minister. And he could congratulate himself for being quick off the mark in outwitting the cameraman. He'd even enjoyed being driven across London with an armed escort, although he'd done his best to look cross. PJ should be pleased with him, although it was hard to tell what his landlord was thinking at that precise moment.

The author of the *Naked Prophet* column had barely said a word since the police had appeared from nowhere in his front hallway. Once at the station he'd allowed himself to be fingerprinted and had given a DNA sample without a murmur of complaint. Only when the admissions officer had refused to accept his name as PJ Walton had he hesitated for a moment before writing Paul Joseph Walton out in full.

"Mr Walton?" PJ looked up as the same officer came into the holding room where the three of them were sitting. "There's a car waiting for you outside, Sir. You're obviously free to do exactly as you please, of course, but the driver asked me to tell you he was sent by the gentleman you had a pizza with at lunchtime. I'm afraid I don't know any more than that."

59

Paul Sinclair held his wife's hands in his own and looked down at them. They stood in the centre of the room like that, almost as if he was about to escort her to the dance floor, for what felt much longer than it actually was. It was Ruth who broke the pose, moving her hand to his upper arm and allowing him to pull her into his body. She breathed in the smell from his shirt and put her other hand against his chest, allowing her fingers to slip between the buttons. "I was worried about you."

He squeezed her body even more tightly as if afraid that if he let her go for a second she might turn around and head back out the door. When he finally spoke, it was in a whisper. "I don't know where to start. I think I'd rather just stand here and hold you for the rest of the day."

"That's a very nice idea, but from what I hear you've taken most of today off already. Don't you think the British people deserve to have their Prime Minister back?"

He gave a little snort that she felt in her hair and relaxed his grip a little. "They seem to be doing perfectly well without me."

"From what you were saying when I came in, it sounded like you were thinking of letting them dispense with your services for good. What's all that about?"

He led her gently to the sofa and they sat down, arms still entwined. "Like I said, I don't know where to begin."

"There's no rush. I'm not going anywhere."

He leant back and looked into her face. "No?"

"No."

"That's the best news I've heard in a very long time. I hope you don't change your mind when you hear what I've got to say."

It had been in this very room three years earlier that Ruth had told him she was leaving. She'd asked herself many times since then if she might have stayed had Paul admitted to an affair with anyone other than Joanna Morgan. If it had been some more recent infatuation she could have accepted, perhaps, that it was just a sadly familiar story about the aphrodisiac of power. Much as she hated clichés, she could have forgiven Paul for lapsing into one. But if Joanna had been able to rekindle his passion after thirty years what was to say she couldn't do it again. She was still in his life and in his company almost every day. Ruth knew she couldn't stay and watch her striding through Number 10 on her way to meetings or standing beside her husband on a public platform. The only option had been to leave.

"I heard that Jo resigned. Is she really gone?" It seemed to Ruth that the answer to that question mattered more than she ever imagined it could.

"Yes. Yes, she's gone."

"For good?"

He longed to be able to tell her what she wanted to hear, to be able to promise with confidence that he'd never let her down again, but first she had to know that the past hadn't finished with them yet. He'd resolved while still at the Castle that Ruth would be the first to hear what he now had to say and while he'd rehearsed his side of the conversation many times in his head in the past few hours he'd never been able to picture Ruth's response. He began hesitantly, so that as he told her Joanna would never again play any part in his life, his personal life or his political life, she began to wonder what he was keeping back.

"What is it, Paul? I can tell there's something else you're not telling me."

He was still holding her forearms in his hands. As he spoke he waited for any sense of her pulling away. "Do you remember that evening on the seafront in Brighton? I told you that I'd seen Jo the night before and had finished our relationship. She'd been remarkably calm about the whole thing. She hardly said a word. Despite what you might think, I found it easy to give up the physical side of our relationship but I was…I was going to say hurt, but I probably just mean disappointed when I heard nothing from her at all for over two years. When I met her again we were both looking for winnable seats to fight at the next election and all I remember us talking about was politics. Well, if I'm right, and while I can't be totally certain I think I am, then Jo was pregnant when we parted." Ruth's arms remained perfectly still in her lap. "I think she had a son who she gave up for adoption and, extraordinary though I know this must sound, I believe I've just spent a couple of hours with him."

Her voice was remarkably level. "He told you this?"

"No. He told me Joanna was his mother. He had no reason to suspect that he was actually speaking to his father. And I didn't say anything. What could I say? I needed time to think."

Ruth had come this far and knew immediately that she had no intention of turning back now. She had analysed her own feelings at great length in the past few years and knew now what really mattered. Paul fathering a child before she'd even met him couldn't fit into that category. She chose her words with care. "It's going to be something we're all going to have to adjust to. Will you tell Jo?"

"That I've met our son? I don't know. I'm certainly in no mood to discuss it with her right now, although I suppose I will have to sometime."

Ruth repeated the question that mattered to her above all else. "Is she really gone?"

"Yes, she's gone. I can't guarantee that she won't be sitting in my chair soon enough, but if she is I'll be just another photograph on the stairs."

"Would you really just let her take over like that?"

He shrugged. "That makes it sound like it's up to me. It may well not be. But if it were to happen, it would have its compensations. I owe it to you and to Josh to give you your lives back. Politics is a selfish profession and I can't go on pretending that I don't know what it's doing to the people I love."

"And what if the people you love don't see it that way?"

He went on as if he hadn't heard her. "Josh needs to be able to have his girlfriends and go to the pub or whatever it is he wants to do like any other kid. And you..."

"What about me?"

"There may be other people you want to spend time with."

"I wondered when you were going to get round to asking me about that. Just because the papers think they have a story about something it doesn't make it true. You of all people should know that. That horrible little man from the *News of the World* may have decided I'm having a torrid affair but, believe me, he couldn't be more wrong. In fact, I think even Mr Neville Standen understands that now."

"How so?"

"Danny told me to ring Donald, Dr Gill, and tell him not to say anything but I was too late. From what I can tell the *News of the World* now has chapter and verse on my so-called relationship, including the fact that I told Donald over dinner how I loved my husband and my son very much indeed." She squeezed his waist to reinforce her point. "Which happens to be the truth."

The Prime Minister realised that he hadn't kissed his wife for a very, very long time and there was nothing he wanted to do more.

When the car pulled up outside a Victorian mansion block in Stockwell there was a woman with a mobile phone to her ear and a very smartly dressed man in leather jeans and an aviation jacket waiting on the pavement to greet them. The driver shrugged and confirmed that this was the address he'd been given and his three passengers had no choice but to get out. The woman looked familiar to PJ but it was the younger man, who had the Mediterranean complexion of an Italian or maybe a Frenchman, who held out his hand.

"My name is Alexander. Sacha to my friends." He hoped Helen's call wouldn't take long. If she had been planning a party she really should have warned him. "It is a very nice evening for September." He was rewarded with three blank faces for his efforts.

"Hi, I'm Helen Griffin." She stuffed the phone into her bag and pushed the hair out of her eyes. "We haven't actually met but I'm the Prime...Paul's Chief of Staff. Paul wants to thank you, of course. He might also want to talk over a couple of things, I think, although he's got some important business to sort out first. I'm afraid the police have left your house in a bit of a mess so we wondered if you'd mind staying here for a little while, until he can see you. It's my flat. There's a full fridge and a TV and everything. You can make yourselves at home. I'm afraid I will have to leave you for a little while, but maybe Sacha wouldn't mind getting you a drink or something." He shrugged and came over to whisper in her ear that he found this situation very strange but that she should know that his hourly rate wasn't negotiable. "Sacha is, well, he works in hospitality."

At that she flagged down a passing cab and jumped in. She was already on the phone before the driver pulled away from the kerb.

~

Kneejerk wiped the sweat from his moustache and made a note on the pad in front of him. If the Director of Communications was in the process of divulging highly classified information then it was nothing less than the Colonel's duty to monitor his calls and decide on the appropriate action to take.

Since being made to feel distinctly unwelcome in the flat, the Colonel had been alone in his office and had taken out the bottle of highland malt he kept in a bottom drawer. He'd eyed the unopened packet of Benson and Hedges and cursed the smoke detectors. For a brief moment the whisky had steadied his nerves. But the effects were wearing off already and he was getting ever more agitated. The situation that he'd thought just a short time ago could still be turned to his advantage now seemed to be in serious danger of running out of control altogether. He took another swig from the bottle.

"You're on your own now, Henry." He was talking to himself. "But you've been on your own before. You can do it, man. Just don't lose your nerve." He put the bottle back in the drawer but took it out again in the same movement.

~

Ruth was at the study window looking out towards St James' Park when she spotted the unmistakable figure of Joanna Morgan striding towards the rear entrance to Downing Street. She called her husband over and pointed in her direction. "It looks like you've got a visitor."

Sinclair picked up the telephone. "Would you tell the…the former Foreign Secretary to wait for me in the Cabinet Room? And see if you can get a call through to President Warren. I'll take it in here."

~

The auditorium was a swirling mass of red, white and blue. Dozens of placards reading 'Go Bunny Go' were being held aloft as the music built up to a crescendo. Above the heads of the crowd vast nets full of yet more balloons were waiting to be opened as soon as Warren appeared. There was an audible murmur of disappointment when it was only the Vice President who ran on to the stage. He did what he could to keep the atmosphere charged, promising that the main man would be with them any time now. From the wings John Warren could hear the chants of 'Four More Years' as he was handed the phone.

"Gotta be quick, Paul. Where have you been?"

"You know what it's like, John. Events. That kind of thing."

"So, hey, it's great news about the hostages. All free and some very bad people dead into the bargain. Who'd believe it?"

"Who indeed?"

"Sorry, Paul, it's kinda noisy here. I'm not getting everything you're saying. But, look, did your guys show you my speech? I should be out there right now making it as a matter of fact. The Senator has been getting some good headlines, accusing me of letting known enemies of America run free. I can't have that, you know. So this is gonna make a big difference. I'm grateful to you Paul."

"And why's that, Mr President?"

"Well I couldn't be too sure. I thought you might be on my case about the raid. I couldn't be completely honest with you back there at Camp David, but you're a big boy. You know how the world works. You Brits took out an important terrorist base and you got your hostages back. Don't worry those guys are well briefed. They'll put on a good show for your media, believe me. It'll play good for you over there, so everybody wins." There was a pause and the only sound on the line was a distant chant of 'Four More Years'. "You still there Paul?"

"I'm here and I hope you can hear me all right because I'm only going to say this once. If you want to fight a campaign based on smears against your opponent, there's probably not very much I can do about that. But if you want to misrepresent me or my motives or what happened in Eritrea then you'd better factor into your precious little grid that I intend to tell the truth. All of it. What you call not completely honest, I call a lie. You lied to me to help get yourself re-elected and while you might think we're a bit old fashioned over here, that's not how we do things. So if that's understood, I'll let you get back to your speech."

"Paul? Paul?" The line had gone dead. The cheers of 'Bun-nee, Bun-nee' were getting louder and louder as the stewards ushered the President towards the stage.

The Prime Minister turned to his Chief of Staff. "I think I'm starting to enjoy myself."

60

Joshua was sitting with his mother in the small kitchen of the Prime Minister's flat telling her about his eventful night out.

"Can you believe it, Mum? That..." he wanted to say arsehole, "that git Kneejerk had me followed and as soon as there was a bit of a ruck up by the bar it was like some cheap TV cop show. He looked so pleased with himself when they brought me back here, I could have hit him."

"I'm glad you didn't."

"Actually I wish I had. I think I could have got away with it. He's hardly going to charge Paul Sinclair's little boy with assault, is he? And he wouldn't have dared hit me back. No, I missed my chance there. But I won't miss it again."

"My goodness, this is a side of you I haven't seen before." She reached over and tousled his hair. He stiffened. "Quite the little toughie aren't you?"

"It's just him, Mum, he brings it out in me. You don't have to live with him watching over you the whole time."

"Well, I was going to talk to you about that."

"Yeah?"

"You know your father and I haven't been seeing a great deal of each other, recently?"

He looked embarrassed. "What do you want me to say? Of course. Not that either of you would ever tell me what's going on. But if you're both happy, I guess that's your business."

"I'm not sure that either of us has been happy. But I think things are going to be better now." So far as she knew, Paul was at that very moment in a room with the one woman who might yet have the power to change all that. "I won't make you any promises I can't be sure of keeping, but I'm hoping life will be a bit easier for you."

"Is this really about me?"

"You're a part of it, of course you are. But now listen, this is important. Your dad isn't as blind to what you have to put up with as you might think. If you told him you wanted him to give up all this so we could go and live quietly in the country somewhere, he'd do it. Do you know that?"

"What? He'd give up being Mr High and Mighty Prime Minister because I said so? Come on Mum, get real."

"I'm serious."

"But that's so cool."

"You mean you want him too?"

"No, of course not. Is just cool that he would. I mean he's been Prime Minister forever." She laughed at the thought that when you're seventeen, four years probably is forever. "I've learned to cope with that. It's just Kneejerk and all his security crap that I can't deal with."

"Well, who knows, if things work out maybe there'll be some changes there too."

When he looked up she could see the heavy bags under his eyes. A lot had happened since he'd woken up in an empty flat that morning. "Well I won't hold my breath if it's all right with you." He ran both hands through his hair. "Anyway, what do you mean, if things work out?"

"Well even if we can persuade him not resign for our sakes, there are one or two people who think they can do the job better than he can. He's not as popular as he used to be, you know, and politicians still have to win elections."

"Yeah, it's funny isn't it? Dad's a good guy, I mean he's a bit crap sometimes, but he's on the side of the angels I reckon and he can be chucked out just like that." He clicked his fingers. "Whereas characters like Kneejerk…"

"The devil incarnate."

"Something like that. They just go on and on."

She stood up and put her arms round his neck. "And what about us? Are we angels or demons?"

"That's easy. We're just the ones who get to live in purgatory."

For the second time that day, Paul Sinclair was alone in the Cabinet

Room with Joanna Morgan. He'd given some hurried instructions to Helen and Danny and asked them to wish him luck. When he closed the huge double doors from the Den behind him, just as he had done that morning, he found her sitting once again in her old seat. The pastel yellow walls and heavy damask curtains of the huge room could have been designed to calm the most bitter of disagreements. The loudly ticking clock, which could be mesmerising if you concentrated too hard on it, was telling both of them it was time to move on. It was the Prime Minister who spoke first. "You surprised me, Jo. I didn't think you'd do it."

"Not as much as you surprised me. Your people did their best to destroy me out there today and they may yet have succeeded. I didn't realise you had it in you."

Sinclair remained impassive. It would probably do her good to think he'd been directing events even if he hadn't. "This conversation can go one of two ways, Jo. We can trade insults and you can storm out again if you want. Or you can tell me why you're here and we can see where that leads us." In a different setting they could have been an estranged couple trying to sort out their differences and the parallels weren't lost on either of them. Paul Sinclair listened carefully as she made her proposal. It amounted to something like a non-aggression pact. She was astute enough to present it as being in the best interests of both of them as well as the Labour Party and the government. Joanna Morgan appeared as much in control of herself as ever, but then Joanna Morgan was not the kind of woman who allowed herself to beg.

"That's very interesting. And if I say no?"

"You'll be right where you are now. You may have won your vote today, but you know as well as I do that this party is split down the middle and divided parties don't win elections. I've been under a lot of pressure from people to announce that I'll run against you, Paul. Your little comeback routine today doesn't change any of the fundamentals. My position will recover and, anyway, if it's not me it can always be somebody else. Do you really want a leadership battle so close to the election? It could get nasty. You might have to justify some of the outrageous things that have been said about me this afternoon."

"And you don't think I can do that, obviously."

"If I didn't even know your mother-in-law was ill, how could I have been responsible for passing that information on to the opposition? Answer me that."

Her composure was extraordinary. Her ability to lie with such conviction was impressive in its way. "That's not what I've been told. Would you mind waiting just a second." He went back to the double doors and opened them just wide enough for a person to slip thorough. As PJ Walton stepped into the room his mother's face showed for the first time that she understood the totality of her defeat.

Helen's call had come through just in time. All Sacha's experience of putting people at their ease seemed to be for nothing when it came to these three. PJ had remained deep in thought and spent most of his time looking out of the window. It was long past the deadline for his *Naked Prophet* column and he hadn't even called the news desk to explain. With luck they would simply fire him and save him the trouble of resigning. Pete was restless but uncomfortable in the unfamiliar surroundings of Helen's flat. He'd accepted Sacha's offer of a drink and then a second and at least had made an effort at conversation, although any common ground had so far eluded them. Helmut watched the slender Frenchman flit around the room obviously as ill at ease as they were and had a shrewd idea what his role in life might be.

When the phone rang Sacha pounced on it like a hungry bird. He hadn't the slightest interest in politics but even he recognised the famous address that Helen gave him. She was proving to be a woman of many surprises.

"I left thirty euro out in the kitchen for the cleaning lady," she said, "so give them that for the cab."

"And what about me?"

She didn't hesitate for long. "Well, if you don't mind waiting a little longer…"

Helen's next call had been to Sergeant Terry Woods, still on duty at the Vortex. She gave him the names of the visitors that would be arriving by taxi any minute and asked him to get them through the security as fast as he could.

The computers had come up with images of Pete and Helmut as soon as the cameras clicked into action. They were clearly recognisable at the heart of a demonstration outside in the Compound. They were down on file in the Colonel's personal code as ODMs, Ordinary Decent Malcontents, 'not to be admitted without prior approval from the Security Supremo'. Terry pondered this for a moment. As he looked down at the screen Helmut was running his own eyes over the interior of the Vortex, a sight he had never expected to see. From memory, and Helmut's memory was very good, it was just as the pictures on the website had said it would be. By the time Terry had decided that Helen's instructions outranked those of the Colonel, Helmut had all the information he needed.

"I wish I'd thought to bring a camera," said Pete as they waited outside the famous black door. Helen was soon there to meet them and herd them straight down the corridor and into the Den.

Just a few metres away Kneejerk's door remained firmly closed. He appeared to have been forgotten, which should have given him time to think. Instead he took another glass of malt and slammed the bottle back down onto the control panel that no longer seemed to give him control over anything.

61

"Well? For Christ's sake, what did she say?" asked Helen.

Back up in the flat, Sinclair had an eager and attentive audience. Ruth sat nearest to him in an armchair with her legs tucked under her. Helen, Danny and PJ were squeezed together on the sofa and only the Prime Minister was standing. The door was ajar and the faint sound of Joshua, Pete and Helmut's subversive discussions filtered across the landing from the kitchen.

"She offered me a deal."

"That was generous of her."

"That's what she thought, actually. She said she would support me from the backbenches, keep her own eager band of friends in line, and help the party at least look united right up to the election."

Helen guffawed. "And in return?"

"I stand down after a year and back her for the leadership."

"Very neat. And she expected you to buy it?"

"Yes, I think she did. She'd actually convinced herself it was in all our interests. Until, that is, I was able to show her that she didn't have the hold over me that she thought she did. PJ here was a great help. He didn't even have to open his mouth. She'd already told him the story of Olive's illness so she couldn't pretend not to know about that. And of course he had told her three years ago that the Circle of Death wasn't what it seemed. The Deputy Prime Minister knew something of that magnitude and said nothing. She saw she was finished immediately."

"I'm impressed," said Helen. And she was. Earlier that day Sinclair had looked like a broken man who wanted nothing more than simply to walk away from it all. When he appeared to have done just that and no trace of him could be found she'd even allowed herself the private horror that he'd thrown himself off Westminster Bridge. And yet here he was, back in charge as never before. He'd won the vote, not that he deserved much credit for that. He'd faced down Joanna and had wrestled back control of his own foreign policy. And now Luke's forensic science contacts had confirmed that PJ was quite probably right about the Circle of Death as well. Sinclair might still have some work to do to get the better of all those who wanted to run the country in his place, but at least he now knew who they were. She rattled off all his achievements and said, "Not bad for one day."

"You're forgetting the most important thing," he said and sat on the arm of his wife's chair with his hand on her shoulder.

Ruth shifted her body round and put her feet on the carpet. "I don't want to spoil all this mutual congratulation," she said, "but where exactly do we go from here?"

"I've been thinking about that," said Paul. "Whether Joanna is out of the equation or not, we have been taken for fools. Not once but twice. We can't carry on as if nothing has happened."

"I should hope not," said Helen. "We'll do what we always do. Cut the crap and get on with it."

"Maybe. You know your journalist friend, Jean?"

"Janine."

"That's right. Didn't you say we owed her a favour? Maybe you should give her a call."

Scott Bolton was not a happy boy. Much against his better judgement he'd done everything Janine Clairmont had asked him to do. He should have been basking in the glory of a fantastic journalistic scoop by now. It was the sort of thing people got awards for. 'Prime Minister Caught in Sordid Squat Shame.' Something like that. If they'd done things his way they'd have had the pictures they needed. Paul Sinclair couldn't have stayed inside the Castle forever. But now, far from thanking him, Janine was blaming him for the fact that they had nothing to show for their efforts. At least that's what he assumed. She hadn't exchanged a word with him since they'd got back to the AM-TV studios. His suggestion of a drink and maybe more to take their minds off it all had been as gratefully received as the vomit on Mrs Alma Gundry's homemade fruitcake.

To make matters worse, Mrs Gundry herself had had whatever the South London equivalent was of a Damascene conversion. Scott had made up his own mind to head back to Wilson Crescent with his camera crew and try to revive his Neighbours from Hell report only to discover that, in Mrs Gundry's eyes, the Castle had been transformed from the gates of hell into something little short of a stairway to heaven.

"It's not every day you have the Prime Minister paying a visit. It's just what the neighbourhood needs. And deserves, if I might say so. It's put Wilson Crescent on the map, this has, right where it belongs."

Scott struggled to keep the frustration out of his voice as he asked the next question. The camera was still rolling. "And have you had any difficulties with your neighbours across the road?"

"Oh no. They're really quite a nice group of men. I had them in my house for coffee just a few days ago. We share an interest in Mozart, you know. I think it's very important in an up and coming area like ours to be neighbourly."

"You did mention something to me earlier about vomit, Mrs Gundry."

"Well I don't think it's awfully nice of you to bring that up, young man. Anybody can get ill you know."

~

The possibility that he might be physically sick was something Kneejerk could no longer ignore. His array of cameras and microphones kept watch on most of what was happening in and around the building, but he had no choice but to admit that right now he had little idea what was actually going on. He'd spoken to nobody since making the mistake of picking up Kapolski's hotline and being told that the President was a very unhappy Bunny indeed. Quite what he'd meant by the serious consequences that were bound to follow Kneejerk didn't like to imagine.

It was the camera in the Entrance Hall that had his attention now. Helen Griffin was welcoming a television crew and in the background the boy Joshua was heading for the door with two of the ODMs that had been admitted without the Colonel's permission. Under normal circumstances he would have had them detained, but he remained glued to his chair, a passive witness to a drama he could no longer follow.

"This had better be good."

"It's very nice to see you, too, Janine."

Janine Clairmont breathed in the strong smell of floor polish and cast her eyes around the walls. Since the advent of the Vortex, journalists rarely made it into the road outside, never mind the house itself, but nothing much seemed to have changed.

Helen was as business-like as ever. "Let's go and set up in the small Dining Room. By the way, you did get your camera back, didn't you?"

"Yes," hissed Janine, "but surprise, surprise there was no tape in it. Now, how could that have happened?" She looked over her shoulder to where Joshua was directing Pete and Helmut out into the street. "Come to think of it, aren't those the goons who stole it?"

Joshua pushed his friends out the door. "Don't worry Helen. I'm just showing Pete and Helmut round. I'll make sure they don't nick anything."

Janine turned to her friend. "I suppose you think this is payback? In return for saving the neck of your precious Prime Minister I get a nice little interview about what a clever boy he's been. Winning on all fronts and being a proper little Action Man, when we both know he's been up to God knows what in bloody Bermondsey. That's not what I call a fair trade."

"Just be patient a little longer Janine. I think that you'll see I've kept my side of the bargain. We might have an extra chapter or two for that book of yours as well."

"Lady Diamond bearing gifts, eh? Now that's a first."

62

Kneejerk watched on his monitor as the camera was set up and listened as the crew did a sound check. When everything seemed to be working properly, the door opened and Prime Minister Paul Sinclair walked in.

This time he remembered her name. "Hello, Janine. Thanks for getting here so quickly. Where would you like me to sit?"

Janine indicated a chair beside the fireplace. The sound recordist attached a small microphone to the lapel of his jacket as the cameraman adjusted his settings.

"Thank you for inviting us in, Prime Minister. It's a rare privilege."

"I know. We really haven't been very helpful to all of you in the media, have we? Well keep it to yourself for now, I haven't talked to my security people about it yet, but I think we can afford to be a bit more open around here in future."

"That'll be the day," said the cameraman under his breath.

"Well that sounds like good news, Prime Minister. After all, we're only trying to do our jobs."

"That's all any of us are trying to do, isn't it?"

The cameraman, who was relieved to be able to do his job for once that day, signalled that he was ready to go.

"I'm afraid Helen hasn't told me what you want to talk about, Prime Minister. So I'm not really sure where to start."

"Well let's just get on with it and see how it goes, shall we?"

Janine looked over her shoulder and was told that they were 'rolling'. "Prime Minister, welcome to AM-TV. Perhaps you could start by giving us your reaction to the resignation of the Deputy Prime Minister? She's been quoted as saying that your government has become so obsessed by security that you don't care who suffers so long as you get your own way."

"Well, you know, Joanna Morgan may have a point there." Janine raised an eyebrow in surprise. "I'm going to do something very unusual for a politician, if I may. I'm going to be very honest with you indeed."

"I think our viewers would appreciate that."

"Sometimes not everything in politics is quite what it seems. I don't just mean that those of us in power have our little secrets, of course we do. But sometimes even we, even *I* don't know what is going on right at the heart of our democracy. In the past few hours, however, I've learned a lot and I have to say that much of it has come not just as a surprise, but as a shock. Now, I suppose I could keep it all to myself and just carry on as normal. That would probably be the easiest thing to do. But it wouldn't be right. The British people have been deceived and they deserve to know how. If they then decide that I'm to blame, that I have let them down, then they have every right to say so and to choose somebody else." He was enough of an actor to know when to pause for effect. "Which is why I've just spoken to His Majesty the King and requested permission to call a General Election for four weeks' time."

Helen had said she'd get a scoop and they didn't get much bigger than this. Janine barely needed to ask any questions. She sat back and allowed Paul Sinclair to explain the true story behind first the Circle of Death and then the Eritrean hostage crisis. A full review of all aspects of security at home and abroad was to be put in place immediately.

As the Prime Minister was promising to put all the facts as he now knew them in the public domain, Colonel Henry Neilson decided he'd heard enough. He put on his coat and tied his scarf tightly around his neck. The bottle with what was left of the whisky was pushed into his pocket. As he went to the door, Sinclair's voice continued to reverberate around the office.

"So you see, this country is at something of a turning point. And now it's up to the voters to decide if they want me to lead them around that particular corner."

"What about Joanna Morgan? As you know, there's been a lot of speculation that she may be about to launch a leadership bid."

"You'll have to ask Joanna about that, I'm afraid. A short time ago in this very building she offered to support me. But if she's changed her mind then I'm sure she'll tell you herself."

"And your wife?"

"For some reason my wife seems to think I'm rather good at my job. She's here now and will be playing a full part in the campaign." There was a brief pause as Janine hesitated to ask her next question. Sinclair saved her the trouble. "If I'm going to continue to be completely frank, things have not been easy these past few years for my wife. And while I'm not going to go into details about my family, much as your viewers might like me too, I can say that Ruth is the most important person in my life and has been for a very, very long time. If she was the only supporter I had left in this country, it would be enough for me."

"That's my boy." Helen was almost dancing around the room. She had hardly been able to contain herself while the interview was going on, but now it was over and they had regrouped in the Den, she gave full vent to her excitement. "We'll show the buggers. And Joanna Morgan can stick it up her prim little arse."

Paul Sinclair had his arms around Ruth's waist. "Don't get too carried away. We haven't won yet, you know. There's still the little matter of an election to get through. I don't know how all this is going to go down with the voters. But I guess we'll find out soon enough."

Danny, who was leaning on the window sill, nodded. "Let's face it, there has to be every chance we'll be out on our ears. I mean, 'I was taken for a fool so vote for me again' isn't the most promising slogan for an election campaign. But who knows, maybe they'll have a soft spot for a sinner repenteth."

"Well I don't know about you lot," said Ruth, "but I'm rather looking forward to this."

There was a clatter from outside as Joshua tumbled into the outer office. He opened the door without knocking and called over to his father. "Hey Dad, I think there's something you should see." He led them all across the corridor to the Colonel's empty office. Helmut and Pete stood at either side of the door like two sentries from a ragtag regiment. Joshua pointed at the bank of screens above the desk, gesticulating wildly. There were so many cameras, Sinclair wasn't sure where he was supposed to be looking.

"There, the third screen from the right."

Sinclair moved closer for a better look. It was an interior view of the Vortex at the end of Downing Street. The image switched between three different angles of Colonel Henry Neilson who was banging on the walls in a state of considerable agitation.

"What's going on?"

Terry Woods could be seen peering into the contraption as the Colonel pleaded to be let out. It was hard to tell for sure but the Sergeant appeared to be smiling. "It looks to me like a technical fault," said Joshua, doing his best to play it dead pan. "What terrible timing. Just as Kneejerk was on his way home."

Paul Sinclair did his best to look stern. "Oh dear, not another security failure? This really isn't good enough. And I'm sure Henry told me that thing was foolproof. Perhaps somebody should go down there and escort him back to the building. There are a few questions I'd like to ask the Colonel before he clocks off for the night."

"I'll go," Joshua was now grinning from ear to ear. "After all he's done for me, it's the least I can do."

THE END

Author's Note

When, in the summer of 2005, I was told by the British government that it wouldn't agree to the publication of the diaries I had kept while working for Tony Blair, *The Times* among others suggested that I had turned to fiction in revenge. The implication was that this novel was written in a matter of weeks and rushed out in record time to spite my former employers. The truth is rather less sensational.

The Spin Doctor's Diary did go to press whether the powers-that-be liked it or not. And, as it happens, I first started writing *Time and Fate* over two years ago and it finished long before the diaries were even offered for publication. Nothing it contains is designed to punish or embarrass anybody. As a former spin doctor, if I had wanted to do that I would have used far less subtle means.

The plot is a topical one, however, and so I wasn't able to ignore the real world entirely. The original story-line involved a bomb attack on the London Underground that came out of the blue while the Prime Minister was at a conference in Scotland. When exactly this occurred earlier this year, I amended the text to take account of the awful tragedy of July 7th. But *Time and Fate* is a work of fiction and nothing more. It doesn't attempt to portray actual events or real people, far less to predict the future.

If I had the gift of prescience I might have been better prepared for just how much time and effort *Time and Fate* would require. The cost in terms of lost sleep and hours spent writing and re-writing fiction in relative isolation is a high one. The worlds of politics and daily journalism, which I used to inhabit, took far less of a toll. But the rewards of seeing this book so well produced and packaged by the Polperro Heritage Press are higher still.

I have been fortunate in receiving a tremendous amount of help and encouragement along the way. Every year a group of gay men get together in the South of France to talk about books and writing.

The sessions are led by the author Patrick Gale and my first thanks must go to him for sharing his own experience with us all and for his patience, dedication and thoughtful advice. Everybody who has taken part in the Lotus Tree Workshops has helped spur me on to keep going when it seemed this novel would never take shape. Thanks guys.

A number of people have been kind enough to read earlier drafts of this book and give me their comments. Scott Gill and Mike Webber, in particular, made detailed and thoughtful suggestions for how it could be improved, most of which were gratefully received and duly incorporated. Sandra Morgan's friendship and enthusiasm meant that giving up was never an option. Guy Burch, Steven Fowler, Natasha Fairweather and Laura Morris were all kind enough to read the book and offer their own helpful thoughts on some of the detail. Thanks to Mark Ormerod for keeping me sano y salvo.

Broo Doherty, my agent, has put more work into this novel than any first-time author could possibly ask for. She has always had more confidence in it than I could manage to muster and that it ever got into a half-way publishable state is more down to her than to anybody else. Better still, she's become a good friend along the way.

Jerry Johns and his team at the Polperro Heritage Press did a magnificent job on the production of this book. Given the contemporary nature of the story, Jerry appreciated immediately that it had to be brought out with unusual speed. And he managed to do that without sacrificing anything in terms of quality or appearance. Very special thanks, too, must go to Simon Reynolds for the cover.

My partner, James Proctor, is a writer himself so he knows what it's like, although he has the good sense to stick to real places and to history as it happened. When the world of fiction made me temperamental and difficult, he never complained and his wicked curries made long days in front of the computer far more bearable. Frankie, who lives with us, is neither as old or as infirm as his namesake in this book. He doesn't limp or fart. Not yet anyway. He would look at me very strangely when I got up at 5.30 to toy with some particularly tricky passage, but he wouldn't bother getting up. Dogs can be a lot more sensible than human beings.

September 2005